Scents of War

J. L. Guyer

To Kim,
Thanks for showing us
hospitality here at Calvin.
Enjoy the book!
Pleasant Scents,
J. L. Guyer

ISBN 979-8-218-09462-1 (paperback)
ISBN 979-8-218-09463-8 (ebook)

First Edition: October 2022

"On the day you break this covenant, your senses will fill with bile; the smell of destruction will fill the air; infants and babes will faint in the streets of the city."

selected words of Manzanita of the Evergreens

Chapter One

The fragrance of freshly cut peonies crept into Agonya's dreams causing her to stir and roll out of her silky sheets. The peonies stood tall in the clay vase next to her bed. Light encased them in a soft glow, enticing her to press her face into the petals and breathe deeply. The scent filled her up, transporting her momentarily to another time and place, before she became aware of someone else in the room. Agonya turned.

A petite woman was bent over the hearth, stoking the gray-orange embers into a fresh blaze. Agonya broke into a broad smile, seeing her there. Even though Maya was a commoner, they had become great friends. At first Agonya had to sneak away to play with the serving girl living in the palace, but eventually she convinced her parents to let Maya serve her instead of cleaning floors.

Maya straightened her small frame, flipping her long black braid behind her, and turned to see Agonya watching her.

"Good morning," she said solemnly. Then she bowed and grasped Agonya's outstretched hand. She sniffed it, as was the custom.

Why was Maya so formal this morning? Agonya laughed and pulled her into a warm embrace, returning the smelif by smelling each of Maya's cheeks. Contentment washed over her. By inhaling each other's scent, it was believed they were able to share of the breath of life. And Agonya never tired of Maya's aroma of rosemary and fir. Somehow it always made her feel content even when she was angry or sad.

Feeling lighthearted, Agonya walked over to the wardrobe and began leafing through the hanging dresses.

"Your father ordered a retreat during the night," Maya said softly.

Agonya's heart stopped, then began to race. Forcing her hands to move over the dresses as if she were still deciding, she focused on breathing normally. Retreat felt very much like defeat. If they lost this war against the Korins, she would be forced to marry her Korin cousin, or more precisely her fetid uncle's son, Prince Lucas. Her father had assured her this would be the last resort and most likely wouldn't ever happen. They had been fighting them for forever. No matter how many times Uncle Reid's armies were pushed back, the Kors were never content to have a truce for very long. Why would her father retreat now? What was his plan?

Inhaling deeply, Agonya let the peonies and Maya's fragrance wash over her again. Retreating was not surrendering, she told herself; they were going to push back the Kors into their own lands and out of the Fertile Basin once for all. Her heart began to slow, and she was able to continue sifting through her wardrobe.

Finding the pale blue dress she was looking for, Agonya pulled it out and let Maya help her step into it, the soft weave flowing gently around her.

Not daring to say anything just yet, she moved to her plush stool and waited for Maya to fix her hair into the usual shape of a peony in full bloom.

Maya picked up the comb but didn't run it through her hair.

Agonya glanced in the copper basin and saw the worried look on her friend's face. "Are you all right?"

Maya shook her head and breathed deeply several times before disclosing what was bothering her. "Many soldiers died in the confrontation yesterday. Division Two was . . ."

Tears leaped to Agonya's eyes, and her stomach twisted into knots. Why hadn't he said anything? When did Hodel's division get assigned to the front lines?

"I'm sorry, your Highness. I only just found out."

"But I saw him last week," Agonya managed to whisper. "I was going to go see him today."

"Your father didn't want you to know," Maya said, beginning to comb Agonya's long black hair.

Anger, now, clawed at the knots in her stomach. "He had no right to keep this from me," she hissed.

"That may be, but you know he never approved of your relationship with Hodel."

Suddenly, her room seemed too small. Thankfully, it didn't take Maya long to tuck the last strand into place. Agonya turned to face her friend. "I want to know everything. Are you certain Hodel didn't survive? Where was the battle yesterday? Are they back to the city yet?"

Maya opened her mouth to answer but a knock interrupted her. She left Agonya still sitting on the stool and opened the door.

"A message for Her Highness."

Maya took the rolled-up parchment and closed the door.

Agonya sighed. "What is it now? Go on, read it."

"Lady Velia requests your presence this afternoon."

Agonya snorted. Of all the things it could have been, and it was Lady Velia! Strangely, she felt like a weight had been lifted from her shoulders even though the knots in her stomach remained firmly in place. "Well, I'm not going to listen to her prattle on and on about how Lady Rebekkah wore a strong violet perfume to Lord Sakima's party last week and how appalled she was at the mere suggestion he would even consider giving her a second sniff. Not when Hodel might be–" The knots tightened.

"I'll let her know."

Agonya stood up, grabbed her mother's necklace off the table, and strode out of her too constricting room. The necklace was delicate with bands of silver that crisscrossed each other like the roots of a plant. A circular pendant hung from it, with a seam stretching down its side. She opened the pendant and inhaled the floral and woody scent emanating from within. Her mother's scent wasn't calming but there was a certain comfort Agonya got from it nonetheless.

* * *

Sitting down in her palanquin, she rapped on the silk coverings. The six bearers picked up the poles, lifted her into the air, and carried her out through the palace gates.

For all her worrying, Agonya wasn't even questioned about leaving the palace. A little oaky pomegranate wine and the guards were under her control. It was the most reliable combination of scents Agonya had found, to make the guards agreeable. How or why the scents did what they did, Agonya didn't know. All she knew was that she tended to get her way when she wore the right perfumes and oils.

The streets of Ithol were packed with people. So much so that her palanquin kept getting jostled from side to side. Sometimes she wished she could do away with the palanquin and walk the same as Maya who was following on foot. Maya hadn't known for sure about Hodel's fate, or when the retreating soldiers would arrive back in Ithol; but, Agonya had to know more. If there was a chance he was alive, mourning for him was out of the question. She closed her eyes and smelled the odors in the air.

Tapping on the coverings again, she said, "Stop!" The bearers lowered her to the ground. Her guards pushed back a few shoppers and motioned for Agonya to come. Maya pulled open the cloth, and Agonya unfolded her legs and stepped out.

A squat man stood beside his little cart of perfumes. "Good morning, your Highness," the man said as he grasped her outstretched hand with his own truffle-colored one, sniffing it as was proper. "Would you like to see what came into the shop last night?"

"Not right now." Resisting the urge to shift her weight from one foot to the other, Agonya gestured to his house behind the shop. "May we speak more privately?"

The merchant's face fell. He knew what she had come to talk about and dreaded it as much as she did. He nodded. Maya stepped forward and held the door open for them.

Leaving the bearers and guards outside, Agonya followed the squat man into the simple room. A bench and table were pulled to the center of it. Other than that, one bed mat lay unfurled on the floor. Another was rolled up and propped against the far wall. Agonya ignored the bench and resisted the urge to run her fingers over the rolled mat. She knew it belonged to Hodel.

"Forgive me, your Highness, but I haven't heard from Ho- from him or any of his commanding officers," he stuttered.

"I figured as much," Agonya said, peeling her eyes away from Hodel's mat. "But I had to check. Your son means a lot to me." Her eyes fell on the two bowls sitting on the table. "Please, can you tell me when he was assigned to the front lines? I didn't even know he'd left the city."

"Hodel was ordered to the field the morning after he saw your Highness last." His voice cracked and he pulled a cloth out of his pocket to dab at his shining forehead.

"I see," Agonya said curtly. "I suppose my father ordered you not to tell me."

The man wouldn't meet her eyes. That was fine. He didn't have to say anything. She knew by the look on his face that her father had done exactly that.

Turning away from this man who, although he answered her truthfully, had been a part of keeping Hodel's scent from her. Pinching her nose in frustration, Agonya tried to remind herself that this man was only a pawn to her father. He didn't deserve her wrath. Her father, on the other hand, had known about her last visit to Hodel. He had all but yelled at her for continuing to see him after he had forbidden it. But she never would have imagined her father would stoop so low as to send Hodel to his death because of her choice to spend time with him. Trying to compose herself, Agonya faced Hodel's father. He was dutifully staring at the ground.

Agonya glanced at Maya who gestured subtly with her hands by her side. Agonya had seen that gesture many times and felt ashamed that Maya had to caution her now of all times to do the right thing.

Agonya nodded and cleared her throat. "Thank you for telling me. I wish I could tell you he is alive and well, but I cannot. Nor can I tell you that he is dead. Let us hope for the first." Agonya glanced at the mat. "Be assured, as soon as I find out where Hodel is, you will be the first to know. But in the meantime, would you show me your latest shipment?" There. That wasn't so bad. Perhaps he wouldn't think she was angry at him for not telling her sooner.

"Th-thank you, your Highness! Of course!" He held the door open for her before Maya even had the chance to reach it. He was a little too eager. Then, walking over to his cart, he riffled through his supplies before presenting her with a small amber colored vessel. "This came all the way from the other side of the Acrid Mountains."

Agonya shivered despite the heat and glanced up at the ever-looming mountains in the distance. Dark clouds encircled the tops of them.

"Don't worry, your Highness. Trouria is a decent place. Here, try it." He held it out to her, being careful not to look directly in her eyes.

The vessel was not made of wood or clay. Agonya had never seen anything like it before. "What is it?" she asked, tapping her nail on the amber container.

"This, your Highness, is what they call glass. It is a new discovery on the other side of the mountains. From what I can tell, the aromas contained inside do not lessen over time in these vessels like they do in our own wooden ones."

"It's beautiful." Agonya opened the vessel, breathing in the smells that wafted into the air. "What do you call it?"

"Blushing Cup. I'm not sure of the exact ingredients, but it has palm tree in it." The little man rocked back on his heels, waiting for her to decide.

"What's palm tree good for? Do you know?"

"It's supposed to help you remember."

"Too bad it wouldn't help with finding someone," Agonya thought. She didn't need help with remembering anything, and she almost gave the glass bottle back to him, but then an idea occurred to her. Maybe the scent could alter a memory. She'd have to test it out. "How much?" she asked; though, he really should gift it to her if she wanted it, for his role in keeping information from her.

"One hundred cinder chips, if it pleases."

Absurd! Even for the rarest of scents. But Maya's concern from earlier reminded Agonya to be nice. However much this man asked for, that was what she would pay. He was the father of Hodel after all.

"I can't imagine how difficult it must be to cross the mountains." Agonya rubbed her thumb across the smooth glass.

"Ah. Hanovi goes *around* the mountains, my Lady. It's too risky to go over. No thorny devils or savage Montanes to get in the way when you go the long way."

Agonya hadn't even thought about the Montanes. They seemed so far off when the Korins were at their gates. But she had heard how backwards they were and agreed with the man. "Do you ever see Montanes? Don't they keep to themselves?"

He hesitated. "Yes. But . . . I would never do business with them. They rarely come down off the mountains, and when they do, they are quite uncivilized." He wiped his forehead again with his cloth.

Agonya reached into her pouch and pulled out the chips engraved with her father's face. "You said a hundred cinder? Here." Before she could exchange the chips, a strong body odor assaulted her senses. Agonya wrinkled her nose and looked up to see an old man hobbling by on the street.

By the time she saw the man, her guards were already stepping over to him. The biggest guard grabbed the man's arm and was about to push him away when Agonya finally found her voice. "Pezi, no." She held out her hand to stop him. "Release him at once."

The guard looked startled but complied.

"What's your name, sir?"

The old man gave an awkward bow because of his walking stick. "Ogi, my Lady."

"Your Highness." Pezi corrected and glared at the man who quickly corrected his mistake, repeating her title and bowing even lower than before.

Addressing Ogi, Agonya gestured to the cart. "Please, forgive the rudeness of my guards. Would it be all right if I bought you something?"

"I'd be honored, your Highness. But there's no need."

"But I want to." Sometimes Agonya liked to do the opposite of whatever her father would do just to spite him, and he deserved it today of all days. Glancing at the cart of perfumes, she noticed a pile of scented soaps. "Would you like one of these? Go on. Pick one out."

Agonya watched the man pluck the top one off the pile. She asked the merchant how much for the soap and added the cinders to her purchase.

"Thank you, your Highness. Your scent is most pleasing," Ogi said, clutching his new soap and backing away with wide eyes.

Agonya smiled. "Your scent is pleasing, too." The man fumbled with his walking stick and tucked the soap into a pocket before disappearing into the crowd.

Turning, she saw Pezi frowning at the ground. If he didn't approve, so be it. He was sent by her father to guard her. And that man was no threat to her.

Agonya felt the cool glass in her hands and tucked the vessel into her pouch. Then, a strong earthy smell, the smell of a storm gathering enveloped Agonya, and a shadow crossed over her. She looked up and gasped. The dark clouds she'd seen hovering over the mountains were above her head, spreading over the entire city. There was no wind to blow them so far and so fast.

She stepped up to the palanquin wanting to escape their building pressure. "Maya, is it supposed to rain today?"
Maya didn't have time to respond. A rider came speeding around the corner through the mass of people hurrying through the streets. He spotted Agonya and came to a halt, blocking their way.

"A message for your Highness."

Agonya took the scroll and carefully pried open her father's seal. It was a summons. Agonya grit her teeth. She doubted she would be able to be civil to him so soon; but looking up at the threatening clouds, she felt the weight as though a heavy blanket had been thrown across the entire valley. The last time they'd had a storm like this, Agonya found herself waking up with no memory of what had happened, only to learn that her mother had died. Suddenly, the palace walls seemed inviting.

* * *

Agonya rushed through the dark halls. The torches that normally lit the way were not burning. The storm had come too fast, and the sun was, supposedly, still high in the sky. But she didn't need the light. She knew the halls better than anyone. She turned a corner, and light seeped into the hall from underneath the doors to her father's rooms. She paused, straightened her dress, and nodded at the guards. They opened the solid oak doors and announced her presence to the king.

She glided past them. The doors shut behind her, leaving her alone with her father. He stood stiff-backed, facing the portrait of the most beautiful woman Agonya had ever known. She gazed up at the graceful woman in the painting. The same intricately designed necklace that now hung around Agonya's neck framed her mother's face. Her black eyes seemed to smile back at Agonya, full of compassion; and pink peonies were woven through her braided black hair falling across her shoulder all the way down to her waist. A sigh escaped Agonya's lips, and her father turned.

Unlike her mother, King Azurarus was hard as stone. When he looked at Agonya, his eyes were harsh and accusing. Agonya wanted to slap him for what he'd done to Hodel, to her. But didn't dare.

Instead, she leaned forward dutifully to smell his cheek and waited for him to do the same. He pushed his broad shoulders back, took three strides, and was by her side. His aroma was heavily masked by frankincense.

Agonya followed the smell with her nose to the incense burning on the corner table: frankincense and sandalwood. She should have guessed. He was trying to manipulate her.

"Come, have a seat," he said, patting her head as if she were still a little child.

Agonya turned to the plush couches and chairs framing the fireplace and picked the one closest to the door. She reached up instinctively for the necklace around her throat, rubbed the delicate bands of silver between her fingers and began to open the pendant, but stopped. She wasn't a child anymore. She didn't need the peony aroma to shield her from her father. She let go.

When she looked back at her father, he was pacing back and forth across the fading rug. "Did you see the clouds?" His voice was tense.

As much as Agonya hated to put aside her anger about Hodel, she understood. They both dreaded the clouds. It was the only thing they shared in common. She opened her mouth to speak but closed it. Better not to say anything until she knew why he'd summoned her.

"There's something you should know about them."

"What do you mean?"

"I mean it was no coincidence that your mother died the last time a storm like this came to Ithol. You were so young then, but now that it's happening again."

Agonya reached for her necklace again. Not because of her father but remembering that day so long ago when her mother died was painful. And now her father was suggesting they had something to do with her death. How could clouds kill someone?

"I want you to leave Ithol."

Agonya gasped. "You want me to–"

"You ought to have heard by now," he cut her off, "that I ordered our armies to retreat to Ithol. Consequently, the Korins are seizing this opportunity to surround us. I do not want you here when they arrive. I have made arrangements for you to leave before they get here."

Agonya rose to her feet as calmly as she could. "What's really happening, father? You want me to flee to safety? Because of a little storm? Or has the war defeated you? Is that why you ordered Hodel to his death? So I wouldn't have any reason to stay or was it because you need me to marry Prince Lucas?"

"We are not so desperate as that, daughter. Besides, marrying him may give us a truce but it won't end the war."

"But I thought–"

"I only threatened to make you marry him because I was mad at you. Prince Lucas is nothing but trouble, I don't want you marrying him not even for a truce. Do you understand?"

Agonya was so taken aback at this that she just nodded silently.

"I have decided," he continued in a softer tone, "you will be safer away from here, and the kingdom will be safer for it. It is my responsibility to—"

"Your responsibility!" Agonya's exterior of civility cracked. "Since when have you ever been concerned with your responsibility? Ever since Mother died, you haven't cared about anyone!"

"Enough!" The king's voice was even colder than before.

Regaining her composure, Agonya stared at the faded rug. She could barely make out the various trees woven into it, trees that grew in the Perfumed Pines and all throughout the Fertile Basin. "But the clouds. Are they connected to the Kors attacking us? Wouldn't I be safer here with you?"

Azurarus' face softened. Before Agonya knew it, he was sitting at her side holding her hands in his. "Don't you see? I'm not safe to be around. I'm sorry about Hodel. No, don't give me that look. I didn't order his division to the battle because of your disobedience. You knew he was one of my soldiers and I made the best decision I could. How was I to know that the Kors would defeat us so thoroughly? I understand your frustration and why you've continued to disrespect me. I know I haven't been the best father to you. I am sorry for that. Truly, I am."

"Then, why are you sending me away?" Agonya rubbed her temples before meeting his gaze. He seemed sincere that his decision about Division Two wasn't about his conflict with her. But she didn't know that she could ever forgive him for Hodel's death. No matter how good his intentions were.

A shadow crossed his face. He let go of her hands, strode across the room, and stopped in front of her mother's portrait. He removed the painting from the wall. Scratch marks indicated the painting had been moved more than a few times. A small opening hid behind it. He reached inside and pulled out a brown package. A woody scent accompanied the package into the room. Agonya wondered what perfume he'd used to scent it.

"I need you to take this with you. You must guard it with your life."

"Why me? You've never trusted me with anything important before."

His hands shook while he stared at the package he was holding. When he spoke, his voice quavered. "Because you are like her. *You* are the only one who can keep it safe." He handed the package to Agonya and caught his breath as he turned away. Was he crying? He dabbed at his eyes before turning back to face her. "You must go to the Montanes and convince them to come to our aid. If they find out you have that," he pointed at the package in her hands, "they will try to take it from you. Don't let them." The words tumbled out of him, Agonya could barely process what he was asking of her.

"But . . . if they want this, why am I taking it with me?"

"They aren't the only ones who want it, and no one will expect you to have it." Azurarus glanced at the locked shutters. "But you may be able to convince the Montanes to come fight the Kors. The man I've chosen to escort you will be able to help you negotiate with them. Trust him."

Agonya clutched the package in her hands. She started to open it but her father stilled her hands with his own.

"Not here. It's not safe."

Agonya nodded. "At least tell me what it is. Why is this so important?"

"I can't tell you, in case we're overheard."

"Who's going to–"

King Azurarus pulled her into his arms, hugging her tightly. "Your mother died to protect this," he whispered. "And, if your uncle gets his hands on it, we'll all be doomed."

Chapter 2

Ever since the darkness had invaded Ithol, all Krillin could smell was oakmoss. "Why oakmoss?" he wondered. There was no good reason for the scent of oakmoss in the palace. It grew on trees and wasn't suitable to eat and no one in their right mind would use it to improve the air.

Grinding his teeth, Krillin groped his way through the pitch-black halls. Not a single candle or torch was lit. He was going to be late. There was no way he could navigate these maze-like halls in time. He was going to be late.

He sniffed the air again. This time a trace of smoke hid under the fungi scent. A light approached from behind. Krillin spun around to face it. A small servant woman with long black hair and equally black eyes, like most women in Ithol, was walking towards him.

"I need that candle."

"Sorry?" she said.

"I need that candle," Krillin repeated. "I have to relieve the other guards from their post."

She was near enough now for Krillin to pick out her scent. She had a unique fragrance: rosemary, honeysuckle, and fir. Her aroma was so refreshing that Krillin almost regretted having to take the candle from her. Almost. Aekan wouldn't be forgiving.

"Maybe you could take me to the kitchen first? I'm sure we could get another candle there," the woman said.

She didn't sound cooperative. He needed speed, not an argument. "No," he said emphatically. "I need it now, or I will be late."

"Surely, they will understand—"

He shook his head. "You can walk with me for part of the way." Before he could change his mind, Krillin swiped the candle from her grasp and started walking.

She had to jog to keep up, but Krillin didn't slow his stride. He needed to get rid of her quickly. "Can you find your way from here?" He tried to remain polite even though every muscle in his body told him to hurry up and get as far from her as possible.

"Yes." She bobbed her head. "There's only a couple of turns."

Krillin smiled. He didn't know what he would have done if she had said no. He sped up, leaving her standing in the dark. He would have broken into a full-blown run if it weren't for fear that the candle might go dark.

He found the meeting place, the planter with the birds of Paradise blooming under the portrait of Jedrek, the first king of Ithol.

Where was Aekan? Krillin shifted from one foot to the other and almost turned to go.

"The birds are gone," came a familiar voice. The smell of cardamom and cacao confirmed it was indeed Aekan. Krillin was good with smells, better than everyone he knew, including Aekan.

That's why he didn't hesitate to reply. Aekan needed to hear it was him. "But Paradise is coming."

Aekan stepped into the light. He wore a servant's uniform. It was a good disguise. His lighter skin was less noticeable. Not that it mattered in the dark.

"Did the storm delay you?" The words were out before Krillin could take them back. The smell of eight metal blades hidden in the folds of Aekan's clothes reminded him to whom he was talking.

"No. I knew it was coming. I was stopped on my way here by someone wanting me to work." Aekan gestured to his uniform. "But that's not why we're here. What did you find out?"

He knew the storm was coming? A shudder ran through Krillin's spine. But he didn't dare ask how Aekan knew. He stumbled over his words. "The king hasn't left his rooms all day. Half a dozen people have gone to see him, and they all carried a package when they left. It could be with any one of them."

"I need names."

"Lord Commander Huren, the head steward, Mikkah. The priest, Lord Tanish, was next to arrive, then Princess Agonya, Sir Marko, and Sir Besnek." Krillin allowed a small smile. He remembered them all. He didn't have time to dwell on it because he smelled . . . rosemary . . . honeysuckle . . . and fir. He stiffened.

"Excellent. We're already watching Sir Besnek and the Lord Commander–"

"Shh!" Krillin interrupted. Yes. He was sure it was that woman he'd met in the hall. Her scent was as sharp as the top layer of a good perfume.

Krillin closed his eyes and lowered his voice. "Someone is here with us. I smell her," he whispered. He hated that he had to tell Aekan about her, but if he let her go, they were both in danger.

Aekan cursed. "Her? You know her?"

Krillin turned towards the sweet smell. "I borrowed her candle to find my way here. A servant woman. She's hiding behind those pillars."

Aekan ran to the pillars Krillin indicated. "There's no one here." He peered down the hall. "But I hear her running. I'll take care of it and contact you later." Aekan ran into the dark.

Even after reciting all those names, doing everything just right, Krillin still felt like he had failed. She didn't do anything to deserve the fate he knew awaited her. Why did he agree to this stench? He didn't like Aekan in the first place.

Krillin stood there by himself for a moment, then headed for the guard tower. He had to put her death out of his mind. It was hard for him to betray his own people, but what gave him the strength was that the very men who were supposed to protect the people often hurt more than helped them–just like they had with his brother. The Korins might not seem much better, but he had to hope for the best. Krillin hurried down the hall, this time not bothering to stay quiet.

***

One change of clothes, the plainest she could find in her wardrobe, the dagger that her father had given her on her tenth born day, and various other items sprawled across her bed. She couldn't figure out why her father had suddenly changed his beliefs about the Montanes. He'd always told her not to trust them. But he was adamant, and then there was the package. Something about that package made Agonya feel like Hodel's death would be for nothing if she didn't succeed. She placed her hands on her hips and let her gaze sweep over the remaining items: two full water skins, her whole stock of candles, incense, and fragrances, a map, and, of course, the mysterious package . . .

The harder she stared at the package the stranger it looked. The air was shimmering around it. She reached to pick it up, but footsteps pounded in the hall outside her room. She shoved it in her satchel barely registering that it was hot to the touch and began stuffing the rest of her things on top. The door opened just as she managed to get her clothes in the bag. Maya entered, shutting the door securely behind her.

Agonya dropped the candles and hurried to her side. "What happened to you? You look like you've smelled blood."

"Shhh." Maya held a finger to her lips. She slid the bar into place and pressed her ear against it. Agonya didn't need to have her ear on the door to hear what Maya heard, running feet and the rattle of doors. Maya quickly jumped back from the door. The handle shook violently. The footsteps paused. A fragrance of citrus filled the room. Agonya could almost see it push through the door. Then, whoever stood on the other side started running again. The citrus aroma vanished.

"He recognized me," Maya panted. "I barely had time to run away."

"Who recognized you? Run away from what?" Agonya tried to process what Maya was talking about but none of it made sense.

Maya took a deep breath and tried again. "I didn't get the food," she whispered. "A guard met me on the way to the kitchen and said he needed my candle. I offered to get him a candle in the kitchens, but he grabbed it out of my hands and left me standing there alone. I might have been able to find my way to the kitchens in the dark but thought perhaps once he'd reached his destination, I could take the candle back. So, I followed him."

"You followed him! But we need to be in the gardens in the next hour."

Maya acted as if she didn't hear Agonya. "When I caught up to him, he was standing there in the middle of the hall. I moved to approach him and ask for the candle back when another man appeared. They spoke some sort of code, and the other man was a Kor, so I hid myself."

"An Itholean guard stole your candle and met a Kor in the palace. And he chased you?"

Maya clutched at her sides. "I heard them say something about the king, and Lord Commander Huren. There were other names. I heard yours. That's when the guard recognized my scent."

Agonya pushed Maya's hair away from her face, tucking it behind her ears. "He's gone now. Can you describe him for me, the Itholean guard?"

"I didn't see his face, but he smelled heavily of frankincense."

"What about the Kor?"

Maya shook her head. "No. There was too much frankincense in the air, I couldn't smell anything else. How he smelled me is a wonder. But I can say the Itholean was taller than most men, and the Kor was short."

"Come. We must warn father."

"But what if the Kor is waiting for us in the hall?"

Agonya grabbed the dagger off her bed and turned back to Maya. "Then, we'll have to be faster than him. But I'm pretty sure that something happened just now to make him keep going. I don't know what, but did you smell the citrus?"

"Citrus? What are you talking about?" Maya's eyes widened.

Agonya shook her head. "I might have imagined it." She pressed her ear against the door. She couldn't hear anyone. She peeked outside. The corridor was empty.

Tightening her grip on her dagger, she slipped out of the room. Maya followed right behind. They made their way towards the king's chambers. Silence filled the darkness. Why weren't the candles lit yet?

Agonya swallowed a cry of horror when she rounded the last corner. The dagger slipped from her hands as they flew to her mouth. A light from her father's room spilled through the cracked door, shining on the blood pooled about the heads of the guards she'd seen earlier that day. She gagged, and Maya let out a short scream. And then Maya's hands were rubbing her back, trying to comfort her even though they were both convulsing. Her head told her this wasn't happening, but the scent of frankincense forced her body to relax. Agonya willed the frankincense to fill her up, to calm her.

It wasn't enough. The smell of blood was too overpowering. Agonya slipped on it when she tried to get past the dead guards. Her hand landed on one of their chests, breaking her fall; then Maya was by her side, pulling her up. Together they pushed the doors open and went inside. Agonya couldn't process what she was seeing. Her father's body slumped in the armchair next to the fire, his head lying on the rug.

"No! No, no . . ." Agonya collapsed on the rug and cradled her father's head in her lap. The smell of his blood made her muscles tense. Not even the burning incense could keep tears from streaming down her face.

"Princess?" Maya's voice shook as she spoke. "Come on, we can't stay here."

Agonya couldn't think straight. Emotions flooded her senses. To see his life dissipate into nothingness like perfume on the wind . . . his soul, gone. "I can't leave him like this. What—" Agonya choked back a cry as her father's head rolled out of her hands.

"Shhh. Footsteps!" Maya hissed, tugging on her arm.

Agonya let Maya pull her off the ground and lead her out of the room. Agonya felt her feet move down the corridor, but her thoughts wouldn't leave her father's side.

She felt Maya stop. A large man in a green and white kurta stood with his arms folded across his thick chest; Mikkah was the king's steward, and he looked like he was about to lecture her.

"Your Highness, begging your pardon, but I was coming to find you."

"He's dead," Agonya forced out.

He didn't hear her.

"I tried to send Lady Velia home, but she insisted—"

"The king is dead," Agonya said again, this time more clearly.

"Shhhhh, your Highness. Please . . ." Maya pleaded.

"The king? What are you going on about? I talked with him less than an hour ago."

Agonya couldn't understand why it was so hard for him to hear her.

He finally looked at her, really looked at her. "Is that blood?"

Agonya glanced down at her favorite cerulean gown, now crimson where the fabric had absorbed her father's blood. Her whole body shook as she tried to control her emotions.

Mikkah reached out and pulled Agonya close. "Quick. Take her Highness to the Sunroom. Do *not* leave her side. I will be with you shortly." Mikkah dashed off down the corridor, his footsteps fading into the distance.

"Agonya?" Maya hesitated.

"Hmmm?"

"Should we go to the Sunroom?"

"What do you mean?"

"Only that–what was Mikkah doing so close to the King's rooms if he were trying to find you? I mean, wouldn't he be near your chambers?"

"What? Mikkah? I can't believe he had anything to do with this. I've known him my whole life. We have no choice, Maya."

"Of course." Maya grabbed Agonya's hand again and guided her up a staircase and through the ancient halls.

***

The Sunroom's normally cheery plants and bright sofas were encased in darkness like the rest of the city. Agonya felt Maya washing the blood off her hands and helping her change into the spare clothes from her bag. When Mikkah arrived, Agonya couldn't help but shrink back into the recesses of the sofa. He brought several guards with him.

"Your Highness," he began, "I've alerted the rest of the king's guards. They are searching the palace as we speak. These men will stand guard outside this room. They will escort you wherever you may have cause to go, but I recommend staying here until we've made certain the palace is safe." Mikkah turned to the guards. "If you would give us some privacy."

The guards sniffed the air and stepped back into the corridor. Mikkah rubbed his palm and faced Maya who was standing by the wash basin, still trying to get the blood out of Agonya's cerulean gown.

"You should do that in the washroom. Not here. Now, go."

"No," Agonya couldn't let Maya leave her side. "Maya stays here."

"But your Highness, with all due respect we don't want any more ears hearing what we're about to discuss than necessary."

"I understand. Maya, come sit with me. You may tell Mikkah what happened."

Maya put down the dress and wiped her hands on a towel before walking over to the sofas.

Mikkah sat down across the small table from Agonya, glancing nervously at Maya. "Your Highness, I need to know if you saw anything or anyone else. At first, when you said he was dead, I did not believe it."

Agonya couldn't force herself to look up. She heard his words, but they meant nothing to her.

Maya did as Agonya asked and spoke, "We didn't see anyone, but there is something you should know. I overheard one of the guards speaking with a Kor. That's why we were on our way to see the king."

Agonya felt her throat tighten and tried to swallow the lump away. They didn't notice.

Maya told Mikkah the whole story from the moment she headed for the kitchens to the moment they met him in the hall.

"And now, I've alerted the guards, one of whom might be a traitor." Mikkah took a deep breath and shook his head. "Did anyone see you come here?"

Agonya didn't know. She didn't remember anything specific since she had found her father dead, except the feel of his head in her hands.

Maya shook her head. "I don't think so."

"Good. Stay here until I figure out who I can trust." Mikkah stood up to leave but turned back. "I'm going to go get Lord Commander Huren, he'll know what to do. And I think I'll send someone to fetch Lord Tanish, too. We'll need a priest to help with the funeral."

"Yes. I trust those two." Agonya let out a breath that she didn't know she'd been holding. She heard Mikkah close the door behind him, and let her mind go blank to keep from dwelling on the pain that threatened to overwhelm her.

Chapter 3

A loud grumble reminded Huren that the last thing he ate was mush at the start of the day. His meeting with the king had lasted longer than expected. Azurarus was convinced his life was in danger. Of course, Huren didn't see how anyone could get past his guards, but he assigned more guards to protect the king anyway and they had come up with a fragrant plan to draw attention away from the king too.

Sending a quick prayer to the Patron of Fortune, Huren put the king out of his mind and approached the kitchen window.

"Kahlilah, you got anything for a starving old man?"

The cook looked up from the pot she was stirring and put her hands on her hips. "You ought to eat more during the day. This is becoming a habit."

Huren shrugged his shoulders. He was the Lord Commander and that meant he didn't have time to spare.

"Oh, don't worry." Kahlilah smiled. "I saved some for you." Then, wiping her hands on her apron, she disappeared behind a wall and returned with a steaming bowl of stew. "Here."

Huren grinned and took the rich venison broth, his fingers lingering on her soft hands. He felt his heart pound faster.

Damn. Who cared what others thought? One of these days he would marry that woman. He turned away without saying another word and sat down at one of the tables.

He dipped his spoon into the broth and began eating. The minted deer melted in his mouth. Three bites in, and he was interrupted.

The king's steward burst through the door. "Lord Commander. You'd better come. There's something you need to see."

Huren swallowed quickly, burning his tongue. "What is it?" he choked out.

"It's the king, sir. He's dead."

Huren's spoon clattered to the floor. He bolted up from the table and dashed after the large man.

When they reached the king's corridor, Mikkah slowed down. "I was looking for Princess Agonya when she found me. She was in shock and covered in blood." Mikkah's hand trembled as he lit the torch on the wall and pointed at the floor.

Huren was also in shock. He had thought that whoever was after the package wouldn't bother with the king if he no longer had it. Yet, two of their best guards, the king's very own, lay dead on the floor, never to smell Paradise again.

"Who else knows about this?" Huren asked.

"The princess and her servant, Maya. I alerted the rest of the guards in the palace to search for the assassin."

"Why didn't you come to me first?"

"I didn't know where you were, and after seeing the princess like that, I knew I had to be quick. I went to Captain Thrush to get guards to protect her. And he told me where to find you," Mikkah replied.

Huren nodded and grabbed the torch off the wall. At least the man was honest. Mikkah was one of the few who had been given a package. And if Huren was right, Mikkah's package was empty.

A dagger lay several paces from the bodies, but it didn't have blood on it. That was strange. Huren bent down to retrieve it. He could smell sweat on the handle and felt an engraving on the back. Turning it over in his hands, he saw the grooves curved in on themselves to make a peony. "Do you recognize this?"

Mikkah took it and traced the outline of the flower with a fingertip. "This belongs to the princess, sir. She must have dropped it when she saw the dead guards."

Huren remembered Azurarus presenting the dagger to Agonya almost fifteen years ago. "But why did she have it with her? Was she already aware of danger?"

"Yes. Maya said that she'd discovered a traitor and a spy. The two of them were on their way to inform the king when they found this." Mikkah waved his arm at the bloody scene. "I ran into them over there. See those bloody footprints trailing off? Those are theirs."

Huren took the dagger back from Mikkah and tucked it in his belt. He squared his shoulders and forced himself to step across the threshold into the king's chamber.

Blood and death usually didn't faze Huren. Most of his sixty-three years had been spent in battle, fighting the king's wars. But this, this was something entirely different. Not even the queen's death compared. Azurarus' body was lifeless in the chair, not even stiff yet. His head lay on the floor.

Huren felt a sharp pain in his chest, but he couldn't look away. The king's head was at an odd angle, and his eyes stared through a film of gray haze at nothing. His expression was sad, as if he had known he was going to die and regretted not having time to make things right. Huren peeled his eyes from his friend's face, unable to look at Azurarus without the pain in his chest growing stronger.

The rest of the room was a mess. The assassin had made a thorough search of the place. Pillows and papers were scattered across the room. Kanti's portrait was ripped in two like her husband. At least whoever killed his friend hadn't found the package. Not even Huren knew where it was.

"Mikkah, help me lay the king down before he's too stiff to straighten."

Mikkah nodded and began clearing a bit of the floor to lay him on. Huren scanned the room again before kneeling next to his friend. He lifted the king's legs while Mikkah grabbed his shoulders. Together they laid him on the rug. Huren picked up Azurarus' head and moved it into place, where it should have remained.

He could hear Azurarus' voice as if he were still alive. "We mustn't give up, even now that we are retreating."

"Did you say something, sir?" Mikkah asked.

Huren hadn't realized he'd spoken out loud. "Just something the king said before he died. He told me, 'It's not our homes but our people at stake. Promise me, Huren, you will not let them down no matter what happens.'"

Voicing Azurarus' words helped lessen the pain in his chest. *No matter what happens*. No matter if Azurarus died. Huren stood and looked down at his friend's body, reeking of death and frankincense. Then he motioned for Mikkah to follow him out of the room.

* * *

Agonya stared at the sofa Mikkah had vacated, her mind numb. How much time had passed? An hour? Two? Everything seemed to be slipping away from her: Hodel, her father, her happiness, life . . .

Maya stood. Agonya knew it was because of the knock on the door. Her muscles tensed. The horror of finding her father flooded back into her body. She had to meet with the men behind the door. Maya went to the door and opened it.

"May I come in?"

Maya opened the door wider. An older man with gray streaking his black hair and wearing priestly robes entered. Agonya forced her body to stand, to go through the customary greetings.

Lord Tanish, one of Agonya's old tutors and a priest, grasped Agonya's hand and sniffed her scent. The wrinkles on his face deepened when Lord Commander Huren and Mikkah arrived. The guards in the hall saluted their commander. He saluted back and joined Agonya and the others in the room, closing the door so they would be alone.

Agonya collapsed back onto the sofa. "Were any of you followed?"

Lord Commander Huren lowered himself onto the opposite sofa. "My men and I have searched the whole palace, your Highness. I haven't seen anyone who shouldn't be here. But we do need to stay vigilant. The king . . ."

Agonya stiffened. She longed to hold onto Maya's hand but couldn't move.

Lord Tanish broke the awkward silence. "Please, your Highness, put your mind at rest. I did not see anyone follow me here."

"Yes, no need to be frightened," Huren said.

"I know you searched the palace and have increased security, Lord Commander," Maya said, startling the men who'd assumed she wouldn't speak to them. "But an assassin did get past."

"About that–" Huren began.

Agonya interrupted, "I should be outside the palace." Her legs twitched below her skirt, ready to run at the first chance as fast and as far as she could, leaving everything behind including the image of her father's severed head and the smell of his blood.

"We cannot ensure your safety outside of the palace without giving away your location." Huren crossed his arms. "We should move you to the room next to your chambers. That way we can have guards posted in the hallway without giving away your location. We can lay a trap for the assassin."

"But your guards didn't ensure my father's safety . . ." And what about the traitor? Agonya felt like someone was watching her, peering into her soul. Her enemies knew where she was. She had to escape.

"As the heir to the throne, I know you must be worried. But let me assure you, your Highness, that we will do everything in our power to protect you. Here." Huren pulled a dagger out of his cloak. It was hers.

Agonya snatched it, then flushed.

Drops of red blood dripped off the pointed tip. The sharp smell of metal filled her nose. Agonya peeled her eyes from the blade and looked up at Huren. He was putting pressure on the wound to his hand.

Agonya fumbled with the dagger before laying it on her lap. "I'm so sorry! Are you okay?"

"It's a small cut." Huren brushed it off.

The feeling of hopelessness began to wear on Agonya again, and she noticed that the incense no longer burned. She reached for her mother's necklace and rubbed it between her fingers. Maya saw and suggested the men leave to pursue their investigations.

❋ ❋ ❋

As soon as the door closed behind the men, Agonya turned to Maya. She felt her chest tighten and her hands shook. "I have to go to the gardens. We have to escape."

"But Huren–" Maya began.

Agonya interrupted. "My father wanted me to go." Speaking it out loud, Agonya felt the truth of it, and her body's shaking ebbed.

Without saying another word, Maya gathered their things. They both looked at the door and knew they couldn't leave through there without being followed by guards. Agonya stepped over to the largest window and helped Maya lift the bar to unlock the shutters. Agonya took a deep breath and climbed out onto the balcony.

The cold night air hit Agonya hard, but she didn't let it deter her. She had to get out. Silently, the women climbed down a nearby tree, crossed the courtyard and wove through the halls. Twice they had to hide from soldiers. But they made it to the gardens on the edge of the palace without being caught.

Agonya led Maya through the rows of plants as they looked for their guide, the one who was supposed to meet them there in the ninth hour. That hour was long past, but Agonya hoped he waited.

Suddenly, someone dropped down from the tree they stood under, landing softly on their feet. "Why are you here?" came a sharp and cold man's voice.

Agonya looked up. The nearest branch was at least fifteen feet above the ground. How had this man jumped so far without hurting himself? And what was this nonsense about her reasoning for being in the garden? Agonya tried to get a better look at his face, but his hood covered it, and it was too dark out. Not a star in the sky, just those thick menacing clouds.

A black cloak hung limp at his sides, hiding him further. But his hands were not hidden. Their lightness stood out. He was a Montane. Her heart pounded in her chest. Had her father arranged for a Montane to escort her? No wonder he said the escort would be able to help her negotiate with them.

"What do you mean, addressing her Highness like that? Don't you know who you are speaking to?" Maya broke the silence, putting herself between Agonya and the Montane.

"You think I should treat her with respect when she does not show it to her father?" he scoffed.

His words pierced Agonya to her core. Somehow this man knew that her father was dead. She'd told Maya she was honoring her father's wishes by going through with the plan, but the truth was she hadn't been able to bear the thought of seeing his corpse again, of burying him in the cold ground away from the scented air.

"How dare you?" Maya poked his chest.

"No. Maya–" Agonya couldn't get the right words out. He was right. She was running away from her problems because she couldn't handle the pain. She couldn't leave her father unburied. Her chest tightened at the thought. But that was just an excuse.

Maya let her hand drop but didn't back down. "Explain," she demanded of the Montane.

Agonya felt him staring at her, but she couldn't bring herself to look at him, not when he spoke the truth about her.

"You need to stay and bury him," he said simply.

"But the king wanted us to leave tonight," Maya protested.

"He did. May the smells of Paradise ever be with him. But he did not know he was going to die." The Montane stopped speaking and bowed his head. After a moment of silence, he went on. "I'm Ashkii. I'm sorry I wasn't able to protect him. Your father was a great man."

"How did you know he died?" Maya asked.

"I was supposed to meet with him one last time before escorting you to Tafka. But when I arrived the breath of life had already left him."

"But how can we be certain *you* didn't kill him?" Maya persisted.

Ashkii didn't respond. A moment later he flipped the cloak over his shoulder and pulled back the collar of his shirt to reveal a tattoo. A peony in full bloom was etched onto his shoulder. The movement released a gust of peony scent, as if the Montane was perfumed with the stuff.

Agonya gasped. That was her mother's flower. He wouldn't have known about the peonies unless . . . "Did you know my mother?"

"No, but Azurarus told me about her." He let his collar fall back in place. "She was part of us, those of us who believe the Kindroots will bring back Paradise."

Every word he spoke only confused Agonya more. But she knew beyond a doubt he hadn't killed her father. She could smell it in the floral and woody scent surrounding him.

"I thought," he continued with sympathy in his voice, "that with his death, you would want to stay a little longer. I had hoped to see him honored."

Maya stepped back, a sign to Agonya that she was willing to trust the man.

"You're right." Agonya decided. "But we leave right after."

❋ ❋ ❋

The soothing aroma of azucena flowers filled the air. The king's dirt grave was covered with hundreds of the little white waxy blossoms. The soldiers lining the path held torches to light the way. Agonya walked between them up the hill in her dark green dress, symbolizing life even in death. Half of her shiny black hair was pinned up in a twist, the other half lay in ringlets down her back. As she walked, music filled the air and Agonya began to sing:

> When the day comes
> and scents, tastes, sounds, touches, and sights
> leave you all alone,
>
> Then surrounded by incense
> cypress, tarragon, cedar, tangerine, sandalwood
> float through the air, immense.
>
> Food is prepared
> and sweets, tarts, sours, teas, savories

burn on the tongue ensnared.

Melodies flow like a fountain
strains, tempos, silence, tones so sharp
flow over the basin.

Textures magnificent and repulsive jar your senses
silky, tough, slimy, tender, soft
waiting for life to re-commence.

Finally, memories blind your eyelids
sensual, teasing, simple, trying, successes
each following the one before, till they are all hidden.

Agonya reached her father's resting place, next to her mother. Images of her parents alive together, walking in the garden, sitting in the great hall floated through her mind. It wasn't until Lord Tanish stepped up beside her that she remembered everyone was waiting for her to pour the sickening scents on his grave. Agonya took a deep breath. She felt dizzy and had to grab Lord Tanish's arm to steady herself.

Breathing in the fresh morning air helped her recover. Agonya let go of his arm and turned to Maya who held out a pail of excrement. She took it, almost threw up, overwhelmed by the half dried half fresh substance, and held it up for all to see. Then she dumped it on top of the grave and said the scripted words. "May these scents help us to remember the pain of losing our king."

Collectively, the lords, ladies, commanders, and all who had come to pay their respect responded, "We remember."

Then Maya handed her a container made of sandalwood. Agonya held it up for everyone to see and smell. She poured the minty perfume over the excrement. "May these scents help us to heal though our king cannot be healed."

Again, everyone spoke as one, "We will heal."

Agonya took the torch offered to her and touched the flame to the excrement and oils. Swirls of smells circled up toward the sky. Agonya handed the torch back to the servant and waved her hand through the air, inhaling the blended scents, trying hard not to choke on them and turned abruptly, walking back down the path towards the city. She didn't look back but knew that Lord Tanish did the same, waving his hand over the grave to bring the scents closer. Then Lord Commander Huren, Mikkah, Lady Velia, and Maya, all of them took their turn breathing in the blend of sickening and cleansing scents before following her back down the path.

The walk back was silent, except for the sounds of feet on the path. When Agonya reached the city gates, her palanquin was there ready to carry her to the palace. Agonya turned back now to see the long line of people following her. Were they following her as queen or just following the customs? Agonya sighed and sat down on the waiting palanquin, anxious to move on.

Smells of roasted meat and vegetables, of sweets and tarts, greeted Agonya back at the palace. She went straight to the great hall where tables were laden with food and drink. This would be the last feast in the city for a long time. Agonya hadn't wanted the feast, but the majority of the council had convinced her to have it anyway.

Even as she smelled all her guests arrive in their fancy clothes with their favored perfumes wafting ahead of them, she knew it was all an act. Agonya took her place at the head table, not bothering to get a plate of food. Lady Velia was the first to join her at the table, her plate heaped with the best of the food. Agonya clasped her hands on her lap beneath the table and waited.

Lady Velia speared the roast lamb with her fork. Before eating it, she leaned across the table. "Where's your food, your Highness?"

"I'm not hungry."

"It must be awful for you to be expected to take on so much responsibility at such a young age." Lady Velia sat back in her chair, chewing the juicy lamb. She swallowed and continued talking. "I had hoped that by arranging this feast in honor of the king, you wouldn't feel so burdened with both the loss of your father and the added duties of being queen."

"You think that you are honoring him by wasting all this food during war? I still don't agree with you and the other council members. We should be more concerned with the kingdom's needs than our own."

Velia's eyes widened briefly before her features smoothed. "Oh, I wouldn't want to do anything to hurt the people, your Highness. But they need to see that we're not worried."

While Velia spoke, a servant appeared, placed a plate of food in front of Agonya, and disappeared back into the crowd of people. "Hope of a swift victory is what they need." Lady Velia raised her fork and continued eating.

"I beg to differ, my Lady," Lord Tanish said as he joined them at the table. "We need to be smarter than that. I respect Queen Agonya's decision not to eat. It shows that she cares for her people. They will take faith in that."

Agonya pushed the unwanted plate away from her and smiled at Lord Tanish, thankful for his support. Lady Velia pushed the plate back. "You really should eat, my dear. You need to be strong for your people."

Anger boiled inside of her. Velia must have arranged that a plate be brought to her, so the people would think ill of Agonya. She clenched her fists and stood up. One by one, Agonya forced her fingers to relax. Raising her voice, Agonya spoke loud enough for the people at the nearby tables to hear her and hopefully spread her words to those who couldn't hear, "I appreciate your concern, Lady Velia. But I cannot and will not feast while I mourn the loss of my father, knowing that war is upon us. I must do what I can to stop the Kors from devouring us." Agonya stood up and left. If Agonya didn't already have plans to leave the city that night, she would beat Velia at her game. She didn't know how long it would take her to reach Tafka and return with help. She hoped her little speech would be enough for her people not to lose faith in her.

Chapter 4

Two guards stood on either side of her bedroom door. They had to stand in front of her chambers instead of the room Agonya would be in to keep up the appearance of Agonya being in her own room. When they saw her coming though, one of them slipped into her new room. By the time she reached the door, he was back in the hall.

"It's safe, your Highness," he said, then joined the other soldier standing guard in front of her real room.

Leaving the feast early was not part of the plan, but what was done was done. She paced the small room, waiting for Maya to get away from the servants' meal.

This was the first time since her father's death that Agonya had truly been alone. The package her father had given her drew her to her satchel. She removed the package and sat on the bed. It wasn't hot like the last time she'd touched it, but the same woody scent she'd smelled in her father's rooms still accompanied it. So, it wasn't perfume. Perfume wouldn't last that long. Peeling off the brown paper, Agonya found more paper beneath. Three times she had to unwrap the package. Finally, the last of the paper fell away, and she saw a plant nestled inside the tiniest pot she'd ever seen. The scent made sense now. It looked like a fully grown tree, but it was smaller than even a sapling.

Why in the name of Paradise would her father want her to guard this with her life? And what kind of tree could survive without sunlight, water, and air wrapped up in paper for over three days? Getting up, Agonya walked over to the wash basin in the corner and scooped up some water. She poured it in the tiny pot and waited. The leaves which had been slightly drooping perked up.

She heard the guards questioning Maya in the hall. Agonya slipped the plant back into her bag, careful to keep it upright, just as Maya walked through the door.

"I came as soon as I heard," Maya said.

Agonya slid her feet to the floor and stood up. "What exactly did you hear?"

"I heard Lady Velia was irate after your little speech." The corners of Maya's mouth turned up in a smile.

Agonya couldn't help but grin back at her. "Velia wanted the people to think I am a selfish little brat who isn't competent enough to be queen. She wanted me to enjoy the feast to its fullest, as if I could. You should have seen the look on her face when I proved that I'm not the child they all take me for, that I can think for the good of others and not just myself."

For the first time in three days, they laughed together. Agonya felt a little bit lighter, though it didn't lessen her headache.

"Your father was honored beautifully today," Maya said, after their laughter died away.

"I keep wondering if we should have left that night. My father ordered everyone to prepare for the Kors' arrival three days ago. They must be close. And for all his talk about wanting to honor my father, I didn't see the Montane there today. Did you?"

"He was there. I almost didn't see him but when my eyes followed the smoke up into the sky, I saw him perched on a branch. As for the Kors, they're pitching tents in the east," Maya said. "The guards assured me that it was safe to go to the burial site."

“Even so,” Agonya rubbed her temples, “if we had left three days ago, we would be that much closer to getting help from the Montanes.”

“But we haven’t been idle, Agonya. I heard the soldiers have been guarding the harvesters, helping them gather as much food as they can. Our storehouses are overflowing.”

“What else have you learned?”

“Since the death of the king, Lord Commander Huren has been sending out troops to harry the Kors and plunder their supplies.”

A clash of swords rang in the hallway. They stared at the door. It burst open. One of her guards backed into the room.

“Run, your Highness!” the other said, following close behind. Then he plunged his sword into the chest of the first. What was happening? Her own guards were fighting each other! Before she could process what was happening, the end of a blade pierced her remaining guard’s chest from behind. Both her guards fell to the floor. A scent of buttery nuts followed the blade in through the door, a man dressed all in black pressed his foot on the guard’s back, freeing his sword.

Agonya didn’t wait to get a better look at him. She ran for the window. Maya was there before her, climbing through with their bags quickly slung over her shoulders. Agonya began climbing after her when she felt hands grab hold of her, pulling her back inside. She swallowed a scream and squeezed her eyes shut.

The hands pushed her to the floor, making her kneel. He was going to cut off her head like her father. Slowing her breathing, Agonya willed her hand to draw her dagger out of its sheath at her waist. The intruder knocked it out of her hands. She tried to crawl away, but he held her in place. There was no escape. Agonya waited for the end to come. In her mind, she saw the assassin aim his sword.

Then, she felt something brush the top of her head. The ring of metal hitting metal followed. Agonya opened her eyes to see someone stopping the assassin’s sword in midair.

“Go, your Highness.” The voice belonged to the Montane. He had come to escort them to Tafka and instead was fighting an assassin.

Agonya heard their sword and daggers dancing with each other. She heard the assassin snarl and then the Montane helped her to her feet, slipping her dropped dagger back into her hands. He gave a push toward the window, and she jumped through. Maya was waiting for her.

Agonya fled into the night, tears soaking her face and gasping for air as she ran. Soon she was breathing in the scent of fresh peonies; they were in the gardens.

"This way." She motioned for Maya to follow her through the maze of plants. Her heart raced faster. They weren't safe yet.

When they came to the ivy on the wall, Agonya pulled it away to reveal a door, one she hadn't seen in sixteen years.

"Wait."

Agonya flinched, smelling the cold rising from her arms.

The Montane walked up behind them. He held a dagger in each of his hands, one of them dripping blood. He noticed Agonya's gaze and wiped the dagger on his cloak, but he didn't put it away. "Let me make sure it's safe."

He pushed past the women, opened the door, and peered down the street. "Come on."

They dashed into the street and ran until the palace walls could no longer be seen.

***

They walked for several hours through streets lit only by slivers of light escaping through broken shutters. Suddenly, Ashkii stopped in front of an oak door. He motioned for them to wait in the street while he made sure it was empty, then directed them inside.

The small home only had two rooms. Ashkii led them into the back. His hood fell onto his shoulders as he stooped and lifted stacked carpets off the floor, revealing a tunnel descending beneath the house.

Agonya's mouth dropped open. She couldn't stop staring at his hair. It was golden like the leaves of an ash tree in the fall. She'd never seen yellow hair like his. She'd heard it existed but had never seen it. Regaining her composure, Agonya climbed down into the tunnel. She felt along the wall until she found what she was looking for. “Maya, do you have a flint?”

“Here.”

The torch caught on fire and lit up the narrow dirt walls. Every few meters, beams of wood framed the wall and roof.

They hurried through the tunnel in silence, as it descended further and further into the ground. Agonya wondered at Ashkii, the Montane. She didn’t know anything about Montanes but if they were anything like this man, a man who valued honor and respect, though in odd ways, and a man capable of killing that assassin when her guards could not, then, she would be glad to have them on her side, even if he was prone to climb trees and jump out of them as if he was just going for a walk. How was it even possible for him to jump like that?

Lost in thought, Agonya continued through the narrow yet straight tunnel. There were no side tunnels and it just seemed to stretch on and on. Agonya wondered when they would leave the city but there was nothing to let her know how far they’d gone, only the time and she couldn’t be sure of that. Exhaustion from the day’s events and the hours and hours of walking clouded her mind.

A large shape rose up beside her. She rubbed her eyes and held the torch up. Bright green eyes stared back at her. She rubbed her eyes again. They belonged to an enormous lizard with large spikes sticking out all over its head and body. Its lips peeled back revealing chiseled fangs, and a noise like the growl of a koliimus but higher-pitched and menacing emanated from the back of its throat. More dark shapes growled from the darkness up ahead.

Ashkii leapt forward, swept Agonya and Maya behind him, and threw something in the middle of the creatures all before Agonya could reach for her dagger. A cloud of smoke exploded, filling the tunnel. Ashkii covered his mouth and nose with his cloak and motioned for them to do the same. Agonya sniffed the unfamiliar pungent and resinous odor before blocking it with her shawl. Her muscles weakened but she gripped her dagger harder.

They backed away from the spiked creatures who were now starting to slink to the ground. What had Ashkii thrown at them to make them lie down?

"This is the first I've seen thorny devils this side of the Perfumed Pines," he said, inching closer to get a better look.

The smoke began to rise to the top of the tunnel, and Agonya could see that the yellow-brown spikes she'd seen earlier were longest on the ridge of their noses and the tips of their tails.

"What is that?" Agonya asked, pointing to the source of the smoke.

"A palantia bomb. Listen. You're going to step where I step. Be careful not to touch their spikes or breathe in the smoke from the bomb."

Agonya held her breath the whole way across the death trap, but they made it without incident. Agonya took the lead again, this time paying attention to what lay ahead of her. If those thorny devils woke up, she would rather Ashkii be between her and them. So far, he had shown his skill at fighting, and she might as well put him to good use. Before long, the tunnel was sloping up towards the surface. Agonya reached the end. Notches were carved into the wall of the tunnel. Climbing up, Agonya pushed on a wooden board. It opened up into a large field of grass. She inhaled the dense night or perhaps early morning air.

"Where are we?" Turning around, Agonya could barely make out lights in the distance, illuminating the city walls.

Ashkii's pale hand pointed away from Ithol. "We won't make it to the mountains for a few days, but there is a safe place not far from here. See that mound? I know the man who lives there."

"How can you see in this darkness?" Maya asked with a yawn.

They all glanced up at the sky still covered by dark clouds that only seemed to be expanding to cover more ground. No one wanted to talk about it. The threatening clouds had brought no rain. Agonya wasn't sure if she felt more depressed by the clouds or the horrible events of the last few days. Either way, she knew they weren't good.

"Follow me," Ashkii finally said.

Agonya picked up her feet and moved them. One step at a time. She stumbled over her green gown, now torn and covered in soot and dirt. It felt like ages before they reached their destination. An older Itholean man, balding on top, opened the door. Agonya wondered if maybe they should have taken more precautions before knocking on a stranger's door, but it was too late now. He took one look at them before welcoming them with an open smelif.

"Oi, Ashkii, long time, my friend."

"Brynn! You stink just like I remember." Ashkii grinned and wiped his hands in his armpits while the Itholean did the same. Then they wiped their hands all over each other's chests.

Agonya watched in utter disbelief. Was this a Montane custom? It was so uncivilized. How had this Itholean become friends with Ashkii?

The man laughed. "I recognize that look," he said to Agonya and Maya. "I remember the first time I saw a Montane greet one of his fellows. My morning meal ended up all over my shoes."

Ashkii cleared his throat. "Brynn, we need a safe place to rest. We've had a rough night and have a long journey ahead of–"

Brynn cut Ashkii off. "I may be old, but I'm not blind yet. Come on in."

Agonya hesitated before following Ashkii inside. The hut smelled minty, very clean.

Brynn walked over to a chest in the corner. He shuffled the contents. When he turned back, he was holding two woolen dresses along with a pair of pants and a cotton shirt. "I know they're not much, but their all I've got." He laid them down on the bench. "There's a basin over there if you want to freshen up." Handing the pants and shirt to Ashkii, he said, "Come, we'll tend the bread and vegetables I started preparing this morning while the ladies freshen up."

Agonya glanced at Maya. Her dress was just as torn and dirty as Agonya's. She picked up the longer dress, grateful that this stranger was so welcoming and unquestioning and was more aware of their needs than she was.

“Let me help.” Maya took the dress from her hands and began undoing the ties on Agonya’s green silk dress.

The women finished donning the brown dresses and sat in silence for a long time, each wrapped up in their own thoughts. By the time the men came inside with hot steaming food, they were fast asleep.

Chapter 5

Agonya looked up at her uncle towering over her mother. She felt small. Looking down at her arms and legs, she saw she was a kid again. She barely reached her mother's waist. Was she dreaming?

Uncle Reid and her mother were talking, but their words blended with the wind. There was someone behind her. She turned. Maya stood on the dirt path.

"Come on!" Agonya beckoned to her sidekick, then ran off into the maze of flowers and bushes, Maya following close on her heels. Her mother and uncle's voices faded the further the girls ran. Agonya stopped.

Maya ran into her. "I'm so sorry, Princess!"

"You count first." Agonya ran down the path and turned before she reached the roses. She knew the perfect spot. Maya would never find her. She rushed over a wall, squeezed in behind the vines, and flattened her body against the secret door.

Agonya could hear Maya calling her name, passing by her hiding spot for the fourth time. That should count as a victory. Agonya decided to jump out the next time Maya came by. But then she heard raised voices approaching.

"Blackthorn doesn't want to go with you. In fact, he is adamant. He will not go with you. He doesn't trust you. And why should I? You lied about why you came." Her mother's voice shook as she spoke.

"Come now, sister. I want to visit with you because you are my sister, and I do care about you. But I need Blackthorn's help to ensure your safety."

"Hogwash. What are you worried about? Our kingdoms are friendly, are they not? And don't give me odors about the dangers of the mountains."

"Oh, but they will leave the mountains soon. I, for one, don't intend to be caught downwind when they do. If you don't surrender him, I'll take him by force."

As her uncle spoke, dark heavy clouds appeared in the sky.

Suddenly, an electric energy surged from the spot they had been standing. Agonya could feel the hairs on her arms stand up. Light blended with a nutty scent and seeped through the vines, blinding her momentarily. The ground shook.

Her body shook. She felt hands on her shoulders.

"Agonya, wake up!" Maya hissed in her ear.

Agonya sat up and rubbed the back of her neck. It felt like her whole body was about to explode. She tried to focus. "What's the matter?" she asked, glancing around the small hut. "Where's Ashkii?"

The Itholean friend of Ashkii's didn't stop packing to answer her. "He said he had something to take care of. He'll have to catch up with us later."

"What do you mean?"

"We're surrounded," Maya whispered.

"Thorny devils?" Agonya dumped everything out of her pack, searching for something useful. The plant tumbled to the floor, glowing. Agonya snatched it up, hoping no one had seen it, and tucked it out of sight.

"No. Korin soldiers," Brynn said.

"How did they find us?" Agonya had so many questions.

Something pounded against the door, bursting it wide open. Brynn tossed Agonya a knife and stepped between the intruders and her. "Why do you barge into my home like this?"

"Food, what else would we want?" The soldier pushed further into the hut, making room for more soldiers to pile in.

"If it's food you want, all you have to do is ask and I'll point you in the right direction."

The Kor grew impatient and pushed Brynn back with the point of his sword.

Agonya held the knife in front of her. But, playing with her dagger in the palace was not enough to know how to fight off soldiers who were pointing large swords at them and ordering them out of the hut as was evidenced by the day before. She dropped the knife and snatched up her discarded incense. It wasn't perfume but perhaps the form didn't matter. Maybe she would be able to convince these soldiers to let her go like she did her guards back at home.

Brynn motioned for the first Kor to follow him to the baskets of food in the corner.

Remembering Ashkii's tip to not be affected by the scent herself, Agonya covered her face with her shawl, then lit the incense. She waved the scents at the Kors. They breathed the smoke in but nothing happened. Agonya closed her eyes and willed the scents to manipulate them.

Their swords lowered. It was working. Agonya imagined the sandalwood and cedar smoke surrounding the soldiers, keeping them in a cage, making them passive. The swords clattered to the ground. Excitement blossomed inside of her. She could hardly believe her success.

A young Korin officer entered the hut, saw the state of his men, then looked Agonya in the eyes. Before Agonya could pull away, he emptied his skins, dousing the sticks in water.

The air took only a moment before it cleared but soon the soldiers blinked awake and grabbed their swords off the ground. The moment Agonya saw the soldiers bending to pick up their swords, she knew it was over. They'd lost. Now she just hoped she wouldn't be recognized by the Kors or everything else would be lost.

Brynn rushed forward, holding his knife out in front. Agonya admired him for it. He didn't even know her name and yet he fought for her. Unfortunately, the officer already had his sword out and was pressing it against Agonya's throat. His square face was hard and unchanging. Both Maya and Brynn stopped mid-stride and dropped their weapons in surrender.

"Lonan, tie them up. Hania, help Lapu search the hut." The officer ordered his men without taking his eyes off Agonya.

"Yes, captain. Right away, sir."

"Where's the food?" he said, still pointing his sword at Agonya.

Agonya pressed her lips together. He may have bested them, but she was not going to give him any more than she had to.

The soldier named Lonan finished tying Brynn's hands behind his back and yanked Agonya's arms behind her. The captain lowered his sword, and she felt the rope tighten around her wrists and tried not to wince.

Another soldier entered the hut and began gathering up their bags. Other men slung Brynn's food and supplies over their shoulders. Lonan shoved Agonya outside. "Move," he said and pushed them towards the distant smoke of the Korin encampment in the valley below.

* * *

Jaylen Dahel was young for a captain, but he wouldn't let his age stop him from moving up the ranks even higher. His capture of a harvester and his supplies was going to help him gain the respect he needed. Most of the farms they'd come across had been cleared out, moved to the city, but here was one yet to be protected. And he had been the one to find it.

There was also the matter of the woman with the incense. It was almost like magic, but Jaylen couldn't see how that could be true. Magic was a thing told to children in the old tales. Only, when he had put out the incense, his soldiers *had* regained their senses. There was no getting around that.

Jaylen continued to ponder this mystery as he steered his company of men past several cook fires in the camp. They had to find General Gad. Nineteen other captains and their men would be setting up in Gad's division, and Jaylen wanted the best location.

The first division's banners—two javelinas under an orange tree—appeared between the tents. Jaylen dismounted. Then, pointing to a group of soldiers close to him, he ordered, "Set up a tent and keep a close watch on the prisoners."

Lonan nodded and sniffed the air before turning to give orders to the others. Jaylen turned to look for General Gad. He walked through the camp, passing groups of soldiers lazing around fires. The darkness was a good reason to congregate around the light, but it might create an unlooked-for opportunity for the enemy to attack. He made a brief stop at one of the cook fires, scarfed down a steaming bowl of gallifowl chili, and found General Gad's tent.

Jaylen stepped up close enough to be seen but not too close to be intrusive. The general was a skinny tree of a man. Not at all like Lord Commander Bannon. But his wits made up for his lack of brawn. Jaylen smiled remembering Gad's victory in their last battle.

"One moment, Captain Dahel." General Gad said and turned back to the guard he was talking to. "I know that's what he said, but these orders came straight from Bannon himself. Make sure they're carried out."

The guard smelled the general's hand and disappeared into the camp.

The general spread his arms wide. "Jaylen! I'm glad to see you made it safely. Did you encounter any problems on the way?"

"Thank you, sir. No problems. You'll be happy to know we found a harvester that hadn't moved his supplies to the city yet."

"That is good news, indeed. But it looks like there's something else on your mind."

Jaylen flushed. Was he so easy to read? He'd have to get better at hiding his emotions. Telling the general about his suspicions was not high on his list. But there was no getting around it now. "These Itholeans, sir." Jaylen cleared his throat. "I suspect they know how to use magic."

General Gad frowned. "What makes you say that?"

"Well, sir, when I arrived in the hut to see what was taking the men so long, I saw they had all dropped their swords on the ground, and there were three Itholeans standing armed and ready to fight. I don't know what made me do it but one of them was burning incense and I doused it with water. When the smoke went away, my soldiers sort of woke up, seeing their swords on the ground, they scrambled to pick them up."

Gad shook his head ever so slightly. "Sounds more like you need to discipline your men, Captain. Magic is for children's tales."

"With all due respect, sir, there is no other explanation. And if this really is magic, then we ought to know about it."

"If they can do magic like you say they can, then I'll be the first to promote you. Your men need to be prepared for battle at any moment. I will not go easy on you if they drop their swords during a raid. Now," Gad said, turning to the papers scattered across his table, "how much food did you bring in?"

Reluctantly, Jaylen didn't push his suspicions further. The general was probably right. Instead, he gave his report on the harvester's stash of wheat, squash, and violets.

"Excellent, these are quite large quantities. It looks like you redeemed yourself despite your men's lack of training. You may go now."

When Jaylen returned to his men, Hania and Lonan stood guard in front of the prisoner's tent.

"Captain." Lonan grabbed Jaylen's elbow, pulled him away from the tent and whispered, "The prisoners are hiding something. I heard them arguing with each other, whispering about someone named Ashkii."

"Ashkii? I don't recognize that name. Should I?"

"I've never heard it before, sir, which is why I don't like it. It's not an Itholean name as far as I know, nor a Korin one. That leaves the Montanes or people beyond the mountains."

Lonan was right. He needed to question these prisoners and find out just who he had caught. If they were linked to the Montanes, perhaps that would explain their strange magic. Jaylen didn't know much about the Montanes, but he did know they were an old people and probably most likely to be tied to the tales he'd heard growing up.

Jaylen nodded and pushed back the heavy flap of the beige tent. He took a moment to study his three prisoners. They sat with their hands tied behind their backs, leaning against the tent poles. They all looked Itholean to him. Their scent gave them away not to mention their darker complexion.

"Shall we start with your names?"

They didn't speak.

"Have my men been treating you well?"

The woman who'd held the incense looked up at him and smiled. "If you think being bound tightly and thrown on the ground, without a blanket to sit on or water to drink is being treated well. . ."

"My apologies," Jaylen said and knelt down in front of the woman. He lifted her chin.

She yanked her head away from his rough hands.

"I'll repeat my question. What are your names?"

Jaylen was met with silence. "Who's Ashkii?"

Again, none of them opened their mouths to answer. "Very well." He yanked the man to his feet. "We're going to have a little chat of our own." He pushed the balding man out of the tent in front of him. "Hania, hold off on the water." Then he took the man over to the waste pits. It might not be magic but perhaps the stench of that moldy refuse might loosen his tongue. If anything, he might learn his name and if "Ashkii" was code for something, or the name of a Montane.

* * *

Back in the tent, Maya pulled her hands from behind her back, revealing a small sharp stone.

"How did you do that?" Agonya glanced at the tent flaps. "You're amazing."

"What took you so long to notice?" Maya grinned and untied her feet and then freed Agonya.

Agonya cupped her wrist, now raw and bloody, putting pressure on them to relieve the pain for a moment.

"What are we going to do about Brynn?" Maya asked, scrunching her eyebrows together.

"I don't know." Agonya tucked her hands into her pocket to bring a little warmth back into them and to try to think about escaping. She felt the plant her father had given her. Thankfully, during the Kors' search of the hut and the rest of the farm they had forgotten to search their prisoners. Carefully, she pulled it out and looked at it. The orange glow she'd seen back at Brynn's hut was gone.

The tree fit inside the palm of her hand. Its branches and leaves were a rich chocolate color with orange streaking the leaves. Tiny green berries not quite ripe hung off the end of its branches.

"Have you ever heard of a plant surviving without sun and water? I wonder what else it can do?"

"I've never seen anything like it." Maya stroked the leaves. "They're soft. And the sweet fruity scent isn't overpowering but refreshing."

Agonya reached to feel the leaves herself, but the moment her finger touched them, a sharp pain shot all the way up her arm. "Smells!" Agonya hissed.

"What happened? Are you all right?" Maya leaned in to examine Agonya's hand.

"I'm fine." Agonya lifted the potted plant to get a closer look. The leaves appeared smooth and soft, just like Maya had said, and there were no thorns that she could see. Agonya steeled herself to touch the little tree again. Maybe it was a fluke. After all, it hadn't hurt Maya.

She touched the soft leaves and then bit her tongue in an effort not to cry out. She almost let go but held on through the agony. Pain coursed through her entire body, spreading through every nerve. What was so special about this plant? Could this be used against her enemies? But why did it cause Agonya pain and not Maya? Once the pain reached the tips of her fingers and toes, it lessened until it was only a slight tingling sensation. There was no guarantee it would help them escape. Agonya continued to hold the leaf between her fingers and wondered what else the tree could do. Perhaps, if she smelled it. . .

Agonya raised the plant and breathed in the faint woody scent of the beautiful bark. The same scent she smelled back in the palace but this time she recognized the woodiness to be like a manzanita tree. The scent grew stronger until it started to block out all the other scents in the tent. She began to wonder if there was any real chance of them escaping. Hopelessness filled her up. The fear and stress of being captured and interrogated pressed down on her. The loss of Hodel, of her father, and running for her life threatened to overwhelm her. Agonya choked back a sob. And the plant fell from her hands.

"What's wrong?" Maya reached over and grasped Agonya's hand in her own.

Her boulder of despair from a moment ago became like a pebble the moment the plant fell from her hands. Agonya carefully picked up the fallen tree, holding it by its pot, and tucked it out of sight. "I'm okay. It just slipped out of my hands. I don't think I'm going to learn anything about this plant right now. We need to come up with a way to escape." Agonya pushed her stray hairs out of her face.

"I don't think we should try and leave without Brynn," she whispered. "I owe my life to Ashkii and Brynn is his friend who was providing shelter to us."

Maya bit her lip. "I agree we should try to help, but wouldn't it be easier to free him after we've escaped?"

"I know it seems better to help him once we're no longer captives, but we are in the middle of the Korin camp. Freeing him at a later time would mean we would have to return with either a force large enough to defeat the Kors which would mean getting the entire army to attack or having a small force to infiltrate the camp, find Brynn, and leave the camp without being discovered. As for the first, there is a reason my father ordered a retreat. We are not ready for another all-out war. And the second, well, I think we've already accomplished infiltrating the camp. And when Brynn returns, we'll have found him. Then instead of escaping to find reinforcements to come back and escape a second time, I really do think escaping with Brynn is the best and easiest course of action."

"But even when–if he is brought back to our tent, how are we going to get out of the camp? We don't have any weapons." Maya rubbed the back of her neck.

"We'll have to escape during the night," Agonya whispered back.

Maya picked up the fallen rope and began to knot the ends together. "We should at least pretend our bonds are still intact, in case the Kors decide to check on us." Then she slipped her bonds back on and tried to get comfortable.

Agonya knew Maya was right, but her wrists were still bleeding and raw. Slowly, she re-tied her bonds and fit them back in place, leaving them as loose as she dared. Then, she lay down on her back and looked up at the sagging fabric above her.

Even with half a plan, the weight of the last few days still enveloped her. She pushed aside the questions she had about the plant and turned on her side. She was a prisoner of war. If they failed in their escape tonight, would Agonya have to make herself known? If she did, she could offer to marry Prince Lucas and end the war before it got any worse. But what would happen to Maya if she revealed who she was? And the Kors would surely discover the plant she was supposed to be protecting. Why hadn't her father told her what was in the package?

Agonya's muscles began to quiver as she thought about her father. *He* was the cause of this war. *He* gave her this tree that hurt her but not Maya, and *he* was the one who left her alone to rule a kingdom that still thought of her as a child. How was it that he was still hurting her even after his death? Agonya turned to her other side and tried to figure out a way to escape the camp once Brynn returned.

Chapter 6

Krillin grimaced as he watched the drunk stagger away down the narrow street.

"Hey! Watch out! Where's your torch?" Eli yelled after the man.

Krillin rested his hand on Eli's shoulder and shook his head. "He's not worth it. Come on."

Eli shook Krillin's hand off. "I was just looking to have a little fun." Eli grinned over at Victor and Xander who were walking behind them, each in crisp red and black uniforms bearing the symbol of Paradise on the shoulder of their cloaks. They grinned back.

Krillin sighed and kept walking. What was the point in trying? He knew there would be an unfortunate person, someone he wouldn't be able to protect from Eli, before the night was over. His whole life, the city guards had been nothing but bullies in uniform. Eli, Victor, and Xander were no exceptions.

Before his memories from childhood could flood back, Krillin sniffed the air. The sky was still covered with clouds and felt like a huge weight, laying on top of the city. He needed to focus on smelling the wooden doors. Cedar, oak, pine. Cedar, oak, pine. The wooden doors and shuttered windows were all connected by one large stone wall. The cedar were the best doors in Krillin's opinion. They smelled exactly like they looked, strong and unyielding.

He kept noting the doors, hardly aware they were nearing Beggar Corner. When he reached the knotted pine, it was too late to steer the others to a safer part of town, at least safer for the residents.

Eli was the first to notice the old man trying to hobble across the street. "Hey, do you smell him?"

"Of course, he smells of pear, orange, and honey. What of it?" Krillin asked.

Victor laughed. "We can always count on Krill to know exactly what perfume someone is wearing."

Krillin started to protest that the man wasn't wearing perfume, but Eli spoke over him. "That's good enough for me."

Before Krillin could even think to stop him, Eli was stalking over to the poor man. "Beggar. Who'd you kill to get that perfume? Hand it over, and I might let it slide."

Xander and Victor began to pat the man's pockets, shoving him harder with each pat.

"Where is it?" Victor yelled as he ripped the man's shirt.

Krillin tried to rush over to stand between them and the man, but he was frozen to the ground where he stood. He wanted to explain it was the soap the man used, not perfume, but his mouth refused to open.

Eli yanked away the man's walking stick, causing him to fall to the ground. Then, he used it to whack the man repeatedly.

"If you won't tell us where it is, then we'll find it ourselves." Victor loosened his short sword from his belt. He kept it sheathed but swung it at the man, hitting him in the head.

Xander joined in the brutality, shouting, "Yeah. Teach the perfume thief a lesson!"

Krillin couldn't move. His mouth was as dry as the wheat in the fields. He no longer saw the old man curled up in a ball on the hard-packed dirt, pleading for mercy. Instead, he saw a small boy. And other men wearing those same black and red uniforms with the Paradise symbols embroidered on their cloaks. Why couldn't he stop this?

The seconds ticked by. Every blow to the head caused Krillin's muscles to tighten. His body was so tight it wouldn't stop quivering. He tried to turn away, but he couldn't move.

Krillin squeezed his eyes shut to block out the sounds. And then they stopped. Krillin opened his eyes but couldn't force himself to look at the man.

"He didn't have it on him after all," Eli said, dropping the walking stick next to the limp man and motioning for the others to follow him.

Krillin smelled the iron in the man's blood, the sweat on the guards, and the soap that had instigated it all. He had to finish their patrol. Krillin prayed to the Patron of Fortune that no one else they saw had washed recently with soap. Then, he moved his feet forward.

* * *

As soon as Krillin's shift ended, he retraced his steps. Cedar. Oak. Oak. Pine. Cedar. Krillin sighed. That poor fellow didn't deserve a beating for no other reason than that he was a disabled beggar who had the luck to wash himself just before they crossed paths!

Krillin shook his head and worked his way back to that street, the one where the houses were barely held together with whatever could be found from the scrap piles. What did these uniforms ever do for these people? He hoped he didn't have to work alongside the Itholeans much longer.

Krillin squatted next to the old man who was propped up against the outside of someone's home. Boards stuck out at odd angles, and the door was nothing but a ratty old cloak. The man had dried blood all over his face and clothes. Krillin didn't know if he could help, but he needed to try. "Excuse me, sir?"

The man didn't respond. Maybe he wanted Krillin to go away. He pressed on anyway. "I want to apologize for what those guards did to you. It was not right. I want to help."

Another beggar stepped between Krillin and the man. "A lot of good your help did earlier! Look at him!" The beggar waved his arms towards the evidence of Krillin's failure.

"I'm sorry I didn't stop them sooner. I didn't know what to do."

"That's not good enough. He's nearly dead! See?" The second beggar bent down and tried to wake his friend. "Ogi! Wake up! Ogi! Do you hear me, lad?" He shook Ogi again and again, trying to wake him up but with no success. Krillin bent down. "Get away from him," the beggar cried.

Krillin backed away with his hands in front of him. "I just want to see if he's still alive." But he didn't need to hold his hand in front of Ogi's nose to know that no air passed through it. The beggar began to weep, still trying to protect his friend from the man in the uniform.

He was too late. Krillin turned to leave, but before he could move, the other beggar straightened up and began speaking loudly. "This is only the beginning of the end. More people will die, and you will lose this war. You will fail to protect the innocent, and the innocent will find you in the end. But there is hope that not all will be lost, even though you will be."

Krillin looked over his shoulder. There were a few stragglers on the streets going about their own business, but they were too far away to hear what he was saying. "Pardon, sir? What do you mean?"

The beggar looked down at his friend, then back up at Krillin. "He's dead. You're too late. Now leave us alone before you cause any more damage!"

"You just said this was the beginning of the end. What did you mean by that?"

"The beginning of the end? Scents! I don't know anything about that. But I do know that you killed Ogi!" the beggar protested.

It had been a mistake to try to help. Krillin turned to leave a second time when the beggar held out his arm to stop him. "You come waltzing back here all proud of yourself for making the effort and that's all you can do? This man died, and all you do is say sorry and leave?"

"I will report the soldiers who did this to your friend."

"What good will that do? They don't care about our kind." He made his case by pointing at the dead man on the ground. "You want to help? Help me bury him. Then you can go do whatever it is you think is more important with your time."

The man was crazy, saying one thing and then another, but he was right about one thing: all Krillin had wanted was to say sorry. But how could he say that when he had essentially killed the man himself. He sighed. He would have to do better than that. "I'll help."

* * *

"Stop!" Krillin screamed. Either they didn't hear him or they ignored him. It had to be a dream. He had to find a way out!

Krillin slapped his own face. "Wake up!"

It didn't work. He couldn't escape the dream.

The guards didn't stop. They didn't have faces.

The old man cried for mercy. Krillin tried to move in between the guards and their victim, but their sticks went right through him as if he wasn't there.

Krillin dropped to his knees and wept into his hands. "Help, please," he whispered through his tears.

"I'm here, Krillin." A soft, familiar voice broke through the agony of not being able to stop the beating.

Krillin opened his eyes. A woman knelt by his bed, her simple braid of silver hair dangling over his chest. "Mother?"

"I'm here, son. It's okay. It was only a dream." She helped him sit up.

He wished his mother didn't have to see him like this, drenched in sweat and tears. He could still smell the blood on his cloak and the dirt in his fingernails. He was supposed to be strong, for the family.

"Do you want to talk about it?"

"It's nothing. Really."

Sari stood up, straightening her dress as she did. "When you're up to it, dinner's hot."

Krillin could smell the steam from the soup drifting through the bedroom door. The hearty blend of meat and vegetables would help soothe his nerves. He could put the dream behind him. He had to. Not only the dream but the man he had just buried outside the city walls. He quickly changed into clean clothes before joining his mother in the other room.

"Is Anya here?"

"She went to play with her friend down the street. She'll be disappointed she missed you. When do you leave again?"

"Soon. Thanks, Mother, for the soup. It's as good as it smells." Krillin took another bite so he wouldn't have to fake a smile. Feelings of helplessness still overwhelmed him, but he couldn't let her know that.

Krillin had to think of something else, anything else. Anya. His beautiful sister. He needed her as much as she needed him. She made him smile and laugh. Krillin closed his eyes and tried to picture her tiny frame in his mind. The more he thought of her, the surer he was that he could smell her scent of gardenias as if she were standing right in front of him.

"Surprise!"

Krillin snapped his eyes open. She *was* standing in front of him, holding a beautiful bouquet of flowers. "Anya!" Krillin spread his arms wide for her to run into. "Aren't you a scent worth smelling? What have you been up to?"

"Rory and I were playing hide and seek. She was so easy to find, but she couldn't find me. Nope, I'm the best."

"Of course you are. So, if she couldn't find you, how did the game end?" he encouraged her.

"Well, I finally made some noise on purpose when she was near so she would find me and we could go jump in puddles. You'll never guess what happened next. This guy came over and gave us these pretty flowers." She smiled and held them out again.

This time he got a good look at the bouquet. His smile faded.

"Aren't they pretty?"

"They're beautiful." Krillin forced himself to look happy for her. "Can I take a closer look?" Krillin took the flowers from her and pretended to examine each flower, smelling their exquisite fragrances.

"That was mighty nice of him. Where were you playing?"

"Near the east market. There are a lot of lanterns there so it's easier to find each other." Anya continued to prattle on about her perfect hiding spots and how she was able to find her friend, even in the dark. "See, it's all about the–"

"So sorry to interrupt, Anya." While she had been speaking, Krillin had found what he was really looking for: a note folded so small and tucked between the stems. "I just remembered an urgent errand I need to complete before my shift tonight."

"Oh, but I never get to see you," Anya protested. "You can't leave yet!"

"I'm sorry, my little flower, but this can't wait. I'll be back as soon as I can." He bent over and smelled the top of her head. "Then, you can tell me all about your awesome powers of hide and seek."

Once outside, Krillin turned east and walked the path previously walked by Anya, only in reverse. Aekan gave those flowers to her as a threat to Krillin. When he'd agreed to spy for Aekan, he had been blinded by rage and a desire to do something, anything that would punish the ones who killed his father and brother. But if Aekan was going to endanger Anya, Krillin wasn't so sure he wanted to be a part of this treason.

Cedar, paliantidia, olive, nutmeg, and other such scents filled the air as Krillin passed the fragrance shops. When he reached the apothecary, he approached the merchant and asked for a cure for achy bones.

"I'm so sorry, we're out of that particular remedy." She smiled politely. "It will be coming soon though. Can I interest you in a little mellified lotion? It's good for most ailments."

The merchant waved him behind the counter and entered the house.

Krillin followed, still wondering if he'd made the right decision to work with the Kor. The wall on his left was filled from top to bottom with shelves, packed with every kind of concoction you could imagine, and many you wouldn't want to. The mellified lotion, for one, was made from the remains of a man preserved in honey.

"Our guest is here, sir."

Aekan, who came up to Krillin's chest in height but was no less intimidating, stepped through an inner door. "It's good to see you got my message." He smiled, then turned to the merchant. "If you would give us some privacy."

"I'll be right outside if you need anything," she replied.

When Aekan turned back, Krillin saw a glint in his eyes that made him shiver.

"What a beautiful sister you have, Krillin!"

"I don't like you using her to get to me. I already told you I will work for you. Why involve my family?" Krillin crossed his arms and tapped his foot on the dirt floor.

Aekan knitted his eyebrows together. "I only gave her the note because it was the quickest way to get word to you."

Krillin let his muscles relax a little. Perhaps there wasn't any hidden motive after all. "You need to talk to me? What about?"

Aekan looked grim. "First of all, the servant got away from me. You may have been compromised." Aekan clasped his hands behind his back while he talked. "But with the king out of the way, we have bigger things to take care of."

"Like what?" Krillin couldn't think of anything worse than his identity getting out. He would be stopped for sure. Then where would that leave them?

"We need to keep a close watch on the people. Do you know what is in this skin?"

Krillin shook his head. "I'm guessing it's not wine."

"It is a potion, compliments of our friend out there," Aekan said, gesturing towards the merchant. "Made to spoil the water supply. I want you to put some in every well in the city if the council doesn't comply."

"Every well? What are we to drink then? Surely, you won't cut off your own water supply."

"Oh, it won't kill anyone, just make them sick. The trick, my friend, is to boil your water before drinking it. That should kill whatever is in here." Aekan shook the skin in his hands. "Don't tell me you're having second thoughts."

"No. I'll do it."

"Good. If the leaders of this city agree to our demands, then no harm done. But if they decide to fight, we will strike. Being a man of resourcefulness, I imagine it won't be hard for you to know what the council decides as soon as they make their choice."

Krillin took the skins from Aekan. "Got it." Then he walked as quickly as he could without running towards the exit. If he could somehow convince the lords and ladies to accept the terms of surrender, then he wouldn't have to worry about the innocent dying. The question was who would listen to him. He was no one special, only a guard. Besides if he approached any of the council members, then they might remember him. They were already looking for a traitor. He knew that much from the rumors flying around about the king's death.

Krillin didn't care that the king was dead. He had been a tyrant who started this whole war. The immediate thing to do now wasn't to dwell on the past but to put this skin pouch in a good hiding place until it was needed. He didn't want to be late again.

Chapter 7

It was no use. Agonya couldn't focus on their plans. She wiped her eyes with the sleeve of her dress and pushed herself up. How Maya had fallen asleep on the ground next to her perplexed her, but it was good for Maya to get rest if she could. They were going to need all the strength they had to escape as soon as Brynn returned. Agonya took the plant out of her pocket again. This time, the pain traveled quicker.

"What are you?" she thought. The pain became sporadic and muddled in a familiar way, almost as if the plant was sad. But that couldn't be right. Plants didn't have feelings. Agonya rested the plant on her lap. It didn't seem to hurt her if she wasn't touching its leaves.

"Why are you so important, little plant?" Her father was adamant that the survival of this plant was more important than anything else. Did he know that he was about to die when he gave it to her?

A noise outside the tent, the crunch of gravel beneath boots, startled Agonya. She tucked the plant out of sight and made sure the rope was around her wrists.

A guard entered a moment later. Brynn followed close behind. The guard shoved Brynn on the ground, eyed Agonya, and left.

Brynn began whispering about how he had been forced to shovel dirt in their latrines. After that, the captain had burned incense, maybe to cover the stench of the moldy pits, and asked questions about who they were. He even asked who Ashkii was; the Kors must have heard them talking about him.

"I don't know what he thought was going to happen," Brynn said. "But no need to worry, I didn't tell him anything, not that I could tell him much. I still don't know your names."

"Better to keep it that way for now." Agonya cringed. If the captain was trying to manipulate Brynn like she did the guards, it was only a matter of time before he'd make Agonya reproduce the magic she'd used upon their meeting. Which meant it was time to escape. They were back together, and they couldn't risk being separated again. Agonya nudged Maya who bolted upright, a question in her eyes.

Agonya tilted her head towards Brynn. Maya slipped over to him and untied his bonds. "You've seen more of the camp than us. Do you have any ideas on how to get past the guards?"

Brynn grinned, exposing his crooked teeth. "We're going to have to fight our way out."

Just then, the tip of a knife poked through the back of the tent. Agonya gasped. It ripped through the fabric all the way down to the ground. Cool air weaved its way into the tent as Ashkii's grim face appeared. He held back the torn fabric and motioned for them to follow.

She crawled forward, resisting the urge to talk. Ashkii had come back for them. As soon as they were all out of the tent, he tossed Brynn a pitchfork, and Agonya and Maya a couple of daggers.

They dodged behind tents and hid in the shadows. Their progress was slow. Every twenty meters they had to avoid another fire surrounded by large groups of soldiers. Hundreds of soldiers had arrived since they themselves had.

Ashkii froze; Agonya bumped into him. He flung out a hand to stop Brynn from blundering past them, but it was too late. A koliimus jumped out of the shadows, baring its teeth. Its long scaly tail curled around Brynn's legs, bringing him down to the ground, and started to howl. Soldiers in the nearby tents stumbled out. A dozen soldiers surrounded them in less than a minute, spears, arrows, and swords were all directed at them.

"Drop your weapons," one of the soldiers said.

Agonya laid her knife on the ground and raised her hands for them to see. Maya did the same, but Ashkii held his daggers out ready to strike. Brynn tried to untangle himself from the koliimus.

"I wouldn't struggle if I were you. Koliis are pretty smart, you know. I heard tell of one of these mutts finding a thief by tracking his smell. If you train 'em right, they can be pretty darn useful, eh?"

"Very useful, indeed." Captain Dahel strode through the crowd and patted the top of the mutt's head. "When I saw that you weren't in your tent, I sent him to find you. What I don't understand is why all of you," he pointed at the soldiers, "are just standing there. Take these prisoners to the pits."

The captain stood there with a smug look on his face while his soldiers tightened their circle around them.

Agonya started to panic. They needed to escape. They wouldn't get another chance if they gave up now. She glanced at her companions. Ashkii wasn't giving up. He was already surging forward, disarming the closest soldier. Arrows flew through the air, narrowly missing him. If he was going to fight, then so must she. Agonya scooped up her knife and ran towards Brynn. With all her might she stabbed the koliimus holding him hostage and kept pushing until the knife broke through the other side. Blood flooded out. The mutt's tail loosened as it died.

Maya followed Agonya. She raised her dagger, blocking a sword from reaching them. Agonya tried to turn and help push back the soldier, but Brynn jumped up and punched the man in the stomach.

More soldiers moved forward, this time in formation. Agonya felt helpless watching Brynn and Ashkii parry the blows of the soldiers. She waved her dagger through the air, clipping a spear by accident. Another spear or maybe the same one hit her behind the knees. She fell to the ground. Then, a horn pierced the dense night air, long and loud. Shouts of confusion rang out. Ashkii took advantage of the distraction and tackled the soldier who was pinning Agonya to the ground. He hit the soldier on the head and jumped so high that he cleared the three other soldiers converging on him. Shouts of disbelief followed him into the night sky. Maya pulled Agonya to her feet and Brynn barreled through the temporary gap, grabbing Agonya's arm and pulling her through with him.

"Keep running."

The soldiers shook out of their stupor and gave chase. She could hear their captain shouting orders in the darkness and pressed on quicker. At the next fire, the soldiers didn't seem to see her. They were fighting. Agonya paused to get a better look. Those were Itholean soldiers. Sending a prayer to the Patron of Fortune, she continued running. That must have been what the horn was signaling. She passed fewer and fewer fires as she dodged tent ropes. The sound of fighting diminished only a little. The closer they got to the edge of the camp, the darker it got. Somehow, she lost sight of the others.

"Ahh!" Agonya cried out as she ran into something on the ground. A man grabbed her legs, pulling her into a cloud of smoke.

"Don't you smell appetizing? Oh, now, don't be like that. No need to struggle, beautiful. Breathe in my perfumes." He pushed his breath in Agonya's face. "Aren't they from Paradise?"

Agonya gagged on the intensity and mixture of scents coming from him. He was drunk. She tried to kick her legs free, but he held on, pushing her down. She hit her head on the ground. The man climbed on top of her. He leaned down and whispered in her ear. "I'll have a nice reward when I deliver you to the Commander, but what's the harm in having a little fun first?"

Her chest heaved with every breath. It felt like her lungs were going to burst. She needed fresh air. Instead, she smelled the man's neroli perfume. The oils of the orange skins in it masked his sweat and the foul scent that snuck out from beneath his skin. Then, intense pain filled her body. She screamed. An orange light burst forth, lifting her oppressor up into the sky, and it kept expanding, reaching all the way up to the clouds above. The light blasted away all the heavy clouds that had been sitting on top of them for the last several days.

Agonya tried to stand, but she couldn't even sit up. Tears burst out of her. All the pain of the last few days spilled out with each drop. Her leg burned where it touched the plant concealed in her pocket. She couldn't move.

But the Montane was there, holding out his hand to help her up.

"Agonya!" Maya cried, pushing him out of the way. "What happened? I saw a light and something dark shoot through the sky. Are you hurt?"

"Where is he?"

Ashkii whirled around.

"You have to get out of here before he comes back."

"Let me help you up." Maya grabbed Agonya's hand and tried to pull her to her feet.

"I can't move."

"Here, let me." Ashkii handed the bag he'd been holding to Maya and bent down to pick her up. "Who are you talking about?"

Agonya tried to push his hands away. "A Kor attacked me. Now's your chance to escape. I'll only slow you down." Agonya's eyes widened with urgency.

"We can't leave you!"

"But you must." Agonya insisted. "Go quickly. Don't you hear them?" She started to reach into her pocket for the plant—A loud thud and crunch sounded nearby. Turning, they saw the soldier, who'd attacked her, dead from his fall.

Chapter 8

Sweltering heat beat down on Lord Commander Huren's head as he sat in the circular courtyard. Huren looked around at the Lords and Ladies sitting on the stone benches lining the edges. Shifting in his seat and folding his arms, he listened to them argue. It was over a week since he had returned to Ithol at the head of the retreating army. The Korins had pursued them relentlessly across the plains and fields, giving them no rest. Now, they were waiting for battle just on the other side of the walls. And these men and women would give him no rest either.

Huren finally spoke up. "Lord Tanish, I beg to differ. Even if we could meet the demands of the Kors and hand over our queen along with our children, they would not stop there. They will rape our people, steal anything of value that we own, and take us away from our homes to be slaves. We can't even meet their demands. The queen has vanished." Huren hoped she was safe. They hadn't found the assassin. "So, this debate is pointless," he concluded. "We have only one option, to fight."

"What do you think will happen if we fight, Commander?" the priest asked. "How long will we last holed up in the city without reinforcements? We may keep the Korins out, but we cannot stop death. We will eventually run out of food. And I don't think we can keep the Korins out. Who murdered our king if not a Kor? Was it one of our own? If it was, should we not surrender immediately, before we are betrayed again, and more innocent lives are lost?"

"Whoever killed the king wanted us to surrender. They want an easy victory. Do not give it to them! We can last . . . what? A year with our supplies as they stand, am I right, Mikkah?"

"Sorry, sir, but the harvest has been much smaller this year. I'm afraid we only have enough for a few months, what with all the outlying villages that came to Ithol for protection before the Kors arrived; you must have seen them in the streets?"

Huren cursed under his breath. Mikkah should have told him about the store houses before this meeting. "All the more reason to fight! Our successful raid last night proves we can defeat them. Don't let them take our home away from us. What would King Azurarus do if he were still with us? He implored me to keep fighting for our home even if he died. I plan to do that."

"I know you met with the king the day he died. So did I," Tanish challenged. "If he told you to keep fighting, well, he also told me to hold fast to sound counsel. The king knew you were our best warrior, but he also knew I was one of his best councilors. We must find the best path forward, together. I believe that lies in finding the queen. If she knew the demands and what was at stake, I'm sure she would do what is necessary." Tanish sat down and crossed his arms over his chest.

"Lord Tanish," Lady Velia piped up. "Will you let our children be taken from us without a fight to be killed or enslaved as the Kors see fit? I understand that it may mean very little to you, seeing as how you don't have any yourself. But I am with Lord Commander Huren on this. Do not be so hasty to surrender. Where is your faith? I appeal to you as a mother. We must protect our children!"

"My faith? You know very well that I am a priest of the Patron of the Woods. You think that fighting will keep our children safe? Remember the sacred words that were written,

‘On the day you break this covenant, your senses will fill with bile; the smell of destruction will fill the air; infants and babes will faint in the streets of the city.’ The sooner we surrender the better it will be for our people.” Lord Tanish took a deep breath. “Not to mention the weather. You all should be praying to the Patron of Storms for deliverance.”

The weather baffled Huren. He used to think Ithol had perfect weather. Now, the valley, like the mountains, was becoming unpredictable in every way. They called this valley the Fertile Basin for a reason. It was Paradise. A river ran along the western side of the city and flowed into the forest not too far away. The fields grew a variety of plants for them to harvest. There was no need for anyone to plant crops. They just grew. The harvesters collected what was needed and sold it in the city. It was never too hot or too cold. It had just the right amount of rain for everything to grow all year long. That is until now.

“You think we’ve broken our covenant?” Lord Tanish continued. “Yes, there is something wrong. It’s obvious. Our Paradise isn’t Paradise anymore.”

“Oh please, it’s not that bad!” Lady Velia said as she wiped the sweat off her brow.

“Not that bad, eh? Why are you sweating? Why are we all sweating? Everything is changing. We’re not fighting for Paradise anymore.” Lord Tanish rubbed his forehead and sat down.

Huren knew only a few would side with Tanish. If only he hadn’t appealed to the gods, none would side with him. But Tanish had a reputation for being too cautious. Perhaps they wouldn’t be duped. “We have heard the arguments for surrender and for fighting. It is time to put this to a vote,” Lord Commander Huren said. “All in favor of surrendering?” Lord Tanish stood. One by one, three more stood, then sat back down.

“All in favor of fighting?” Sixteen lords and ladies rose from the hard benches. Huren’s smile broadened in victory. “It has been decided. We fight!”

“You all are making a huge mistake. Mark my words. This will not end well.” Tanish shook his head and marched out through the archway.

***

The training yard was mostly empty when Krillin arrived. He paused to take note of the early risers sparring with swords and spears. He didn't recognize any of them. The warring sounds of metal on metal clashed with the pleasant resinous and nutty aromas from the soldiers' oily skin wafting through the air. Not that he'd met many of the soldiers in the city. Most of the men and women in the army had been out on the battlefield when he joined. Now that they were back home, Krillin felt trapped, as if it were these older soldiers who were invading, when really, he was the one infiltrating their ranks.

Krillin fingered the long curve of the bow that lay across his chest. He had plenty of time before he had to report for duty. Turning away from the others, he climbed the stone steps all the way to the top of the wall. The first light of the sun was beginning to turn the sky a light gray, a sight Krillin hadn't seen in days.

He strolled along the rampart until he was past the sparring arena below. The wall continued out of sight as it encircled the city, but he stopped and turned to face the Korin camp outside the city, resting his hands on the rising stone merlons to either side of him. He peered through the dip in the wall to where the tents rose out of the fields.

Krillin's eyes drifted to the part of the wall on which his hand rested. He marveled at the chiseled shape and texture of the stone merlons. They were beautiful, if only they smelled of the cedar, oak, and pine that they represented. The rise and fall of the merlons which extended over his head and the crenels that dipped down to his waist were fascinating. Each merlon was slightly different from the one before as you might find from tree to tree. Some were curved up and others were curved down. Some were pointed in the middle and some on the tops of the side.

From what Krillin's mother told him, the design had to do with the Kindroots who lived here before Jedrek the First arrived from the sea. They had burned some sort of covenant with each other, making a long-lost agreement about who knew what. But Krillin didn't care to know the details. He just knew that Jedrek had the wall built to honor the Kindroots. That was the story anyway. Krillin had never met a Kindroot. He didn't know anyone who had or if they even existed, but the pattern of the crenelation was mesmerizing.

Krillin turned away, back towards the practice arena. He lifted his longbow gently off his chest and notched an arrow from one of the buckets lining the edges of the wall. Several target boards were scattered across the ground. Some were large but most were small, hiding in little holes or behind hay bales and in trees.

He let an arrow fly. It hit the center of the closest target board below. There really was no challenge in it. He notched a second arrow and hit the next target just the same. Soon all the obvious targets were killed.

He closed his eyes and sniffed the air. Even though they were all made from pine, every fake bird or squirrel had a unique smell. He wasn't sure why he could smell the difference, when no one else did. He just could. All he had to do was focus on them individually and he would find them.

He let another arrow fly. It soared through the air in a downward arch, piercing what appeared to be solid ground with hay sprinkled on top. Krillin smiled, knowing the wooden gopher was dead. He continued to work, letting the joy of discovering each one push out the dread of seeing Eli, Victor, and Xander later that day.

After much debating with himself, he had written up a report about Ogi. Captain Dawson took his report and thanked him. He said he'd "deal" with them, whatever that meant. But Krillin saw that all of them were on the roster for duty with him later that day and felt sure that Captain Dawson hadn't done anything at all, or maybe this was how he was "dealing" with Krillin.

"Hey, Krill!" Don strode out onto the arena floor and picked up one of the arrows jutting up from the ground. "Wow! This is amazing!" A small wooden squirrel was attached to the sharp pointed tip. "I didn't know you could shoot like this."

Krillin grinned. Don was all right, as far as soldiers went. He never made fun of the unfortunate or joined the others when they wanted to have "a little fun". Krillin respected him for that. “It’s mighty brave of you to offer yourself as a target. I needed a new challenge.” Krillin aimed his bow straight at Don’s chest.

Don dropped the arrow as if it had burned his hand and quickly recovered his composure. “My pleasure, friend. A moving target would be just the thing. Unfortunately, I’ll have to pass. I’ve been looking for you. Lord Bykan let slip the council's decision.”

The blood drained from Krillin’s face. After a moment, Krillin prodded his friend. “Well, what is it? You shouldn’t keep a comrade waiting.”

“It looks like you’ll get your moving targets after all. We’re fighting!” Don said, pretending to shoot his own arrow into the air.

Krillin forced a grin in response, lifted his bow, and let his last arrow fly true. It swooshed about five centimeters from Don’s ear, landing in the middle of a haystack behind him.

Don’s hands flew up to protect his head. “What’d you do that for?” he shouted.

Krillin shrugged. “I hate rats.”

“Rats?” Don whirled around. Sure enough, a small, brown rat was pinned between Krillin’s arrow and the haystack. It twitched for a moment longer, then lay still, reeking of refuse and blood.

Krillin replaced his bow across his chest so that he wouldn’t be tempted to shoot anything else. This was bad news. He would have to contaminate the wells.

Don backed away from the rat and hurried off the arena floor to the bottom of the stairs, still clutching his chest. “Krill,” he laughed, “that was amazing! But I’m going to have to ask you not to gamble with my life next time. I know of a few other living targets you can shoot at soon.”

Krillin left his perch and joined Don on the ground. “You know I would never hurt you. Was there anything else you needed to tell me?”

“Oh yeah. I was supposed to tell you there’s a mandatory meeting tonight at dusk for division five, at the palace no less. I bet they’re going to officially tell us the news. See you later, Krill.” Don slapped Krillin’s shoulder and waltzed out of the arena.

“Thanks for the heads up,” Krillin mumbled. While he liked Don as a person, he had no idea how cruel war was, how Krillin was going to poison the wells now because the council hadn’t surrendered.

* * *

Krillin left the arena and went to find Anya. Random strangers roamed the street, going from shop to shop, most walking away with empty hands. Even before the real siege had begun, prices were as dense as the richest perfume. Thankfully, Krillin didn’t need to worry about getting enough food. Soon after the king had died, the army had started rationing the food. Too many people were panicking and trying to hoard as much food as they could.

A small girl with curly hair ducked behind a large oak rain barrel. He knew his sister wasn’t too far away. Her floral scent was coming from the nearby alley. He grinned as he watched her sneak up behind her curly-haired friend.

“Got you!” Anya squealed.

Rory jumped, falling to the hard-packed dirt beneath her. “How did you find me? I thought you were over there.” Rory pointed in the opposite direction and then turned back to face Anya, but Anya was already moving again.

She was headed straight for Krillin, who was leaning against the shaded wall watching the two girls play. Smells! Anya was good. How did she know he was there? He’d only been hanging around a few minutes. She beamed up at him. Krillin stepped away from the wall and held out his arms to embrace her.

“Krillin! Oh, I’m so glad you’re here! Rory and I are having so much fun. Aren’t we?” She gestured towards her friend who nodded in agreement. “Are you staying for supper? Oh please, do!”

“Sorry, Anya. I’ve got to go to work soon. I just wanted you to let mother know it’s happened.”

“What do you mean, it’s happened? What’s happened?”

“Never you mind. Mother will know what I mean. Run along. I’m sure she’s expecting you for the midday meal anytime now.” Krillin couldn’t help but smile when Anya hugged him again before racing down the street with Rory, laughing and playing tag. What he had to do next, he had to do for her. He had to look at the bigger picture.

Even so, Krillin had doubts, but what choice did he have? He started walking. At least his family would be safe. By this evening, they would be in hiding and boiling their water before drinking it. He hated that they needed to hide because of him, but if he didn't do it, the Kors would simply find someone else to take his place.

Krillin craned his neck, but he didn't see anyone watching him. He gritted his teeth as he ducked into the alley. There he pulled the skin from its hiding place, stood up, and tucked it in a pouch beneath his cloak. Again, he didn't see anyone watching him. He tried to relax and look normal as he left the alley. But before he could take a step toward the first unsuspecting well, a commotion broke out.

"Help! Guard!" a woman shouted at him, pointing towards the intersecting street.

What now? Krillin found himself clenching his jaws again as he jogged up the street to see what was so urgent. "What's going on?" Even before he finished his thought, he smelled it. Smoke crept around the corner of an old building. People were running to barrels of water like the one Rory had been hiding behind earlier.

Krillin raced to the nearest barrel. "Boy, throw me that bucket!" He caught it, and the hard work of scooping water and carrying it to the blazing fire began. Krillin continued to bark out orders. It was amazing how quickly the fire spread. Mounds of trash and sewage lined the streets, feeding the fire. Smoke and ash mingled with the fetid smells, causing several people to heave up their last meal.

But they persisted. Bucket after bucket was tossed on the fire until they were scraping the bottoms of the rain barrels, and the fire was extinguished. Krillin set his bucket down and wiped the sweat off his face. All he could think about was how late he was, but he knew his job wasn't over yet. Someone or something had started that fire. And he'd used up precious water putting it out.

Krillin turned to the ones who had called him over to help. "Is anyone hurt?"

“No, it doesn’t look like it.”

There were no answers, and he had to get to the meeting before it was too late. It was too late to drop the damning skins before the meeting. Hopefully, he’d have another opportunity later that night, under cover of darkness.

Chapter 9

The Kor lay sprawled on the hard ground, dead. Yet, fear gripped Agonya. She tried to stand, to get as far away as she could from the man who had tried to hurt her. She couldn't move, the pain in her leg was too much. Ashkii finished picking her up off the ground, despite her protests for them to save themselves, and jogged after the others. The dust beneath their feet kicked up into the air, filling their nostrils so that they could hardly breathe. Shouts and the clash of swords sounded behind them. She tried to see what it meant, but she couldn't see anything. Brynn stumbled to a stop, and Ashkii's grip tightened around her. Why had they stopped?

A steep ravine stretched out in front of them. Prickly bushes rising up from the cracks in the boulders hid it from view. If they had been twenty paces to the right, they would have missed it completely.

"I'll go first," Brynn said. "Then you can hand her down to me."

"No need." Ashkii bent his knees, and Agonya felt her stomach drop as they rose into the air, up and over the bushes. Agonya clenched her teeth and squeezed her eyes shut, as they fell through the night air. One. Two, three. . . six.

"You can open your eyes."

Agonya gasped for air as he pried her hands off his shoulders and set her gently on the ground. How had he jumped so far? She'd seen him jump out of a tree before, but this was something entirely different. They had to have fallen at least six meters. Not to mention how he had jumped over those Kors during their escape, too. She tried to form a coherent question to ask him about this, but he suddenly bent his knees and leapt back up to the others. He made it look so easy.

A moment later Ashkii set Maya on her feet, kicking red dirt into the air. Agonya choked and tried to stand up for fresh air but couldn't force her body to move. Her heart raced inside her, but her legs felt like sacks of grain; and the plant in her pocket hurt. The realization that it had been burning against her leg this whole time alarmed her. Yes, the pain was fading now; but, instead of feeling curious about this plant, she was afraid. This package her father had given her really was dangerous. Why did she ever agree to protect it in the first place?

"Don't bother to help me, Ash," Brynn hissed. "I'll climb down on my own." Then, bracing his feet against the few tufts of plants stubbornly hanging on to the rock walls, he made his way to the bottom of the ravine and squatted next to the others.

Agonya reached for her mother's necklace, she needed the scents to help her remain calm. Her hand touched her chest, but it wasn't there. How long had it been missing? Did she have it in the Korin camp? She couldn't remember. Sudden tears pricked the corners of her eyes. She tried to blink them away and looked up at the sky. The moon and the stars shone bright, but what could they do to help her?

"How bad is it?" Ashkii asked. "Can you move your legs at all?"

How could she think about her legs when her mother's necklace was missing? When the plant in her pocket hurt her and yet she was supposed to protect it? She wished her father had never given it to her. Knowing she had to answer him, she tried to move her legs again; they wouldn't budge.

"Do they hurt?" Maya asked.

"Not anymore." Agonya finally managed to speak. "I can't feel them at all. My arms are weak, too. I'm not sure how I was able to hold on to you when we fell through the air."

"There was no reason to be afraid. I wouldn't have dropped you. Besides, we didn't fall. I jumped."

"Yes, but how did you do it? I've never seen anyone jump as high or as far as you have these last few days." Agonya leaped at the chance for a distraction.

Ashkii shrugged. "Was it the Kor who did this to you?" he asked, completely ignoring her question.

"I'm not sure what happened." Agonya tried to remember. "He was on top of me and . . ." Her throat constricted, and she gasped for air. It was as if that man's sweat was choking her all over again. She was being assaulted again, but she wasn't. She knew she wasn't. She'd lost her mother's necklace. Yes, she should think about that; it was safer. She tried to stand again to show she was okay and in charge, but her legs refused to do what she wanted. And she remembered the Kor again.

"Agonya, breathe." Maya pushed back a strand of hair from her face.

Memories flooded her mind, one after the other, over and over again. Sometimes they were exactly the same, but sometimes they were slightly different. She tried to push them away. She didn't want to think about anything. But the memory of the power bursting out of her and the pain she'd felt from the tree in her pocket wouldn't leave her alone. They seemed to be one and the same. This plant her father had given her *had* pushed the Kor into the sky. It had helped her! But was it also the reason she couldn't walk? Regardless, she had to regain her composure. She was a queen. She had escaped from her enemies and still had the plant in her protection. Air slowly seeped back into Agonya's body, and she began to breathe again.

Maya rubbed her back. "We don't have to talk about it if you don't want to," she said.

Agonya nodded appreciatively. She could tell them her suspicions, but only Maya knew about the plant she was protecting, and it was better it stayed that way.

"Brynn, we're going to need to make a stretcher."

“No.” Agonya couldn’t allow them to carry her all the way to Tafka. “Let me rest a bit.”

“I’m not so sure resting this close to the Kors is a good idea,” Ashkii said.

“Don’t mind him. We can spare a few more minutes. Did you see what I snagged from an unsuspecting horse on our way out of the camp?” Brynn held up a saddle bag in one hand and a wineskin in the other. He tilted his head back, pressing the skin up to his lips. “Here. Smell the berry oak wine and drink. You’ll feel better.” Brynn held the skin out to Agonya. She took it in her shaking hands and raised it to her mouth. The smooth liquid slid down her throat and warmed her insides.

Maya lifted the flap of another bag. She pulled out a small torch, a flint stone, dried fruits, and some jerky — a soldier’s traveling bag. “It’s not much. But, here, you should eat.” Maya held the fruit out to Agonya.

“You eat it. You’ll need your strength to find more food.”

“Just one.” Maya popped a berry into Agonya’s mouth when she tried to object again. She let the berry rest on her tongue. A little energy flowed back into her just like with the wine. She allowed herself to chew it slowly, releasing the sweet flavorful aromas.

“We should get into the Perfumed Pines,” Ashkii said, swiping a handful of berries from Maya and standing up. “If we follow this ravine we should reach the forest soon, though it does curve further east than I would like.”

Agonya sighed. She wished she could walk on her own two legs.

Brynn tucked the wineskins back into his bag. “I’ll take a turn carrying you; though, I still don’t know your name.”

Agonya hesitated for only a moment. “My name is Agonya, and this is Maya. Thank you for helping us though you do not know us.”

“It’s nice to officially smell your scents. They are pleasing.”

“And yours,” Agonya and Maya said together.

The ravine continued as it started, rocky and dotted with brush, making the trek slow and bumpy. The up-and-down movement of walking became monotonous. After a while, her thoughts drifted to the dangerous and yet mysterious plant.

Agonya tucked her hand in her pocket and felt the tiny branches and soft leaves. The pain didn't come like it had before. "What happened?" she wondered.

"Are you all right, little one?" a deep voice echoed in her head.

Agonya snapped her eyes open. The voice wasn't Brynn's or Ashkii's, but there was no one else near them. Whoever was speaking to her continued. "I did what I could, but your own magic was stronger. I should have realized after . . ."

"After what? Who are you? Where are you?"

Brynn frowned at Agonya. "Are you talking to me?"

"They can't hear me. You only need to think your questions and I will answer."

Agonya blushed. "Sorry Brynn, I was remembering a conversation I had a long time ago. I didn't realize I spoke out loud."

Brynn seemed to accept her explanation because he didn't inquire further, but Agonya noticed Ashkii looking back at her suspiciously.

"After your mother . . ." the voice spoke again.

"My mother?" she answered the voice inside her head, though she didn't know how this person would hear her. Would he be able to hear her every thought? Agonya felt her whole body tense, but Brynn didn't seem to notice. "Did you know her? Do you know what happened to her?"

"Yes, I knew her, child. Kanti was my friend. But forgive me. I haven't introduced myself properly. My name is Blackthorn, and I am the plant in your pocket."

This voice belonged to the plant in her pocket. But how was that possible? Plants didn't talk. Those were just stories about Kindroots, right? But Kindroots didn't exist. They couldn't exist. Agonya hesitated, "You're the one." If the plant had been the source of that power that had pushed the Kor off her and broke the storm clouds overhead, how would he respond to her accusations of hurting her?

"I'm sorry to have caused you so much pain."

Had he heard her? Was he listening to even the thoughts she didn't intend for him to hear?

"I thought," he continued, "it was best if you didn't know me, easier for you not to betray me. I have been betrayed many times."

Agonya tried to wrap her mind around the reality that a plant was talking to her in her mind. She couldn't even begin to process what this Blackthorn was telling her. "Why are you talking to me now? Aren't you still afraid I'll betray you?"

"After our encounter with that horrible man, I couldn't not talk to you."

"Wait, were you responsible for killing him? Are you the reason I can't walk?"

"Slow down, child. We are both responsible for those things."

"Do you . . . will I be able to walk again?" Agonya wasn't sure why she was asking a plant about healing her legs. She didn't know it/him at all. Only that she needed to protect him, and she wasn't even sure she wanted to do that anymore, not that she could do much for him.

There was no reply for a long time, then she heard him say, "I think so. You will need some fragrances."

Fragrances sounded plausible. After all, Agonya used various scents to manipulate the guards and she was pretty sure that the smoke bomb the Montane had used in the tunnel only worked because of its scents. "There are fragrances that will heal me? Which ones? How do you know all this?"

"I'm a Kindroot," he simply said.

So, they did exist. Agonya couldn't believe her ears, or well, what she was hearing in her mind. "You're a Kindroot? But that means . . . I thought Kindroots didn't exist."

"We exist, but that is a story for another time."

If the stories were true, the Kindroots were friendly and wise and powerful. But if he really was a Kindroot, what reason would this plant have for lying to her? Perhaps he was trying to trick her? He did say he'd been betrayed many times before. She doubted he trusted her yet, but what other choice did she have except to find out what he knew or was willing to share with her? "Will you teach me everything you know about this, this magic? Which scents will heal me?"

"I have no other choice. You'll die if I don't."

She would die? The claim seemed incredible. If she hadn't just lost the use of her legs, she would have dismissed it as exaggeration or just plain false, but her legs still refused to move at her command. Agonya closed her eyes. She could smell the tree through her dusty clothes. His scent was familiar. Then, she remembered. "You were there! In my dream. Uncle Reid and mother were arguing about you."

"Orinberries," he said.

"Orinberries?"

"They will help you to walk again."

"Orinberries. Okay, but—"

"Yes, I was there in the garden that day. Your mother saved my life. Now, the sooner we can find the berries the better."

Agonya opened her eyes. The ravine walls were slowly disappearing, and the ground was getting flatter. She could see the Perfumed Pines in the distance. Agonya tried to look behind Brynn, but it was too hard to see around his broad shoulders.

Should she ask the others to help her look? Would Blackthorn feel betrayed if she told the others about him?

The image of her mother arguing with her uncle seared the back of her mind. Uncle Reid was the reason her mother had died that day. She had died protecting Blackthorn from him. Agonya wasn't sure she was ready to die for this plant, but she needed his knowledge. "I won't tell them, Blackthorn. But how am I supposed to find orinberries without their help?"

"By smell of course," Blackthorn said in her mind. "You will have to learn how to detect its scent." Then, by some miracle, a sweet fruity scent filled her mind, and she knew what to look for.

* * *

Although he was proud of his men for pushing back the Itholean soldiers, he was irate at them for allowing the prisoners to escape. If only the Itholeans had attacked later, Jaylen was sure he could have prevented the prisoners from escaping, though losing his koliimus was a huge loss. He'd personally trained that kolii, and that woman had killed him!

He watched his soldiers spread out across the field, searching for them. Even with the prisoners on foot and with the sun beginning to rise, his soldiers were not finding any sign of them.

"Captain!" a soldier called out, pulling his horse up next to Jaylen's. "Message from General Gad."

He took the scroll and kept pushing his horse forward. He knew, without opening it, what it would say. "Double guards on supplies, Itholean raids must be prevented." The only thing he wasn't expecting was the part about moving the prisoners to the pits. He'd thought the general wasn't interested in them. But now he wanted to interrogate them himself?

Rolling up the scroll, Jaylen turned to the messenger. "Tell the general I'll look into it, but if he wants the prisoners in the pits, then I'll need another koliimus to assist in the search. The only reason we were able to stop the Itholeans from causing more damage was because we let the prisoners escape." Jaylen clenched his fists around the horse's reins. How dare she kill his koliimus!

The messenger nodded and rode off back the way he came. Jaylen waved over a handful of soldiers.

"Gather the men. Meet back at the place we saw the lightning strike. We need to go about finding them logically." Jaylen waved his arm, and they galloped away.

The field was mostly flat with grass and dying flowers about knee high. Bushes were sparse, and trees non-existent. Jaylen scanned the ground, looking for the slightest depression. He heard a rustling of a bush and swirled around in his saddle only to see a rabbit hopping away.

"Smells!" He made it back to the designated spot without a hint as to where they could have gone.

Dismounting, he strode over to the dead Kor, surprised he hadn't been moved yet. There wasn't a lot of blood considering the unnatural way the man lay. His legs and arms were twisted awkwardly beneath him, and his head looked like a baked squash that had been stomped on. Turning away from the gruesome scene, Jaylen looked around for other clues.

About six meters away, there was a small indentation in the ground. Was that where the bolt struck? He could still smell the burnt grass in the air. But it was so far from where the man lay.

Jaylen strode over to get a closer look. Several footprints overlapped each other, making it difficult to figure out how many people had been there. If Jaylen had to guess, though, they would match up with the prisoners. He walked a few paces away and found three pairs of footprints heading into the fields. Three? But what happened to the fourth, the one who had helped them escape? Did one of them die like the soldier? Maybe. But how would they have gotten away so quickly if they were carrying a dead body?

Jaylen turned back and found Lonan and the rest of his squad approaching. "Look at this." Jaylen indicated the trail he'd found. "How did you miss this?"

Lonan started to stammer an excuse, but Jaylen cut him off. "Men! Form a line. Sweep forward along this trail. General Gad wants these escapees found!"

Jaylen's speech was followed by a chorus of muttering and scrambling back out into the grassy fields as quickly as they could to do the job properly this time.

Chapter 10

Lord Commander Huren looked at the men and women standing in front of him, his personal guards. They were the ones who had fought alongside Huren repeatedly over the years. Looking at them now confirmed what he already knew about them: none of them were traitors.

He took a deep breath and held up a small parchment with a sketch of a young man on it. "You all have seen this likeness before. Unfortunately, we can't be sure of his scent. The only report we had was that he smelled heavily of frankincense. But we know he had been in or near the king's chambers where frankincense incense was burning all day. I'm showing it to you again now because I want you to help me. During the next several meetings, we will interact with all ten divisions. We need to be on the lookout for this man."

Huren tapped the sketch and held it higher. "We know he wears one of our uniforms and that he is taller than most men with short spiky hair. I want you, the people I trust most in this city, to pull aside anyone who fits this description so that I can talk to them after the meeting. We need to learn names and their division. Trust me, we are going to find this traitor before the week is out."

That is if the traitor didn't know they were looking for him. If the traitor knew how much detail Maya had provided, he might hide or flee, and then they would never catch him. That's why it all had to be handled with the sensitivity of the lightest perfume.

The head guard cleared his throat. "Sir, a lot of men fit this description."

Huren nodded. "That is precisely why this will take so long. But we must start somewhere. We can take down names and stations and more importantly I can meet them face to face. If any of them look like they're hiding something or seem overconfident, then we'll start with them. Even if none of them fit, we'll be that much closer."

The guards sniffed the air in agreement, drawing it towards them with their right hands. They turned towards the door, but Huren stopped them with one last word of caution. "Remember, I don't want them to suspect that we suspect them. We'll say they're being considered for a special job. Take one more look at the sketch." Huren stepped next to the door and held the picture up for them to study on their way out.

* * *

Soldiers poured into the hall, marveling at the rich decor. Lord Commander Huren watched them look at the room. Each one seemed to be ill at ease in such finery.

Huren was used to it. He grew up among the nobility. What was strange to Huren was not the elaborate paintings and curtains nor the embossed stone pillars, but how every soldier reacted the same way. Even though the great hall was filled with soldiers from wall to wall, they still managed to edge away from anything that looked fancy.

Huren patted his pocket, the one that held the traitor's likeness, and began his address to the soldiers. His deep voice echoed off the high ceilings and walls as he praised the good works the soldiers had done up to this point. He scanned the room while he talked, wondering if the traitor was sitting in the crowd.

"The Council has decided not to acquiesce to the demands of the Kors." He paused to let the soldiers cheer. "We will fight."

Huren waved his arms for quiet. "You will have your chance at glory, but we will also be responsible for enforcing the new rules. A curfew of sundown will begin tonight. We will continue rationing all the food but with better diligence. If any try to circumvent the rations, we will decrease that person's share."

Huren watched the soldiers' faces change from pure excitement at the prospect of winning honor, to concern. They began to realize what it was going to take to win. He continued to dole out the new rules and how they were to be enforced. He smiled to himself when he saw his guards lead a few men to stand against the wall.

"You may have noticed that my personal guards have been pulling some of you aside." Huren looked at Joshua standing by the door. He nodded. "I would like that group to remain here for a brief interview. There is a special job that needs to be done. If any of you who weren't chosen would like to be considered, you may stay behind for an interview. That is all for now. You can find your assignments on the boards as usual. You are dismissed."

Huren ignored the chaos of soldiers stumbling for the exits and tried to keep his eyes on the few with whom he meant to have words. That was another reason he had chosen one of the great halls to meet. It had the capacity to hold so many but only two exits: the one he was standing in front of and the one Klah and Joshua were guarding. Huren waited for the vast hall to empty of everyone not lining the walls.

Huren waved the men forward. "Please, come closer." He studied each one as they approached. A few were too short but otherwise looked like the picture. Others were the right height but didn't look anything like the picture. Even with all those men eliminated, there were still far too many. He only had ten personal guards, and they couldn't all be following suspects and protecting him as well as the others.

"I'm looking for someone with precisely the right skills." Huren clasped his hands behind his back. "This is a very important job, and whomever I choose must be of the highest quality. You were chosen because someone spoke highly of you. I will need all your names, stations, and skills before you leave. Joshua, take down their information."

"Yes, sir. I've got parchment right here."

"Good. Now, who among you have been with the army between one and five years? More than five? Ten?" Only a few raised their hands for the last one. "You there! When did you join?"

"In the fifteenth year of King Azurarus, sir."

"Why did you join?"

"For glory and honor, sir. And to ensure the safety of Paradise."

That would be the answer of all these soldiers. "And have you found what you were looking for, soldier?"

"Yes, sir. If there is anything I can do, I'd be honored to help, sir."

Huren nodded and turned back to the group at large. "Have any of you traveled anywhere apart from on campaign?"

A man in the second row raised his hand. "I have, sir. When I was little, my father took me to Trouria."

"Tell me, soldier, did you go over the Acrid Mountains or around?"

"We went over, sir."

"Talk to Joshua before you go. I have many questions for you, but now is not the time."

"Yes, sir."

Huren continued to ask questions and took note of any hesitancy on their parts. By the end, he had narrowed it down to fifteen men, with others to remain on the suspicious list. One looked like he'd been through a dust storm before the meeting. Either that or he was covered in soot.

"You there. Why are you covered in filth?"

"Sorry, sir. I was on my way when a fire started by the flower market. There was no time to bathe."

"Your name, soldier?"

"Krillin Boged, sir."

"I see. Turn in your report when it is ready. Even if you don't get chosen for this task, being here for this initial interview has been a service to your kingdom. Make sure Joshua has all your information, and you are free to go."

Huren watched the men form a line and relay their name and rank before leaving through the main doors. Krillin looked familiar. Had he seen him somewhere before? He hoped he was not the one he was looking for. Not many men, including soldiers, would stop to help put out a minor fire when they were off duty.

Why did he recognize him? Of course, he'd probably seen all the soldiers in the army at one point or another, but somehow, he knew Krillin's face. Huren put him out of his mind and prepared for the next division to arrive.

Chapter 11

The scent of the Perfumed Pines was such a relief, even though she still hadn't found the scent of orinberries that the plant, the Kindroot, had put in her mind. But pine trees meant shelter, meant that they were blocked from view. Finally, after relentless walking and walking away from their enemies, they were able to rest, to focus on finding some allies. Ashkii hadn't been able to tell Agonya if the Montanes would be willing to help or not, but they were now further from Tafka than they had been at Brynn's hut.

And now, all Agonya could think about was how she was failing her father's last request of her. Yes, they'd escaped from the Kors, but he'd asked her to go for help ages ago, and yet she couldn't walk, was farther from her goal, and was forced to rely on people she barely knew to help get her there. There was no turning back. How could a queen rule a kingdom as a cripple? No, she needed to learn to walk again before she returned to Ithol.

Ashkii and Brynn were working to make a stretcher for her, but even with that she feared she wouldn't make it in time to help her people. The only comfort she had was that, at least, the package her father had given her was still safe; though, she couldn't protect this plant any more than she could walk. If someone wanted to take it from her, she wouldn't be able to stop them.

And she hadn't been able to talk to Maya about any of it. They hadn't been able to discuss anything other than each moment's survival since the night they were attacked. So much had happened since then and she had had no peace until now. Maya wasn't there to talk to, but she would be grateful for any time to herself.

Breathing in the fresh forest air, Agonya decided to get another look at the tree, now that she knew it was a Kindroot and now that there was no one to look over her shoulder. Pulling the tree out of her pocket, she tried to talk to it in her mind. "Do you need anything? I wish I had more water to give to you."

The little green berries shook on their tiny branches, as if he was laughing at her. "I don't need as many provisions as humans, child. The water you gave me back at the palace has sustained me and will be sufficient for now. I have food in the soil of my pot," he said out loud with a surprisingly high-pitched voice. Then he waved at her with one of his branches. "You should really be searching for those orinberries."

So, he could talk out loud. She knew why he hadn't until now, but that was good to know. "Yes, but as much as I've tried, I haven't smelled anything but dust, sweat, and now the pine trees."

"Close your eyes, little one."

"I'm not so little anymore."

"You are to me. I'm still a youngling among the Kindroots but old to you."

"How old are you?" Agonya laughed, unable to imagine the owner of this squeaky voice being older than a child.

"Never you mind. Now, close your eyes," he said again.

Agonya did as he asked, wondering why he didn't want to tell her his age, and inhaled deeply. The Kindroot's scent was much stronger now that he was out of her pocket. A warmth radiated throughout her body that she hadn't felt in days, in weeks really. There was something about Blackthorn's very scent that made Agonya feel as if she'd never known fear or pain. She knew the fragrance wouldn't heal her; her legs still refused to move, but perhaps he was healing a little bit of her soul.

"Go on, reach out with your mind. Tell me what you smell?"

Reluctantly, she tried to smell beyond the tree in her hands. Occasionally, she smelled the dirt beneath her and the pine behind her, but mostly all she could smell was the Kindroot. "I can't," she finally admitted.

"You can, though perhaps not right now. Your friends are returning," he said, this time in her mind.

"What?" Agonya rushed to put him back in her pocket, out of sight. He must have smelled them. How else did he know they were coming back?

A moment later, Brynn's voice boomed across the small meadow just as Blackthorn's last branch was tucked safely inside her dress. "Look what I found," he said.

The sun shone down on him as he strode towards her. It was directly overhead, the middle of the day and no cloud in sight.

"Close your eyes," Blackthorn said in her mind.

"But I want to see what Brynn found," Agonya thought back.

"If you're going to learn to identify orinberries by their smell, you must start identifying everything by its scent before seeing it with your eyes."

"But the only thing I remember about these berries from my tutor is that they are used for decoration and taste like bark."

"Ha!" Blackthorn shook in her pocket. For a brief moment, Agonya thought she smelled something sour, but Blackthorn continued speaking. "I remember that day," he said. "You were terrified that you'd eaten something poisonous."

Before Agonya could respond to this new revelation, Maya, Brynn, and Ashkii were all at her side. She closed her eyes, trying to make it look like she was blinking from the intense sunlight and focused on the scents around her. She couldn't smell Blackthorn as clearly anymore, and her pain and fear were beginning to return.

Maya urged her to look at what they'd found. Agonya looked up at them, standing around her. Ashkii had trimmed branches for the base of the stretcher slung over his shoulder. Both he and Maya were chewing on something. Brynn squatted and held out his broad cupped hands. Wild currants were piled inside them. She tried to not let her disappointment show that they hadn't found, by some chance, orinberries. But how could they? They didn't even know Agonya was looking for them.

She took the currants and lifted them to her nose. They smelled sweet like most berries, but they also had a floral scent to them. "Are there more?"

Brynn grinned, showing off his crooked teeth. "There's a whole patch of them over there next to a small stream we found. Don't be shy. Eat them. Maya, do you have those skins?"

"I filled them with water but I'm afraid they're going to burst."

The mention of water made Agonya reach for her throat. It was so parched. They'd finished the wine while they walked but she'd breathed in so much dust. "Thank you," she said, taking the old skins as carefully as she could.

"Drink your fill, we can refill it."

The water was glorious, and the skins didn't feel that old in her hands, they had more life in them yet. Too bad they didn't have more wine to put in them. The currants would have to do in its place. She hadn't realized how hungry she was until she didn't have any more currants left to eat. She was hungrier now than she had been only moments before. But to her surprise, she didn't feel quite so weak. She couldn't move her legs, but she did feel like she had more strength than before. "You said there's a stream, can we wash in it?"

"I'm afraid not, my Lady. It only takes one stride to cross it and wouldn't even cover your foot if you were to step in it," Brynn said.

"Yes, and as much as we would all like to freshen our scents, now that we've all had some food, we should get back to work." Ashkii set down the stretcher they'd been working on. "Maya, why don't you fill the skins and pick more currants while Brynn and I finish this?"

Maya nodded and took the stolen bags and skins to fill them up. Agonya wished she could go with her. She'd be willing to do servant's chores if she could only walk. Even if the stream wasn't much, she could at least wash her face. Agonya sighed and turned to see Ashkii hacking off fresh branches from a nearby cedar. They were lucky Ashkii hadn't been captured by the Kors. He still had all his supplies except for the weapons he'd lost in the fight.

Agonya closed her eyes again and sighed. She didn't feel lucky but knew she should be grateful for what they did have. Thinking about Blackthorn in her pocket, she tried one more time to identify the scents around them.

"Don't worry, my Lady," Brynn said. "We're safe now and I'm sure we'll find a safe refuge at Tafka. I've been there before, you know."

Agonya sighed again and abandoned her task. She couldn't concentrate anyway.

"That's a story to remember," Ashkii said with a laugh. "But, yes, Brynn's right, you know. You will be safe in Tafka. I wish I could tell you what the chief's decision will be about helping Ithol, but we won't know until we ask him."

Yes, she worried about that, but that wasn't what she really needed to hear in this moment. Agonya studied the two men who had helped her escape the Kors. Should she be honest with them? They were so different from each other, so different from her.

Brynn was old enough to be her father, balding, crooked teeth, and yet strong from working in the fields his whole life and kind to strangers. In the short time she'd known him, he'd remained positive and was able to make them laugh despite their trials. She realized she trusted him. But perhaps, she didn't need to tell Brynn she was the queen of Ithol . . . yet. There would be no harm for him to continue to think of her as an ambassador.

Now, Ashkii, in contrast, was probably too serious. Even though he was a few years younger than her, he was one of the most skilled warriors she'd ever known. He had strange ways of talking and his smelif . . . well, that was best forgotten. But he hadn't failed her yet. Her father had picked him to escort her to Tafka, and that meant he had trusted Ashkii with her life.

They really did seem concerned for her, and she wanted to be able to talk freely with them like she could with Maya. Of course, she wouldn't tell them about Blackthorn, but she could talk about all the other things weighing her down.

"I'm not worried about the Kors anymore. Well, not with regards to our safety," she said softly. "I do still worry about the siege. I'm just tired and upset about not being able to walk to Tafka on my own two feet."

There. She'd said it. She wasn't as strong as they thought she was.

Ashkii paused his hacking and turned to face her. "I can't imagine not being able to use my legs, but there is hope. We have healers in Tafka. I don't know if they will be able to heal you completely, but I do know that they can help make things easier for you."

Could it be true? Could she trust him? He had proven himself several times over, and her father had trusted him. Of course, she would continue to look for orinberries, to learn as much as she could from Blackthorn. But what if she never found the berries? What if she wasn't able to learn about this magic of fragrances? Ashkii was holding out hope to her, hope that perhaps she wouldn't remain crippled the rest of her life after all.

***

General Gad had been furious with Jaylen for letting the Itholeans escape and asking for resources to recapture them was out of the question. "Dahel," he had said, "those prisoners may have had knowledge that would have helped us win the war, but they might not have. Do you expect me to send valuable resources after them on a whiff? You let them escape! What makes you think you'd be able to find them and bring them back?"

"But we were being attacked!" he'd protested. "We didn't *let* them escape."

Gad had slammed his fist on the table in response. "You don't get it. You're far too young to have been promoted to a captain. We're at war for smells sake! Wake up, Dahel. We must focus on the task at hand. There is no looking back in war. We can't afford to chase possibilities. I've reported this incident to the Lord Commander, and I expect you to show him that you are capable of managing fifty men and women through your tunnel duty." Then, Gad had turned and left the tent.

Tunnel duty. Perfect. It wasn't quite a demotion but near enough. His men were going to hate him for it, though they deserved it. They would have to work at night when the Itholeans who patrolled the outer walls wouldn't be able to see them. Even in the dark, the archers could hit anyone who came within two hundred meters. Not to mention the other dangers of working the tunnels, like cave-ins.

Jaylen sighed, stood up, and left his tent. His troops stood at attention. Clasping his hands together, he faced the eager men and women. "We've been assigned to the tunnels."

A chorus of moans floated through their ranks. Jaylen held up his hand to silence them. "You did well, protecting our supplies last week, which means you will do well building the tunnels. But I'm disappointed with your lack of vigilance concerning our prisoners. From now on, I expect nothing but the best from you. You must remain watchful, ready to always defend. It isn't just me that you must prove yourselves to, but General Gad and the Lord Commander himself, too. We must build the tunnels quickly and without any mistakes. After the tunnels we build succeed, no one will be able to say we're fetid anymore. Be ready to dig as soon as night falls. Laniel, come with me." Jaylen turned and walked back into his tent.

"You're our tunnel expert, Laniel," Jaylen said, sitting down across from his friend with a table covered in maps between them. "I know that if we're going to get these tunnels built quickly, we need to get as close to the wall as we can before we start digging, which means we might be within firing range of the Itholean archers. What do you think is the best way to go about this?"

"I'm no tunnel expert, Captain," Laniel replied.

"You know how to build, don't you? How many stories have you told me about working on the King's palace back home? Surely you encountered secret passageways and what not." Jaylen leaned back in his chair.

"Do you know how many people worked on the palace?"

"I do."

"Then you would know that I–"

Jaylen cut him off. "In order to succeed, I need you to use whatever knowledge you have to help me. I've marked out a few potential places to start tunneling here, on the map. What do you think? Will these work?"

Laniel leaned over the table and studied the map for a few minutes. "In theory they look like good starting points, but we won't know until we actually see the area. A lot depends on the soil, rocks, and vegetation in those areas."

"I knew you would have good insight. Let's go look at the sites. Don't give me that look. We won't get close enough for them to shoot us." Jaylen rose, grabbed a shovel, and left the tent before Laniel could protest.

The first site he'd picked had two bushes guarding it. They would help hide them from watchful eyes since most of the land was grassland. Laniel dug down half a meter to test the ground.

"What exactly are you looking for?" All Jaylen could see was a bunch of dirt with a few rocks mixed in.

Laniel set his spade in the dirt and leaned against the handle. "The bushes hide us from unwelcome eyes. It'll also help keep the soil at the entrance from collapsing on us. But this dirt is too dry. See over there, beyond this bush?" Laniel pointed towards the city.

"What about it?"

"There's not much more vegetation between here and there, right? That means we'll have to find a way to keep the tunnel from collapsing on us."

"So, you're saying this isn't a good spot?"

"Not at all, sir. This may be the best we have, but let's take a look at the other locations before deciding."

Jaylen couldn't help thinking this tunneling business was going to be the end of him. He'd never done anything like it before, and from the way Laniel was talking, it seemed the potential problems were insurmountable, especially since most of his men didn't have any experience in tunneling either. At first, he had thought, "How hard can it be? Filling buckets with dirt and dumping them out in a different location." Now he was glad for Laniel's experience. Everything could have been jeopardized if he had done it his own way. He had stumbled into a pile of dung when he lost his prisoners. That is, Jaylen suspected Gad was using it as an excuse to get rid of him. He would not make another mistake like that again. There was no way he would let Gad win.

* * *

Krillin wasn't a fool. He knew the men pulled aside after the mandatory meeting looked a little too much like himself. That is, they were all men with short black hair, tall, and skinny. The servant girl with the candle must have given a description to the Lord Commander. It was a good thing it was dark that night. She wouldn't have gotten a detailed description. He could hardly remember what she looked like except that she was short with hair down to her waist and her scent of rosemary, honeysuckle, and fir. He doubted she could recall his scent. But would have to talk with Aekan after he did what he had to do.

The smell of the poisoned skins in his cloak outweighed his concern about being discovered. Seven years after his father and brother died, and Krillin still woke up from his dreams feeling helpless. He had learned to turn that hopelessness into anger, anger at the Itholean soldiers, anger at the now dead King for not doing anything about the injustice. Krillin knew of others like his brother, beaten for no reason other than being different. In some ways, Krillin was like those poor souls but only someone who knew what to look for would know: larger width between the eyes, lower and fatter nose . . . Krillin's face was not as distinguished as theirs and so he was able to hide his abnormalities. Mostly.

"Watch out!"

Krillin started. "Sorry, mister. Are you all right?" The man didn't answer but walked away muttering about too many people in the city, not enough space.

"It's good to smell you, Krill," Don said, standing in a fetid uniform near the well. Krillin smelifed his friend. "You've got rations duty, then?"

"Just making sure people don't panic and take more than they need or start fighting over it. It's only been one day since the tighter restrictions, but people can be irrational. Simply because there is a limit now, they think the end of the world is here." Don shook his head.

Krillin's heart beat faster beneath his skin as he stepped up to the well and drew the water bucket up. Even though the task was simple, Krillin didn't want Don to see the sweat on his hands as he pretended to fill his old empty skin. All he had to do was to make it burst so the contents would leak into the well.

"So, where are you assigned?" Don focused his attention back on Krillin just as the skin split and all the contents spilled into the well.

"Incense Sticks!"

"Hey, don't get your nose in a scrunch." Don handed him an extra skin.

"Thanks."

"Don't mention it." Don winked at him.

Krillin smiled. "I'm manning the wall in a few hours. Maybe I'll see you around later." He didn't want to tuck the new skin in his coat lest he confuse it with the poisoned ones still waiting to be dumped into the other wells. That would not be good.

Krillin left his friend and headed to the next well and then the next. It wasn't as hard as he thought. No one seemed to suspect anything. Each time he spoiled a well, he visualized the guards who had killed his brother getting sick, perhaps dying. It helped. Aekan had said that some might die. Krillin was hopeful that the innocent people would use their noses and boil the water instead of trusting blindly that the enemy couldn't touch them inside the walls.

Now that the deed was done, he was surprised that he didn't really feel guilty. He was nervous, but not sorry.

✻✻✻

Two of the usual men were playing Twenty Squares in front of the apothecary when Krillin approached. "The Patron of Fortune surely smiles on you," he said.

"She can't smile on all of us, but maybe she will smile on you." The man to the right of the table stood up and went inside to talk with Aekan while Krillin took his place.

"It's your turn, lad. Go on, roll the dice." The man across from him had an overwhelming mix of various scents. He was almost as bad as Captain Thresh. He couldn't even remember what he'd been thinking about moments before, the scent was so strong.

"What is that perfume you have on? It's awful!" Krillin did his best not to gag too dramatically.

"I beg your pardon?" The middle-aged man sat up straighter. "Well, don't you smell fabulous!"

"Thanks. I think cedar, frankincense, and rosemary is the best blend ever." Krillin picked up the square bones and rolled them on the board. "Ha! Look at that!"

"We'll see if the patron continues to smile on you," the man replied and picked up his quill to write Krillin's score.

Krillin pointed at the parchment. "You wrote my score incorrectly."

"It looks like I did. An honest mistake." He moved to make his roll.

Krillin started to reach out to stop the man but hesitated. "Aren't you going to correct it?"

"No."

"Why not?" Had Krillin said something wrong, again? His mother was always telling him to think before speaking.

The man ignored Krillin and rolled the bones. Krillin replayed the conversation over in his head while they continued to take turns but couldn't figure out why the man was cheating so blatantly.

While Krillin pondered this, the man who had given his seat up for him came back out. "You can go in now."

Krillin threw the bones down one last time and carried his new water skins inside.

Aekan greeted him with a smelif, sniffing each cheek, then straightened his small stature. "What gift did you bring me?"

Krillin tossed three empty and broken water skins at Aekan, who barely caught them all in time. "It's done. I don't have a lot of time. They are expecting me on the ramparts."

Aekan set the skins down on the table and pulled a small rolled-up paper from his bright blue cloak. “Yes, by all means, I don’t want to keep you. Here is your next assignment, a note you must deliver while you are there.”

Krillin hesitated.

“What’s the problem?” Aekan asked.

“I think the guards have my description.”

Aekan snorted. “You were sloppy. If they have your description, then be extra careful when you shoot that arrow.”

“But didn’t you take care of the serving woman?”

“She got away. But so did you. Look I did what I could, but a complication presented itself, be happy that I tried.”

Krillin felt the lump in his throat double in size. He tried to swallow. He couldn’t blame Aekan for not catching her. He would have to be more careful. At least he was finally rid of the poison, even if he had a damning note to carry in its place.

Chapter 12

She couldn't remember how many days it'd been since they escaped. Every morning Agonya woke up to the sad songs of the birds. More times than not, her companions were already gathering food and wood or making weapons when she woke; no one wanted to be caught off guard again. When the morning chores were finished, they packed up. Ashkii and Brynn would transfer Agonya to the stretcher, and then they would walk until it became too dark to go any further.

The trees were beginning to grow closer together, making the days darker than before, and the ground was gradually sloping up towards the approaching mountains—the Acrid Mountains that Agonya had seen from Ithol, heard so much about, and never wanted to visit. How the Montanes lived there alongside thorny devils and other horrible creatures baffled Agonya. But perhaps that was how Ashkii had become so skilled in fighting. She looked at the Montane now as he carried her feet. Were all Montanes warriors like him? She hoped so, otherwise what would be the point asking for their help?

A slight breeze washed over her, bringing fresh fragrances with it. Agonya pushed her thoughts about the Montanes out of her mind and tried to focus on the scents. She needed to learn to distinguish every individual scent in the air. Some days she thought she had mastered it, but other days the fragrances overwhelmed her senses to the point of nausea. Maybe it was just the smell of her own body odor getting stronger by the day, reminding her that her oils had been stolen. The others stank, too, and she would have gladly shared her oils with them.

Agonya had yet to smell orinberries and the scent Blackthorn had given her wasn't in this breeze either. She was reluctant to ask the others to look for them when orinberries weren't considered food and they were already working hard from the moment the sun crested the horizon until it disappeared again behind the mountains. She would have to explain why she wanted them and that would lead the conversation dangerously close to Blackthorn.

Inhaling her own stench again, Agonya asked, "How far is the river?"

"We're not far now," Ashkii assured her.

"About time," Brynn chimed in. "I'm getting sick of Ashkii's stink."

"You're one to speak. Rancid polecats would welcome you with open arms." Ashkii smirked.

"I love rancid polecats!"

Agonya laughed. "Who loves polecats? You are kidding, right?"

"On the contrary. They're so cute with their big fluffy tails, and it's fun to launch old water skins at them. They hate getting wet, and if you throw them from far enough away, you get blessed with the musky smell of their spray without actually getting hit."

"You must have a good arm," Maya said.

"I know they're not polecats," Ashkii said in a low voice, "but, I see deer over there. The river is closer than I thought."

Suddenly, Agonya felt like she was falling. She gasped. Her head was tilting towards the ground but the rest of her remained straight.

"Brynn! Set her down." Ashkii lowered his end of the stretcher, leveling her out. Agonya couldn't see what Brynn was doing but she wasn't about to fall off anymore.

"Sorry." Brynn reached behind his back and unhooked the weapon he'd been working on. "I wanted to show Maya the atl."

Agonya strained to see what he was talking about. "I don't understand. A stick?"

"It's not just any stick. Look." Brynn brought it closer. The wood curved up at one end, creating a slot for the shaft of a spear to rest in. "If I flick my wrist and throw with my arm, it'll send the spear into one of those deer over there." Brynn nodded his head to the left.

"They must be a hundred meters," Maya said in disbelief.

"They are." Ashkii shrugged and offered Brynn a spear.

He accepted it and placed it on the atl, raised his arm behind his head and flung it hard. The spear sliced through the air faster and farther than Agonya knew was even possible. As soon as it hit the closest deer, blood squirted from its neck, and it collapsed on the ground. The other deer scattered in every direction.

Ashkii patted Brynn on the shoulder. "Nice shot. My turn."

"But why do we need two deer?" Agonya asked.

Maya looked at Ashkii. "We can use the skin to make the stretcher better and make a bag to carry the meat."

Ashkii smiled and took aim at the fleeing animals. The spear struck the deer above and behind the front legs, killing it instantly.

"Show off."

"Come now, we both got one. Though, you're right. Mine was the better kill."

"Humph." Brynn picked up his end of the stretcher and Ashkii his.

Agonya took one look at Ashkii's face and grimaced. "I suppose I ought to thank you for finding the deer, but now I have to watch Ashkii's smug face the whole way there. You know, if your places had been switched, Brynn would have hit the moving deer, too."

"Who do you think taught Brynn how to use an atl in the first place? Ever since the bow was created your people don't see them as being useful anymore," Ashkii replied.

Ashkii had a point. "You're right. As accurate as the spear and atl were just proven to be, I do think a bow and arrow can go a lot further and be more accurate."

Ashkii smiled. "Yes, but it takes time to make a bow and when you need weapons quickly, an atl is better."

Before she knew it, they were lowering her to the ground again and disappearing behind the trees to find and clean the deer. Thankfully, they weren't doing it in her line of sight. She couldn't handle seeing or smelling so much blood, not after seeing so much death recently.

"A lesson on the insides of a deer might be beneficial to you," Blackthorn said in her mind.

"You can't be serious," Agonya thought back. She had forgotten he was always listening. "How on earth could that be good for me?"

"Understanding the way a body works is one step closer to healing it."

Agonya perked up at that sentiment. "I'm listening."

"Sense of smell is vital to life. When one loses their head, they lose their sense of smell. That's why Ashkii's shot was better than Brynn's. Although, it didn't look like the deer was beheaded which would have been worse for the deer."

Agonya recoiled as the scent of the deer's blood reached her nose. Images of her father's head flooded her mind. She couldn't hold them back. Agonya suddenly felt like she was drowning. She could still see his eyes staring into nothingness.

"Maybe that was the wrong example."

Agonya took a deep breath.

Blackthorn pressed his point. "It isn't the sense of smell that makes it so abominable. You forget how important blood is to life."

"I don't think I can talk about this right now."

"It is important that you understand. Smells enhance our magic. But that is all they do. The smells are not the magic as some assume. The magic is separate. It flows inside us like our blood."

Agonya did her best to not think about her father and thought back to what she had felt when the power filled her up and pushed out of her. "Did that man's scent of neroli perfume have anything to do with the magic we did together?"

“Yes, there were many scents on that man and in the air but you are right. The citrusy scent makes it easier for us to defend ourselves. And my sweet berries, though not quite ripe,” Blackthorn pushed his scent toward Agonya, “allow us to speak in our minds.”

The scent of his berries grew stronger. She could almost see it traveling through her body, blending with her blood like a silvery wind. Agonya knew the silvery wind was the source of her magic, and she could feel it flowing out of her. “Can I speak to others like this?”

“You can. But I would caution you against it. Especially with Ashkii.”

“Ashkii? Why?”

“I don’t trust him. He has a wall around his thoughts. I think he is hiding something.”

“What do you mean you don’t trust him? Why haven’t you said so before?”

“I mean what I said. You shouldn’t trust him either.”

Agonya couldn’t possibly think Ashkii would harm her. He’d done everything to protect her. Instead of trying to reason with Blackthorn, she focused on the other thing Blackthorn had said. “You mean to tell me; I can block others from knowing my thoughts?”

“I don’t listen to all your thoughts. I know sometimes I eavesdrop on what you’re thinking but your thoughts help me.”

“I don’t really want to block you, Blackthorn. But can Ashkii read my thoughts? I mean, if he can block others from reading his own? How will I protect myself? You will teach me how to do this, right?”

“I don’t know Ashkii’s ability yet, but I must urge you to use caution in case he can.”

Agonya liked Ashkii, not in a romantic way, but as a friend and even though he had been blocking his thoughts from them, she couldn’t help but wonder why she had to be as cautious with him as Blackthorn claimed. As soon as she thought it, she cringed. Blackthorn could probably hear her questioning his advice. If he was listening, he was decent enough not to say anything.

***

Maya knelt next to Agonya and placed the deer skins on the fallen pine needles. "Do you have any more feeling back yet?"

"A little. I can feel these branches sticking into me." As soon as she said it, she regretted it.

The look on Ashkii's face when he stepped out from behind a pine said he thought she should have said something sooner.

"I wish you would have told me," he chided.

Agonya frowned. "While I appreciate your concern, I need you to let me carry my own burdens in so far as I can."

Ashkii studied her for a moment then gave a quick nod. He scooped her up and gently placed her next to the tall pine. Then he and Maya laid the deer skin on top of the stretcher and tied it with the grass Maya had woven together. When they were done, they moved Agonya back on. "How's that?"

"Better." Agonya admitted.

Ashkii's face smoothed out, satisfied. Then, he rejoined Brynn.

When he disappeared, she turned to Maya who was weaving grass ropes through the other deerskin to make a bag in which to carry the meat.

"I think Ashkii likes you."

Agonya nodded. "That is a problem."

"What are you going to do about it?"

"Nothing. If he does like me, there really isn't anything I can do about it. He's probably just being nice to me because my father asked him to."

Maya nodded. "Shouldn't you take advantage of the situation though?"

"What do you mean?"

"Well, he's a Montane, isn't he? Do you know how to convince them to help us yet?"

She had a point. But Agonya couldn't pretend to like him back. She still didn't know if Hodel had survived or not. Besides, Agonya thought to herself, according to Blackthorn, he wasn't trustworthy. The very fact that Ashkii knew how to guard his thoughts from unwanted visitors was a little worrisome. “I can’t, Maya. It’s too risky. But don’t worry. We’ll find a way to convince them.”

Agonya closed her eyes and smelled the various forest scents surrounding her: oak, pine, deer musk, blood, Maya’s body, her own body . . . How many days had it been since she bathed? Shaking her head, Agonya focused again on the earthy aromas and then thought about her magic. It was like a never-ending pool inside of her that she didn’t know existed until recently.

“Now, direct the power. Try guiding it towards your mind.”

Agonya was getting used to Blackthorn chiming in when she least expected it, but she couldn’t keep her concentration this time.

“Pull the magic to your mind and picture that wall you want to build.”

“Thanks,” Agonya thought sarcastically. “Who knew a tree could be so bossy?”

“I did,” he said. “Now concentrate. Once you master that, you’ll have to practice putting it up when you are distracted.”

Agonya started over, taking a deep breath. This time she couldn’t quite identify the smell that came to her. Opening her eyes, she was startled to realize it was coming from Ashkii who had returned from helping Brynn and was sitting across from her. He flushed and turned his eyes away. Does he actually care for her? It doesn’t matter, she told herself.

“Do you need anything else, Maya?” Ashkii asked.

“I’m almost done.”

“May I see your bag?” Agonya tried to crane her neck to get a better look.

“Sure, here.” Maya moved closer so she could see. The bag was well done for the materials that were available to them. Maya had tied the front legs to the back legs and cinched up the sides so they wouldn’t gape. “I’ll want to make some adjustments when we have time and better materials. But it’ll do.”

“It looks fine to me.” Agonya tried to pass it back to Maya, but Ashkii grabbed it, his fingers brushing against Agonya’s. His face hardened for a second before he turned and headed back to the roasting meat.

Chapter 13

Jaylen learned early in the process that they could only fit three men to a tunnel. Maybe more could join once they got a bit further underground, but for now he divided up his men into groups of three and sent them to the spots he and Laniel had found. In the beginning, two dug down and one carted the dirt off. Once the hole was big enough, one of them would jump inside and start passing the dirt to the others. They had to dig down three to five meters before they could head towards the city wall. Laniel said they needed as much dirt above them as they removed below to help prevent the tunnel from collapsing.

That was a problem. Where to put the soil and rocks they pulled out of the ground? If they piled it up next to the tunnel opening, they'd give away their plans to the enemy. After a lengthy discussion with General Gad, they decided to use it in the latrines and sprinkle the rest evenly throughout the camp.

The men worked in six-hour shifts. Jaylen needed to meet his deadline of two weeks if he wanted to be forgiven for his earlier lapse in judgment.

"Captain!" one of his soldiers shouted across the field, motioning for him to come.

He looked upset. Jaylen dashed away from the tunnel he was supposed to be inspecting. "What is it?"

"Lonan was down in the tunnel, digging, sir, and then he was kicking and flailing his arms at me for no apparent reason."

"Where is he now?" Jaylen peered down the shaft.

"It took the both of us to pull him out. He was covered with sweat. When we got him out, he calmed down, but then he vomited all over himself. Hania took him back to camp."

"I see. Are you hurt?" Jaylen asked. This reeked of headaches. He didn't have men waiting to help. If Lonan was too sick to work, who would take his place?

"I'm fine. Just a little bruised from that initial kick."

"Tell you what, take a short break. I'll go check on Lonan and send Hania back to help." Jaylen took a step towards his horse but stopped. He needed to find out exactly what had happened in that tunnel. Not bothering to explain, Jaylen climbed down the rope ladder into the shaft and crawled inside the tunnel. Its diameter was just shy of a meter. There were a few sticks and rocks piled up on the entrance edges and then again, every few meters. Jaylen crawled to the very end. All he could feel was dirt and rocks. His throat filled with dust. He tried to breathe again and then he knew. Scrambling back out of the tunnel, and out of the shaft, Jaylen found the soldier still pacing back and forth.

"Stop the digging, immediately. Everyone is to meet at our main campfire for further instructions." Jaylen wiped his hands on his pants. "Well? What are you waiting for? Go." Jaylen watched his puzzlement turn to comprehension before he took off running. Here Jaylen had thought he had been doing everything he could to keep his men and women safe, but he was actually endangering them instead.

It took the better part of an hour to gather the soldiers who were on shift as well as the men off shift. He didn't want to have to repeat himself. While he waited for everyone to gather, Jaylen consulted with Laniel about his suspicions. Then, he visited Lonan, who seemed to be in good spirits after a little rest. All the same Jaylen told him he didn't have to come to the meeting. Lonan came anyway.

"Today we had a little scare. While one unit was digging, the member near the front started fighting his teammates. No one was seriously hurt, but things might have gone differently. Upon further investigation, I realized that we have yet another dangerous task to accomplish. It may cost some of you your lives."

Jaylen took a moment to search the crowd of faces. None of them seemed surprised or scared. They looked resigned to whatever Jaylen had to tell them. "It's the air in the tunnels or, more accurately, the lack of it that we've got to be worried about. You see that brave soldier didn't have enough air to breathe and consequently to think straight. To fix this, we will dig air drafts every fifteen to twenty meters. We can do some of it from the tunnel, but we'll have to finish it from above which will put you at a higher risk of being spotted by the Itholeans."

A few soldiers groaned.

"I am open to suggestions for getting a good air supply all the way through the tunnel if you have any. For now, when you aren't on a tunnel digging shift, you will have to work on air flow. Three men should suffice. One to dig. One to shield. One for support and scouting of enemy forces. If you see Itholeans on the wall, hide or retreat. We don't want to give away the locations of our tunnels."

After a few questions, they dispersed back to their duties.

Jaylen watched the men leave then headed to his command tent to figure out his next move. Perhaps he should go through the prisoners' belongings again to see if anything would help him.

* * *

Lonan came to Jaylen before the next shift started. "Captain, sir? I think I'm ready to go back to work."

"How are you feeling? Are you sure you're up for it?" Jaylen asked without glancing up from his project. Incense, candles, a dagger, perfume bottles, a green dress with rips and covered in dirt, and one not as fancy but still indicating one of them was rich were all strewn across his make-shift table. He couldn't seem to gain any new understanding as to why the prisoners had been carrying all these things.

"Yes, sir. I'm feeling better. I know I can do it. Please don't make me lay in my bed any longer." Lonan looked at the ground and rubbed his palms.

Jaylen looked up from what he was doing and saw the sincerity in the man. Even the best trained soldier could have panicked like that lacking proper air. "You may go back to work, then. Stay out of the tunnel though. You can cart dirt or help work on the air drafts from above. Work it out with your team. If there are any more signs of sickness you will be back in bed before you can smell the roses. Understand, soldier?"

"Yes, sir. Thank you, sir. I won't let you down." Lonan trotted off to find his team.

Jaylen turned back to his thoughts. They had retrieved a lot of these items from the hut where they had captured the prisoners. The bags told him they were ready for a journey, but where to? One of the bags was empty. Maybe it had contained some of the items that were found throughout the hut. It was hard to tell what might have been in the bag and what was normally in the hut. He could still smell the incense fragrances lingering in the bag.

Who did each of the bags belong to? One of the bags had men's clothing in it. They looked like they would fit the Montane man who had come to their rescue, which would also explain the strange items that Jaylen didn't recognize. He didn't know much about the Mons. It was strange enough that he was traveling with the Itholeans.

It wasn't so much the Montane that interested him but that woman. Who was she? The way they all had surrounded her and looked to her for the final say told Jaylen that she was the one the green dress belonged to, she was someone important and he really messed up letting her go. Why wasn't she safe inside the city if she was an important person? Had she been attacked? That would explain the rips. Could she potentially tip the war one way or another? Jaylen prayed no one else discovered his enormous mistake.

***

Time without anyone nearby was rare. Agonya had to take advantage of every moment that would let her think. This was one of those times. The men were off collecting wood to burn for the cold night ahead, and Maya was bathing in the river upstream. The running water was both comforting and distressing. On the one hand, they all could use a bath. But that also presented a problem for Agonya. Maya couldn't carry her into the stream for a bath by herself. Either Ashkii or Brynn would have to help. Maybe she could try healing herself again.

Breathing in through her nose, Agonya tried to pick out the smells around her. Neither she nor Blackthorn had found any orinberries yet.

Agonya focused harder and tried to draw on the silvery swirl of magic inside her as she searched for the elusive berry. She remembered Blackthorn saying the smells only enhanced her magic. And if her magic was the reason she couldn't walk and continually made her feel drained, how could the berries heal her? She knew frankincense calmed her nerves and relieved anxiety, but what did the orinberries do? She'd never find out if she couldn't locate them.

Tugging on the magic, she thought about the scent of orinberries and imagined the swirl of silver flowing out of her. A thin silvery line seemed to zigzag away from her, traveling along the ground, up and over rocks, dashing behind bushes and around trees. Agonya followed it with her mind, but it never stopped. She could feel the little strength that had returned to her leave her body and was forced to let the magic go.

"You did well," Blackthorn said in that high pitched voice of his. "It's not easy to find things that are so far away. The closer we move to Tafka the more chance we have of finding what we're looking for."

Agonya glanced around. Seeing the others weren't back, she pulled the Kindroot out for some fresh air. "Blackthorn, can I ask you a question?" Hopefully, he hadn't already read her thoughts.

"What's on your mind?"

He hadn't been spying on her, or maybe he was just polite enough not to say. "I was wondering about my mother."

"What do you want to know?"

"I've been dreaming about her for a while. About the day she died. You were there?"

"I was."

"Why didn't you save her like you saved me?" Large teardrops began to cloud her vision, giving her away.

"I'm not sure I did save you."

"Of course you did. I wouldn't be here if it weren't for you." Agonya was beyond baffled.

"It's true that I lent you strength. But you saved yourself. I may have even hurt you in the process." Blackthorn's voice sounded sad.

"Please, explain."

"Kindroot magic is different from yours."

There was a long silence. "That's it?" Agonya felt let down. "I have so many questions. How was your helping me different from your not helping my mother?"

"I did what I could for her. She was my friend. And I hers. At least, that is what I told myself. That day your uncle came to visit, he wanted me for his own purposes. He did not care about your mother. He tried to take me by force. But your mother. She was strong. She used her magic to push him away and to hide me from him. I thought I was helping her, but when my magic combined with hers, it killed her. I killed her." Blackthorn's leaves drooped so low they almost touched the soil in the pot.

Agonya pressed her lips together. Had Blackthorn really killed her mother? But why had he tried to help Agonya if he knew it might kill her, too?

"I should have known the effects my magic would have when combined with hers. I should have been able to sense how powerful she was. Did I stop to think about it? No. I killed her."

Agonya hardly knew what to say. But then, why would her father tell her to protect him? "Did my father know?"

"He did. I insisted he punish me. But he refused."

"What happened? After she died, I mean?"

"Your uncle started to search for me in her pockets, but your father found him, accused him of killing her, and sent him back to Korina."

"But then how did my father find you?"
"He didn't, you did. Don't you remember?"
Agonya hesitated. "I remember them fighting. I remember the light and the ground shaking. I was so scared I soiled my undergarments. The sun had set by the time Maya found me." Agonya's mind began to whirl with thoughts. "One minute I was staring at the vines in front of me wondering if Mother needed me but being too afraid of Uncle Reid, and then the next minute you were . . . Were you hovering in front of me? How did you get there? I showed Maya, but she just said it was a nice plant and that I needed to come inside to talk with my father." Agonya couldn't believe she hadn't remembered all that until now. Even the dreams left out Blackthorn. All they ever did was repeat one of the worst moments of her life.
"Your brave mother used the last of her power to hide me."
Agonya's brain began to whirl faster like the untamed magic swirling inside her. "What exactly did she do? Did you float through the air? If you did, Uncle Reid would have seen, right?"
"Slow down, you ask too many questions. All in good time, your Highness. For now, tell me where your friends are."
Agonya looked around. "I don't . . ."
"No, feel them in your mind. Smell them."
"Fine. That doesn't mean I'm going to forget my questions."
"All in good time, little one. Find your friends."
She tried again, this time closing her eyes and picturing Maya's pretty face in her mind. Her rosemary, honeysuckle, and fir scent surrounded Maya, clean with wet hair, as she walked back from the river, carrying both water skins. How was she seeing Maya in her mind?
"Focus. Where are the others?"
Agonya shifted her thoughts to Ashkii. When she finally conjured his blue poppy musk scent in her mind, she could see him with several branches tucked in his arm, jumping down from a dead tree that still stood tall. His ability to jump like that had to be magical. But whatever he was doing didn't seem to make him weak like it did for Agonya. A light breeze interrupted her thoughts, and she lost sight of him. Brynn was

the only one left for her to find. But he was hard to see. Maybe she didn't know his smell well enough.

"How am I seeing them in my mind?" she asked Blackthorn. He didn't answer. Maya's image took over her thoughts, becoming clearer and clearer as her scent became real. Agonya quickly tucked Blackthorn back in his hiding place. She would have to remember to ask him again at the next chance that presented itself.

Maya arrived a moment later and sat next to Agonya. "Are you doing all right? You look like you've been crying."

"I was just thinking about my mother. I wouldn't mind a wash in the river though." Agonya put on a smile for her friend and told herself everything would be fine.

"Ah. I noticed you lost her necklace."

"I can't remember the last time I had it. Do you?"

Maya wrung her wet hair while she thought back. "I think it might have been in the palace, but so much happened so quickly that I can't be sure of it."

"I hope it's in the palace, otherwise, I might never smell it again."

"Well, if it makes you feel any better, Ashkii and Brynn will be here soon to carry you to the river."

"It does."

***

The trees were just far enough apart for Agonya to see the sky while she laid on her stretcher. She breathed in her clean scent and gazed longingly at the stars. The stars who didn't have to endure any hardships. But she did. That had been the hardest bath Agonya had ever had. Not being able to move from the waist down was the worst thing that had ever happened to her. Well, not really, but it felt that way. Losing her mother and father were definitely worse. But Agonya hated needing help washing in the river, hated needing help taking care of all her bodily needs.

A shooting star streaked across the sky. It was over. She was clean, for now. So were all the others. And in the morning, they would continue toward Tafka. There was an urgency to her mission, she understood better the predicament her people were in. They were paralyzed just like her, unable to leave the city or keep it going without help.

"Is it very much further to your village, Ashkii?"

"We should be there in a fortnight," he said, rolling onto his side to face Agonya.

His tone was somewhat annoyed. Was he irritated at her for slowing them down? For needing them to help her? "Maybe we should split up. You or Brynn could go on ahead."

"No way." Brynn shook his head in the light of the fire. "We're in this together."

"We all saw the Korin army. What chance do our people have if we don't move faster? I'm slowing us down. The longer it takes to get there and petition for help the longer the Itholeans must hold out against the Kors. I would feel better if my message were received sooner than later."

"I burned a contract with your father. If I left you before you got there safely, I would be breaking that contract."

Agonya sighed. "But what was his intent in the end? My father could be over-protective, believe me I know. I've got Brynn and Maya here with me, and we haven't smelled any enemies for a long time. What could go wrong?"

"More than deer roam these parts. Some are not so friendly," Ashkii said grimly. "Thorny devils are descending lower every year, as evidenced when we encountered them in the tunnel. And there are other creatures from the Acrid Mountains who are doing the same. We haven't quite figured out why though. The Itholeans are not the only ones fighting you know."

"Did my father know all this?"

"Yes, he knew. That is why he chose me to guide you. Because I am familiar with these horrible beasts and can protect you."

If she was going to convince him to split up, to send ahead for help she had to press. Taking a deep breath, Agonya let her words sting. "Can you?" she asked, raising her eyebrows.

A flicker of emotion crossed his face. "What do you mean, can I?"

Had she gone too far? He seemed hurt. Maybe Maya was right, and he did care for her. "I only meant we don't have our supplies anymore. Yes, you protected me from the devils, but you had that odor bomb with you. Now what do you have in defense, an atl?" Agonya couldn't look at him. There was an awful silence from everyone. She knew she had made him mad, but she needed to know what exactly he thought he could do better than Brynn or Maya. What justification would permit them to stay together?

"We have been collecting the items needed to make more 'odor bombs' as you call them. But my knowledge of this forest should be enough."

"What about you, Brynn? You've been to Tafka before, right?"

"I have," he said cautiously. "But I don't know the Perfumed Pines as well as Ashkii. I'm afraid I wouldn't save us any time."

Agonya nodded. She could accept that, but Ashkii could still go on ahead of them. He would be way faster on his own. "Why aren't you using your magic to help us?"

Ashkii stood up from his once comfortable bed. "Magic? What are you talking about?"

"I'm talking about the way you can jump unnaturally far and high." Agonya refrained from mentioning the whole mind barrier, considering Maya and Brynn didn't know anything about that.

"We're staying together. I don't want to hear any more crazy ideas, especially coming from you." Then he turned and jumped out of sight.

Yes. He did like her, too much. and yet, Blackthorn was right. What was he hiding from her? She needed him to go for help. Ithol needed him to go for help.

"Princess, if I might . . ."

"Not now, Blackthorn. Not now."

Chapter 14

The report about Eli, Victor, and Xander beating Ogi to death had earned Krillin nothing but a constant change of duties, without any consequence for them. That is if you don't count latrine duty which Krillin had not been given.

This was the first night he was scheduled to work with them since the incident. His throat dried up as he walked to the wall. He could barely swallow. Usually, he enjoyed wall duty—the feel of a bow in his hand and the scent of the open fields beyond, but the stress of having to deal with Eli and get that message from Aekan to the Kors without them noticing was just too much. He couldn't prep the arrow beforehand because the arrows were kept on the rampart in buckets. Nothing was going unrationed.

Each of the twenty towers along the wall had been outfitted with its own armory, securely located at the base in case the city needed to quickly mount a defense. Krillin picked his way through the streets toward one of these armories. When he stepped up on the threshold, a guard was lounging at a table with parchments for keeping track of who took what equipment. Beyond the guard, the room was filled with hundreds of bows hanging at various heights along the circular walls and spears stacked together in heaps. The swords were orderly like the bows, resting in tiered racks, each of which held up to twenty. Most of the bows were exactly alike but there were a few of different sizes and shapes. Krillin wanted a specific bow, so he took his time looking for it.

"Hurry up, soldier," the guard complained. "You're being paid to watch up on the wall, not linger here like a fart."

"Sometimes it's worth the scent to take your time." Krillin lifted the rosewood bow from its hook. The smooth wood had a leather grip in the middle. Deer sinew stretched between the upper and lower arms, pulling just the right amount to make the perfect curve. He placed it across his back and marched out the door. Then he climbed the winding staircase to the ramparts.

He liked to be on top of the wall, to look out across the Fertile Basin. The grasses weren't green anymore, and the trees were few and far between. But Krillin still hoped. He hoped the Kors camped out there would change things. They promised to bring back the Paradise the Itholeans had ruined, which reminded him of the tiny scroll in his pocket. He had to prepare an arrow before anyone saw him.

Krillin moved further down the rampart until he found a stash of arrows. He bent down, pulling several from the bucket while glancing both ways. Krillin saw someone in the distance coming toward him. As fast as he could, he attached the scroll to one of his arrows and rose up, slid the arrow into his quiver, and turned to meet the fast-approaching man. The sun was getting ready to disappear beyond the mountain any minute. He needed to find some brave Kor within firing range.

"Hey, Xander." Krillin greeted the callous man. He had to pretend like everything was fine. "Have you been patrolling long?"

Xander shrugged. "Not long."

"Looks quiet up here, much better than the crowded streets down below." Krillin nodded back at the city.

"You mean, you like it more than latrine duty?" Xander raised his eyebrows.

It was Krillin's turn to shrug.

"I don't understand you, Krill. Why'd you have to report us? If it bothered you so much, why didn't you say something?"

"I–"

"No. Don't tell me. Anyway," Xander continued, "Captain Dawson has Hani, Victor, Mikkah, and Don in the towers. He told me to find you and Eli to patrol between the east and north towers. The others are between the north and west. Every once in a while, the Kors try to send arrows over the wall, but they always fall short. I see you're ready to fire back." Xander pointed to the arrows on Krillin's back.

"I hope to shoot them before they shoot us."

"That's the scent!" Eli said from behind. "Well, now that I'm here we can get to work killing stinking Kors."

Krillin tried to hide his gag reflex as Eli fell into step with him, his perfume was overwhelming.

"Did I hear we on the northeast side?"

Xander nodded, his long hair falling in front of his shoulders.

Krillin needed to think about something other than Eli's perfume. "Who's on the south? Do you know?"

"Captain Thresh." Xander flipped his hair out of the way. "You know the big balding man with the Patron of Rituals symbol tattooed all over his body?"

"Let's hope we don't have to meet up with him tonight." He hated that man with a passion. Krillin was not a religious man, and Captain Thresh was more than just religious. He embodied the worst of religion: self-seeking, single scent-minded people wasting good perfumes on the gods as if the gods cared about them.

"I like the man. What do you have against him, Krill?" Eli asked as they walked to their section of wall. "Did you file a report against him, too?" He laughed. When he thought Krillin wasn't looking, he gave a meaningful glance to Xander.

Krillin hesitated, unsure where Eli was going with this. He didn't want to spend all night with Eli if he was going to hold the report against him. He would just say as little as possible and hope Eli moved on. "Thresh makes the hair in my nose stand up."

"Gives you the creeps? How so?" Eli pressed.

"He smells bad. I mean who wears a mix of dungess mushrooms, neroli, and cedar in his perfumes?" Krillin closed his eyes. So much for saying as little as possible.

"That's what creeps you out? His choice of perfumes? You're hilarious sometimes, you know that?" Eli laughed so loud Krillin was sure everyone would hear him.

"Shhhh." Krillin raised his finger to his lips.

"Calm down, Krill, Eli's not that loud."

"I see Kors out there. Do you think they heard us?" Krillin's exclamation quieted Eli.

"Where? I don't see anyone." Eli stepped closer to the merlons and peered out into the basin.

"They're far away, but we should get ready in case they come any closer." Xander pulled out a string and tied his black hair securely behind him.

Krillin felt the feathered arrows on his back, picturing them in his mind, the order they'd been in when he put them there. He selected the one with the scroll attached and notched it. He hoped the others were too focused on their own bows to notice his. Then they waited. The small group of Kors crept closer and closer, pausing every so often. Krillin squinted but couldn't see what it was that they were doing when they stopped. Two of them were holding shields in front, protecting the third man as they went. They were about two hundred and fifty meters away when Krillin spoke. "I can hit them now."

"No one can make a hit that far," Xander replied. "Save your arrow."

"No, I want to see if Krillin is as good as he says he is. Go ahead," Eli goaded him, clearly expecting Krillin to miss.

Krillin took a deep breath, inhaling all the various scents rising up from the ground far below and aimed. Eli and Xander watched him pull the arrow back.

"You're totally going to miss."

The tension in Krillin's muscles reflected his nervousness. He let the arrow loose. It flew through the air in a wide arc. The arrow penetrated one of the shields and might have hit the soldier behind it.

Xander and Eli cracked up laughing. "I can't believe you actually made that shot."

Krillin couldn't help but grin. It was a superb shot, and he'd delivered the scroll just like Aekan wanted him to.

"The captain ought to know how good you are. Maybe he can finagle more shifts on the wall," Xander said, his smile fading halfway through his words.

Krillin's mother had told him to pay attention to people's smiles when they spoke. Was Xander saying something different than what it sounded like? Did he see the note tied to the arrow? Krillin reached for another arrow to help steady his hands.

"This is way more interesting than rations duty," Eli chimed in. "Can you get the other one before they get further away?"

Krillin already had his next arrow ready. "Sure, no problem." True to his word, it too landed in the center of the other soldier's shield. The Kors retreated. Krillin's worries of being discovered did not.

***

Two soldiers stood before Huren's desk. He didn't want to give them the time of day. He was already worried about Agonya. He'd tried to send her a message bird, but the Kors had shot it down. It was a good thing the message had been coded. And then there was the news from Lord Tanish. Huren pushed the thoughts aside and focused on the men in front of him. "Let me get this straight. You were on rampart duty when you met Krillin Boged who was bent over doing something to an arrow?"

Xander nodded. "I didn't think anything of it at first. I thought maybe he was just checking the head to make sure it was secure."

The knot in his stomach started to turn sour thinking about the possibility of that soldier, the one who had helped put out that fire and was brave enough to report his cohorts for killing that beggar, being the traitor. His guards had reported nothing suspicious about him, and he had been hopeful Boged would prove to be a good asset. "What happened next?"

"Eli joined us, and we started walking, keeping an eye out for any suspicious activity from the Kors."

Eli put his hand on Xander's shoulders. "Yeah, and we were laughing because Krillin didn't like Captain Thresh's perfume!"

"Is that relevant?" Huren taped his fingers on the desk.

Eli wiped the grin off his face. "No. It was just funny, sir."

Xander shook Eli's hand off his shoulder. "Krillin spotted some Kors in the distance and boasted that he could hit them."

"I didn't believe it was possible," Eli chimed in.

"Let me guess: he hit them with one shot?" Huren asked.

"Yep. But it wasn't until after the first arrow hit the Kor's shield that I realized there had been something attached to it: a note of some sort. I'm sure of it."

Huren picked up the report that was on top of his stack of papers. Why hadn't he tried to send a bird instead of risk being caught? "And you're not just making this up because he reported your actions from the other night?"

Eli coughed into his hand. "We didn't know who reported that false allegation."

Huren raised his eyebrows, making Eli backtrack a bit. "We suspected it was him, but we didn't know for sure. This proves it was false, if he's working for the Kors and all."

It didn't prove it was false. Huren knew that. He had looked into the case when he'd first received the report against Krillin, and sure enough a man had died that night, and Krillin had been vouched for by a beggar no less. It just proved that Krillin was more complicated than he knew.

"Anything else you need to tell me, gentlemen?" Huren waited.

They shook their heads.

"You may go." Eli and Xander were halfway to the door when Huren added, "Next time you kill a cripple, I won't be so generous."

After they were well out of the room, Huren rose from his chair and walked over to the guard, standing at the door. "You know what to do?"

He sniffed the air and left.

* * *

An hour later Krillin stood before Huren's desk. Huren took him in more fully this time. Krillin was the right height, and the uniform was the one Maya described. He also had short spiky hair, a detail that Maya was only partly sure of because of the darkness. But for him to hit a target from that far away could only mean one thing. His sense of smell matched the traitor's. He used his nose to know that Maya was nearby. Huren stared at the man sitting before him and wondered why his skills hadn't been brought to his attention sooner.

Krillin shifted uncomfortably and broke the silence. "Um, sir? You needed to speak with me?"

"Do you remember that job we interviewed you for?"

"The special job? I don't think I'm your man, sir."

"Oh, but I think you are. Someone with your skills would be perfect."

Krillin frowned. "My skills? What exactly are my skills, sir?"

Huren smiled. "No need to be modest. You hit a Kor that was over two hundred meters away?"

Krillin's shoulders relaxed, and Huren knew he was the man he'd been looking for. He'd finally found his traitor. This man wasn't worried about his abilities being found out, there was something else that was making him tense.

"Oh, that," Krillin replied. "It was two hundred and forty-nine meters if I had the height of the rampart correct. But I can't be the only one good with a bow."

"I knew of one other that good, but he died in the last battle." Huren raised his hand to silence Krillin's reply. "I have one question for you. How long have you been working for the Kors?"

Raising his scrunched eyebrows in confusion, Krillin replied with an even tone, "Kors? You think I'm working for the Kors? The ones I just shot arrows at and hit?"

"What was on the scroll?"

"What scroll?"

"You know very well what scroll I'm talking about. Where were you doing yesterday before your evening duty?"

Krillin tensed for only a moment. "I was with my family, sir."

If it hadn't been for Krillin's response before he spoke, Huren would have believed him. But Huren had seen the fear of being caught flicker across his face. "Joshua, arrest this man."

"On what grounds?" Krillin rose from his seat, stepping out of reach of the guards in the process.

Huren walked around the desk so that he stood right next to Krillin. "Passing information to the enemy, witnessed by Eli and Xander." His guards blocked any escape Krillin might try. Seeing his predicament, Krillin surrendered without another word. No more protests. Huren would have to figure out a way to make him talk. It felt good to be making progress again. Not only had Krillin been stopped from leaking information but Huren hoped he had just caught the man who had ransacked Lord Tanish's rooms. He breathed in the burning frankincense and let his anxieties of being trapped in the city with an assassin and not knowing if the queen was safe fade into the back of his mind.

Chapter 15

"Captain!"

Jaylen heard the heavy tent flaps burst open. Who would barge in like a maniac unless something was terribly wrong? He spun around to face the newest complication. Lonan's big frame stood at the entrance. "What is it? Are you ill, again?"

"No, sir. It's not that." Lonan shifted his weight from one foot to the other, taking in his surroundings and seeing that Jaylen was not alone. "I need to speak with you."

The man looked like he was about to explode but kept glancing at the general which prompted him to bite his lip. "One moment, Lonan. Please wait outside. I'll be with you as soon as I can."

"No need. I'm leaving." General Gad stood up. "I approve of your progress with the tunnels. I expect a report at the end of every day going forward. Stay focused on the task at hand and not that." Gad waved his skinny hand to the stack of confiscated items in the corner of the tent then left.

Jaylen gestured for Lonan to take a seat. "When you're ready."

Lonan sat on the very edge of the wooden bench almost as stiff as the board he sat on. Then he launched into his tale.

“We were attacked. Lapu is at the healer’s tent getting stitched up.

“Is he all right?”

“Whoever shot the arrows at us was not aiming to hurt us.” Lonan fumbled with his cloak and pulled out a wrinkled scroll.

Jaylen flattened the parchment spotted with Lapu’s blood.

> To: Lord Commander Bannon
> Sent on the fourteenth day of the sixth month
> in the twentieth year of King Reid
>
> Everything is falling into place
> in the swirling gray water.
> The people will not be able to hold
> out in these conditions much longer.
> I’m still looking for what we discussed.
> It may have disappeared with the princess
> On the twenty-eighth day of the fifth month.
> Paradise is Coming.

Jaylen read it again. “Quick, Lonan, go find the Lord Commander and give him this. Tell him I have something that might be of interest.”

Once Lonan left, Jaylen sat on his stump of a chair. The twenty-eighth day of the fifth month was the day before he arrived in camp. The possibility of one of his prisoners being the princess just increased tenfold. Not only did the dates line up, but this would also explain the dresses they’d found in the hut. He stood, went to the corner, and retrieved everything Gad had told him not to focus on. Spreading it all on the slab of pine, he looked at it with new eyes. What had he missed?

“I heard you have something for me?” Lord Commander Bannon strode into the tent with Lonan at his heels. Jaylen was relieved the note had convinced him to come at Jaylen’s request. It saved him the headache of having to go through the proper channels. The Commander hardly ever spoke with captains without going through the generals first.

“Lonan, go find Hania. You need to get that air vent dug today.”

Lonan saluted and left.

"Please have a seat, Lord Commander. I take it, you have read the scroll?"

"Yes." Bannon frowned.

Jaylen took a deep breath. This was his chance to prove he could be more valuable to the Lord Commander than as a frontline captain. "I believe we had the princess in our grasp and let her slip away."

"You what?" Bannon's face turned red for a moment, before he continued speaking. "Did you suspect she was the princess when you let her escape?"

Jaylen had enough sense to look ashamed. "I didn't. I knew that it was possible one of them was rich, but I didn't think she was a princess. Let me fix it. Send me after her." Jaylen tried to wait for Bannon to give him an answer but couldn't stand the silence. "If I had a koliimus–"

"You would what? Do you have her scent? Because if not, you can forget it." Bannon turned to leave.

"I do have her scent."

Bannon looked pleased when he turned back and saw the items spread out on the table. He rifled through them. Then he frowned. "I was hoping it was here, but perhaps you didn't search your prisoners thoroughly?"

"What are you looking for?" Jaylen began but fell silent when Bannon lifted his hand.

"A package of high value. I like you, Jaylen. Even though Gad doesn't think you should have more important responsibilities, I want you to go after her. You know what she looks and smells like. The tunnel work can go on without you. Is there someone you would like to leave in command during your absence?"

"Leave in command? You mean for me to go alone? For my men to keep working on the tunnels?"

"Not alone. Some of my personal guards will go with you. Someone has to get those tunnels built. Don't you want to get home before the cold hits?"

Jaylen tried to cover his disappointment and stumbled through his next words. "We . . . we should put Laniel in charge. He worked on King Reid's palace."

"Good. Laniel will report to General Gad. I will send a koliimus with my guards first thing in the morning. Don't spill the perfume." Bannon knocked the table with his gnarled hand as he rose.

Jaylen watched him leave and tried to sort out what had just happened. He felt bad for leaving his troop behind on the frontlines, but the moment he thought about bringing the Lord Commander the princess and whatever she was carrying with her, pure excitement wanted to burst out of his chest.

***

Maya combed her fingers through Agonya's wet hair. "I think you should let it go. Ashkii is looking out for us. I know you worry about everyone trapped in Ithol, but Lord Commander Huren and Lord Tanish are great men who will do everything to protect the city."

"Oh Maya, if it were only that simple. There's something else, some other reason Ashkii doesn't want to split up. You know as well as I do that Brynn can protect us just as well." Agonya took a deep breath. "I touched a nerve. He's never volunteered information about his magic before, and he avoided answering my question once he realized his mistake."

"You know what I have to say about that."

"Yes, you would say it's because of his affection for me, but I disagree. Something smells off about the whole thing. How long has it been? Didn't Brynn go after him over an hour ago? For all of this talk about protecting us, why aren't they back yet?"

"Sounds like they just returned."

Agonya closed her eyes and sniffed the air, expecting to smell Ashkii's scent nearby, but detected a different musk. The pungent scent lacked Ashkii's floral one and resembled a wild animal's. Dread started to creep through her body. Her voice shook in a whisper. "Maya, that isn't them. Can you see anything? The scent is behind us."

Maya stiffened then slowly shifted to look over her shoulder. "It's too dark, but I can see an outline of something large." Maya froze in place and after a moment whispered, "I don't think it's seen us."

"How close is it?"

"Twenty meters or so. Maybe I can get the atl before it notices us." Maya lifted Agonya's head off her lap and laid it back on the stretcher. Then she crawled over to the small stack of weapons.

"Be careful. It might ignore us if we leave it alone."

"I don't want to take any chances." Maya grabbed a spear and put it in the atl like she'd seen Brynn and Ashkii do. The spear was taller than her and was hard for her to manage, but she did her best to aim it at the creature. "It's turning now. I feel like it can see right through me. I wonder how well it can see at night."

"What does it look like?"

"It's as big as a horse and has a couple of nasty tusks."

"A horvelina?" Agonya was shocked. Never in her life did she think she would actually see a horvelina, and she felt absolutely helpless. Maybe Maya could hit it with the spear, but what if she missed? What then? Why weren't Ashkii and Brynn back? Agonya tentatively reached out to Ashkii's mind. She could picture him in her mind like before but when she tried to speak to him in his mind like she did with Blackthorn, she was blocked. Blackthorn was right.

She tried Brynn instead. She could sense his presence near Ashkii, so she called out to his mind as though she were talking to Blackthorn. "Can you hear me?"

Without warning, the creature charged, trampling the plants in its path. Maya flung the spear. It flew a few meters before falling flat.

"Incense sticks!" Maya threw the atl on the ground and scrambled for another spear.

Agonya sucked in a deep breath and smelled the horvelina's heavy musk. It never would have occurred to her to get inside the mind of an animal, but she did it without thinking. Pure rage swirled inside the creature's mind. Instinctively, Agonya knew it wasn't hunger making her mad, but there was no time to figure out why she was intent on goring Maya to death. Agonya concentrated on her love for Maya, Maya gave everything to Agonya whether it was letting her win hide-and-smell as a child or standing between her and a charging horvelina. Maya loved her. Agonya wrapped the silver thread of magic around that feeling and pushed an image of Maya brushing her hair and laughing at something Agonya had said into the creature's mind. To her great relief, the horvelina halted a meter from Maya who had dropped her spear and stood frozen in place.

"Are you okay?" Agonya whispered.

"Yes," Maya squeaked back. "What's going on? Why isn't it attacking?"

"Um. I think I just told that creature to stop, and it did. Come here slowly."

Maya glanced at Agonya, her mouth hanging open. Then she slowly backed away from the creature and made her way over to Agonya. The horvelina followed her movements with its eyes but stood quite still. She was majestic, with legs of a horse, and two curved tusks on either side of her snout. She had tough folds in her skin, and her scent was stronger than ever. Even if Maya had been able to hit her with the spear, it would have bounced off.

Brynn suddenly barged between two oak trees, leveling his spear at the creature.

"No! Wait!" Agonya cried. "She won't attack."

"I wouldn't be so sure." Ashkii followed close behind Brynn, aiming his spear at the horvelina. "What now? Are you going to tell this horvelina to go somewhere else before she changes her mind?"

"She's magnificent."

"Olfamancy is dangerous, Agonya. Send her away before it's too late."

"Wouldn't she solve our problem though? I could ride on her back, and we would get to Tafka quicker without splitting up."

"Bad idea. Yes, you calmed her mind, but how long will that last before she fights back? When she does, she will be angrier than before for being controlled."

"Won't she come back if I send her away?"

"She's not that smart."

"Where should I send her?"

"Either back the way we came, to find whoever might be following us, or to the mountains where she belongs. Or we could kill her."

Agonya didn't think anyone was following them, but if they were, would she want this creature to harm them? Or them to harm it? Now that she had been inside its mind, she didn't want to see anything happen to this fragrant horvelina.

"I think back to the mountain is best." Then Agonya pushed thoughts of the horvelina going to her home in the mountains toward the creature. Slowly, the horvelina turned and walked away into the night.

Agonya turned her head to look at Ashkii who was still pointing his spear in the direction the horvelina had gone. He looked satisfied that she had listened to him and that made her mad. She listened to him because it was the right thing to do. But the problem of getting help for Ithol remained.

"Olfamancy?" Brynn asked, looking at Ashkii, then Agonya. "What just happened?"

"I'm not sure," Agonya said.

"Agonya can do magic, Brynn. She just controlled that horvelina's mind with her own."

Agonya's next words came out harsher than she intended. "You still think we ought to stick together? You weren't even here when we were in trouble. Between the two of us," Agonya nodded at Maya, "we handled the situation quite well."

"I told you; we're not discussing this. We are staying together." Ashkii folded his arms.

"Don't stomp away again like a little child," Agonya warned him. She tried to sit up and failed. She needed Ashkii to talk with her, not at her. "I thought you agreed to help me. Instead, you're just like my father, thinking you have all the answers."

Ashkii took a deep breath, walked over, and squatted next to her. "Would you like to sit up?"

"Yes, please." While Ashkii helped her, Agonya saw Maya motion to Brynn to follow her towards the riverbank.

"Agonya," Ashkii said, sitting back on his heels. "I burned a covenant with your father and with the god of Jedrek to look after you and what you are protecting. I couldn't leave you if I wanted. And I don't want to leave your side. Not now that I know you."

"What do you mean, 'now that you know me'? And what, exactly, do you think I'm protecting? I'm useless." Agonya gestured to her immoveable legs and fought back the overwhelming feeling of darkness. Everything she'd been feeling in the last hour threatened to take over her body now that the danger had passed.

"I meant what I said. I care about you now. Surely, you knew that. And you're not useless." Ashkii stared into her eyes. "You saved Maya from that horvelina. Yes, you are paralyzed, but we'll fix that."

Agonya had to look away. "How? Every time I feel like I'm making progress I make it worse."

"Every time you use your powers, it feeds on your strength."

That much was obvious, and Blackthorn had already explained that. "Powers?"

"Don't pretend. I know it was you who brought the lightning down on the Kor."

"But how? What do you know about this power inside me? Why haven't you said anything before now?"

"You didn't ask."

"Will I die if I keep using it?"

"It's possible, but I think you'd have to use a lot of it really fast. From what I've gathered, I think that's what happened to your mother."

"What do you know about my mother?" Agonya was too exhausted to hold back the tears any longer.

Ashkii didn't tell her not to cry. He simply brushed the salty tears from her cheeks. "I didn't know your mother personally, but your father told me what happened, how she sacrificed herself to save the Kindroots."

"The Kindroots?" Agonya swallowed the lump in her throat as she remembered when they first met. He had shown her the peony tattoo on his shoulder and said he believed the Kindroots would bring Paradise. "What do you know about them? I have so many questions. My father never told me about any of this."

Ashkii rocked back on his heels and re-balanced his squat. "You've heard the story of Jedrek the first, how he came over the mountains and found Paradise in the Fertile Basin."

Agonya blinked the tears away. "Those stories are told to every child in Ithol."

"That is when the Kindroots were discovered. They are the reason the basin is so fragrant and plentiful. They welcomed Jedrek with open arms—so to speak." Seeing the confusion on her face, he clarified, "Since they don't have arms."

Agonya laughed. Then with all seriousness, she asked, "Have you actually met one?"

"Once, a long time ago."

"Yes, but, how did you?"

"Please, let me continue. You don't understand my relationship with your father. He was my friend."

"Why don't I remember seeing you around the palace?"

"Mostly because your father came to me. We would go hunting together. A lot of Itholeans are uncomfortable around Montanes, and I've never cared much for being in Ithol myself. So, Azurarus would come to me." Ashkii stared off into the distance.

"Go on." Agonya felt a calm wash over her as she listened to Ashkii's melodic voice.

Ashkii drew his eyes back to Agonya's face and continued. "One day when Azurarus and I were hunting, I noticed he was more discouraged than normal. He said it was the anniversary of your mother's death. He told me about your Uncle Reid and his thirst for power. How he wanted to enslave the Kindroots. He told me your mother died protecting the last free Kindroot. Though your father didn't understand that her olfamancy was what ultimately destroyed her, he did know why she died." Ashkii paused. "She was a fragrant woman. Her scent was better than all the others, with the exception of one woman I know."

Agonya tried to ignore his pointed look and spoke quickly. "I was there when it happened. I didn't know what was going on. Not until the night we stayed in Brynn's hut did I start to figure it out. It was–" Agonya bit her tongue. She had been about to say it was because of Blackthorn that she knew so much, but Ashkii didn't know Blackthorn was there, so she finished her sentence by saying, "It was my nightmare that helped me remember."

Ashkii gave her an understanding look and continued. “Your father was back from his latest battle. He knew the tide was turning and that he could trust me to help him protect what needed to be protected. I know you want to split up because you think it will be faster to save Ithol, but there are bigger things at stake. What if your olfamancy had failed you earlier? What then?” Ashkii stood up.

What could Agonya possibly say to change his mind? He spoke of good things, things to think about, and yet she just didn’t feel right about not sending someone for help.

“We all need to sleep before we move tomorrow morning. We can leave at first light.” Ashkii moved back to his original resting spot and closed his eyes.

“Ashkii?”

“Hmm?”

“I’ve got one more question.” Agonya heard him sigh. “I tried to reach your mind when the horvelina was here, but you were blocking me.”

“That’s not a question.”

“Why do you have a wall around your mind?”

There was a long pause before he answered. “I’m sorry I wasn’t there for you.”

“That doesn’t answer my question,” Agonya interrupted.

“If you really must know. I’ve had a wall around my mind since I was little.”

“What are you afraid of?”

“If you don’t know, I can’t tell you.”

Agonya watched him turn his back to her and wondered if she felt the same way towards him as he did about her. She wanted to believe him, to trust his words but he clearly didn’t trust her yet. By the time Agonya figured out how to reach Maya and Brynn’s minds to explain this power she had and to let them know they should come back and get rest, his chest was rising and falling gently in the rhythm of sleep.

Chapter 16

The main door to his rooms was already open when he arrived. His clothes were strewn across the floor, the drawers were emptied, paintings were smashed into pieces, and broken clay vessels lay in heaps. Huren rubbed his temples and tried to take calming breaths. The dull throb that had been keeping him company all day was getting stronger.

Why did his room smell of burnt peonies? He must be imagining things and needed to clear his mind. Lord Tanish had come to him earlier in the week telling him that his rooms behind the temple had been ransacked. Who would dare to even touch a priest's home? And now the Lord Commander's? Huren's instinct told him it was the assassin. But that couldn't be possible, because the traitor was currently locked away. He thought after arresting Krillin that no more break-ins would happen. Did he have the wrong man? Who else was Krillin working with? Was it the man Maya said he'd met with in the hall?

Looking around him at the mess, Huren finally let himself smile. Even if the assassin knew every man and woman who had talked with the king before his death, he didn't know where the package was. First Lord Tanish, now himself,

Huren knew who was next on the list: Mikkah, Sir Marko, Sir Besnek and the queen. The last of which was safely away from Ithol.

He had to warn the others and set up a guard for them. Then he could find the other spies and assassins. Huren scooped the scattered papers off the floor and rifled through them. A report of people falling sick lay on top. Huren suspected the wells had been poisoned but he wasn't sure. Just that morning Kahlilah told him that her sister and her family had gotten sick all at once. In a matter of days, several of them had died. At the time, Huren was only thinking about comforting her and finding the cause of their deaths. But this was information he could use to make Krillin talk. He had kept silent the last time they talked, but after Huren warned the others, he would make Krillin tell him everything.

Huren crossed the room and found his stash of perfumes. The majority were broken. Clay and wood pieces lay exposed to the air. They smelled of boiled fat now, no longer of the scents they had once contained. He grabbed the unbroken jar of peppermint, unplugged the bottle, and dabbed it on his temples and the back of his neck. Instant relief. Huren tucked the small wooden vial in his pocket and left the room.

"Mikkah!" Huren called down the corridor. "Just the man I wanted to see."

The tall steward turned, spotted Huren, and walked over to greet him. "What can I do for you, Commander?"

"I know you've been taking precautions since the king's death and the attempt on the queen's life, but someone is still snooping around. They've already ransacked Lord Tanish's home and now they've gotten mine."

"Is Lord Tanish well?"

"Yes, he was at the temple when it happened. Do you think you could send someone to clean up my rooms? It's too much for me right now, and I must warn the others."

"I'll send someone right away. Have you had any word from the queen?"

"Nothing. But I do know she made it out of the city safely. Beyond that there's been no word."

"I guess it was a foolish hope."

“I’m sure she’s all right. We would have heard if the enemy had captured her. No news is good, right?”

“I suppose when you put it like that.”

“I’ll send a couple soldiers to keep you safe.” Huren slapped Mikkah’s back and continued on his way. Doubts about Agonya’s safety crept into his thoughts. He’d told Mikkah she was safe, but was it possible that she had been captured? He knew she was smart enough to hide her identity. Hopefully, Ashkii and Maya would keep her safe. And Blackthorn. *He* would guard her.

“Commander! Commander!”

Huren closed his eyes. He knew that tone of voice. It was the voice of something unthinkable. He slowly turned to face the bearer of ill news.

“Come quick! It’s Sir Besnek!”

“His home has been destroyed?”

“How did you know? Come quick!”

“Has he been hurt?” Huren’s hands started to sweat.

“He’s barely hanging on.” The messenger took off back the way he had come. Huren had to rush to keep up. “He called your name. But won’t say anything else.”

Huren pinched his nose when the door opened. Besnek reeked. He was, also, translucent from massive amounts of blood loss. Huren forced himself to release his nose and pulled up a chair next to his friend’s bed. “Who did this to you?”

Besnek snapped his eyes open. “Mon . . .” his shoulders shook as he drew in more air. “. . . tane,” he breathed out.

“A Montane? Are you sure?” If that were true, the implications were not good. “You mean a Montane saved you, right?”

Besnek moved his head to one side, then to the other. “Tried . . . to . . . kill . . .”

Besnek attempted to say more but coughed up blood instead. Huren put his hand on Besnek’s shoulder. “Don’t. You need to rest.” Then he stood. “I will find this man. Be assured, friend, he will not get away with this.” Huren ran from the room.

* * *

Darkness seeped into Krillin's bones. It was so thick that it pressed in on him, right into his very being. He curled up on the hard bench as if that would help keep the darkness out and longed for his perfumes. All he could smell were the plain brown trousers and cotton shirt they'd given him after they locked him up and stripped him of his uniform. He didn't even have the lingering scent of the guard's fragrance.

Krillin ignored the ache in his nose as best he could and forced his bruised limbs to stretch out on the bench. His legs hung off the end, but it was better than lying on the cold damp floor.

Aekan would be pleased to know Krillin hadn't given anything away when they questioned him. It was easy, really. He imagined the guards questioning him to be the guards who had killed his father and brother. Their stench kept his nose determined not to say a word. Every blow they delivered to him confirmed that they were planning to execute him without evidence.

Krillin forced those morbid thoughts from his mind and stood up. He couldn't see very far in front of him, even now that his eyes were adjusted to the darkness. But his nose and fingers still worked. Krillin searched the cell for the umpteenth time, his fingers running along the walls and his nose investigating every inconsistency which wasn't much but at least it alleviated his need for perfumes even if only turning it to a dull ache.

He was on his hands and knees feeling the edges of the wall when a burst of sunflower, rosemary, and oak entered the room. A light flickered through the crack at the bottom of the door. Krillin scrambled up and felt his way back to the bench. The lock squeaked, and the door opened. Krillin squeezed his eyes shut to block out the blinding light.

"Wait out here. It may take some time."

"Yes, sir."

Lord Commander Huren stepped in and closed the door behind him. Krillin heard the guard lock the door. Why was the commander back? Was he that desperate for information?

Krillin cracked open his eyelids just enough to see Huren place his torch in the bracket that hung on the wall. The commander faced Krillin with his arms crossed. "Are you ready to talk?"

Krillin remained silent. They didn't have solid proof of his treachery. All they had were two questionable witnesses.

The commander saw Krillin's blank face and nodded. "You want out of here, right? Well, if you help me, I will help you."

Krillin's body tensed. Help? What kind of help did he want? And how would the commander help Krillin? By killing him? Like he killed the others?

"Tell me, to whom do you report? How many are you working with? Give me names, and I'll make sure no harm comes to you."

Krillin relaxed his shoulders. He could handle the Itholean commander. "I report to Captain Dawson who reports to General Leon who reports to you," Krillin replied.

Huren tsked. "Still claiming innocence. I thought you wanted to get out of here."

"I do, but you've got the wrong guy. I am not working for anyone other than you, my lord commander." Krillin kept his face earnest while he spoke.

"There are witnesses who say otherwise."

"You believe those two? They want to get back at me for reporting them."

Taking the bait, the commander demanded, "Why didn't you stop them from beating the old man before it was too late?"

Even though Krillin meant to distract the commander with the report, Ogi's bloody face flashed before his eyes, and he grimaced.

"Who helped you kill the king?"

Krillin nearly gagged. It took every ounce of his concentration to swallow normally. He focused on breathing in the commander's fragrance and keeping his face unreadable. But inside, he was outraged at the accusation. If the commander thought he'd killed the king, there was no hope Krillin would get out alive.

"Your silence condemns you." The commander crossed the small room, picked up the torch, and headed for the door. The scents he'd brought with him into the small room moved with him and the darkness began to creep into Krillin where he sat.

He knew, then, that he had to say something. He couldn't let Huren take the fragrances away again. The darkness was waiting for him if he did. Krillin didn't know that he could survive the scentless darkness much longer. He had to convince the commander he was innocent. The only way to do that was to tell him all of it. Well, most of it or he wouldn't believe the lies Krillin needed him to believe. Krillin took a deep breath and answered Huren's first question. "I didn't kill the king."

The commander turned back to face Krillin, his hand still resting on the handle.

"I froze." Krillin rushed his words now that the commander was staying. "I couldn't stop them from beating Ogi. I wanted to, but my body wouldn't obey my thoughts."

"You froze?" The commander raised his eyebrows.

"You don't believe me. See why I didn't say anything? All I could do was remember the guards who beat up my brother." Krillin closed his eyes and hung his head in shame.

He felt Huren sit on the bench next to him. "Tell me about your brother."

Krillin grimaced. This man didn't want to know about his brother. He just wanted Krillin to talk. Krillin told the commander about the day his brother was born. How his mother and father bribed the healer to not say anything about his condition. Sani couldn't stay hidden forever though. Krillin was a boy who didn't understand why he couldn't play outside with his brother. Sani had seizures, but Krillin knew how to catch his brother when it happened. He knew how to hold his head, to protect him. One day they snuck out of the house to go play. They ran into a group of soldiers patrolling the city just like he'd run into Ogi.

Krillin fell silent. He couldn't bring himself to go on.

Lord Commander Huren finished the story for him. "They beat him for his condition, didn't they? Then he started convulsing, and they beat him more, yelling at him to stop even though it was out of his control."

Tears forced their way down Krillin's cheeks at the memory. How did he know?

"That's why you froze when they started beating up that man. Come with me. I still don't know if I can trust you, but I do believe your report about Xander, Eli, and Victor. There's something I want to show you." The commander stood and waited for Krillin to do the same. He knocked on the door. The guard unlocked it.

"Tie his hands. I know we just talked with Sir Marko, but that is precisely why I think a visit to see him is necessary."

* * *

The room the commander took him to was the same one his father had been tried in. The one where he was found guilty of assaulting the officer and guards who'd killed Sani. Sir Marko stood at the center front of the large room. His red robes billowed around him while he frowned down at a middle-aged woman. She was alone, kneeling on the packed dirt, though the room wasn't empty. Salty tears streaked her face. It wasn't the woman at the judge's feet though that made Krillin's veins pulse with hatred. His robes were all that Krillin saw. The tip of a dagger brought Krillin back to the present. He felt it press into his ribs until he stepped closer to the people lining the walls.

"Calm, soldier. He is not the enemy."

Krillin's head snapped to the commander. How did he know what Krillin was thinking? Ah. He let his jaw relax and unclenched his bound fists. He needed to be more careful. If the commander knew everything he was feeling, he would never have the advantage.

Huren shook his head. "No, he was not the one who sentenced your father for execution. I checked." Huren motioned for Krillin to stand against the back wall, right in the middle of several guards.

The commander really had done his research. Krillin stumbled around several men and women because he refused to take his eyes off of the judge until he reached the guards. When he glanced at the people around him, they avoided his eyes. The few who met his gaze didn't hold back their disgust for him. Did everyone think he was a traitor? It was obvious he was a prisoner, but this was not his trial. Not that Krillin had much hope for a fair trial when it was his turn.

Sir Marko cleared his throat, drawing Krillin's attention back to the woman's trial. What was special about this trial or was it the judge that the lord commander wanted to show Krillin?

"You are Saar, daughter of Niyol, are you not?"

The woman at Sir Marko's feet took a feeble breath. "Yes, sir."

"You have been accused of boiling your own child and eating him. What is your defense?" Sir Marko puffed out his chest and waited for her response.

"I didn't!" she protested. "How could I do su-such a thing?"

Sir Marko nodded toward a young woman standing on the side of the room. "Lady Otekah, please tell those present what you saw and heard."

Lady Otekah pushed her hair behind her ears and stepped forward. "I was on my way to the well for some water. The western well." Otekah wrung her hands and spoke to the ground, "When I passed by her house, I heard a baby crying. Screaming. I could tell the infant was in intense pain. My first thought was that the child was sick, and there was nothing to be done. I know how little medicine is left in the city, so I kept walking." She paused and wrung her hands. When she spoke next, her voice shook. "It was the sudden silence that stopped me in my tracks. I raced back to the house and knocked on the door. If there was anything I could do to help, I would do it."

Lady Otekah covered her mouth. Her whole body started to shake.

Sir Marko hushed the accused's protests and addressed the witness. "Whenever you're ready to continue."

The hatred Krillin had felt upon seeing the red robes was now shifting towards the woman on the floor. This was the most horrifying thing he had ever heard! Lady Otekah was not a guard defending herself but a witness. All the more reason to betray these people. They were wicked to the core. Did the commander think showing him this would convince him to return his loyalty to the Itholeans? If so, he was dead wrong. It only solidified the choices he already made.

Lord Commander Huren approached Lady Otekah and offered her a cloth. She accepted it, blew her nose and took a deep breath. “I waited for a moment at the door, but when there was no answer, I forced it open. This woman,” Otekah pointed at the slumped woman on the floor, “was standing with her back to the door by her cauldron, licking her spoon. So, I asked her. I said, ‘Are you all right? I heard a baby crying. Where is he? Maybe I can help.’

“She just shook her head. ‘It’s too late. You’re too late. He didn’t make it.’ she replied. I searched the room but saw no trace of the baby, until she stirred the pot and a tiny red leg boiled up. I turned and fled.” Lady Otekah sobbed into the commander’s cloth.

One of the soldiers led Lady Otekah out of the room, probably to get away from that woman who was responsible for the unshakable images. Krillin, too, wanted to flee her presence, but that wasn’t possible. If the commander wanted him here, he wasn’t going anywhere.

Saar began to shake. Instead of tears of repentance though, her laughter began to bounce off the stone floor, mocking everyone in the room. No one made a move to go near her. Even Sir Marko seemed at a loss for words. After a few tense moments, he found his voice again and ordered her execution to take place as soon as they could get her to the chopping block.

“I think we’ve seen enough. Wouldn’t you agree?”

Krillin pulled himself from reliving those vivid pictures Lady Otekah painted, to see the commander standing in front of him with ten guards encircling him. All the other guards were escorting Saar from the room. Her laughter was still pouring out of her, leaving her stench wherever she went. “You’re all doomed to rot!” she yelled.

Krillin forced himself to the present again, acknowledged the commander, and followed him out, his wrists chafing against the ropes.

❋ ❋ ❋

Huren pushed open the oak door and stepped onto the busy street. The sun hung directly overhead. He watched the people hurry by with scarves or bits of cloth wrapped around their heads to help keep cool. Once everyone was outside, they regrouped with Krillin in the center.

It was a risk bringing Krillin here, but it was a risk he had had to take. He was running out of time. While it was possible Krillin might escape, he really hoped Krillin would do the right thing which seemed to be why he was helping the Kors in the first place. He truly thought it was the right thing to do. And no wonder. The Itholean guards and judges had been wrong to kill his brother and father.

Huren hoped that by bringing Krillin to witness a trial done properly, he might be convinced that not all Itholeans were bad. He clenched his fist as he walked, that that particular trial might not have been the one to convince him. Either way, the deed was done and now Huren had to help Krillin see things his way. He needed Krillin to help him find the assassin who killed the king and very nearly succeeded in killing Sir Besnek.

Huren glanced to the corner of the street they were approaching. One of his men waited in the shadows for the signal. "You know where to go," he told his guards. "I want to talk with Krillin while we walk." He stepped inside the circle of guards, matching their pace. "Why do you think I brought you here?"

Krillin's face was unreadable, but there was something in his glance that made Huren think something had changed in Krillin's mind.

"Not ready to talk about it? Then let me talk." While Huren tried to reason, he gave the signal to the man in the shadows, who immediately moved into action. "I brought you here to show you that we are not all corrupt."

"Ha!" Krillin jerked away. "You call that justice? I call that doing the obvious. Anyone would agree she was guilty and the only punishment for what she did of course is death." Krillin spat on the ground then wiped his face with his sleeve.

Huren couldn't react to him in kind but had to stay calm. "I was not aware of the specific case Sir Marko was judging today. Only that I know he is a fair judge, contrary to whatever belief you have about our council of judges. The fact that a woman resorted to eating her own child doesn't mean he is any less of a good judge."

Krillin kept his face stony.

Huren understood. The mere thought that someone could boil a child was revolting, but at least she didn't get away with it. "I know what you must be thinking," Huren continued. "That she represents all Itholeans. It's not true. You, yourself, are an Itholean, are you not?"

Huren watched Krillin's head tilt ever so slightly. If he had been looking anywhere else, he would have missed it. Having seen it though, he knew he could get through to him with a little time. But he didn't have time, so he pressed on. "You've got to see that everything isn't one flavor or another. More often than not they blend together to make something else entirely."

Krillin started to reply, but the sun disappeared behind dark clouds. Huren quickened his pace.

When they turned the corner, he noticed the shapes of two men waiting for them. It was too dark to see them properly, but the hoods of their cloaks made their forms appear larger.

The men attacked so fast that it wasn't Huren's first or second guard who called out but the third. The guard was on the ground by the time Huren saw what was happening. He didn't wait to see the other guards move to protect him but grabbed Krillin and tried to pull him back the way they had come.

Krillin fought back, yanking his arm out of Huren's grip and swiping his leg at Huren's. Huren didn't fall. He had already planted his feet firmly in a defensive stance, knowing that even in retreat the tide could turn quickly. The menacing clouds and the smell of rotten eggs worried him more than the ambush. At least now he knew without a doubt that Krillin was guilty of treason.

Huren lunged for Krillin, tackling him to the ground. "Help me, Krillin. You don't have to do this."

Huren glanced up just in time to see his best guard fall to the ground. The man standing over him held a dagger in his right hand, dripping with blood. Their eyes met briefly before the attacker leapt over the guard's body and dodged the remaining guards effortlessly.

The attacker was untouchable. Huren scrambled to his feet and pulled his sword free as fast as he could. Unfortunately, as soon as Huren stood up, so did Krillin.

The man with the dagger dodged Huren's blade just like he did the other men. Huren switched mid-stroke to change course, but by the time his sword reached the man, he was gone. No, not gone, just far enough away to not be touched. There was no explanation for how quickly this man moved.

Instead of attacking Huren, though, the attacker reached Krillin and slit his bonds loose. "Go on!" he shouted. "Don't worry about him. He'll hold them off and come when he can." The attacker waved his dagger toward the other man who was ducking beneath the swipe of one guard and meeting another sword with his own.

It was an amazing dance. Huren had never seen anything like it, and that was saying something. Huren shook his head clear of the dust being kicked up into the air and ran after Krillin.

He motioned for one of his guards to follow. But there was no need: the guard already had his arrow notched into place. Huren ran to the side to get out of the way. It flew past him. How the man in black knew to dodge was a mystery. It looked like the arrow might have grazed his arm, but regardless, Huren was satisfied when it landed squarely in Krillin's back. Krillin wouldn't suspect his contingency plan. The one that would follow Krillin to the others.

Krillin fell to the ground but the man in black pulled him to his feet and forced him to run. They started to zigzag back, leaping over rain barrels as they went.

"Hey! Watch where you're going." A woman shoved Huren in the chest. Huren stumbled and backed away. "Pardon? Look who you're talking to."

The woman bowed her head and hastened out of his way. "Forgive me Lord Commander, I didn't know it was you."

By the time Huren got past the woman he couldn't see Krillin anywhere. He couldn't see his own hand let alone where they had gone. No worries. Even in this sudden darkness that was happening more often and lasting longer, his man hiding on the roofs could still smell. Yes, Sitsi would be able to track them, especially with the stink of a blood trail.

Huren heaved to catch his breath. His veins pulsed beneath his skin. Turning back towards his men, he started to feel his way through the dark. He'd find out soon enough if his plan was working, but for now he needed to help his wounded guards.

Chapter 17

Jaylen heard a rap on the leather tent and looked up. He could see torchlight on the other side, so he slung his satchel over his shoulder and pushed aside the flap. The cold morning air hit him hard. He took a moment to breathe it in before holding out his hand. “Good morning.”

The soldier took Jaylen’s hand and smelled it. “Sergeant Kyler, sir. And this is Sergeant Razya.” The man gesturing to Razya had several piercings in his nose and ears. Not unheard of but Jaylen never understood the appeal.

Taking the hand of Sergeant Razya, he noticed the man’s hands were covered in tiny little scars. Jaylen let go as soon as the smelif would allow.

“I see you brought a koliimus.”

“Her name is Kloo,” Commander Bannon said, walking towards the tent holding a sleek black raven in his large hands. “And his name is Darkwing.”

Darkwing flew over to Kyler’s horse and started pecking at the saddle bags. “Here. Take this token. If you need to send me a message, let Darkwing smell it and he’ll find me.”

Jaylen took the perfumed cedar token from Bannon and was about to ask about their progress towards getting the

Itholeans to surrender when Bannon just walked away. Razya shrugged. "He does that all the time."

Jaylen shrugged and tucked the token safely in his cloak. "Who else are we waiting for?"

"No one. It's just us."

That wasn't good, but what could Jaylen do about it? Bending down to Kloo's level, he held out a piece ripped off the green dress for her to smell. "Let's go find her, shall we?"

Kloo's whiskers twitched in rhythm with her nose as she smelled the cloth. After a moment, Kloo set off between the tents, her long hairless tail curled up behind so that it didn't drag on the ground. She knew the exact path the prisoners had taken to escape. She whined when she came to the place the other kolii was killed before continuing. Even though it was still dark outside, Kloo didn't miss a turn. The men let Kloo set the pace.

The ravine was the same one as before. Jaylen grimaced at the lost opportunity. The steep descent that had made them turn back before didn't have control over him this time.

They rode along the edge of the cliff until they found a way down. Jaylen held his torch out to look at the narrow path the ravine formed. "They came this way. Look. That bush has broken branches."

"Yeah, but they've got more than a week's head start," Kyler countered.

That was a pessimistic way of looking at it. "Surely, they haven't gone very far, in a week, on foot. We are on horses. We'll overtake them in a few days. You'll see.

"Remember that dead soldier we found at the edge of camp?" Jaylen changed the subject. "The way he died doesn't make sense. And there was that lightning bolt and then the heavy storm dispersed . . ."

"We were protecting the Lord Commander that night and never saw the man. What happened to him?" Razya asked.

The smell of that night came back to Jaylen. He had had to wrinkle his nose in protest to the burning smell rising from the dead Kor. "Did you not see the lightning?"

"To be sure, we did, but only from a distance."

"It struck one of our soldiers. I can still smell his burning body. But I was wondering if that lightning had also hurt one of the escapees."

"I've only been close to lightning once in my life," Razya said, rubbing the scars on his hands. "And it wasn't close enough to be hurt but my hair stood up into the air. It is possible if the soldier had captured one of them that they both were hurt, but wouldn't that one be dead too?"

"I suspect we'll find a grave soon, if one of them has died."

Kyler and Razya nodded. They were easy to talk to, one of them may be a bit negative and the other a clear thinker, but they balanced each other out. More importantly they worked for Bannon, and this was Jaylen's chance to impress the Lord Commander. When he returned with the prize, he'd be promoted to general and then Gad would be forced to think better of him.

"I think we've learned what we can from this spot," Jaylen said, as he mounted his horse and waited for the others to do the same. "So, Sergeant Kyler, how long have you worked for Bannon?"

"Um." Kyler fingered the ring in his ear. "Just a few years. My father was a general and so I've known the Lord Commander my whole life. When he died, the commander promoted me to sergeant and to his guard. I suppose he thinks I need looking after or something like that."

"Ain't that for sure!" Razya laughed. "You know, Captain, Kyler is a good enough soldier mind you, but odd scents do tend to linger near him. The other day–"

Kloo barked and bounded on ahead of the horses following the contours of the ravine.

"Go on. The other day?"

Kyler looked back at Razya and glared.

"I was just going to tell the captain about how the nutty smell around you must have misplaced your sword." Razya coughed, covering his mouth with his scarred hand. "Many times," he coughed again and cracked a smile.

Jaylen laughed. "Got any scents to share about Razya? How did he get those scars, for instance?"

Kyler nodded solemnly. "That's not my story to tell. But he'll tell you, won't you, Raz?"

The grin left his face. "My father died a year ago," he said. "In the battle of the Neroli Fields. When I tried to remove him from the dead orange tree, thorns about this long," Razya held up his fingers spaced apart, the length of an orange from one side to the other, "pierced my hands."

That would wipe the grin from anyone's face just to think about it. "I'm sorry for your loss. May his smell linger on," Jaylen offered. The death of Razya's father was part of the reason they were there fighting the Itholeans. The death of their princess though was unforgivable.

The horses trotted after Kloo, creating a steady rhythm. Jaylen looked up at the white moon and recalled the day he heard about the princess' death. Aha! "Razya! You're a fragrant scent to the nose."

"How so, Captain?"

"One of the prisoners resembles Kanti. I knew she looked familiar, but I didn't make the connection, but it's proof she really is the princess. We only suspected it when Commander Bannon agreed to let us go on this hunt, but now I'm certain."

"You figured this out because I told you my father died?" Razya asked in astonishment.

"Right, well, I got to thinking, he's one of the reasons we're fighting this war, right? That thought led to how the Itholeans killed our princess that we gave to them in marriage, our Princess Kanti!" Jaylen studied Kyler and Razya's faces but they still looked skeptical. "Come on men! It's her. And we just let her slip through our fingers." Jaylen shook his head. This was good news but also bad news. No way did he want to mess this up a second time.

Kloo picked up her pace and they were out of the ravine and into the Perfumed Pines before the sun set. When the darkness invaded, Jaylen was still thinking about the princess: every word she said, every word her companions said, everything they did. The Montane worried him the most. How had he slipped through their camp undetected? He was skilled when it came to fighting too. If it weren't for that man, the princess would still be in his custody.

Jaylen sighed and was grateful Kloo kept them going at a steady trot. He knew they'd have to stop eventually, to rest before they found her, but he hoped they'd only have to stop a couple of times. Their horses were the best of the best. His mother would be so jealous right now if she knew he was riding such a magnificent creature. These particular horses were bred for speed and could run for days at a time before they would need a break. Granted they were slowed down a bit by the maze of trees, having to turn this way and that. But for the most part, it looked like the prisoners had already laid out the easiest route for them to follow.

"They stopped here for a night. Maybe we should, too." Razya broke his train of thought.

"Did the sun set already?"

Kyler pulled his pale horse up to Jaylen's. "Where have you been? The sun left us hours ago. But you're right, it is darker now than it was before. We've got another storm. Didn't you notice? The clouds moved in swiftly."

Jaylen looked up at the sky and shook his head. He had to do better. "I wonder what's causing it. Where's the rain? Look at these plants. Do they look like they're dying?"

Razya shrugged and pulled up on the other side of Kyler's horse.

"All right, Kloo has decided to follow every little step our prisoner took around their site. We can stop for a little bit."

"I could stretch my legs a moment," Kyler agreed, and hopped off his horse.

Jaylen slid to the ground after him. "Be quick. We're staying just until Kloo figures out which path to take. Then we keep riding."

"Yes, sir." Kyler ducked behind a tree while Razya lit a torch.

Jaylen started for Razya. "Could you bring the torch over here?" Kloo's soft white fur was easy to spot. "Hey girl, how's it going?"

Kloo barked in response, fluffed up her furry ears, and wagged her scaly tail. Then she put her nose to the ground, darting into the woods momentarily before coming straight back. She did this a few times. Finally, she bounded back and howled for them to follow.

"Looks like Kloo's found the path again. Time to go."

They rode in silence through the night, letting Kloo lead the horses. Even though koliimuses didn't have very good eyesight, they were able to get around in the dark just fine by following their noses and trusting their ears and whiskers to lead them right. The horses had better eyesight, but mostly they stayed in single file and followed Kloo's bright white fur. Jaylen rode in front. Kyler followed next and Razya brought up the rear.

The morning brought a little more light to see by, but the trees only grew thicker together counteracting any light the sun forced through the clouds. All day they rode, stopping once at another site of the prisoners for about an hour of rest before continuing. It was hard to say but Jaylen thought it was night again when they finally reached the third resting place the prisoners had used.

"Let's stop here. We could all use a good night's sleep, including the animals." Jaylen didn't wait for the others to respond but hopped down from his steed. After he removed his bags from the horse and gave her a good brushing, he rolled out his sleeping mat and went to sleep, listening to the sound of crickets chirping, content with the progress they had made.

The next morning, as they were preparing to ride, Kyler suddenly bent down. "Do you know what this mark in the dirt is from? I've seen it at every campsite," Kyler pointed out.

Jaylen walked over and studied the ground with him. The fine ashy sand was compressed in the middle with straight edges marking off the bed shape. But they didn't have any supplies when they left. If it was a bed, it was weird. Jaylen traced the picture formed in the dirt. "I think those are poles. Maybe they made a stretcher to carry stuff on."

"Or someone," Razya remarked. "Remember? We thought maybe someone in their party was injured from the lightning. Maybe whoever it is can't walk."

"I think you might be right. I suppose that's good for us. It'll slow them down. Kloo! Are you ready girl?" Jaylen patted Kloo's head.

Kloo bounded in front of the horses and waited for the men to mount up. The hunt was back on.

* * *

“Agonya, wake up! We need lavender, Agonya!”

“It’s still dark. Why are you waking me?” Agonya spat.

“There’s no need to be angry. I didn’t wake you,” Ashkii said.

Confused, Agonya tried to look around. “Didn’t you call my name?” She could see Ashkii sitting on a rock not too far away, keeping watch while they slept.

“I called you,” Blackthorn’s voice reverberated in her mind.

“Oh, sorry, Ashkii. Don’t mind me. It must have been a dream.” Agonya closed her eyes and pretended for Ashkii’s sake to sleep. “What is it, Blackthorn? What’s the matter?”

“The storm has gotten worse.”

Agonya opened her eyes again. This time she looked up. The stars and moon were still hidden. The only light in the sky was coming from the fire Ashkii was tending. She took a deep breath. The very air was different. “I do feel it. It feels so . . . heavy. And I smell . . . is that rotten eggs and oakmoss?”

“You have a good nose to be able to smell that.”

“Did it smell like rotten eggs last time?”

“No, just oakmoss. I fear she has figured out a way to control people from far away.” Blackthorn shuddered inside her pocket.

“She? Who is she?” Uncle Reid was the only one Agonya could think of who would want to control people that way. “Does she have anything to do with my uncle?”

“She has everything to do with your uncle. And she has finally found a way to harness my peoples’ magic.” Agonya could feel Blackthorn’s branches shudder again. “They must be in so much pain . . .”

“This woman and my uncle found other Kindroots?”

“Almost all of them.” Blackthorn took a moment before he continued. “Your uncle’s great great great grandfather, Markus the third, learned about us and started harvesting us up like peonies. Wait. Let me start over. If you’re going to understand, I need to tell you what happened before that. We were hiding because of the sorceress. At first, she was our friend. But she started to get greedy. She wanted us to help her do more magic than was healthy. When we refused, she started kidnapping us. So, we went into hiding.”

"When did this happen?"
"Many generations have passed."
"How old are you?" It had never occurred to Agonya that Blackthorn might know her grandparents and their parents, too.
"I'm but a youngling. By your reckoning, I'm over one thousand three hundred years old."
"But that means--"
"Do you want to hear my story or not?" Blackthorn yelled in her mind.
Agonya's hands flew to her head. She squeezed hard to alleviate the pain.
"Forgive me," he said in a much calmer voice. "I didn't mean to yell. The oakmoss scent makes me angry."
"Oh. Do you know if we can stop it?" Agonya tried to think of a scent that might help counteract the oakmoss but could only think about frankincense.
"Do you smell any lavender nearby?" Blackthorn asked.
Agonya didn't. But that gave her an idea. She pretended to stir from her sleep. "Ashkii?"
"What?" He growled at her. Ashkii rubbed his forehead. "I didn't mean for it to come out like that."
"It's okay, I yelled at you first. Which is why I need to know if you remember seeing any lavender growing nearby?"
"Lavender is a good calming scent. I'll go check."
"Wait. Can you also look for orinberries?"
Ashkii gave her a funny look but gave her a slight nod of the head before disappearing into the forest. Agonya appreciated that he didn't ask her why, even though she could tell he was curious.
"Clever, asking about orinberries."
A moment later, Ashkii reappeared. "Lavender and orinberries. Just like you asked for." He held several twigs.
"Thanks, Ashkii. I think we're all going to need some. I mean incense or perfume would be better, but a twig will help. This storm has a rotten egg and oakmoss fragrance."
Ashkii held up his hand for silence and sniffed the air. A moment later he grimaced. "I thought you didn't know anything about olfamancy."

"I don't. But I am pretty good at knowing smells. I grew up with access to one of the best perfume libraries in the Fertile Basin."

"I'll go see if I can't find more lavender. But what are the orinberries for?"

Agonya bit her lip before replying. Knowing that Blackthorn's family was in pain at this very moment increased her sense of urgency to be healed and to keep Blackthorn a secret. "I remember my mother saying something about how they have healing properties," she lied. Explaining her need for orinberries was easier than she thought, and a huge weight lifted off her shoulders.

"In that case, I'll try to find more of those too." Ashkii got up, leaving Agonya alone with Blackthorn.

"I want to know more, Blackthorn." Agonya pulled him out of her pocket and held the lavender up for him to smell. She was curious about the Kindroots and how this was the first time she'd heard about what had happened to them. They were part of the tales told to children before bed, but they had faded out of the histories.

"Where was I?"

"The part about when you went into hiding from this sorceress. Who was this person?"

"Dana. She is beyond beautiful . . . The best part about her though was her aroma. She had the perfect blend of cedarwood, ylang-ylang, and peppermint."

"Um, Blackthorn, we're talking about the person who caused you to go into hiding, right?"

"Yes. You've got to understand why we befriended her in the first place. She was quite frankly a lot like you: beautiful, smart, fun, easy to like, pleasant to the nose."

"Um… Thank you?" Where was he going with this?

Blackthorn spread his branches wide. "This is why I did not want to talk to you when you first met me. You reminded me of her and what she did to us, but I've seen you learn and grow. You have your faults, but you don't hide them like she did."

Agonya remembered that Blackthorn had hurt her when she touched him. He never did that now.

"Sorry about that."

“I’m okay, but what about you? All this time . . .”

“Dana was our friend and then she started to hurt us. But that’s not all. She started calling herself the Patron of Life, befriending the King and Queen of the Kors.”

“My Uncle?”

“Eventually. She was friends with his parents and their parents and so forth starting with Markus the third.”

“She’s still alive?” She could hardly fathom Blackthorn’s age but a human living that long?

“Not only has she prolonged her life, but she has also perfected and discovered everything olfamancy can do. You mentioned your mother’s perfume library. Well, Dana’s is unmatched.”

“I see.” Agonya felt the hair on the back of her neck stand up and goosebumps covered her arms. She felt the darkness closing in on her, surrounding her, filling her with anger and pain and despair.

“The lavender! Smell the lavender, Agonya.”

Slowly, Agonya fought the despair and pulled the lavender up to her nose. The agony she felt only a few moments before dissolved to nothing as the fragrance filled her up. “This Sorceress Dana is very powerful. Why does she want you if she has so much power already?”

“She thinks, with my power, she’ll be able to bring the dead back to life.”

His words sounded in her head as she fell back asleep.

Chapter 18

Krillin clutched his side even though it was the back of his shoulder that throbbed with intense pain. It happened so fast. First, he was a prisoner bound for death. The next minute there was an arrow sticking out of his back. If he didn't do something about it, he could still die.

Aekan crossed the small room to where Krillin sat facing the door that led to the dark streets of the city. "It lodged into your bone. That is good. Even though that makes it harder to remove."

Krillin flinched when Aekan touched the shaft. He clenched his teeth and inhaled through his nose. Aekan's aroma was beautiful! The most prominent of the mix was a sweet cardamom, sweet healing cardamom. Pain shot through his back when Aekan broke the shaft off near the skin. A small cry escaped despite his efforts to remain quiet. Krillin tightened his hands on the stick he was holding. If it hurt that much just to break the shaft, how much would it hurt to remove the arrowhead?

Aekan slapped something cold and slimy on his back. "Someone else will have to finish the job."

Krillin nodded and loosened his grip on the stick. He drew Aekan's scent into his body. The cardamom came with the scent of olive leaves and rose petals. Was that also cacao he smelled underneath the others?

Aekan broke into Krillin's savoring moment by saying, "We need to make sure we weren't followed. I'm not going to risk going back to our hideout until I know for sure."

Then he disappeared, taking his aroma with him out into the street. Without the aroma to keep him distracted, the memory of that vile woman who killed her own child overwhelmed his mind. Krillin shuddered thinking about her. And the commander thought that would be enough to convince him to change loyalties? If anything, Krillin was surer that he was doing the right thing than he was before. Besides, Aekan had come for him like he promised he would, despite Krillin's mistakes.

Aekan ducked back inside. "Yiska's almost here."

Krillin sniffed the air flowing in from the open door. An animal scent floated in from just down the street and yes, he smelled the other man who'd come to his rescue too.

Aekan peered outside. "What do you smell Krillin?"

Before Krillin could respond, Yiska walked inside. He was almost as tall as Krillin, and he smelled of fresh pine and vanilla.

"Glad to see you got away. Are you hurt?" Aekan met Yiska's outstretched hand and took whatever it was he was holding.

"I'm fine. They really are a bunch of imbeciles. How they call themselves guards is beyond me." He barked a laugh.

"If you're not hurt then we need to find a solution to our new problem." Aekan nodded toward Krillin. "Our friend took an arrow to the back. I've done what I can for him, but he really needs to see a healer sooner than later. And someone did follow us here." This time Aekan pointed overhead.

Yiska rubbed his chin. "They'll have everyone looking for him even after we take care of the stray."

Krillin admired Aekan for smelling the Itholean on the roof, but he would have mentioned the other scents if he'd noticed them. Krillin cleared his throat. "I, also, smell oakmoss and rotten eggs. I think it has to do with this storm."

"It's nothing you need to worry about." Aekan snapped back.

Why had Aekan yelled? Why did Krillin want to yell back at him? "But—"

Aekan cut him off. "The most important thing right now is to get you to safety. We can't do anything about the storm, so forget about it." Aekan paused, then reached into his pocket and pulled out a bottle of perfume. "This might help with your emotions," he amended, squirting it into the air for all of them to inhale.

The lavender scent did make him less angry, but the rotten egg smell transported him to a different place altogether, one he'd never been to. Aekan and Yiska's discussion of the best way to get out of the city faded. The last he heard was something about the number of guards surrounding all the exits. Krillin blinked and looked around. He stood in a cave, filled with . . . Krillin didn't know what they were but for some reason this smell made Krillin think they were in trouble. And it wasn't just whatever was in the cave but almost like the whole world was in trouble. Krillin looked for a way out, seeing none, he closed his eyes. When he opened them again, he was back in the room with Aekan.

An hour later, Krillin, Aekan and Yiska were on the ramparts. This section had been abandoned recently, though probably not for very long. How they expected him to climb down the outside with a wound on his back was beyond him.

"Here. Tie this around your waist. We'll help lower you down. Quickly now."

Krillin grabbed the rope. "You're sure there's not another way out?"

"We've already discussed this. All the gates are blocked. Besides, we want them looking the other way. Go on, wrap the rope around you." Aekan gestured at the line in his hand.

Krillin tried to do as he said but couldn't reach around himself. The pain was too much. Aekan took the rope back and did it for him, tying it in front so it would be easier for Krillin to undo once he was on the ground.

"Now, when you get down, retreat out of range and wrap around to the northeast side. There's a battle there. It's the fastest way to get you help. The soldiers will help you. Here. Give them this. There'll be no questions asked."

Krillin tucked the note in his cloak. "What about you? The Itholeans know you too."

Yiska patted Krillin's shoulder. "Don't worry about us. We've got a plan. Besides, neither of us are injured. That bandage won't last long."

Krillin gave up trying to get an answer out of them and climbed up on the crenellation, wincing from the sharp pain in his back. Aekan and Yiska held the rope which they had tied around one of the stone merlons and began to lower him down. The rope held him at just the right places so as not to cause him any more pain than he already had.

Krillin placed one foot after the other on the wall and began to walk down. He twisted the wrong way and pain pierced his body. Krillin clamped his jaws shut and angled himself until his wound wouldn't feel the stretch.

After what seemed like an eternity, Krillin touched the ground. The worst part was trying to undo the rope. He almost let slip a cry of pain, but he eventually got it loose enough to let it slide to the ground and stepped out of it. He watched the rope retreat up the wall and made his way out of range into the trees.

* * *

"We're under attack, Commander!"

Huren looked up from his stack of papers he'd only just sat down to work on. "Hmmm?"

"The Kors are firing on us."

"In the dark?"

"Yes, sir."

"Send reinforcements to the wall. Who's on duty?"

"Captain Dawson's team is on the north side, and Captain Thresh's team is on the south."

"Are they both being fired on?"

"I have had reports from both sides."

Huren sighed. What he really needed was to focus on how to warn the princess. But he gave the order. "Don't just stand there! Go wake the other troops! I'll follow as soon as I can."

If only the birds would travel. Ever since the first storm rolled in, the day Azurarus died, the ravens were refusing to fly. He tried to send word as soon as the storm ended but the birds stayed in their nests or were shot down by the Kors. Huren gathered his papers and stuffed them into his satchel. Smooshed on top lay his letter of warning for Agonya. Perhaps he should take it with him. Just in case.

Huren quickly pulled out the letter for Agonya. Then he placed the satchel in the vault. He would send it that very night if he could get a rider out of the city. Huren clutched the scroll in his hand and ran to find Dawson.

* * *

One. Two. Three. Four. Every step brought a new smell to Krillin's nose. Grass. Oak. Cedar. Pine. The forest reached out to him where he hunched over next to the city wall. If he could reach the trees, he'd be safe. There was no need to bother the Kors fighting the Itholeans at the moment. He could just make his way to the camp the long way.

Every jostle from his steps made Krillin cringe. But he embraced the pain because he deserved it. His whole arm ached from trying to keep it still. His other shoulder was hurting too. That's usually how it went in Krillin's experience. His body had to hurt equally or not at all.

Krillin made it to the trees, leaned up against a pine with his uninjured shoulder and looked back at the city. He was leaving his home. He didn't know if he'd ever go back. He was an exile now. If only he'd been able to get his mother and sister out, too. He'd just have to trust Aekan would keep his word and take care of them for him. The alternative was unthinkable.

As Krillin listened to the distant shouts and battle cries, he noticed movement coming from the other direction. What could it be? He turned to see it more clearly. A rider was coming towards him, directly away from the city gate. Sticks! There was no way he could outrun a horse! Did they see him escape and send someone after him?

Krillin slipped his bow off his back as fast as he could, which wasn't very fast at all. He tried to notch an arrow, but the pain was too much. He dropped it and grabbed the dagger from his belt. He preferred to stay at a distance but if the rider discovered him, he would be as prepared as he could be.

The rider slowed his horse as he entered the forest. Krillin's heart beat faster. Shock and confusion crossed the rider's face when he saw Krillin standing among the trees. Krillin leapt into action before the rider had time to process what was happening. He slashed the rider's leg and sliced through the strap holding the saddle in place.

The rider cried out as he tipped off the horse on the other side. Krillin grabbed the horse's reins before it was too late and mounted him bareback.

The soldier was now on his feet. He pulled his sword from his belt and aimed it at Krillin. "Surrender or I'll kill you right now!" he yelled.

Krillin threw his dagger in the man's chest. He wasn't sent for him after all, or he would have known Krillin wasn't about to surrender. The soldier dropped to the ground, clutching the dripping dagger in his sweaty hands. That was his second mistake. If he had left the dagger in his body, he might have survived but now he was bleeding to death. Krillin slid off the horse and crouched next to the unconscious man, rifling through his pockets. Just as he suspected, the man carried a message. Krillin unrolled it but couldn't read it in the darkness. He pulled out his flint and struck it. In the brief glow, Krillin saw the note was for the princess. Krillin grinned; it looked like he now had a gift to bring the Korins.

Grabbing his dropped bow and dagger, Krillin remounted and rode towards the camp. His heart slowed and the pain returned, now the adrenaline had burned off. Riding a horse was a lot more painful than walking. The journey seemed like it would never end, but then he smelled them.

"Hey you! On the horse, Stop or I'll shoot." Several guards surrounded Krillin with bows all aimed at him.

"Whoa! I bring news." Krillin tried to raise his arms to show he wasn't holding his weapons, but he could only get the one arm above his head. "I have a message for Lord Commander Bannon. Actually, two."

The soldier in charge stepped closer. "Dismount and put your weapons on the ground."

Krillin obeyed.

"Good. Now let me see the messages."

Krillin pulled Aekan's note out first and handed it to the man who read it and nodded.

"He's one of us. Let him pass." The soldiers lowered their weapons and parted to make way for Krillin. The captain pointed at one of the soldiers nearby. "Lapu, take this man to the Commander."

"Yes, sir." The man called Lapu walked up to Krillin, and they smelifed each other. "Your aroma is pleasant," they said together.

Krillin picked up his weapons and followed Lapu. One of the other soldiers took the horse to brush him down.

Lord Commander Bannon was studying the maps spread across a table when they entered.

Lapu cleared his throat. "Commander, I bring you Krillin Boged, a messenger from Aekan Firikyi." Then Lapu backed out of the tent, leaving Krillin alone with the commander.

Commander Bannon smiled and stood up. "What a pleasant surprise. I heard you were captured. Please do take a seat. I would love to hear the whole tale."

Krillin gratefully took the seat gestured to. Bannon moved to the chair opposite him.

"Aekan and Yiska helped me escape, sir." Krillin recounted the whole of it and then tagged on, "They sent you a message. Here." Krillin pulled out Aekan's second message, the one meant for only the Commander's eyes and passed it to him.

Bannon took it and read it briefly. "Very good."

"Sir, may I go see the healer now? For my arrow wound."

"Yes, yes. Of course. After you see the healer though, I will find you your next assignment."

"Um. There's one more thing. I almost forgot. Once outside the city, I ran into an Itholean messenger who didn't survive my dagger. Here's his scroll. I thought you might like to know what it said."

"Indeed, I would." Bannon read the warning to the princess and grinned even bigger than he had before. "I think I've found your next assignment, Boged."

"Sir?"

"I want you to take the place of that messenger you killed. Deliver the note to the princess and help Captain Dahel. You see he was sent after her to capture her. You can help him."

Krillin wasn't sure how he was going to find her but perhaps the Commander had more information for him to go on. "Yes, sir. I'll return as soon as my shoulder is taken care of."

***

Movement came slowly. Not because of the darkness but because Agonya just couldn't seem to control the magic long enough. Every time she got a little more strength in her arms, she felt weaker than she had before. It was as if an endless pit feasted on her energy and strength.

Agonya sucked in a deep breath. If the Sorceress Dana could find a way to use magic and not be crippled and to live hundreds of years, then surely Agonya could find a way to heal herself and still use olfamancy. She exhaled. She didn't want to become like her. The things Dana had done to Blackthorn, to his friends and family, and if Agonya was smelling things right, Dana was responsible for what happened to her mother. Dana might not have killed her directly, but she might as well have. The moment she threatened Blackthorn's life and convinced Uncle Reid to do the same, that was when Kanti had died.

Agonya clenched the rough poles of her stretcher in frustration, not caring if she added another splinter to her hand. She couldn't forget that this sorceress, however bad she seemed, still knew the secrets of healing. Why couldn't Agonya figure it out? Agonya tried to breathe in the orinberry scent from the twig tucked into her braid, but the fragrance was faint. She felt the stretcher tilt in the air and then Ashkii spoke.

"You do know that we're not going to dump you on the ground, right?"

His comment only made her tighten her grip on the poles. After a moment though, Agonya opened her eyes to look at him. He must know by now that the mere fact that he was carrying her was frustrating. She would much rather be walking on her own two feet.

"I know," she said.

"Then why are you hanging on so tightly?" Ashkii asked.

Agonya relaxed her grip and crossed her arms. "Better?"

"Not really. What's bothering you, your Highness?"

"Your Highness?" Agonya raised her eyebrows at him. He never addressed her by her proper titles. "Perhaps it's your stoic face that I have to look at day in and day out."

"What? This handsome face?" Ashkii wrinkled his nose like he was a boy assigned to trash duty.

Brynn let out a burst of laughter. "Don't you go getting her riled up like perfume in a storm. She might have to hold on again to keep from falling out."

"Don't worry, Brynn, she's not even going to dignify me with a response. Are you, Cinnamon?"

"Cinnamon? I'd rather you called me your Highness. Or are you ready to talk about that wall around your mind?"

"Pardon, your Highness. I didn't mean to offend you."

The words he spoke didn't match his tone. Ashkii wasn't anywhere near ready to explain himself to her. She didn't even know why he asked if she was well.

"Wait, you're being serious. You are the queen? I thought you were an ambassador."

Agonya sighed. "Yes, I am your queen. You understand why I didn't tell you sooner?"

"I do. No wonder you always have that regal way of talking," he said solemnly. "The Kors couldn't know who you were. That was very wise."

Agonya let him fall silent. He would need time to process who she was. Besides, she wasn't done talking to Ashkii. Without thinking about the consequences, Agonya summoned her magic and reached out to Ashkii's mind. She pushed on the stone wall blocking her path. It didn't budge but it did get a response out of him.

"What do you think you're doing?"

"I would like to talk with you."

"You are talking with me."

"Alone."

Ashkii's eyes softened. "Look. I've told you before that I don't want to talk about it. I'm going to ask you to not ever try that again."

"But why? Ashkii, what if we get separated again and we're in danger? How will I warn you? You won't always have Brynn or Maya to help."

"You're right. I don't want to talk about it. But it isn't like you to not talk about what's bothering you. Is it me?"

"Yes and no. You aren't being honest with me so why should I trust you?" Agonya hadn't meant to say that. "I think I need some lavender."

Ashkii had the good sense to look ashamed of his actions before sniffing the air. "Ahh, yes. I can smell the oakmoss. Does it seem stronger to you?"

Blackthorn shook his branches. "It's not stronger. It's just been building up," she said, repeating what Blackthorn said in her mind. "We've been breathing it in for a long time."

Maya jogged closer to the stretcher and held some lavender up for Agonya to smell. The fresh herbal scent filled her up, and the headache that had been growing stronger by the minute disappeared.

Maya withdrew the twig from Agonya's nose and shared it with the men since they had their hands full carrying her. "Is that better?"

"Yes, thanks, Maya. To change perfumes, if I might, are you sure we're going the right way?"

Ashkii nodded. "If we keep the river to our left we should stay on track. I can still hear it rushing over the rocks. Brynn? Do you know where we turn to go northwest?"

Brynn cleared his throat. "The Burned Boulders, right?"

"Yes. We should have a hard time missing those giant striped towers. Hopefully, this storm will have passed by the time we reach them, or we will have to slow down to find our way."

No one spoke after that. They just kept climbing through the forest, up the base of the mountain, listening to the river far off to their left. "Isn't it a little too quiet around here? Where are the squirrels and birds? Something smells wrong?" Agonya wrinkled her nose.

Brynn stopped in his tracks. Ashkii stumbled to a halt. Agonya's hands flew to the poles and clung to them.

Brynn stabilized the stretcher just in time. "You're right, your Highness. Something is wrong."

"Set me down, please."

The men obliged. They reached for their weapons and Maya came to sit next to Agonya.

"I can't see anything," Ashkii remarked.

"Smell it then. It smells like burning pine and skunk."

"Well, that's a relief. Skunks aren't bad." Brynn laughed. "Let's keep going." He let his atl slip down into a loose grip.

"It's not a skunk," Ashkii hissed and crouched, ready to move Agonya out of harm's way if need be.

The hatred in his voice made everyone stiffen. "What is it?" Agonya whispered.

"Dranks," he spat.

Maya lifted her shaking arm and pointed toward the river beyond the trees. "I see yellow eyes staring at us through those bushes."

Ashkii moved in the direction Maya pointed. His movement sent an animal no bigger than a koliimus scurrying back a few paces, but it didn't run away. Brynn stepped up next to Ashkii and tightened his grip on his atl. "Should I spear it?"

"Agonya? Can you tell what it's thinking?" Maya asked.

"Something's blocking me from its mind," she said. "But I can tell you it's not alone."

"I smell six. How many do you detect?" Ashkii spun around, peering into the darkness.

"Six are nearby but more are coming," Agonya confirmed. She wished she could help more, but for some reason she couldn't get in this creature's head like she did the horvelina.

Brynn fit his spear in the atl and aimed. Whoosh! It glided through the air and hit the dirt that had been underneath the creature. The drank sped toward them, his companions following close behind.

"Here come the others!" Ashkii held his daggers in his hands and braced himself. A small dark furry animal suddenly flew toward Ashkii. Its black shiny fangs spread open the closer it got. Agonya was sure the pine-skunk, or drank as

Ashkii called it, would chomp down on his arm. She tried harder to break through to its mind. But Ashkii was quick. He moved with ease, slicing its neck and tossing it into another one advancing from the side.

Maya took some dried deer meat out of her pack and threw it as far as she could. It disappeared into the trees, to no avail. They weren't interested in food. Two were attacking Brynn who gave up on the atl and just held a spear, whacking them whenever they came close. One of the creatures, the one who had been knocked out of the way, was now advancing towards Ashkii again but with more caution than before.

A sudden screech bellowed from its small body and green liquid spewed forth. Ashkii flung his arm in front of his face and jumped. He wasn't quick enough.

"Aack! It burns!" Ashkii stumbled back to the ground and charged the animal with his good arm.

Agonya tried again, pushing her thoughts on the creature that was coming toward them. It faltered, then kept coming. How could this animal create a wall around its mind? She imagined she could see the wall in its entirety and focused her energy on ripping a stone from the wall to make a crack.

The creature snarled and opened its jaws wide, but before it could screech and squirt acid, Agonya tugged that stone with all she had, and it came loose. Surprised, Agonya didn't know what to do next. She felt some other force repairing the wall. Quickly, Agonya squeezed through the breach. "Stop!" she said in its mind. The drank stopped.

Maya picked up a stick and moved in front of Agonya. It fought her for control, but Agonya held fast. Brynn caught a different one under his spear and flung it into the forest. He spun around and saw the drank facing off with Agonya and Maya. He stabbed it in one fluid motion, ending its life.

"Are you hurt?" he asked.

Agonya shook her head. She had to stay focused. Even now that it was dying, she was aware of the other dranks connected to its mind. She could see its leader.

Ashkii beat another one back and joined Brynn. Their backs faced Agonya. They were surrounded. Fifteen maybe twenty of these horrible creatures were closing in from every direction. They were trapped.

Maya reached out and grabbed her hand. Agonya squeezed it tight and breathed in the scents of the battle. She pictured the leader in her mind's eye. She smelled the stench he reeked of. Even though she could barely see his shadowy form in the darkness, she *could* see his wall. The stones were intricately connected as if a master builder had created it. Again, Agonya couldn't help but wonder how these wild creatures could have walls around their minds, but they did.

Both Ashkii and Brynn continued to fight the dranks, taking turns stepping away from the group to push the animals back. Brynn jabbed his spear at one that was getting too close. It backed away.

Ashkii stabbed one as it flew towards them. "We have to get into the trees," he said, shaking the drank off his daggers.

"How are we going to do that?" Brynn asked. "They keep attacking us."

"I'll have to carry Agonya first, then I'll come back for Maya, then you." Ashkii laid out his plan.

Agonya didn't reply. She inhaled deeply. A slight breeze enclosed her, and she could smell it all. Blackthorn's ripening berries stood out above the rest. She reached for their fragrance and felt him give her permission. Then she used his aroma to enhance her strength. She focused on the leader's wall and pulled. Back and forth between the berries' scent and the wall. She felt like a kid's toy ball that bounced up, then down, then up, and back down again.

Then, the screeching began again. Acid squirt through the air. Brynn turned his back to it and covered Maya from the attack. Ashkii was already bending over Agonya to lift her up and take her into the pines. Together, they cried out in agony.

The smell of burning skin nearly made Agonya lose her focus. She grasped hold of her ball of magic and threw with all her might. A brick fell, a hole opened up. Agonya wrestled with the drank's mind. "Stop attacking us," she commanded. To her surprise, not just the leader but all of the dranks stopped whatever they had been doing.

"Let go of my friend," Agonya directed her thoughts to Brynn who had a drank latched onto his burning leg. The creature obeyed. Agonya let out her breath in relief.

Ashkii tried to pick her up, but he buckled under the pain.

"There's no need, now, Ashkii. They will listen to me." Then, she pictured the dranks leaving. The leader resisted, but Agonya was stronger. The drank turned and walked into the darkness. The rest followed. Agonya would not let go of its mind, not even after they were out of sight.

"My lady!" Maya shook Agonya's shoulders. Agonya could hear the fear in her voice, but she didn't dare open her eyes. She had to get those creatures far away.

When their scents were finally gone, Agonya opened her eyes. She saw Brynn curled up in pain, lying on the ground. Ashkii was also on the ground beside her. Maya was still shaking Agonya, trying to wake her up.

Agonya tried to speak but she couldn't. Fear pricked at her. This was worse than not being able to walk. Reaching out to Maya's mind, she tried to convey as much as was needed without using more of her strength. "Help them."

A worried look crossed her face, but Maya nodded, wiping her tears from her eyes, she went to help the men. Agonya watched Ashkii accept Maya's help and wondered why he hadn't stopped the creatures with his own mind. He obviously knew how to build one of those walls. He should know how to take it down too, right?

Chapter 19

The Korin Commander had told him to leave at first light. So that's what Krillin was doing. He was thankful for the healer who had removed the arrowhead from his back, applying a thick honey-apple aromatic paste over the wound which eased the pain and allowed him a full night's sleep. The next few days were not very promising as far as comfort was concerned. Especially with his back still healing.

Walking as fast as he could, he made his way through the camp. At least he wasn't being ordered onto the front lines.

"Who goes there?" a stable hand inquired at Krillin's approach.

"Krillin Boged, sir. I was told this is where my horse would be waiting." Krillin stepped into the light of the lad's torch.

"Ah, yes. I remember someone with the Itholean emblem would be coming. This way."

The young man led Krillin into the horse pen, passed several war horses and up to that beautiful horse he'd stolen the day before already saddled and packed. Just to be sure, Krillin opened the saddle bags.

Inside, he saw enough food for the journey and more. Captain Dahel should be pleased with a few extra supplies. There were also extra clothes that he doubted would fit him, since he was unusually tall. There were candles and latrine towels, a knife, the map Bannon had shown to him in the command tent, and a few other odds and ends. But what Krillin was most grateful for was his repaired bow and a few quivers full of arrows hanging on the side of the horse.

Krillin ran his hand the length of the bow and in that moment, he was also grateful he wasn't a prisoner of the Itholean commander anymore. He owed Aekan and not just for helping him escape but for the gift he'd given him too.

Pulling the vials of Krillin's favorite perfumes and oils from his cloak, he placed them in the saddle bags. He knew what it was like without them. He needed them; they comforted him and reminded him of his family. Aekan's gift was thoughtful and kind.

Krillin rode the mare out of camp, straight for the Perfumed Pine Forest. He knew the direction the others had gone and made sure to stay out of sight of the city wall. He felt a twinge of guilt at the thought of leaving those children behind to faint and die in the streets, to be eaten by those horrible people who would consume their own children, but there was no way he could have stayed and saved them. He was a wanted man.

Having this mission made him feel like he was doing something about it all. Yes, he knew his mother would still do her part. She had taken every child he'd brought to her, but she still only got rations for two. There was no way to get the ration for the child unless you found their parents and they gave it to you. These kids' parents didn't want to be found. Without their child they got twice as much to eat or stock up on, however you wanted to see it. Krillin could see his mother tending to the children, finding a way to make the food stretch. She would fuss over their clothes and hair and wash them with a scented cloth. She'd tuck them into bed and smelif them before she sang a song about Jedrek the first or Kindroots who made things beautiful.

Sari was the best mother even when things were bad. He remembered her after his brother died. She had been heartbroken. They all were. His father did his best to comfort her but, in the end, it was she who comforted him. That is, until he'd sought justice.

Krillin didn't want to remember that part of the story, so he started to recount the song of Jedrek the great, the one his mother used to sing to him, while he rode:

"He fled from the sea,
over the Acrid Mountains,
through the deep, deep freeze,
until he found the fountains.

Jedrek, the first, he found them,
eternal fountains of the fertile basin,
Flowing with ten fragrances:
floral, resinous, fruity and rank,

Rotten, sweet, and nutty,
citrus, fermented, and spearmint.
Ten scents blending into
Towers made from tree and stone . . ."

* * *

She couldn't talk, breathing was only possible through her nose and even that was a struggle. Agonya tried to breathe normally and think about something else. But seeing Maya strip off Ashkii and Brynn's shirts to tend to them was no better. Their backs were spotted with burn marks, some of them still burning.

Maya poured some water on Brynn's back. He cried out in pain as soon as the water touched his skin.

"I'm sorry! So sorry!" Maya backed away reflexively and bit her lip.

Ashkii took a deep breath. "Don't be afraid. It's going to hurt no matter what."

"I know. It's just. Oh! I hate this!" Maya pulled the water-skins back, even closer to her body.

"Maya." Brynn inhaled sharply. "Come here."

As soon as she was close enough, Brynn took her hands in his. "It's okay. You don't have to do this. The water can't break me, it'll just cleanse me like Jedrek burned the Kindroots."

Laughter erupted from Ashkii, promptly followed by wincing.

"What's so funny about that?" Maya asked.

"Don't you get it? Jedrek broke the covenant with the Kindroots."

Brynn grinned and before Maya could stop him, he had the water-skins out of her trembling hands and was turning towards Ashkii. They weren't far apart. So even though his movements were painstakingly slow, he was pouring water on Ashkii's back before she knew what he was doing.

"I still don't get it," she said, stretching her hand out, then withdrawing it. "Can I help?"

Shaking his head, Ashkii began to sing a song that Agonya's mother used to sing, grimacing when the water touched his back. She didn't know he could sing like that. She felt both awe and sadness at the same time. The peony carved into his shoulder stood out now. This song, that she'd heard as a child, sang about the Kindroots taking refuge under peony bushes. It was a wish to go back to the way things were before the covenant was broken.

Agonya tried to ask him about it but she still couldn't speak.

Maya, on the other hand, was just as curious as Agonya, and she could speak. "But Kindroots are just a children's tale. Do you really believe in all of that?"

"I do."

"There." Brynn finished washing Ashkii's back with the little water he had in the skins. "Can you stand?"

Ashkii pushed up to a sitting position. "Aghh!"

Maya rushed over to help him up. Between the two, he was able to rise.

"We need to get to the river." Ashkii grabbed a low-hanging limb from a nearby tree. "We have too many wounds to wash them all here."

Agonya wondered exactly how much Ashkii knew about Kindroots. Why, if he was a part of this group that wanted to fix the covenant that was broken, didn't Blackthorn trust him?

Brynn stumbled, drawing Agonya out of her thoughts. She wished she could help. She hated seeing them like this. If only she had broken through that creature's mind sooner! She could have stopped this from happening.

But she had failed. She hadn't been able to protect them. And now what? They could barely walk to the river let alone carry her to Tafka. Agonya's chest started to constrict, and her head became light, thinking about what this meant. Each breath was harder than the last. Slowly, she closed her hand into a fist where it lay until they were out of sight. Tears welled up in her eyes, and Agonya let out a muffled sob.

"My lady?" Blackthorn's voice was full of sympathy.

Agonya strained with the effort to shake her head. What she did to control those horrendous creatures had used up all her strength. She had hidden it from Maya just now, but she was in a much worse place than before.

Blackthorn persisted. "Forgive me, your Highness. For not helping you sooner. I was afraid I'd hurt you even more, but Ashkii's song reminded me of a time long ago. There may be a way for me to help. And you were right. Maybe I should trust Ashkii more."

"Blackthorn?"

"It is dangerous and partly what caused your current situation."

"If there is a chance it will help." Agonya dared to hope there was some relief either for her or for Ashkii and Brynn or all of them.

"In theory, it should work."

"In theory?" That didn't sound promising.

"I was only a baby when Dana captured my family. I wasn't old enough to have a teacher." Blackthorn sighed.

"You've never done this before?" Agonya asked.

Blackthorn's branches drooped a little. "I've tried, but remember what happened when we were fleeing the Korin camp? I lent strength to you, but when it combined with your power it was magnified a hundredfold and caused you damage. Typically, our magic isn't supposed to harm others.

It is intended to help. But that was the second time I tried to help and caused harm instead."

"Maybe, since we aren't running for our lives, you'll be able to help this time."

"I need you to relax."

Agonya closed her eyes and tried to do as he said. She took a deep breath and waited. A moment later she started to feel that tingling sensation she had felt the first time she met Blackthorn. Her fingers buzzed. The feeling crawled up her arms, slowly spreading throughout her entire body.

Agonya tried to move. "I can't . . . "

"Shhh . . . Keep still." Blackthorn continued to send magic through her body. He did his best to not cause her actual pain but every once in a while, it hurt.

"I can't do any more right now. How do you feel?"

Agonya thought about her legs. She still couldn't move them, but they did feel a little stronger. The same went for the rest of her body. She tested out her voice. "I can speak. Thank you, Blackthorn. And I have more energy; I can feel my well of magic filling up faster than it was before."

"Good. I'll try to help again in a little while after I've replenished a bit. Maybe when they return from the river you might be able to relieve some of their pain?"

"Yes, I can give it a try." Agonya thought about the orinberries Ashkii had collected for her. She still didn't know how to harness their fragrance. Perhaps she could try burning some like incense. It was the smoke of the frankincense that allowed her to manipulate the guards back home. Perhaps, the berries' smokey fragrance would allow Agonya to heal them; if not completely, maybe a little bit.

The sound of heavy slow footsteps drew nearer. "Brynn? Is that you?" Agonya figured it must be Brynn since he was the biggest among them.

"No. I don't believe we've met before." A deep gravelly voice startled Agonya. She automatically tried to turn her head to see who was behind her but her muscles refused to budge.

"May I ask for an introduction?" Agonya did her best to not show her panic. Was he friendly? An enemy? What could she tell him?

The man moved around to where she could see him. He was holding a torch in one hand and an atl and spear in the other. He was average height and well-built with a beard almost as long as his dirty blonde hair. A Montane.

"Why do you not rise to greet me?"

"You'll have to forgive me. I would, if I could."

"Are you hurt? Here, let me help." The Montane squatted down in front of her and set his weapons on the ground. "Where does it hurt?"

Agonya shook her head as much as she could. "You can't help me unless you know how to heal a cripple."

"Have you always been crippled? How did you get here, then? Forgive me for prying, but if you were injured recently there may be a way to heal you."

"It was recent," she admitted. Though, she didn't want to tell him how it happened. She still didn't trust Montanes. Ashkii was one thing, but a stranger?

"If you come back with me to Tafka, I'm sure Old Wise Kylie could help make you better."

"Tafka? Do you know Ashkii?" Agonya held her breath, letting it fill her with a glimmer of hope.

"I know a few Ashkiis. Perhaps I know the one of which you speak. Perhaps not."

"Indeed, you do! Hey, Tse, how are you?" Ashkii did his best not to show how much pain he was in as he walked slowly into the clearing, but Agonya saw his face muscles twitch.

"Ash? Is that you?" The Montane held his torch up to see better in the cover of the forest canopy and storm above. "It's been a very long time." The man Ashkii had called Tse rose up and began the Montane version of the smelif, but Ashkii raised his hands in protest.

"Please, I'm hurt and your smelif will have to wait. I know we ought to get all the pleasantries out of the way first, but I must ask you to help my friend." Ashkii motioned over his shoulder towards the river where Maya could barely be seen helping Brynn walk up the slope.

"Of course!" Tse rushed to their side, lending his strength to them and lighting their path.

Agonya wanted to help Brynn herself but was unsure how much she could trust Tse. Yes, he and Ashkii were friends or so it seemed, but she still didn't know what sort of person he was. He had insulted her, but he'd also been quick to try and help.

"Tse, meet my friends," Ashkii pointed to Agonya, "I know you've already met . . ."

"You can call me Kanti," she said quickly.

"And this is Brynn and Maya." Turning to the others, he said, "Meet Tse. He and I go way back. Tse is good friends with my older brother."

"I'm glad I've smelled you all. If you don't mind my asking, what happened?" Tse asked again as he looked at the burns on Brynn's back and legs.

"Dranks. Here! Of all places."

"Dranks? Are you sure?" Tse looked worried.

Ashkii nodded, sharing a knowing look with him.

"I'll go see what I can find to treat it." Tse strode off into the woods.

Once he was gone, Agonya breathed in the cool evening air. "Ashkii? Can we trust him? I mean, about what I can do? I think I might be able to heal you, maybe." Agonya hesitated long enough for Brynn to get a question in.

"That would be great and all but if you can heal us, can you heal yourself, too?"

"About that, I caused the Kor to fly into the air and the clouds to dissipate. I don't know how I did it but I'm pretty sure using that much magic is why I can't walk. It drains me of strength and energy whenever I attempt to use it. Before, when you were singing, Ashkii, I wanted to sing with you but I couldn't because my tongue wouldn't move."

Ashkii started to speak, but she shook her head. "Let me finish. While you were at the river, some strength returned to me, and I can talk again. Well, now, I would like to try and help heal you while I have a little strength left."

There was silence as they all processed what she'd said. Ashkii sat down next to her. "I think he is trustworthy. I wouldn't worry about it. If you think you can help, you ought to start with Brynn. He got the worst of it."

"Are you sure, Ashkii? You look like you're in as much pain as I am."

"I'm sure."

"I will try to heal you both, but it all depends on my strength. Maya? Could you get some orinberries from the pack? I want to try and burn them."

Maya crossed quietly to the pack and retrieved a handful of berries. Then she gathered a few twigs and started a fire. The berries were starting to smoke when Tse returned.

"I found some of these." He held out more orinberries for them to see. "But it looks like you already have some."

"Perfect! We don't have very many. Do you know how to use them?" Agonya asked.

"To be honest, I only ever saw my mother use them. I've never done it myself."

"Come hold my hand, Brynn, and I'll see what I can do."

Brynn hesitated but saw her glance at the Montane. He joined hands with her.

She focused on the smoke rising from their little pine fire. The fragrance seemed stronger than before. She drew it into herself and mingled it with her well of magic. Then she willed it to travel through her arm and into Brynn's hand. She pushed it all the way to his back and down into his legs. Whenever it hit a burn mark, she felt it diminish and she would try to focus on putting more of her strength into it.

The berries burned up and became ashes and Agonya lost the fragrance. She sighed and closed her eyes. "That's the best I can do for now. Any better?"

Brynn pulled his hand from hers. "Are you kidding? What kind of contract is this? I hardly felt the burn at all!"

Tse looked at Agonya in wonderment. "That's not how my mother used the berries. That's amazing! I have so many questions right now. If you can do that for him, why are you still crippled?"

"It's not for lack of trying," Ashkii offered. "If we can get her to the village, Old Wise Kylie might be able to help her get better."

"I was just telling her that before you showed up." Tse's face was aglow for a moment before he realized the realities of getting to the village. "I should go for help. I can travel faster than you all and bring back help. Will you be okay if I leave you here?"

"We will manage," Ashkii replied.

"Um . . . I think we need to get off the ground if we're to stay here. I don't want to be attacked again with no way of escape," Brynn countered.

"How do we do that? We can barely walk." Agonya wondered.

"I'll help you get into the trees and then I'll go for help."

Chapter 20

Krillin stood panting in the alley again, watching his brother suffer beneath the clubs of the guards. He couldn't do anything but stand there and watch, to listen to every painful cry Sani uttered.

The scene changed. Krillin sat in the middle of a crowd. There were guards at all the exits to the circular courtyard. Everyone sat facing the same way, looking towards the front. Krillin's mother was there, tears streaming down her face. His father was standing in front of the crowd although not facing them. And then, Krillin saw the man in the red robe, the man who condemned his father to death. He just stood there, stern and uncaring. He sentenced Krillin's father to three moons for assaulting the guards even though he'd only been trying to protect his son. The judge had sided with those murderers.

The dream shifted again. Krillin watched his father walk away from his prison. Watched him find his way home to see his family, to finally be reunited but not before the guards found him. They beat him for no other reason than that he had accused them of the very thing they had done.

His mother knelt by his father in the alley, bent over him, crying and trying to stop the bleeding. It was no use. Krillin watched him die, knowing that he would. But being in a dream, he couldn't do anything to stop it.

Emptiness. Anger. Frustration boiled up inside his chest. And then, sharp pain pierced his shoulder. Krillin bolted upright and glanced at the ground. A sharp rock sat there unapologetic for hurting him where he'd already been wounded. He rubbed around his injured shoulder and the pain didn't go away.

Krillin stood up to see if the pain would lessen. The uniform he wore was so tight; the pants only came down to the middle of his calf. Standing was more comfortable. It would have to suffice. He needed to wear this uniform to keep up his appearance as an Itholean messenger, in case he found the princess sooner than anticipated. Lord Commander Bannon had sent someone to retrieve the uniform of the man he'd killed just outside the city, that way he could trick the princess into trusting him.

He could smell the river in the darkness somewhere off to his right. "Follow the river until you reach here," the commander had said, pointing to a map. "Then go northwest until you find the village." Krillin bent down to pick up his bag. He lit a candle and pulled out the note he'd found on the Itholean soldier, the one meant for the princess.

The note said something about Montanes not being trustworthy. That meant he had to be careful if and when he found the princess. Commander Bannon had said she was traveling with a Montane and two others. And Jaylen's note said he suspected the escaped prisoners were on their way to a Montane village. The thought of trying to figure them out started giving Krillin a headache. He hated it when people were tricky. He hated being tricky himself. He only did it because he hated those murderers more. That meant he had to keep going. He couldn't go back to Ithol no matter how much he wanted to see his mother and sister.

After he ate some dried bread and fruit and took a swig from his water skin, Krillin pulled out his perfume and uncorked it, bringing it to his nose. He couldn't function during the day if he didn't get his daily dose of cedar-wood mixed with frankincense and rosemary. He shuddered, remembering those long days in the dark room without his perfumes. He dabbed it on his neck and stashed the bottle back in the saddle bags. He picked up his bow and quiver, securing them on the horse's back, then jogged next to his horse toward the river.

A path ran next to the rushing water. Krillin wondered who had made it. He didn't know anyone who visited the Montanes, not one merchant, as far as Krillin knew. Most people wanted to stay as far away from them as possible. Or maybe the path was a hunter's path. Although, he had been surprised when Commander Bannon had said the princess was traveling with a Montane and going to ask the Montanes for help. He couldn't let that happen. He needed the Itholeans to be defeated. Only then would those murderers receive justice. Justice. Not the so-called justice his father had received. He let his anger build up inside of him. It was all he wanted to think about. His anger fueled his energy and numbed the pain in his back. He ran a little bit faster and further. Once he felt refreshed from his restless night, he mounted the horse. He kept replaying his imprisonment and the injustice in the Itholean court. This was what would get him there in the end. His anger. His desire for real justice.

* * *

It was only a matter of time before Gad would have to recant his comments about Jaylen being incompetent. He was closing in on his prey and could smell his victory already. Once he found them, he would capture the princess, kill the rest and return to the praise of the Lord Commander.

Reaching into the bag behind him, Jaylen pulled out a handful of roasted eyeballs to munch on while they rode. The squirrel ones were the best but the others were fine too. His lovely mother wouldn't like them; she loved animals and wouldn't eat meat of any kind. She always had a story to tell about one animal or another. Once, she told him about the invisible cheemas that Markus the third had defeated. But his favorite stories from her were the ones about the Kindroots that used to live in the Fertile Basin and Perfumed Pines. Many thought they were extinct or never existed at all. Jaylen wanted to believe they'd just gone extinct because who could ever imagine these magical tree-like creatures on their own? Sure, they were probably exaggerated in the things they could do and maybe they weren't as treeish as they became in the stories, but he thought they probably had existed hundreds of years ago if not longer.

Jaylen shook his head. His mind seemed to be drifting off track. He needed to be on the alert even if they had another day or two of traveling before finding the princess. He never knew when Kloo would disappear and where she'd pop back up. There were many dangers in the Perfumed Pines, cheemas were one of them; not to mention they were entering Montane territory.

Jaylen glanced around and noticed Kloo up ahead. "The ground is sloping higher."

Kyler leaned forward to get a better look. "I think you might be right."

"Keep a lookout for signs of the Montanes," Jaylen ordered.

"What do you know about them?" Kyler asked.

"They are smelly and ruthless. But they've probably had to be, to live at the base of the Acrid Mountains."

"Do you think we might have to fight them?"

"I hope not." Maybe they could find an agreement of sorts without fighting, but then again there had been a Montane helping the Itholeans. Negotiations might be off the table. "We might be able to sneak up on them and snatch them in the dark. We only need to get the princess. We can kill the others or leave them."

"Kill them. Don't want them hunting us, do we?" Kyler pointed out.

Jaylen agreed and checked the rope tied around his waist to make sure it was secure. Then, he closed his eyes and let the rhythmic walk of his horse lull him to sleep. He needed to stay awake during the first watch later that night, but even as he drifted to sleep, an idea of how to capture the princess was beginning to take shape in his mind.

***

In the end, they chose not to go up in the trees. Tse had offered to jump them into the trees since Ashkii couldn't but then they would have been stuck. Instead, Agonya watched Tse and Maya build a shelter on the ground that would hide them from unwanted visitors and act as a shield.

"If another horvelina comes it will easily knock it down," Ashkii pointed out. "But it will have to do. I owe you one, Tse."

Tse turned from placing one more branch on the shelter and gave Ashkii a slight bow. "It's the least I can do." Then turning towards the mountains, Tse jumped. He jumped like Ashkii.

Could all Montanes do this?

"Don't worry. He'll fly like the wind and be back in no time," Ashkii said.

Agonya raised her eyebrows as she turned to look at the Montane. "But couldn't you have done this thing too?"

"That's different. If I had left–"

"No," Agonya interrupted. "If you had left help would already be here or almost here. But you are just ash on the wind."

Brynn tried to smother a chuckle.

What had she said that was so funny?

He laughed again, this time not bothering to hide it. "Ash! You're burnt to a crisp," Brynn bellowed.

Ashkii grimaced. "If only it didn't hurt so much."

"I know," Brynn said solemnly. "I can smell your ego sizzling to ash as we speak."

More laughter erupted from the group, even Ashkii joined in the laughter this time. It felt good to laugh. Agonya had to drop the what if argument. It did no good. And they were in need of a little good right now. Both Brynn and Ashkii were in pain, unable to move without it hurting more. Even their laughter was punctuated with wincing and a hand to their sides. The only one not in need of help was Maya, the smallest of them all. She did what she could for them but that wasn't enough.

Agonya recovered from her laughter and breathed deeply. She needed to focus on doing everything in her power to help heal them. Because no matter how much she insisted they would have been better off if Ashkii had gone for help, he had saved her life.

Inhaling the scents surrounding her, Agonya tried to identify what she was smelling. Finding the fruity scent she was looking for, she tugged on it and tried to blend it with the raging, swirling mass of magic inside her.

"You're getting better at that." Blackthorn's voice seemed distant.

"It doesn't feel like it. Are you ready? I need your help if I'm going to help them." Agonya glanced up. Ashkii and Brynn were resting on their sides, their backs exposed to the air. Agonya cringed at the sight.

Blackthorn did his best to impart his gift of strength and energy to Agonya. He kept the perfumes of magic washing over her for what seemed like a long time but when Agonya opened her eyes the sun had barely moved.

"Ashkii, would you like for me to try to heal you?"

"I'm sure my ego will continue to sizzle a little longer. Brynn though. . ."

Agonya smiled and turned to Maya, but she was already starting a fire. A pile of berries sat at the ready. The flame licked the pine needles and oak branches, releasing their fragrances. Maya lifted one end of Agonya's stretcher and pulled her closer to Brynn and to the fire. Maya helped Agonya move her hand onto Brynn's right leg that had received the worst acidic burn.

It took but a few seconds for the berries to start burning and the smoke to reach Agonya's nostrils. Instead of trying to spread her magic throughout his whole body like last time she focused on his leg. It was probably more important that he be able to walk again than being able to lean against a tree or lie on his back. She sensed his burns and used all her strength to bring healing to that one burn. Occasionally, it would try to move on, to travel through his body, and Agonya had to focus even harder to make it stay and work on the one spot. At last she didn't have the strength to control it and she just let it go where it willed, evaporating as she relinquished control.

"Thank you, your Highness."

"No need to call me that, Brynn. Please, call me Agonya."

"Of course, Agonya. You cured my ego real fast," he said with a laugh. "No, really, my leg feels so much better. I might even be able to walk on my own now. Maya, would you be a flower and help this old man on his feet?"

"Look! That burn is completely healed!" Maya said, as she leaned down to help him up.

"Is it?" Agonya couldn't believe it. After days of struggling to do the least bit of healing and now she had accomplished it!

Agonya's mind immediately raced to Blackthorn. "I couldn't have done it without your help," she sent.

There was no answer.

"Blackthorn?"

Still no answer. Was he okay? Why wasn't he answering? Usually if Agonya wanted to talk he was there waiting for her. The brief energy she got from being successful vanished. She started to realize how tired she was. Before she could inquire about Blackthorn anymore, darkness enveloped her.

Chapter 21

Birds chirping in the trees woke Agonya. She felt groggy, not at all like the birds. How long had she been out? Her friends were still asleep, so it must be the morning. Sunlight was filtering in through the cracks of their small shelter, its warmth creeping down between the pines, half of which were brown and brittle. Not a good sign. The hair on her arms stood up and she remembered.

"Blackthorn! Talk to me. Are you all right?" Agonya reached into her pocket. Her fingers wrapped around the Kindroot. As gently as she could she pulled him from his hiding place.

"Catch your scents before they fly away," came a rasping voice inside her mind.

"My scents?" Agonya laughed. "Oh, it's good to hear your voice even if you sound like you're in desperate need of water."

Blackthorn stretched his branches in anticipation. A water skin did lay nearby. Agonya was barely able to reach it but she did.

"You were so focused on helping Brynn," he continued, "that you forgot about me. I know you didn't mean to do it, but I am angry with you."

"I don't understand. Did I hurt you? Why didn't you say something?"

"I did say something! You were too busy stealing my powers so you could heal Brynn's leg to hear me. You completely emptied me dry."

Blackthorn's leaves didn't have their usual glow, now that Agonya thought about it. His berries, too, looked dried out like the juice had been squeezed right out of them. And Agonya noticed something else about his berries. They were starting to turn different colors, but it was hard to tell since they were so shriveled. Did she cause that? "Please, forgive me. I didn't mean for you to get hurt. All you've ever done has been to help me. I wanted to . . . I was determined to heal his leg. I really did let my scents fly away, didn't I?"

If she couldn't safely heal herself or the others, what was the point of learning how to heal? Is this what he meant about Dana the Sorceress using Kindroot powers? Was she just as bad as her?

"No."

"What?"

"You're not anything like her."

"Were you listening to my thoughts?"

"I'm not sorry for it. I'm glad you're thinking about these things. It proves you are not like her. The sorceress would not regret taking my powers as her own. Scents! Did you notice something different this morning?"

Agonya looked around the small shelter. It slowly dawned on her. "The storm is gone. That wasn't us, was it?"

Blackthorn shook his branches from side to side.

"But that must mean . . . Did she lose control or drain her magic?"

"Maybe both but either way that means she still hasn't met her goal."

"You said she wants to make the dead live again, right? What I don't understand is how these storms she's conjuring help her accomplish that."

"How, indeed?" Blackthorn mused. "We know that she has been seeking me for centuries. We, also, know she can control our emotions and maybe even our actions through these storms. Knowing those two things, we could assume she's trying to control you and others to bring me to her. How many people," he continued, "and creatures can she touch through these storms? Many will die because of it." Blackthorn's trunk shivered.

He was right. A chill ran down her own spine and Agonya thought she knew what her father had meant when he said they would be doomed if her uncle got a hold of Blackthorn. She felt cold and raw as if the sorceress could touch her even now that the clouds were gone. Agonya needed to feel the warmth of the sun on her face, to dispel this scent of dread looming over her.

Putting Blackthorn back in her pocket, she willed her voice to break the silence. "Maya? Ashkii? Brynn?"

No one stirred. She hated being so dependent on them. Agonya spoke louder. "Wake up and smell the sunlight!"

"I don't want to wake up! Leave me alone," Ashkii murmured.

"Ashkii!"

"We're not going anywhere today," he snapped.

"Who woke up on the wrong side of the bed? If I could have gone out on my own, I wouldn't have bothered to wake you. But open your eyes and see that the storm is gone, the sun is shining. All of us need to get out of this tiny shelter and enjoy the light while we can."

"Fine!" Ashkii pushed himself up and cried out from the sharp pain that came with the movement. "Sticks!"

"What's going on?" Brynn rubbed his eyes and began to slowly push himself up from his sleeping position.

"Good morning, Brynn. Ashkii is having a hard time waking up. How are you feeling this morning?" Agonya cringed inwardly at her forced cheerfulness.

"My back is killing me but thanks to a certain fragrant woman, my leg feels great." Brynn smiled.

"Oh good," Maya said, sitting up. "You know, you guys are making a lot of noise this morning."

"How long was I out?"

"You passed out mid-afternoon yesterday." Maya chimed in.

"Well, would you help me outside? I'd very much like to get into the sun."

Ashkii just grunted and closed his eyes, lying back down gingerly.

Maya and Brynn helped her through the tiny opening. The cool scented air filled her lungs, and she looked around. It was so beautiful! After so long of being in the dark, now she could see the pine and the oak trees.

"There." Agonya indicated a tree with a small bush next to it. "I'd like to rest against that tree. Please."

They propped her up against the large pine. When they turned their backs to her, she quickly placed Blackthorn on the ground between her and the bush, out of plain sight. Then, she soaked in the warmth of the sun. She pulled it inside her like she pulled in fragrances. In a sense, it was a smell all of its own, a bright, cheery smell that filled Agonya with peace.

"Well, if it isn't the princess taking a nap after waking us all up." Ashkii walked towards her.

"What do you want?"

"Apparently, I was mean to you this morning. I'm supposed to be apologizing to you."

"Hmmm . . ." Agonya closed her eyes again. She heard Brynn's footsteps nearby. He was the one who had sent Ashkii to apologize for something he clearly didn't want to apologize for. He was probably giving Ashkii the silent eye. Agonya cracked an eyelid open. Yes. He was.

"I'm sorry for yelling at you."

"Do you want to talk about why you feel so angry?"

Agonya could hear Ashkii take in several deep breaths before he answered. "No, but I see I can't blame the storm anymore. Maybe I can blame my battle wounds for causing constant pain?" Ashkii shook his head. "Smells! I'm mostly angry with myself. We shouldn't be here right now, waiting for help. I should have done everything differently. Not just because of what that Kor did to you, but we shouldn't have gotten caught in the first place!"

"Ash, none of that can be helped," Brynn said. "Now that we are here, three out of the four of us injured, all we can do is wait for Tse to bring help."

"No, that's not the only thing we can do." There were ways they could prepare. "Now that both of you can walk again, you can follow Maya's example and collect more orinberries and lavender . . . "

"But the storm is gone."

"It will be back and stronger next time. There are lots of things we can do. We can cook up the rest of our meat before it goes bad. But the most important thing is having as many berries as possible. I would very much like to keep working on healing you, but my strength is spent. Sitting here in the sun is the best thing I can do to regain my strength."

Ashkii looked surprised. "You wanted to come out here to have the strength to heal us? Now I really feel bad for yelling at you earlier."

"Apology accepted," Agonya said in her most regal tone. "But I won't be healing anyone else like I did for Brynn's leg. The risk is too high just to speed up the healing process. It was too much. But I can bring you some relief. I've had a better idea."

"Agonya?"

"It's time for you both to have another rinse in the river." Agonya saw both the men wince. "I'm no healer but I do know that we need to keep those burns clean. Then after you're clean you can collect berries."

They worked hard all morning, that is as hard as they could with the injuries they had. Once they had a good stash of berries and lavender, they moved on to making traps and weapons. Agonya liked to watch the venison roasting over the fire. Whenever the wind blew her way, she savored the juicy scent.

After the mid-day meal, they dug a pit between the two trees they had come through. In the pit, they hammered spears into the dirt so that they stood upright just below the top of the ground. Then they covered it with branches to disguise it.

Agonya was impressed. But that would only be useful if someone was following them which she highly doubted at this point. It was possible the dranks would return. It sort of made sense to put the trap there, she supposed. And if someone was following them, it was likely they'd catch up while they had to sit and wait for help.

It took all day, with many breaks, to get it all done. The burns on their backs stung from the sweat dripping into them and if they moved just the wrong way the skin would tug the burns and they would feel the pain all over again. Agonya tried several times throughout the day to try and heal parts of their burns, but her strength had not returned yet.

"Let's try one more time. I feel like I might have enough strength now."

"You go ahead, Brynn." Ashkii tried to seem nonchalant about it.

"What? No, she's already helped me twice. Don't be so altruistic with me. I know you're in pain and need help."

This was a real struggle for Ashkii. Agonya watched him start to respond and closed his mouth several times trying to decide just what to say. So, she didn't give him a chance to say anything. "It's your turn, Ashkii. Shall we get situated closer to the fire?"

Then all he had to do was nod and accept his fate. The moment her hand was resting on his back she could feel his whole body tense up.

"Relax. It'll make my job easier if you do." Agonya called over her shoulder, "Oh, and Maya, would you take this bag into the shelter?" She wouldn't risk having Blackthorn so near her again. As smoothly as she could she slipped Blackthorn inside the bag and lifted it for Maya.

This time Agonya paid more attention to the beginning and ending of her magic. She went slow at first. It was amazing how a few days before she barely knew what lay under their skins and now, she could find her way around through what felt like little dirt paths but not made of dirt of course. Agonya could feel his pain and every point of origin. Breathing in deeply, she started blending the scents and magic together to weave its way to the spots that caused the most pain.

Every few minutes she checked to make sure she didn't accidentally steal magic that wasn't her own. That's partially why she didn't want Blackthorn at her side. It was harder to communicate over distance so she figured it would be harder to take his magic without knowing.

"Thank you," Ashkii said quietly.

"For what?"

"I don't deserve this."

"What? Don't be ridiculous!" Agonya had to stop the olfamancy so she could make sure he understood how much he really did deserve this. "How many times have you saved my life? The night the assassin came for me and then not even a day later from those thorny devils! And we couldn't have escaped the Kors without your help. You carried me away from that dreadful place when you could have escaped and been done with me. Not to mention the other close encounters we've had and the most recent of which these burns are a reminder."

"I didn't mean . . ."

"What did you mean, then?"

Agonya didn't miss the brief hesitation in his voice. "Just thank you for this. Already it feels much better."

"You're welcome. No more talking. I need to concentrate."

Chapter 22

"We must be getting close," Jaylen called back to the others, "see Kloo's excitement! She can hardly contain herself."

The Koliimus was bouncing lightly from rock to rock, between trees and bushes. Her long tail was curling up tighter and tighter, wagging back and forth. Yet, even with her pure excitement she never missed her footing, never tripped on a root.

"When we get to their camp, it should be dark again. Better to surprise them." Jaylen grinned. "Both women were dressed the same, but I believe the taller one is the one we want. If we can't figure out which one is which, we'll grab both."

"Why don't you just grab her yourself, since you've seen her? And we can make sure the men don't get in the way," Razya reasoned.

"All right let's go then. No more talking in case they hear us." The last few days of chasing after the Itholeans and they were almost there! He could taste it on his tongue. He would return, a hero. He might even return in time to help conquer Ithol and win glory there, too. It all depended on how this next phase of the mission played out. He didn't think the princess would be anticipating them since no one had gone looking for them in so long. That meant they'd have the element of surprise on their side. They also had horses and the princess did not.

Then, he heard a heart-wrenching howl followed by eerie silence. Kloo! Jaylen's heartbeat sped up. He barely reacted in time to stop his horse. He wasn't going to chance the same fate happening to him that had happened to Kloo.

Kyler pulled up beside him and slid from his horse. He crept forward with his sword drawn.

"What do you see?" Jaylen hissed.

"Shhh." Kyler crept back to his horse and motioned for the others to follow him away from the trees where Kloo had disappeared. As soon as they were a good distance away, he told them what he'd seen and heard. Their element of surprise was lost.

***

The howl was so intense, Agonya hoped whatever it was was a creature that wished them harm. She also wished the trap would have killed more instantly. Agonya was about to ask what they thought it could be when Ashkii motioned for her to remain silent. Then he was gone. A few seconds later he returned with a grim look on his face.

"They've found us!" he hissed. "A koliimus fell in the trap. I don't know where they are or how many." He fell silent.

Agonya checked her pocket. Blackthorn was back in place. She breathed a sigh of relief and tried to hold up a finger for the others to remain silent. Her body didn't cooperate. Ashkii had his back turned, ready to go out again.

"Wait," she whispered. She had an idea and she hoped it would work. She closed her eyes and inhaled the scents around her. The scent of a sweet night flower filled her body. Grabbing it and pushing it out into the darkness, Agonya followed the scent to their attackers. She breathed in again, this time she was able to smell the essence of the Korins. "Three men on horses. They circled around to the north," she said pointing.

Ashkii and Brynn nodded and grabbed their spears.

There was no way Agonya was just going to sit and wait for Ashkii and Brynn to come back safe. She could know exactly what was happening even though she couldn't see it. Quickly, she found one of the men in her mind, sneaking up on Brynn. Agonya jumped her thoughts to Brynn as fast as she could. "Brynn! Behind you!"

Brynn spun around, crying out in pain as he did so. But he parried the man's sword with his spear. Agonya couldn't jump from one mind to another without getting confused. It was too hard to follow.

Before she could warn him, the tip of the sword grazed Brynn's arm. He tried to back away and stumbled. Then Ashkii was there, fighting his own soldier and the one attacking his friend. How he didn't cry out in pain like Brynn did, Agonya didn't know. But he fought like he wasn't injured at all and better than Agonya knew was even possible.

"Agonya!" Blackthorn shouted in her mind, breaking her concentration.

"What is it?"

"Someone's coming!"

"Maya," Agonya used her mind to talk so the approaching Kor wouldn't hear. "We've got company."

Maya nodded and grabbed an atl and crouched next to the shelter's entrance. Agonya recognized him at once. The Korin captain was coming into their shelter, the one who'd captured them what seemed like an eternity ago. It was such a small doorway that he had to crawl to get in, making it easy for Maya to pound him over the head with the atl repeatedly before he was able to grab hold of it and wrench it from her hands.

"That wasn't very nice. Let's start over, shall we? I feel like we got off on the wrong foot." Captain Dahel finished coming into the little shelter and took a look around. "Ahh. I see the princess is the one who was injured. Looks like you won't be able to fight back when I take you to the Lord Commander."

"You're not taking me anywhere!"

"Oh yeah? Why not?" The captain smirked.

Agonya closed her eyes and then she was in his head. It startled him long enough for Maya to push him onto the ground and leap out of the shelter, leaving her alone with him. She wasn't quite sure what Maya was up to, but she trusted Maya knew what she was doing. Not to mention with Maya out of the shelter, the captain wouldn't be able to use her against Agonya.

The captain was fighting back from Agonya's intrusion into his mind. He swiped his arms through the air till he latched onto Agonya's leg. Agonya couldn't shake him off. Doubling her efforts, she increased the pressure on his mind.

"Aghh!" The captain's hands tightened on her legs. She felt him yank her toward the entrance.

"Oh no you don't!" Agonya pushed harder on his mind. She forced his thoughts of capturing her to fade to the back of his mind and thoughts of sleep to flood his body. He fought back.

"No! I'm not going to sleep. Get out!" He clutched his head between his hands.

"No. Not until you leave or go to sleep. Your choice." Agonya sniffed the air. What plants were close by? What smells might she use to influence him? She really couldn't force him to sleep, she could only put that thought in his head. Now that he was fighting back, pushing her out, she needed help. She caught a whiff of the pines and lavender . . . lavender could work. It was meant to counteract anger, maybe she could use it to calm him down enough to go to sleep.

All those thoughts were not fast enough. By the time she drew the lavender scents in and blended them with her magic, the captain had her halfway out of the shelter. She didn't let it phase her but continued to focus on sleepy thoughts riding the wave of scents and magic light into his mind.

He almost had her to his horse when the magic overcame him, and he fell face first into the dirt.

"Aghhh!" Agonya had the air knocked out of her as the captain landed on top of her. Brilliant, Agonya. Now what? How long would he be asleep and how long until someone rescued her? All she could see were oak branches stretching over her. She could hear fighting somewhere off to her right but had no idea who was winning or losing. The rocks and sticks beneath her were not helping her focus on any one idea. She had already exerted all of herself on controlling his mind and was now feeling the effects of it. She would just have to wait.

Time seemed to stretch on as she lay between the hard ground and the Kor. But it was only a matter of a few minutes before Maya was by her side rolling the captain off her.

"Maya!"

"Shhh. I'm going to try and lift you on my own. Can you help me at all?"

"I can try."

Maya squatted down and lifted Agonya's hands to rest around her shoulders. Agonya held on with all her remaining strength. Maya slid one hand under Agonya's legs and the other under her back.

"Umph!" She barely rose off the ground.

Agonya caught the scent of pine trees in her next breath. "Try again." When Maya moved to lift her again, Agonya focused on the scent of the tree and willed it to lend strength to Maya's legs. Working together, Maya was able to stand up while holding Agonya. She walked a few steps and tripped on a root jutting out of the ground. Brynn caught her elbow. He lifted Agonya from her hands and saw where she was headed. It took only a moment for him to reach the horse. His body tensed as he braced himself for the pain, then he raised Agonya up onto the pale steed as quickly as he could.

"Can you ride?" He turned to Maya.

"I've done it before, yes."

"Get that horse over there. I'll ride with her."

"No." Ashkii sauntered over. "I'll ride with her." He jumped on the horse and was sitting behind Agonya before Brynn could protest. "What are you waiting for? Let's get out of here."

"Our things," Agonya's voice came out as a whisper, "don't leave them."

Maya rushed back to the shelter and grabbed their pack and raced back outside. Agonya got a glimpse of the captain she'd put to sleep, and another Kor spaced several meters apart, laying on the ground and wondered what happened to the third. But then they were out of sight and Agonya's mind was overwhelmed with exhaustion.

***

Sticks and smells! Jaylen couldn't believe what she did. How on earth had she forced him to sleep? It was unheard of. Kyler! Razya!

Jaylen leaped to his feet and ran back to the small clearing. He found Kloo in a pit, Razya on top of him with several spears piercing through his chest. His face was stuck in an expression of surprise at landing on the spikes. He had died just like his father, being pierced by a tree. Jaylen gagged and had to turn away. That's when he spotted Kyler.

Jaylen rushed to his side. "Kyler!" He held his hand below Kyler's nose. He was breathing. Praise the Patron of Fortune! Just unconscious. Before he even looked, Jaylen knew the horses were gone. Splendid. Just splendid.

He had her in his arms and she still got away! And Razya and Kloo were dead! Kyler wasn't in any shape to pursue them. Jaylen moved Kyler inside the shelter. At least there was that. Should he leave Kyler and go after them? They couldn't have been gone long. If he ran, he might be able to stay close on their tail, though he had no hope of catching up.

To make matters worse, all their supplies were on the horses' backs. Good thing they didn't take all their supplies with them. Jaylen saw a water-skin and picked it up. He took a swig and then poured some on Kyler's face.

"Kyler? Can you hear me?"

Kyler moaned and tried to open his eyes. Jaylen splashed more water on his face.

"Rotten Stench! What was that for?"

"Glad to see you're awake! Can you run?" Jaylen grasped Kyler's hand, pulling him to a sitting position.

"Of course! But why would I, when I've got a perfectly good horse to do the running for me?"

"Because they have the horses and we do not. Not too far ahead of us. Ready?"

"Razya?"

"Dead."

No words were needed. Kyler pushed his way out into the open and took off running.

"They went this way," Jaylen called after him.

Kyler did an about turn and ran after Jaylen. It appeared they were continuing along the path that followed the river. If Jaylen hadn't needed to stop for a rest, they might have missed the part where they had turned off the path.

As it was, Jaylen leaned against large slanting boulders that stood just off the path and stared at the ground they'd just ran over. The moon was full, casting shadows across the ground.

"Kyler? Can you see any hoof prints on the path?" All Jaylen could see were his own boot marks and Kyler's behind his.

Kyler stood and retraced their steps. "Here! They turned north, right here."

Jaylen rushed over to see for himself. "Are you ready to keep going? We'll have to slow down." Following their prints was going to be tricky without a path to follow.

"Sure am, Captain." Kyler sounded falsely enthusiastic about it.

Razya kept intruding on his thoughts and must be doing the same for Kyler. He didn't know how long they'd known each other. Long enough to be friends. Because of that Jaylen was grateful Kyler hadn't seen Razya in the pit. Kyler probably didn't want to know how his friend had died. That was something they all agreed about: sometimes less knowledge was better.

"It looks like they are headed in a straight line." Jaylen pointed in the directions of the hooves. Then, to reassure Kyler, he added, "We will come back for him, you know that, right?"

"Yes, I just wish—"

"No need," Jaylen interrupted. "His smell is pleasing to the Patron of Death." Jaylen stepped off the path and kept his eyes fixed on the ground. Kyler followed without a word. It was a comfortable silence between them. They understood each other. Maybe Jaylen was more determined to finish what they started, but that didn't mean Kyler wasn't behind him in this endeavor. If anything, now Kyler was more determined than before to avenge his friend's death.

Losing Razya was a tragedy they shared. Jaylen couldn't help but to think about what went wrong. It all happened so fast. They were about to fall back and regroup when the Montane jumped down from a tree straight on top of them, forcing them to go through with their original plan. Razya and Kyler had ganged up on the Montane while Jaylen slipped away to find the princess. Jaylen urged his horse closer to the shelter where he assumed the princess was hiding. With the men distracted, Jaylen was sure he could snatch her, and they'd be gone before the Itholeans knew what hit them.

Scents! He was so wrong about them, about her. He should have completely destroyed the shelter, making it harder for the women to fight back. Even then, Jaylen didn't want to think about it. What had happened to him? He was weak! He had let her control him like that. His mind had not been safe! Jaylen felt his foot squish into something warm. "Ahh!"

"What is it?"

"I stepped in horse shit!"

"We've been stepping in shit ever since we found our prey."

"At least this shit is still warm." Jaylen tried to scrape the dung off his boots with a nearby rock. Most of it came off, but it was going to stink until they could find some water.

"Kyler?"

"Yes?"

"Did you see what happened to me during the fight?"

"I saw you trip and fall with the princess beneath you. I don't remember anything else except pure pain on my head."

"I didn't trip." Jaylen paused. "She put me to sleep." There, he voiced it. She had used magic. He waited for Kyler to understand what he'd just said.

"Uh? Say that again."

"She controlled my mind and made it go to sleep," Jaylen repeated.

"Didn't she do something similar when you first caught her?"

"How did you—"

“That story was all over camp. We had many laughs at it too! I can’t believe you are just like they said you were. I mean, you seemed so normal these last few days.”

“I suppose you heard the story from General Gad?”

“I sure did. Isn’t he good with the stories?”

“I hate to disappoint you, but he wasn’t there and so he can’t have known what happened or didn’t happen. Whether you believe it or not, it’s true. She has some sort of magic. The first time we caught her she had incense that she was burning and using somehow to make my men stop attacking. I doused the incense and was able to capture her. This time it was something different.” Jaylen knew Kyler was rolling his eyes at him even though he was behind him.

“So, next time we make sure nothing’s burning when we capture her?” Kyler clearly didn’t believe him.

Only to avoid an argument, Jaylen thought his retort instead of voicing it. “Exactly. We’ve got to figure out what her weakness is so she can’t affect us.” Jaylen thought about how she had gotten inside his mind and if he could find a way to block her somehow. Then, he picked up the pace.

Chapter 23

What happened after the fight with the Kors was all a blur. Agonya knew she was on a horse and that someone was sitting behind her. She could feel the steady stride jostle her as they rode. Sometimes, she could hear people talking around her but mostly she was drifting in and out of sleep. Every muscle in her body ached.

It seemed like they were riding for days, but she really had no idea how long it had been. She was vaguely awake now. Were they slowing down? She mumbled something about what was going on. She heard someone mumble something back. The horse stopped.

Whoever was sitting behind her, maybe Ashkii, was talking to someone else, a voice she wasn't familiar with. They talked but she couldn't listen. It was like her ears refused to work. Then she was asleep again.

"Agonya? Where have you been?" King Azurarus glared at his daughter. "You were supposed to meet Lady Velia today for tea."

"But she's such a bore. Father, have you ever sat through tea with her before? Besides, Moki received a new shipment today. I simply had to go check it out." Agonya knew she was in big trouble, but she said it just to rile him up.

"What did I say about that? You will apologize to Velia in person this time. I will not make excuses for you anymore. You need to learn to take responsibility for your actions. I will know if you don't do it."

"My lady?" Maya's voice startled Agonya awake. "We're here! We made it to Tafka."

Agonya opened her eyes. She was no longer on a horse but lying on a soft fur bed with plump pillows under her head. Above her, squares of pine showed growth rings cut off at the edges. The swirling lines blended from one section to the next, broken up by long beams stretching from one end of the room to the other. In the very center, dim light seeped through the small crack, outlining the largest square tile.

She turned her head as far as she could and saw Maya sitting next to her on a bed of her own. "Where are we?"

"We're in Tafka. The Montanes have been very fragrant towards us."

Relief flooded Agonya's body. She'd finally made it to the Montanes. But that meant she needed to speak to the chief as soon as possible. She tried to place her hands on the floor to push herself up but they wouldn't move, again. She wouldn't let it distract her. Through gritted teeth she asked, "When will I speak with the chief?"

Maya shook her head. "I told His Honor you needed to speak with him, but he wants his warriors to return first."

"Return? From where? Are they at war?" This made no sense. "Where's Ashkii? I want to speak with someone even if it isn't the chief."

"I don't know where Ashkii is. I think he went to see the healer." Maya twisted her fingers together. She was probably upset that Agonya was upset.

"How long?" Agonya started to wonder. "How long have I been like this?"

"From the moment we started riding until now. Every once in a while, you would mumble something, but we could never quite understand what you were saying. We arrived midday today. They expect the warriors to be back by breakfast."

"And we started riding last night?"

Maya nodded.

"At least it hasn't been days and days. Won't I get a chance to talk with someone at dinner?"

"You can try, but I think, because of your condition," Maya bit her lip.

"Because I can't walk. Is that it?"

"They said they'd bring us some food and their healer will be in to see you soon to determine what would be best."

"I see." Agonya pressed her lips together. Just because she couldn't walk on her own or push herself up to a sitting position, she'd be trapped in this room the whole time they stayed there. But now that she was actually with the Mons, she didn't want to stay. Her last dream was still fresh on her mind. It was her responsibility to help her people. It was time she accepted that role and did what she could.

"Here, let me brush your hair."

"I might as well look my best when I finally get to meet them," Agonya mumbled.

Maya helped Agonya sit up against the back of a chair. Then, she sat in it and moved her legs behind Agonya to give her a cushion and began to work.

"Where's Brynn?"

"He went with Ashkii to the healer's and then to see Ashkii's family."

Agonya wondered what his family must be like. Did he still have both his parents? She knew he had a brother, but did he have a sister? Why hadn't she ever asked him about them during their long journey? She knew the answer and hated to admit it. She had been solely interested in herself. She wanted to heal herself. She wanted to get here for herself. She told herself it was for her people but really, she just wanted to be safe again. Since being in Tafka aligned with her desires, she might as well petition help for her people.

Agonya was deep in thought when a door creaked open. Agonya heard it, but she couldn't see it. She looked at all the walls, yet there were no doors in them. Then Maya tilted her head up towards the ceiling.

"Look up, my Lady."

The door was on the roof. The square outlined in light earlier was lifted, and Agonya could now see a rope ladder being lowered down into the room. It took only a moment before someone climbed down and pulled up another chair next to them. She reminded Agonya of her grandmother. Her white hair was pulled back in a bun, tightening the wrinkled skin on her face just a little bit.

Agonya wanted to hold her hand out to be smelled as was tradition but couldn't, so she waited for the newcomer to speak.

"I've heard so much about you," the old lady said, skipping formalities.

"You have?"

"Pardon. I'm the healer of the village. You can call me Kylie. I heard all about your adventures." Her smile was warm and inviting even though her teeth were yellowed and crooked with gaps where missing teeth should have been.

"Oh." Agonya cleared her throat. How much had Kylie heard? If she was like Tse, she probably already knew about olfamancy, more than Agonya, probably. "What do you know about magic?"

"Straight to the point, I see. Good. I know enough not to use it unless absolutely necessary." Her voice changed slightly from welcoming to more of a mother scolding her child.

"Yes, well, it was necessary. I didn't mean to do what I did. I didn't even know I could do what I did!" Agonya felt like she had to defend herself, just like she felt every time her father would confront her behavior.

"No need to get upset, child. I will teach you what I know. You don't even have to tell me what happened. Ashkii, that sweet little boy, told me the whole story."

Agonya had to choke back a laugh. Sweet little boy! "Can you help me then?"

"Perhaps. I heard you already know about orinberries. Let's begin there."

"Maya, would you be kind enough to retrieve the berries we have left from our travels?"

"Of course, my lady." Maya started to move when Kylie motioned for her to stay put.

"No need to get up, child. I brought my own." She dug inside her pocket until she pulled out a glass vial filled with something as fine as dirt.

"You have glass? But how? I heard you can only get glass bottles from the other side of the Acrid Mountains."

"You're quite right, my dear. Glass can only come from there. A long time ago I acquired this one and a few others that I can continue to use time after time."

"But won't the previous smells contaminate whatever else you want to put in them?"

"I simply have to wash them out and then they're as good as new.

Agonya sat stunned. She had no idea that the treasure she'd bought was the glass bottle and not so much the perfume inside. Not that she still had the perfume she bought so long ago. The Kors had taken all of her perfumes.

"Now, let's focus. I'm sure your fresh orinberries won't be ready for proper use for a while yet. It would be good for you to understand how to do it yourself, but first let's see if we can't get you moving more on your own.

"Once your berries are completely dried, you can grind them into small particles like this. But you can't dry them until you've steamed them and caught the vapor in something like this." Kylie pulled another glass vial out of her pocket.

This time the smooth amber glass looked foggy but like nothing else was inside it. Agonya barely had time to ponder this when Kylie went on speaking. "When you have both of these, we can make our drink. It helps to also have some of this." Kylie reached into her pocket and drew out not only a vial this time but some bark from a pine tree.

"Bark?"

"Yes, bark. If you had known about it you might have been able to do a better job on their burns. As it stands you did a fine job without any experience."

"How are they?"

"I healed them. Mostly. They're not in pain anymore. There will be scarring from it but they'll be fine."

"Thank you. They sacrificed themselves to protect us." Agonya sighed. Her emotions were bouncing all over the place: frantic, angry, thankful, surprised. Kylie wasn't what Agonya had expected. Overwhelmed by all of the new information, Agonya was reminded of her failures.

"It wasn't your fault," Kylie replied as if she had read Agonya's thoughts. "You mustn't blame yourself, child."

"But it was my fault. If I hadn't paralyzed myself, they wouldn't have had to carry me all the way here! I could have helped them fight or we could have climbed into the safety of the trees!"

"Your Highness! Is that what you think?" Maya rested her hand on Agonya's shoulder. "I'm glad you used your magic! If you hadn't done it, you might not have survived or gotten away from those horrible men."

"Listen to the little lady. She's wise. You must never play the 'What if?' game. You can't change the past. All you can do is focus on what needs to be done in this very moment, to breathe in the scents surrounding us before they disappear." Kylie nodded at Maya and inhaled deeply. "Right now, I think we've had enough chat and should start the fire."

Maya helped her build a fire below the open door, and let it burn down to coals. Then Kylie placed the pine bark on top. When it caught fire, she poured some berry dust on it. Smoke from the small fire rose through the air in one small stream. Agonya watched the kind old lady direct the smoke into the vapor filled vial. It was a wonder how she was able to get the smoke to do what she wanted.

Even then before Kylie was finished, Agonya was starting to feel better. Slowly her muscles were starting to relax. Muscles she didn't even know were tight.

"Here, child," she held the vial up to Agonya's nose. "Breathe it in. All of it."

The smoke and vapor mixed together into a beautiful burnt orange color of fall leaves swirling together in a dance. The first inhalation, Agonya started to choke and cough.

"Easy now, just a little bit at a time. There. That's better."

With each subsequent breath, it got a little easier. She could feel it flooding her body. It was as if her muscles were drawing it to themselves. They were feasting on the wonderful new smell of orinberry and pine together and they were loving it. Agonya could feel pure strength returning. Her well of magic was replenishing. She started to draw on it.

"Stop! Don't do that, child! What did I tell you about using it only when necessary?"

"But--"

"Shhh. Don't talk until it's over."

Agonya inhaled the last of the mixture. Immediately, her muscles cramped up again. They were out of food and refused to stay relaxed. It was excruciating! Her whole body was racked with pain. After a few moments, the pain lessened.

"What happened?" Agonya exclaimed in horror. "One moment it was amazing! The next, I was back to where I started!"

"Are you? Turn your head to look over your right shoulder. Good. Now to the left. Look up. Down. Already you have more movement in your neck. Let's try the arms. First the right arm. Can you bend it or raise it at all?"

Agonya felt her arm in her mind and told it to move.

"You did it!" Maya exclaimed.

"I did?" Agonya opened her eyes to watch, knowing she wouldn't be disappointed. A strange sensation came over her as she watched her arm bend back and forth. She saw it but couldn't feel it. She tried to lift it higher. To her amazement, she was able. Granted it was only off the ground by a hand span, but that was more than she could do before. She didn't need encouragement anymore. She moved her attention to her left arm. Same results as the right. She tried the right leg. Nothing. Then, the left. Still nothing. Her excitement started to wane.

"Good." Kylie nodded in satisfaction. "Yes, that's a good start. We'll get you up and walking in no time. Until then, rest."

Rest! She was tired of resting. "Um?"

"Yes, child?"

"I appreciate you helping me, but I really need to be better quickly."

"It won't be quick if you push yourself too hard."

"Then, I need to speak to someone about my people as soon as possible."

"You'll get your chance. I'll see you later when it is safe to treat you again."

Agonya watched Kylie disappear up the ladder so fast she found it hard to believe Kylie was doing everything she could to help her.

Chapter 24

The pounding of hooves grew louder and louder as Jaylen ran. Except they weren't the hooves of horses. The footfalls galloping toward them sounded heavy and larger than anything Jaylen knew. His mother might know what the sound belonged to but even if she was there, there was no time to figure it out. As it was, they neither had the time to jump behind a bush or to climb a tree.

Ten men wearing dark cloaks with hoods that covered their faces except their eyes surrounded them in seconds. Three of them were indeed on the stolen horses. The others sat on seven furry beasts of various colors, so large their riders were head and shoulders above the men on horseback. Sharp spears from every angle made Jaylen and Kyler put their backs together in defense.

"Drop your weapons. Come peacefully and we will prolong your life."

"That's a real comfort," Jaylen said, considering his odds for a moment. These men must be the savage Montanes he's always heard about. Then, he unhooked his sword and threw it in front of him.

"More shit." Kyler spat on the ground.

"Just do it, Kyler."

Clunk. Kyler's sword fell on top of Jaylen's. Two men slid off their massive beasts. One tied Jaylen's hands behind his back while the other tied Kyler's.

"Wise move. I hate to see a life wasted," the leader said from his perch. "Blindfold them."

Jaylen felt a sac slip over his head and then hands pushed him forward. The hands picked him up with ease and jumped. They must have landed on something high off the ground. Jaylen could only assume he was now on top of one of the furry beasts. He was lowered to its back and a moment later the man's arms wrapped around Jaylen as he grasped the reins.

"Can I ask for an introduction?" Jaylen asked, hoping for something to help him talk his way out of this.

"Move out!" the man called.

So much for conversation. Jaylen would probably be doing the same to him if their positions were reversed. With nothing better to do and no way to see what was going on, Jaylen did his best to recall the name of this creature he was trapped on. There was a slight chance his mother had told him about it and if she had there might be something useful Jaylen could use against his captor. If only he had been as interested in all the different animals she was fascinated with. Its head had been gray (all of the creatures had gray heads), rough and almost hairless which was the complete opposite of its body full of thick coarse fur (the color of the fur was different with each beast). Its ears were almost as big as his head, but its nose was nearly a meter long and still it didn't drag on the ground. If only he didn't have a sack on his head, he'd be able to inspect the creature more closely.

"Well, if I can't have an introduction, can I at least know what sort of creature we're riding?"

The man sitting behind him was silent for a long time before he finally decided Jaylen's question was harmless. "He's an elephantus. Very useful creature if you ask me."

"What does he do, apart from carrying cargo?"

"That is mostly what he does, but he does it so well. He is stronger than any other creature I've met. He is faster than a horse. Even though they are intimidating with their tusks, they don't normally hurt humans. Only if provoked. Just like you and me in that regard."

"Good to know you won't suddenly chop my head off for no apparent reason." Jaylen laughed. He tried to cover his laugh with a cough when the man didn't reply.

Perhaps he could get the ropes on his wrists to loosen. Maybe he could get the man's weapon and fight his way to freedom. Then again if he had wanted to fight, he shouldn't have given up so easily to begin with. He was going to have to do this the stealthy way. The way that got him into this mess. The good news was that both he and Kyler were still alive, though he had no idea why. Everything he'd heard about the Mons said they were vicious animals. He was happy they weren't as blood thirsty as he'd heard. It was pleasant to be riding instead of running, and they were being taken exactly where they wanted to go. He'd just have to figure out the rest, once they got there.

✻ ✻ ✻

A young Montane woman delivered two bowls of steaming stew and helped Maya move Agonya to a chair at the table. Then she left without saying a word. Agonya inhaled and felt revived by the mushroom scents wafting up from the stew.

"I thought perhaps you might get a chance to eat with the others even if I can't," Agonya said.

"Someone has to help you, my lady. I'm happy to do it. To be quite honest I feel a little bit out of place here. Everything is so different from home. Staying in here with you where I don't have to worry about doing or saying something wrong is a huge relief." Maya pulled up the other chair close to Agonya.

The food was very flavorful and bursting with more than mushroom scents. There was a sweet and sharp smell of onions that made Agonya think she was back in the Sunroom again, enjoying a carefree afternoon with her mother. The scents were all the best foods but there was something foreign about it too.

"Thanks, Maya, again. I am glad that we get to rest. I am tired of constantly being on the move," Agonya spoke in between mouthfuls, "You are right. It feels good not to have to put on a face for others." Even while Agonya spoke, she couldn't help but worry.

Already, she had been gone almost a whole month. It was sure to take time to gather up an army to go rescue the Itholeans and to move said army through the forest to even be able to come to the rescue. If any of them were like Ashkii and could use odor bombs, she'd be able to go back to her people in a few months.

How long had it been since she'd given any real thought to them? Lady Velia, she could do without, but Lord Tanish and Mikkah, they were like father figures to her. She hoped they were doing well, and that Commander Huren was listening to Tanish and not putting everyone in further danger.

Agonya took another bite. She would ride back to Ithol with the Montanes at her side. She would be the queen they needed.

***

The next morning Maya made Agonya presentable, dressing her in the simple yet beautiful dress the Montanes had provided for her. By the time Brynn and Ashkii came to get them, she was ready. Agonya blushed when she saw Ashkii's stare. He really was taken with her. He would just have to learn the hard way. The only way he would be with her was to help her kingdom. But what could he offer her? Agonya put those thoughts out of her mind just as quickly as they had come.

The main square had people sitting sporadically, mostly around scattered fires. "Do we sit anywhere? Where are the tables?" Agonya asked.

Ashkii smiled. "For the most part, we don't use tables."

"But there was a table in our room."

"For you. The table was there for your comfort." Seeing Agonya's confusion, he went on, "We know you are accustomed to tables, so we made sure there was one available to you."

Ashkii lowered Agonya into Brynn's waiting arms before jumping down to join them. They found seats around the central fire, and Ashkii explained how the whole village was like a family. They did everything together. They cooked their meals together. Ate together. They all had their individual tasks such as collecting firewood or hunting or cooking but it was all for the collective. No one was left out. No one was homeless. Agonya was so used to passing beggars in the streets back at home as the way life was, she had never thought about how to change that. She couldn't help but wonder at the Montanes. It appeared everything she had known about them was false except that they did have strange customs like their smelif and eating on the ground without tables.

After they ate their porridge and the dishes were cleared away to be washed, a man with skin as pale as Ashkii's, wearing warrior garb, approached the small circle. A beautiful woman followed behind him. Her auburn hair framed her round face and complemented the brown and yellow dress that touched her feet.

"Good morning! We welcome you to our home. I am Chief Golar, and this is my lovely wife, Mazali." Golar wiped his hands in his armpits and offered them to Agonya to smell.

Not quite sure how to respond, Agonya lifted her hands as far as they would go. Being the gracious host that he was, Golar smiled. He moved his hands closer for her to sniff then he grasped her hands in his, bringing them up to his nose to smell her fragrance in return.

"Your fragrance is most pleasant," he said, still smiling.

"And yours as well. Your welcome of us has been most fragrant. Thank you for opening your home to us weary travelers. I am Queen Agonya Kanti Nakai of the Itholeans. Here is my faithful companion, Maya. And, you know Ashkii who has been our guide these many days. Brynn, too, has come from just outside of Ithol."

The shocked look on Golar's face disappeared just as quickly as it had come. "I was not aware the Itholeans had a new queen."

"Yes, I bear ill news of my father's death. He died at the start of the month. His scent still lingers."

"That is hard news indeed. King Azurarus was a good man. My son," Golar gestured to Ashkii, "has told me that he thinks you are a good woman."

Agonya caught her emotions at this revelation, remembering how to compose herself. Why hadn't he told her? "That is very kind of you to say. I have come a long way to discuss the fate of my people. It is my hope that you will hear what I have to say."

"We will hear. Shall we go somewhere more private?"

"That smells good." She needed more time to process this new revelation.

***

The room Agonya found herself in an hour later was lined with simple cushions against the walls. Opposite Agonya hung a beautiful tapestry of Paradise on the mountains.

Had the Acrid Mountains ever been a place of refuge? Agonya couldn't picture it. The mountains weren't called Acrid for nothing. Dangerous creatures and plants thrived on them, not to mention the burning lakes, though they hadn't climbed high enough to encounter any of those. But there was something about the depiction before her that was appealing. If there was hope for even the Acrid Mountains to attain Paradise, then there must be hope for her.

Ashkii finished straightening the pillows around her, brushing the skin of her hand as he did so. Did he do that on purpose? Didn't he know she didn't like him like that?

"Are you comfortable, your Highness?"

Agonya opened her mouth to reply but Chief Golar spoke for her. "Yes, thank you, son. Please show Miss Maya and Brynn around the village, I'll send for you when we're done talking."

Agonya couldn't believe Golar would presume to speak for her. Quickly, before Ashkii could leave, she thanked him for herself.

He winked at Agonya. Then he jumped through the door in the roof to where Maya and Brynn were waiting. The moment he left, Agonya let her frustration at the chief take over. Just because she couldn't walk didn't mean she couldn't talk.

"I see you have met Wise Kylie," he said, oblivious to what he'd done by speaking for her.

Breathing deeply, Agonya tried to let his arrogance flit away on the wind. She needed to think about her people. Kylie was a good place to begin their conversation. She had visited Agonya again earlier in the morning and now Agonya could lift her arms up and over to a new position but only up in the air for a few seconds before they were exhausted. "She is indeed wise. I have learned much from her. I am so grateful for her teaching and healing. If there is anything I can do to repay her, please let me know."

Agonya was hopeful she would find an ally in Chief Golar despite his impertinence. She was still a little bit nervous though. All the council members in Ithol were crafty and good with words. She was never any good at that herself. Too often Agonya would speak her mind and hit herself later for saying too much. Golar held himself in a confident manner that reminded her of Lord Tanish and yet he shared similarities with her father.

"Kylie finds joy in helping others and she would not accept any payment even if you tried."

Agonya straightened her shoulders as best she could. "You have been so kind to us. I hate to ask anything more of you than you have already given but I fear that I must."

"Don't be afraid to ask me anything. Please speak your mind freely. I will listen. If it is possible, I will be glad to help in any way I can."

"When I left Ithol, the Kors were surrounding our city. We were preparing for a long siege, but I'm not entirely sure how long my people will be able to hold out and so I'm asking for not just your help but a speedy help. If we do not act fast, we will arrive too late."

Golar leaned forward on his cushion and searched her eyes. "If we help defeat the Kors, what will you give us in return?"

Agonya forced herself not to look away. "I do not know what it is that you would desire or need but I would give almost anything to you in return for your help. What is it that you desire?"

"Perhaps there is something . . ." Golar rubbed the beard on his chin and stared at the tapestry on the wall. "I would like you to tell me everything you know about Kindroots."

Agonya gasped involuntarily. Did they know that Blackthorn was with her? "Kindroots? My mother told me stories about them when I was little." Agonya's words came out steady even though her first thought was a warning not to say anything at all. She had to protect Blackthorn at all costs.

Golar's shoulders slumped. "I was hoping you knew something a little more recent than that."

He knew! He had to know Blackthorn was with her. But how? Did Ashkii know Blackthorn was with her? She had been very careful not to reveal Blackthorn to Ashkii, but it was possible. Agonya couldn't believe Ashkii would do anything to harm her and putting Blackthorn's life in danger would most certainly hurt her. He was her family now.

"I'm sorry I don't know what it is you are looking for. Perhaps there is something else I can give you in return for your help?"

The chief gave Agonya a sad little smile. "It was a vaporous hope. Do you know why the Korins are attacking your people?"

"They claim we killed their princess, my mother. But it was King Reid who killed her," Agonya spat.

Golar sighed. "I'm afraid that may only be a part of the reason. What you do not know is that they are looking for the last of the Kindroots which are said to be protected by your family. Since your father has died, I had hoped you were protecting the Kindroots."

Agonya's mind raced. She was protecting Blackthorn, but she wasn't about to tell him that. "But why are they looking for Kindroots? I thought they were just made-up creatures in the old wives tales," she lied.

"Oh, they're real, all right. They are the reason we came to live here so many years ago. You see, Kindroots are the bringers of Paradise. Where they are, life permeates the air. This is where you are wrong, the Korin King is working for a sorceress to bring the last of the Kindroots to her."

"A sorceress? How do you know this?" Agonya had to pretend she didn't know any of this. But it was proving harder and harder knowing just how much Golar knew.

"You're right, not many know this. But I know her because she tried to get my father to do the same for her as she has convinced King Reid to do. The Sorceress Dana wants revenge on the Kindroots for many of the reasons the Kors want revenge on Ithol. For me to send my men into this battle is asking more from us than I am perhaps willing to give. But I do not wish to see you fail. To see Dana succeed would be far worse than if all my people died protecting the Kindroots."

"Then, what would you have me do?"

"Find out if the Kindroots are in fact hiding in Ithol."

"But how am I supposed to do that? By the time that I get back to Ithol and find them it may be too late."

"There is a way to communicate across distances. Ashkii told me you are one of the few capable of this."

Agonya's mouth fell open. "I don't understand."

"But don't you? Did you not cause a horvelina to return to its home instead of letting it harm your friends?"

"Oh. But the horvelina was right in front of me. How can I possibly communicate with something or someone in Ithol?"

"With practice, you will be able to."

"I am willing to try."

"Then it is agreed. I will send Kylie to you so that she can help you. There is one more thing that perhaps you would be able to offer."

"Yes?"

"I would like you to consider a marriage between yourself and my son, Ashkii, as a sign of our friendship."

This was something she had dreaded he would ask as soon as she heard Ashkii was his son. Not because Ashkii wouldn't be a suitable husband. He would be fine, she actually liked him as a friend, but because she may yet need to marry her cousin instead. She had to keep her options open. And she had a creeping feeling that even though Golar expressed a desire to protect the Kindroots, he had an ulterior motive. "I will consider it," she finally said. "Ashkii is a fine man, your Honor. If I may, I'd like to consider these options and give you an answer in the morning."

“Of course. At your leisure.” Golar stood up and knocked on the closed door above him. The door opened and a man Agonya didn’t recognize popped his head inside.

“Your Honor?”

“Please find my son and his companions so they can escort her Highness back to her room.”

“Yes, sir.” The man did some sort of finger salute and disappeared.

“Pardon. I have other issues to attend to now. Ashkii should be here shortly to help you.” Then Golar bent his knees and without touching the rope ladder he jumped up out of the room, pulling himself up the rest of the way once he caught hold of the ledge.

* * *

“Blackthorn?” Agonya sobbed his name for the twentieth time. He wasn’t in her pocket. But she had changed clothes. She just couldn’t reach her discarded dress or bags to see if he was inside. She’d been in the village for a whole day now and she didn’t think to check on his safety! She didn’t even get suspicious when he didn’t add some snide remark to her thoughts like he normally did.

Breathe, Agonya. Breathe. Did they know about him? Did they take him from her? But then why would they ask about the Kindroots if they’d taken him from her. She was overthinking this. She just had to reach her discarded dress in the corner. But Agonya could barely move her arms. She inhaled sharply and was overwhelmed by the scents.

Which one was Blackthorn’s? He had a wonderful smell. If only she could find him somewhere close by . . . clay, dirt, pine, oak, dungess, venison, potatoes. Oh . . . where was he? It was so hard to pick out individual smells among all the smells around her. Every person had a unique smell and the floors and walls of each room, and the clay mixed with trash that filled the cracks of the walls, the food being prepared for the evening meal, the smells were endless! Maya! Agonya could smell Maya!

“Maya? Can you hear me?” Agonya thought the words.

“Yes, my lady? Is everything all right?”

"No, I need your help. It's important no one knows we are speaking. Who are you with?"

"I'm surrounded by the village women. We're weaving rugs. Well, they're trying to teach me how to do it their way. I'm okay in a pinch but rugs?"

"Are any of them looking at you funny, like they don't understand what you are doing? You've got to be careful not to move a muscle on your face unless it's in reaction to what they are saying or doing."

"Yes, my lady. I understand. No one seems to be inquisitive as you suggest."

"Good. Just keep an eye out to make sure no one does catch on to you. When was the last time you saw the plant my father gave me to protect?"

"Didn't you put it in your pocket? Is it missing?"

"I thought I tucked it into my hidden pocket before the Korin captain found us. But maybe not. We'll have to check our bags to make sure we didn't forget we put it in there."

"I'm pretty sure you put it in the pocket of the dress you wore into Tafka, but it might be in our bags."

"It might have fallen out when we were galloping through the forest up the mountain slope, or he could have taken him."

"Who took who? What are you talking about? Are we still talking about the plant?"

Agonya realized her mistake too late. "I'm sorry I didn't tell you sooner. That plant is the last of the Kindroots. His name is Blackthorn. He has been teaching me how to use my magic and helped me heal Brynn and Ashkii. He has become like a father to me. I couldn't bear it if I failed to protect him."

Maya was silent for so long, Agonya thought she hadn't heard her explanation.

"I'm sorry you've lost him. I really think he must still be in your pocket or in our bags because I didn't see anyone go near your pockets."

"Thanks, Maya, but there is still the possibility he fell out which means he might have been trampled by the warriors who went to make sure the captain and his soldiers weren't following us anymore."

"The ladies are looking at me now. I'll come to you as soon as I can."

Agonya lingered in Maya's thoughts which were focused now on pacifying the ladies before retreating into her own lonely mind. She had to believe Blackthorn did not get trampled. He just couldn't be dead.

A vague memory of slipping from her seat while they rode to Tafka came back to Agonya. Ashkii had grabbed hold of her and drew her back onto the horse. She remembered his hands had grabbed her waist before slipping back to unconsciousness. But if his hands had been on her waist, they had also been on top of her pockets.

Cold seeped into Agonya's thoughts. Her mind refused to even think about what she felt in that moment. Blackthorn had been right. She couldn't trust him. Were all his affections just an act to get her to trust him? Agonya pictured Blackthorn in her mind and couldn't shake the idea that he'd been kidnapped.

Chapter 25

The pain wasn't slowing him down anymore; and he didn't need to rest nearly as often with the wound on his back almost healed. According to his map, he was halfway there. "The princess must already be in Tafka," he thought, "maybe the Kors too." Krillin sped up. He must not be late. This mission was important to the war. If he could find the princess in time, the fighting could stop. Then, his family would be safe again.

When the sun started to cast shadows across his path, Krillin dismounted and leaped from shadow to shadow giving his horse a rest. This was his favorite time of day. The forest changed somehow and became more interesting. It felt great to stretch his legs.

Suddenly, a scent of musk wafted from behind. Krillin froze on one of the larger shadows. He wasn't the only one to smell it. The horse whinnied and tossed his head, tugging at his reins in Krillin's hands.

Turning around, he saw a huge beast watching him. It had legs like a horse and a head like a hog. There was only one thing it could be, a horvelina. Its tusks were larger than Krillin had imagined. Before he could contemplate the creature any further, it grunted.

Doing the only thing there was to do, Krillin tried to leap onto the horse's back. But he bucked in fright and Krillin lost hold of the reins. The horvelina charged. It rammed its tusks inside the horse's belly.

There was no time to mourn the horse or even think about what was happening. Krillin instinctively drew his bow and notched an arrow, aiming it at the creature who was stomping its feet on the ground and trying to dislodge itself. He had a heartbeat to think. Did he want to kill this creature? His horse was dying, and he didn't have time to walk the rest of the way to Tafka. Krillin was going to be late if he didn't acquire a new steed. But this creature had killed his horse!

The creature kicked the horse off its tusks and turned towards Krillin. Instead of shooting, Krillin dashed around the animal for the bag now squashed beneath the horse on the ground. He heard a snort. Before he could change his mind, he yanked the bag free. The creature pawed the ground and eyed Krillin. As fast as he could, Krillin pulled out a piece of jerky and held it out in front so the animal could smell it. Krillin slowly walked toward it. Stupid idea, he knew, but he couldn't walk the rest of the way. The beast continued to stare at him and started to snort in anger. Krillin stopped advancing and threw the jerky at the creature's feet. The creature gobbled it up so fast Krillin barely had time to get another piece ready. This time the horvelina came to him and ate it straight out of his hands.

Krillin was ready. As soon as the horvelina was next to him, he grabbed hold of a bloody tusk and used it as a stepping stool. Krillin scrambled up the rest of the way and held on for dear life. The beast's back legs flew into the air, then his front, and then the back legs, again and again. He tried so hard to buck Krillin off, but he held fast. One. Two. Three. Four. Five. Six counts before the beast stood still.

Krillin slowly let go of its neck. He reached above him and broke off a branch from the nearest oak tree. Then he got a third piece of jerky out. He tied it to the end of the branch and dangled it as bait in front of the wild creature. The horvelina followed it onto the path, picking up speed the angrier it became for not having the meat. Good. He was going faster now than he had been with his horse. Maybe he wouldn't be late.

***

"Your Highness," Kylie curtsied slightly as she approached, "How are you feeling since our last healing?"

Agonya noticed Kylie's addressing Agonya as royalty came only after Chief Golar had addressed her as such, as if she hadn't been deserving of the title before then. She put it out of her mind. "I have more movement in my arms, but I still can't hold them up for very long before they get tired. How long before you think I can walk?"

"Now, dearie, it's best not to get our hopes up and then be disappointed. I suspect at this rate you might be able to walk for short periods in a few weeks, but then only very briefly. You haven't been able to walk for a long time now. Your muscles need to relearn how to work properly. Just give it enough time. I think you'll be back to normal in a few months."

"A few months! I've got to get back to my people. I can't be lying around here for that long. They need me."

"I'm sure the Honorable will be willing to help if you just ask. Now, let's get started." Kylie held the vapor-smoke up for her to inhale.

Clearly Kylie wasn't interested in really healing Agonya, not if she wanted the process to take months! Agonya opened her mouth and let the vapor in, letting it fill her body. Then, taking the tiniest bit of her magic she blended the two substances and directed the energy to her legs. Kylie didn't seem to notice.

Agonya continued with her deception. With each breath, Agonya added drops of her magic, careful not to use too much like she'd done on the first day. Kylie mustn't know what she was doing.

"There! How do you feel? Shall we test your movement?"

Agonya obliged but held back. She could already tell that her plan was working. She was definitely stronger than the last time they did this. Her neck was almost all the way back to full movement. She didn't mind if Kylie knew that. So she moved her neck in every direction as far as it would go with Kylie's instructions. Then for her arms she remembered what she could do before and added a little bit more movement but did not go as far as she could. She tried to let a little disappointment show on her face.

Her leg muscles felt stronger, but she didn't move them at all. She would test them after Kylie left.

"Good. You are getting stronger. I will see you again tomorrow." Kylie stood and climbed the ladder, leaving her supplies on the table. She hadn't even talked to her about mind-speaking like Golar said she would.

Agonya's chest started to fill up with joy at having accomplished the first part of her plan. She almost burst with excitement but knew someone was probably standing guard on the roof. She could hear him moving around every once in a while. At first when they had just arrived, Agonya thought it was because they wanted her to be able to get help if she needed it, now she suspected it was because she was a prisoner again.

A knock sounded on the door, then slowly opened. The whiff of his scent blew down into the room. "Can I come in?" Ashkii called down to her.

Agonya's mind flooded with indecision. She hadn't begun to think about the chief's proposal of marriage. How could she, with Blackthorn missing? How was she going to confront him about Blackthorn when he thought she didn't know he knew about him? She wasn't ready to face him.

Not waiting for a reply, Ashkii jumped through the door with ease. He was just like his father in that regard. He was tall, handsome, and charming and she needed to try to find out what he knew or didn't know.

Ashkii smiled at her as he pulled up a chair next to her bed, "How do you like Tafka so far?"

Every nasty word she knew came to her lips. How did she like being there? Kept prisoner under the guise of friendship? Why couldn't he just say what he wanted to say and be done with it? Calming her insides, she replied, "Everything is so different from what I'm used to. I'm sure you know, having seen my home. I do like how there are no homeless people or beggars lining the streets. Everyone pitches in and benefits from one other."

"I don't know if that's entirely true. There are those, like in your city, who choose not to work or can't work."

"But you don't keep them from enjoying the community meals, right? That was my impression from eating with you today."

"There are rules we must follow and there are consequences if they're not followed. But yes, for the most part everyone gets along. Uh . . ." Ashkii shifted in his seat. "I really came here to talk about what you and my father discussed earlier."

Agonya looked away, biting her lip. It occurred to her that he might be willing to answer her questions now that he wanted to marry her. She would have to play the part of the indecisive and shy woman.

"Don't worry. You still have until the morning to make your decision."

"So, what we talk about here stays here?"

Ashkii nodded.

"What do you know of what we discussed?"

"Well, I know my father was going to try to arrange a marriage between us but beyond that I don't know anything of your conversation. I tried to get a word out of him, but he would not budge," Ashkii replied.

"He did propose that we marry as a sign of our friendship." Agonya tried to think fast. If he really did have feelings for her, she needed to know if he had betrayed her.

"So? Are you willing to marry me?" Ashkii scooted to the edge of his seat, almost too hopeful for her answer.

"I don't know yet. Do you want to marry me? Not just for our people but for you."

Ashkii scooted back a tad before answering. "I'm not sure. I mean I like you and all. You are the most beautiful woman I've ever met. You smell like peonies in full bloom mixed with cinnamon and myrrh. You are smart. You can be annoying though. I don't know."

"I'm annoying, am I?"

"That's not–no," he ran his fingers through his blonde hair, "all of us are annoying at times, but what has that got to do with anything? I like you."

"I am glad for your friendship." Agonya hesitated. "I don't know how many times you've saved my life since we met. And you, too, are pleasant to smell and look at." Agonya's cheek flushed redder as she spoke. She'd said it because she wanted him to think she thought it. But did she really think that? A part of her did, she realized.

"But that's it, huh? Just a friendship?"

"I'm not saying it can't be more with time. But I will need time."

Ashkii stood to go, his shoulders slumping lower than she'd ever seen before.

"Wait." He couldn't go yet. She hadn't asked him her questions yet.

Ashkii straightened his knees. "Yes?"

"Tell me why you have a wall around your mind."

Understanding flooded his face. She knew she had him. He thought she needed to understand him more before making a choice. He moved to sit back down in the chair but then he surprised her and squatted next to her instead.

"You must be wondering, if I fancy you as I do, why I still hide behind my wall. Part of it is because I am afraid."

Agonya shook her head in astonishment. "You. Afraid? But you're the best warrior I've ever met."

"No, I'm not. You talk about how many times I've saved your life, but I have failed you too. I failed to keep you undetected from the Kors. I failed to fight our way to freedom when we were surrounded. I failed to protect you from using your magic when I knew it could harm you. I have failed in so many ways. I am afraid."

Agonya tried to respond but Ashkii put his finger to her lips, and she forced herself not to pull away. "I am afraid that if I break down my wall, I will not be able to build it up again in time. I am afraid that if you get inside my mind, you won't like what you see. I am only able to tell you all this now because I am afraid you will reject me if I don't tell you these things."

Then he leaned forward and kissed her full on the lips. To her surprise she kissed him back. It was only a moment before he pulled back. How dare he kiss her without her permission! But why had she kissed him back? Was she in denial about the way she felt about him? Or was she just tired of being lonely? Did he really feel that way about her or was he playing the game too? It was hard to imagine he might have stolen Blackthorn from her. But that was the most honest answer she'd ever had from him. Before she had time to say anything else though, Ashkii left her with jumbled thoughts.

****

The sack came off Jaylen's head and he saw that they had arrived in a small settlement, but what really drew his attention was the Montane leaping across the rooftops. How did he do that? The motions of jumping looked just like anyone preparing to jump but when he left the ground, he flew through the air further than was possible. He'd done the same thing when they escaped; he'd jumped over his men. He wasn't the only one on the roofs, but he was the only one coming to meet them in the town square, except it wasn't a square, it was a circle.

The Montane jumped down, landing directly in front of their elephantus. "That was quick, Tse!"

"These fools were trying to follow, making it easy to track them." The man sitting behind Jaylen slid off the elephantus to stand next to the other man. "What would you like us to do with them now?"

The Montane looked up at Jaylen. "I want to question them," he said. "Take them to the second aromatic house, sixth room. I'll be along shortly. You know what to do." And just like that he leaped back up onto the nearest roof and bounded away.

As Jaylen watched the man leave, he noticed that the buildings beneath him seemed to be connected into extra-long homes. Each building had large letters painted on whichever side faced the center of the settlement. Several doors which all appeared to be on top of the roofs, could be seen propped open. Yet, there were no ladders to be seen anywhere. Even the children had no problem leaping up onto the roofs with the help of a few well-placed water barrels.

As it turned out, aromatic house two, sixth room, was exactly that, the second house with a maple leaf painted on the walls from the south end of the village and the sixth room also counting from the southern end. The room itself was simple. Although the metal rings and chains hanging from the walls were a bit disturbing. But Tse didn't lock them up. They merely stood in the room directly beneath the door and waited.

There were no chairs to sit in, which explained the standing. Jaylen considered sitting in the dirt but there was no need. The door opened and the man from earlier dropped in and placed a torch in a bracket on the wall. The sky was darkening and though they didn't need it now, they would need the light in a few minutes.

"I'll be up here if you need me." Tse motioned to the roof and jumped out. The door shut behind him.

"Why do you want the princess?"

Straight to the point. Jaylen never liked wading through layers and layers of scents. "Orders."

"What exactly were they?"

Jaylen studied the Montane for a second, he had an air of authority about him. That meant if he made a deal with him it would hold. So, he gambled honesty. "To bring back the princess or the package that she carries. Look, if you want the princess, I'll let you have her. I just want the package."

"What's in the package?" The Montane's face remained free of emotions.

"Don't you know already? Has she not shown it to you?"

"Oh, I know. I just wanted to know if you did." He smirked.

Jaylen let the jibe go. "You haven't answered my offer. I will let you have the princess, if you give me the package."

"Absolutely not. But you can switch sides. What do you say to working for me?"

"Why would I do that?"

"Because, I have the package. Well, my father does. And soon the most powerful person alive will have it and trust me. You don't want to be on her bad side."

So, he wasn't on her side after all. "What, exactly, did you have in mind?"

"Captain." Kyler shook his head.

Duty to their commander, to the king, was their first priority. But if they could turn it to their own ends . . . "Let's hear him out, Kyler. It can't hurt."

The Montane watched their exchange and shook his head. "I see, you've already made up your mind." Then he rapped quickly on the door.

Tse and two others appeared a few seconds later and Jaylen found himself attached to the wall, metal rings and chains wrapped around his wrists and ankles.

"Wait! We'll work for you."

"No. You are still loyal to that imbecile King Reid. I'd rather not work with you." He bent his knees and flew out the door.

"You shouldn't have said anything to him, Captain."

"It's true, I may have given away too much but he too gave away the information we needed."

"You don't think he was lying?"

"It is possible, but I don't think he was. No. I'm sure his father has the package, and we needn't bother with the princess anymore. Have you figured out how to get out of these yet?"

Kyler shook his chains. "We just got in them."

For the next several hours that was all they worked on with no success. The walls were strong, and the chains were tight. Before too long they were both exhausted from trying to get free and fell asleep.

A deep rumbling blast woke them up sometime in the middle of the night. What in the name of smells could warrant a call to arms at this time?

Shouts filled the air, though Jaylen couldn't hear what the orders were. And then the high-pitched screeching began. Something horrific was attacking the village. Men were screaming in pain now.

"Captain? What was that?"

Jaylen could only see Kyler's shape slumped against the opposite wall in much the same position he had been when they fell asleep earlier. “I don’t know. I wish I knew what sort of creature could inflict that kind of pain on our enemies.”

“I thought you were going to join forces with them. Glad to hear you still think of them as the enemy. Nothing good can come from working with them.”

Just then, a screech so high pierced the night air just outside their room. “Pray to the Patron of Fortune that thing doesn’t get in here with us.” If whatever horrible creature was attacking got inside the longhouse and started attacking them, they were done for. They had no way to defend themselves.

“What about escape? They are rather occupied at the moment.”

“If you can think of a way to get out of these, I'm all ears.” Jaylen shook his hands, clanking the chains.

They sat in silence listening to the battle outside their little walls for a while after that. The human cries of pain were fewer now, maybe they figured out a way to fight these things without getting hurt. The creatures were still screeching every few minutes. That meant they hadn’t killed them off or scared them away yet.

“Captain, I get why you wanted us to surrender, but it smells all wrong. We didn't even try to fight our way out of their clutches. We probably would have lost but I would rather die fighting our enemies than by these creatures.”

“You're right. If we had shown so much as one ounce of desire to escape, we would have been killed on the spot. We were greatly outmatched. But our orders were to bring back the package and the princess. This way, we at least got to our destination and were able to regain our strength. Also, we know that the princess doesn’t have the package anymore.”

“So, we just wait, then? For an opportunity to present itself?”

Jaylen nodded. “My prisoners escaped, right? So why not us?” After a short pause he continued, “And after tonight, it sounds like they will be in worse shape, easier for escaping. Who knows, maybe our fortunes will change for the better.”

***

The night was young when Agonya and Maya were left alone. Agonya immediately linked her mind with Maya's so they could talk without being overheard.

"I'm sorry, but they have been so welcoming to us. I love how much they are one big family. They take care of each other. Look at how much better you are!"

"About that. I don't think they want me to be healed as quickly as they make out."

"Why would you say that?"

"Because I wondered if I could heal faster if I used my magic."

"But Kylie said not to use it unless absolutely necessary. Won't it hurt you?"

"That's what I thought, but both times today when she came, I decided to try using just a little bit in combination with Kylie's perfumes. Well, look!" Agonya pushed herself up into a sitting position with ease. She tried to bend her knees which moved a little. Her feet were even more flexible.

"That's wonderful! And using your magic didn't hurt you like it has in the past?"

"The thing is, I think it hurt me before because I used too much of it too fast. And Blackthorn's powers were combined with mine then too."

"But when you tried to heal Ashkii and Brynn you were so weak afterwards and needed to regain your strength in between sessions."

"I was trying to heal them quickly and without help from the right perfumes. And before you object with the time I was unconscious after using my magic to defend myself, that took all my strength, and again, it was too much magic, too fast. And I'm afraid that because Blackthorn was helping me, he couldn't defend himself when he was taken from me."

"I still think he fell out of your pocket. Does Kylie know how much you've healed? It's amazing that you can sit up on your own and have some movement in your legs!" Maya seemed genuinely happy for her.

"No, Kylie doesn't know. And she can't know. Please don't tell her. I showed you because I trust you and I don't want to keep you in the dark. We've been through so much together."

"Of course. You know I'm here for you. It's just that I think if Kylie knew, she could help you more than you're letting her. I want to see you completely better."

"The thing is, Maya, Chief Golar said he'd help rescue Ithol."

"That's great!"

"If he was indeed offering a hand of friendship, but in exchange for his help he wants Blackthorn. He knew that my father was protecting a Kindroot, I think he knows that I have been doing the same if he hasn't already stolen him from me. But since I denied any knowledge of the Kindroots, he asked me to marry his son. But the only one who could have stolen him was Ashkii."

"No!"

"He must have taken him from me when I was unconscious."

"But he's saved us so many times. Why would he do that? He likes you."

"You know very well, how many men have decided they like me only to win my father's favor. Ashkii's no different, except he knew how to get what he wanted without me returning the feelings. Please, Maya, I need you to do some sleuthing for me tomorrow."

Maya removed her arm and sat up straighter. "What can I do? It's not like I get to wander around on my own. Now that I think about it, someone is always with me."

"Well, you can look for potential hiding places. See if there are some rooms that might be off limits, or ones that only the Chief and Chieftess go in and no one else, except maybe Ashkii." Agonya rubbed the back of her neck. "I don't know what's going on with him."

"I'll do my best. But I have a feeling I'll be stuck in the weaving room again. With winter approaching they are focused on making blankets and cloaks. Maybe I can request a different job."

"That's a good idea. Maybe you could collect firewood or help with the butchering or cooking."

"Butchering! Eew!" Maya pinched her nose closed at the very thought.

“I know it's not the easiest job. It is pretty gross, but you've seen Brynn and Ashkii do it to the deer.”

“Seeing and doing are two different things.”

“You shouldn’t even have to work, Maya. We are supposed to be guests. I need some time to think.”

“Well, if, you’re sure. I'm tired anyway. Wake me if you need anything.”

The room grew quiet and the guard on the roof walked to the edge. They couldn’t hear her thoughts, could they? Ashkii knew how to block unwanted listeners and Golar knew something about communicating over distances, but wouldn’t Agonya know if anyone had tried to listen to her thoughts? She needed the Montanes to be generous towards Maya and let her move around Tafka more freely.

Chapter 26

Agonya had too many thoughts whirling around in her mind. She needed to be back to normal. She hated being a cripple. She hated not knowing if Blackthorn was safe. He never explained his powers very well to Agonya, but the things he did say pointed at one thing. His survival was more important than Ithol's. Would agreeing to marry Ashkii be enough? Would she be able to save both Ithol and Blackthorn? No, not if she married Ashkii. He was too secretive, and she was too weak. She'd have to find a different way to save her people. There was always the possibility of–

Something heavy thudded above her head. The guard must have flattened himself on the roof. The snarling that followed made the hairs on the back of her neck stand up. "Watch out!" she cried. "They squirt acid when they start to screech!"

She heard the guard's spear bang against the roof as he loaded it into his atl. Wham! The drank howled. "How many are out there?" she called up to the guard.

"Don't worry. You'll be safe in there."

That's not what she'd asked. Agonya breathed deeply and tried to identify the dranks' aromas to know just how many were attacking.

Agonya's heart started to race. There were so many, she couldn't count them all. Would they be able to get on the roof? She hoped they couldn't jump up the walls or climb trees. That would be bad.

Maya was sitting up again. There would be no sleeping tonight.

"I'm coming in." The guard pulled the door closed behind him.

"Can you seal it?" Agonya asked.

"With what?" The guard looked around the small room.

Maya grabbed her scarf, pulled a chair beneath the door, but she was too short still to tie it onto the handle.

"Here, let me." The guard took Maya's scarf and hooked it onto the door and tied the other end to one of the beams in the roof.

In the time it took to secure the door, the screeching and screaming began. Someone blew the horn of battle long and loud. The whole village was awake now. Acid ate away at the walls. But what could Agonya do?

She closed her eyes and breathed in the smells that were all around her. She focused on the dranks. She couldn't find the leader controlling them.

Then, she smelled Brynn. She linked her mind with his. "Brynn! Can you hear me?"

"Ashkii, wait up!"

She could hear him, but he didn't hear her. "Brynn!"

"Agonya? I mean, your Highness?"

"I need your help. We've got to find the leader or leaders of the pack. Can you tell which one is guiding the dranks? I need to know where he is so I can focus my energy. I can't find him in this large of a group."

"On it. Hey Ashkii, after we get our weapons, we need to find the leader of the pack."

Agonya let him go. She needed to contain her strength, to build it up for what she was about to do. After a few minutes of agony listening to the terrified children crying and that awful noise the dranks were making, Agonya checked back in with Brynn.

"Have you found him?"

"We've only had time to gather our odor bombs and bows and arrows. Headed out to look now."

"Please, hurry." Odor bombs! Those things were incredible, the way Ashkii made those thorny devils lie down.

Agonya hated waiting and not being able to do anything to help. That's all she'd done for the last several weeks! Then, she saw her guard just sitting there in the chair. "Don't you need to go help the others fight?"

"My job is to make sure you stay safe, no matter what happens."

"What's your name again?"

"Seni."

"Seni, I think you helping the others kill these creatures would be very much protecting me. Besides, it's not like I'm all alone here." Agonya gestured to Maya.

"Sorry, your Highness, but my orders are clear. I'm staying here. Don't worry. There are plenty of warriors to take care of the situation."

Agonya looked at Maya and raised her eyebrows. This is what she was talking about earlier. They were prisoners. That's why he wouldn't leave them alone. Well, if he was just going to sit there at least Agonya could help Brynn.

"How's it going, Brynn?"

"We think the leader is in the forest to the north of the village. It's hard to tell from up here. We can't get close enough without getting sprayed and it's dark out here too."

"What about your odor bombs?"

"They aren't working! We've tried several times, but it doesn't seem to affect them."

Agonya sighed. She knew why they weren't working. She had hoped it wasn't true. "They've got walls around their minds. You've got to break through those before the bombs will work."

"And you're just now telling us this?"

Agonya didn't answer but searched the edge of the village. There were five of the dranks standing still.

"There are five leaders. Go for the one on the farthest side of the village from me and kill him, maybe that will put whatever dranks are under his command into chaos. Have

Ashkii or someone else go for the one next to him. They're about fifteen meters apart."

Agonya smelled the one closest to her. She took a little bit from her swirling river and sent it to the creature. She hit a wall just like before. She stretched her magic all over and around the wall looking for a weakness. She found none. She pulled it all back together and pushed it through the clay holding the stones together. Once inside she was able to flood him with enough magic to take command. About twenty dranks answered to him. She made them all go to their leader and lay down. Leaving his mind though was not a good idea. If she left, they would surely just get back up and start attacking. She should have thought of that before she told Brynn to start his attack on the farthest one from her. She just had to wait for the soldiers to find them and kill them. Twenty out of commission improved their chances. Maybe one of the warriors noticed their odd behavior and followed them.

Nope. The minutes stretched on, one after the other. She could hear the dranks on the street snarl and screech. Occasionally, a warrior would hit one and it would howl in pain until it died. No one came to kill the easy prey she'd made for them. Her attention was drawn back to the leader who was fighting her hold on him.

How odd? One by one she could feel the dranks in the pack start to disappear from her control. It didn't seem to matter that she still had control of their leader. Maybe someone was killing them for her. They continued to disappear until the leader was gone too. Agonya smelled for them. They were still physically right where they had been when she lost mental contact with them. Were they alive? She couldn't tell.

Was that sandalwood mixed with rotten eggs? The blend didn't belong to any one individual that she could pinpoint. Where was it coming from? Something about it was off.

"Ashkii?" A solid wall. So, irritating!

"Brynn?" What could be causing that smell? Why were the dranks staying where she'd left them?

"Maya, something is wrong. Do you have a weapon?"

Maya's eyes widened. "I'll find something, my lady."

"No need to worry." The guard held up his spear. "That's what I'm here for."

"Just the same, I'd like her to not be completely defenseless."

"I'm a little busy right now." Brynn's voice in her head gave Agonya a start.

"We've got bigger problems."

"You're joking right?"

"Nope. Not a joke. Everyone must change tactics. Right now!" She didn't need to focus to smell the sandalwood and rotten eggs. It was filling the air, washing over the village like a flash flood raising a river so fast that it didn't give time to get out of the way. Agonya started to feel an unspeakable anger fill her mind, cutting off her communication with Brynn. She had to build a wall, to force it out.

First, she had to warn Maya. "Don't breathe it in! Breathe through a cloth; anything to help dilute it!" She didn't look to make sure that Maya had heard.

Instead, she placed a stone at the base of her mind. Then another one. And another. Little by little she built her wall, using the anger she felt to build faster and faster, filling every crack as she went until she was ready for the last piece. Then she pushed the twisting clawing anger out the little opening until it was all gone. Finally, the last piece of the puzzle completed the wall. She was safe. For now, anyway. Was this why Ashkii kept a wall around his mind? He said he was afraid. She was afraid too.

She tried to reach out to Brynn again, but she couldn't get past her own wall. She didn't dare remove a stone to find him. He was on his own.

"My lady! Something is trying to get in!" Maya squeaked out so fast Agonya barely understood what she said.

"Let us in!" It was Ashkii.

As fast as he could the guard fumbled with the knots in Maya's scarf until it came undone. The door swung open. Brynn dropped inside, then Ashkii, and Kylie followed, landing in Ashkii's arms. He set her down gently before slamming the door shut above them. Seeing the scarf still attached to the handle he quickly tied it back to one of the beams of the roof to lock them inside again. "Good thinking, Seni."

Ashkii raced over to Agonya's side. "Are you okay? Brynn said you were in trouble. We came as fast as we could."

The room seemed to be shaking, the walls, the ground, Ashkii, everything was shaking. She wanted to hide. She heard them talking to each other, but she couldn't figure out what they were saying. There was constant pressure on her wall. It wouldn't stop. The tears began to streak her face which soon became dirty from someone trying to wipe away the tears.

"Don't cry! Kylie, can you do anything? Help her, please."

"Calm down, son, and move out of the way. Open your mouth, sweetie." Kylie gently pried Agonya's jaws open. "That's it." Then she placed a leaf in Agonya's mouth. "Chew."

Agonya obeyed. She could feel the stress leave her body with every bite. The pressure was still there but she felt fresh and able to resist it. She continued to chew until there was nothing left. She opened her eyes to see three faces transfixed on her.

"I'm okay." Agonya took a deep breath. It felt like she had just been riding a river and fell off a cliff and that she resurfaced, amazingly in one piece. "Something, or someone, is controlling those dranks. Something is very wrong. I understand, Ashkii, why you have a wall around your mind."

Kylie glanced at Ashkii then back at Agonya. "I feared this was the case. I'm going to ask you to do something now, your Highness, because it is absolutely necessary. The Honorable would object if he knew, but then again, he thinks he knows everything."

Agonya had a feeling she knew what she was being asked. It frightened her to no end. "Where is he?"

Maya and Brynn both said, "Who?" at the same time Ashkii and Kylie both said, "Hidden."

Ashkii finished his sentence without meeting her eyes. "On the other side of the village."

He had taken Blackthorn from her. Ashkii had betrayed her and pretended that he hadn't. The only consolation she had in that moment was that she had avoided asking him about it so he never had to lie about it. Would he have lied, if she had asked? Now when they needed Blackthorn the most, he was as far away as possible with every obstacle in the way. "I'm coming for you, Blackthorn!"

Kylie already had a fire going and her ingredients at hand. "Ready?"

Agonya nodded. She would talk to Ashkii later about what he'd done. In the meantime, she had a chance to fight. This sorceress had to be stopped. How did she get so powerful? Powerful enough to reach into the minds of all these creatures at once and to direct their attack on this innocent village.

Ashkii squatted next to her and held her hand. "You can do this. I know you can."

Despite her recent resolve not to say anything, the words flowed out of her. "I could have done this if you hadn't taken him from me and acted like nothing had happened, leaving me to wonder if he was still alive."

Before he could reply, Brynn shoved Ashkii to the floor and started knocking over the ingredients Kylie was preparing. Seni was on top of him in no time, pulling him back. Ashkii scrambled to his feet and helped Seni force Brynn onto one of the chairs. Kylie grabbed another sash and started tying him to the chair.

It all happened so fast. As soon as Brynn was secured everyone turned towards Maya. But she was just in shock like Agonya. Her cloak hid her nose and mouth. That was good.

"Brynn, I'm sorry for tying you up like this. She got in your head, and we can't have you getting in the way."

***

The fire burned the berries and pinecones letting their smoke escape into the air. Kylie caught it in her vapor filled bottle and brought it to Agonya. This time Agonya didn't pretend. She let the magic flow and mix with the sweet burning aromas. She felt the effects immediately. She also knew what she had been doing wrong all this time. Quicker than any other time, Agonya felt her muscles embrace the new energy. She remembered the first time she used the magic.

Knowing that she wouldn't be able to draw from Blackthorn, Agonya didn't hold back.

"Agonya?" Maya stepped back in surprise. "You're glowing!"

"Am I?" Agonya glanced down at her hands. Maya was right. A slight glow emanated out of her. The key, Agonya figured out, was to focus on the fragrances of what she wanted; to see them in her mind, to smell them in her senses. The fragrances worked together to build or heal what she wanted to build or heal. They wanted to help. Agonya imagined herself standing and walking and felt the power rush throughout her body.

"I've never seen anyone with this much control. That is, besides the sorceress." Kylie continued holding the bottle beneath her nose. The smoke-vapor was almost all gone. "Can you build a wall around all of us?"

Agonya breathed in the last, making sure it passed through all her muscles, strengthening them as it moved from her nose all the way to her toes. "Help me stand up please."

Ashkii grabbed one arm and Maya grabbed the other. Together they lifted Agonya onto her feet. The sensation was amazing! She hadn't stood on her own two feet since that night they escaped from the Kors. The moment Maya started to let go of her arm, Agonya started to crumble. "Don't let go!" The glow disappeared. Although the fragrances had melded with her muscles, it'd been too long since she stood on her own and her legs were not accustomed to her weight.

"Brynn, you have to stay here. We can't risk you turning on us when we're out in the open." Ashkii turned away from his friend. Then he and Maya helped Agonya take a step closer to the door.

"This isn't the way. I need to stay here. I'm still too weak to do this. You would be much faster without me."

Ashkii looked to Kylie for her opinion as if it was better than Agonya's.

Thankfully Kylie agreed with her. "Yes, Ashkii and Seni will go together. You can leap across the roofs and easily stay out of reach. I'll stay here with them."

Seni quickly hopped on the chair and untied the scarf, peeking through the door. He couldn't see anything in plain sight, so he pushed the door open and climbed on top. He unsheathed his daggers and turned in a complete circle just to make sure.

"I think it's safe. Can't see any of them," Seni called down.

"Take care of her. Don't let anything happen to her." Ashkii waited for Kylie to acknowledge the responsibility he'd just given her. Then he jumped onto the roof, letting the door drop back in place.

* * *

Ashkii had admitted to knowing where Blackthorn was hidden. She couldn't trust him. She had been seriously considering marrying him in an attempt to make an alliance, but without being able to trust him, a marriage like that meant nothing. She couldn't forgive him that easily. Even if he kept his word and brought Blackthorn back to her safely. She couldn't be sure he wouldn't do it again if he thought it was the best thing to do.

"Kylie, tell me why he did it."

The flickering torch highlighted melancholy wrinkles around her eyes and mouth as she spoke. "You must ask him yourself if you want to know. But we all had orders. Why I confessed to you that we knew where he was is the better question."

"Why did you answer me?"

"Because none of us here know how to fight back. Yes, we have magic just like you, but it's different. All I know how to do is make perfumes and potions and heal people. I should be out there healing. There are many people getting hurt and yet I'm in here."

"Why are you here? More orders?"

"No, because Ashkii asked me to come. He was worried about you."

Agonya coughed.

"Yes, he cares about you whether you believe it or not. He thought I might be able to heal you if you were hurt."

"So once you helped me, why did you stay?"

"Because you feel her, too, and are afraid. Because you have a chance to fight her, and maybe win. I don't believe you will win but there is a chance. There are too many dranks out there. Our elephantus are afraid of them and won't go near them at all. We will run out of arrows and spears before they're gone. She will send more. I'm sure of it."

Talking about Dana the Sorceress scared Agonya. She just learned about the woman, yet it seemed Dana knew about her ages ago. The way Kylie spoke about her made Agonya wonder how many times she'd attacked the Montanes, and why she was so intent on destroying them. What was she after?

"Have you met her?"

"Once. A long time ago. I was a little child. She came to our village looking for something. I didn't understand much of what was going on at the time but have since been told the story. Every child in our village knows it. Chief Ofri met with her. They talked for a long time, and no one really knows all that they discussed. She was pleased at the end of it. I remember her jumping out of the Chief's rooms with her head held high, her glowing silver dress flared out behind her. She walked the length of the village with a smug smile on her beautiful face and disappeared into the forest never to be seen here again."

Kylie's story was puzzling. "If she never came back, what makes you so sure this is her doing and not just wild creatures attacking?"

"You said it yourself, your Highness, you felt her enter your mind."

Agonya knew it to be true. "But why is she attacking you now? Did Chief Ofri fail to keep his end of the bargain?"

Kylie nodded. "When Chief Ofri left his rooms, he ordered a feast to be prepared for the day he made an alliance with Dana the Sorceress, the Patron of Life. Deer were slaughtered and the wine was brought out from storage. It was the best feast I have ever been to. The cake was scented beyond anything I'd ever smelled before. A few of us children were allowed to play with the deer bladders." Kylie laughed at the old memory.

"Was that feast the last one he gave?" Agonya could picture it now. He either deliberately broke his agreement or he couldn't fulfill it.

"Yes. What she asked of him was too much. Chief Ofri spent a good deal of his days taking scouting parties up the mountains and down to the river and traveling all over the place in search of the last Kindroots. He never found them. The protection from the creatures of the Acrid Mountains lasted a little while, but as the months turned into years, we started seeing dranks and thorny devils and all sorts of evil creatures creeping out of their caves from way up high."

Several dranks screeched in the night air, emphasizing her point.

"They all came to us, but none of the glory and riches she had promised. Chief Ofri doubled his efforts until he died on one of his scouting adventures, pierced through by a tusk of a horvelina."

"And Chief Golar is trying to find the Kindroots too. That's why he took Blackthorn from Agonya?" Maya asked, trying to make sense of it all.

"His older brother, Chief Amiri, started fighting back. He believed she was the one to break the contract, not us. Instead of searching for Kindroots, he gathered our warriors and warriors from the other Montane villages and challenged her. But they couldn't find her. One night when they were camping in the mountains, Chief Amiri disappeared. He was nowhere to be found. Without him there to unite the tribes, everyone dispersed and went back to their own villages. Now we just try to defend ourselves. There has been nothing we could do to change the way things are. Until now."

Someone landed on the roof. Thump. Thump. Two more people followed. Ashkii jumped inside followed by Seni and Chief Golar. Golar was red with anger, but Kylie didn't quail at his look.

Golar crossed the short distance to where Agonya sat leaning against the wall. He squatted down to her level. "She told you everything?"

Agonya clasped her hands together. "Most of it, I think I can figure out the rest." She remembered what Ashkii told her about her father. Once he knew about Blackthorn, he had to be Azurarus' friend, to get close to him. It made sense. She would have done the same. "I think you are blinded by your past."

"I am not blinded. I see more clearly than you. I have thought through every possible outcome and have made the best choices that I could make. Do not say otherwise." Golar's expression became even more murderous than when he first entered the room. Agonya didn't realize that was possible.

"I will not say I'm sorry. You, and I mean all of you," Agonya glared at Ashkii who was hiding behind Seni, "thought to befriend my father so you could trick him into giving you Blackthorn or make it easy for you to steal him. No, I'm not finished. You did steal him from me. You are thinking like she wants you to think." The more she spoke her thoughts out loud the surer she was about them. It made her angry and hurt and sad. "Blackthorn is not a bargaining chip. Do you think she will keep you safe once you hand him over? At first, I thought you wanted him to use his power yourselves to build your own Paradise, but I see now you were going to hand him over to this evil sorceress from the start."

Ashkii had the decency to look ashamed.

"Why not get Blackthorn's side of the story? Where is he?" Agonya reached out to him with her mind, but she felt nothing, smelled nothing. "You didn't!"

Golar fell backwards, no longer being able to hold his squat. Good thing. Her anger was building up inside her. Kylie, Maya, Seni, and Ashkii were all backing away too, leaving Agonya sitting by herself. Why did Maya back away? She wasn't afraid of Agonya, was she?

Brynn was the first to speak. "Your Highness, you're glowing! Orange!"

"And you're emitting a fragrance like nothing I've smelled before," Ashkii added.

Again? She looked down at her hands and indeed there was an orange glow surrounding them, brighter than before. And not just her hands, but her whole body. The glow did have a scent, one she couldn't place or maybe it was many scents. Either way, she felt strong. Stronger than she'd ever felt in her whole short life. Knowing she could do it, Agonya stood up and brushed the dirt off her dress. She could feel the swirling, raging power inside her, but it didn't frighten her anymore. She understood it. "Here is what is going to happen." Agonya pointed at the Chief. "You are going to gather your warriors in the main square and prepare to go to battle."

"But the dranks!" he cried.

"She knows Blackthorn isn't here. They are leaving even now, as we speak."

Golar stood up defiantly. "I will not be told what to do."

"But you are being told what to do, by Dana. Why do you serve her when she sends dranks after you?"

Golar's face remained stony.

"Why, Golar? What has she offered you in return? Has she kept any of her promises? I may not be as powerful as Dana, but I do know that sending an army of dranks to attack an entire village filled with men, women, and children who have done nothing but try to meet her demands is wrong." Agonya paused to let her words sink in, and still Golar couldn't meet her gaze.

"I need you to smell me, Golar. I am asking you to do the right thing. I am asking you to help me protect my children, my women, and my men; to fight alongside us against the evil that Dana is bringing against us."

Golar finally looked at her. "Will you marry my son?"

"You lost all your rights to ask anything of me the moment you stole Blackthorn." Agonya looked at Ashkii standing underneath the door. He had betrayed her. But she needed Golar's help. Ithol needed his help and as long as there was a possibility of getting what he needed, Golar would continue to work with Dana. "I will," Agonya said, still looking at Ashkii, "*after* you help me defeat the Kors and bring back Blackthorn safely."

Golar clenched his jaws, clearly not wanting to show weakness. But he was an intelligent man and knew when he'd been bested. Reluctantly, he stepped forward and smelled Agonya's outstretched hand. "May it be done." Then he jumped onto the roof.

"Thank you, Kylie, for not hiding the truth from me. You have done what you can for me. Now, go. Do what you can for the others. There are many wounded tonight."

"Your scent is pleasant, your Highness." Kylie bowed and went to do as she was told.

"Seni, you were a good guard to me. Now you must prepare yourself for battle with the others."

For the first time since arriving, the four of them were alone again. Was it only two days ago? Agonya walked over to Brynn and untied his bonds. "Her scent has left us. I do not think you are in danger anymore." Agonya delayed as long as she could. She had to face him sooner or later.

"Agonya, Your Highness," Ashkii said, bowing low before her. "Forgive me. I did not know my father would send Blackthorn to her the moment he had him. I believed Blackthorn to still be in the village."

"Oh, Ashkii! You shouldn't have taken him in the first place! My father trusted you! I trusted you. Your scent has soured." Agonya's glow intensified. "After you answer my questions, you will go join the others who are preparing for battle."

"Agonya? Please don't send me away. Don't you want our help bringing Blackthorn back safely? I want to help before it's too late. Besides if I don't go with you, Aiden will fight you, he will not gladly let you have Blackthorn without an order from his Honor. If I were with you, he would take my word for his."

Agonya wanted to believe Ashkii was sincere. He was right about needing at least one Montane with her. "I said that I would marry you, and I will. But I do not trust you. You may come with me on one condition."

Ashkii stood up. "Anything."

"Remove your wall."

Ashkii recoiled. "I can't!"

"You can. And you will if you are going with me." Agonya would not budge on this. "I take it Blackthorn left here within the very hour of our arrival. Is that right?"

"No, Aiden did not leave until the next morning when my father returned with the warriors from taking care of the Kors. I thought Aiden was going hunting."

"So, he's one day ahead of us, flying fast on the back of one of those huge bear-like creatures."

"Elephantus," Ashkii corrected.

"What chance have we got in overtaking them?" Agonya resisted the urge to rub her temples. Too much to think about in so little time. What did he say about the Kors?

"It will be difficult, but I believe we can do it. Elephantus are expert climbers and know their way around the wilderness better than we do."

"One more thing." Agonya rested her glowing hand on his shoulder as he started to make for the exit.

Ashkii flinched but didn't pull away.

"What became of those Kors?" They were a risk she couldn't ignore.

Chapter 27

The sun still wasn't awake when Agonya stood before the gathered warriors. The torches were starting to go out but the glow emanating from her body cast a small light on their weary faces. Many looked like they were about to fall asleep right there on whatever log they were sitting on. There were no more than eighty men and women that were able to ride forth to war. The others were injured or too young or too old. They would need more warriors if they wanted a chance to defeat the Kors.

"Good people of Tafka, I stand before you this morning because I know what you have been through." Agonya swept her hands from one end of the group to the other. "We have a common enemy. I am asking you to unite with me and with your fellow Montanes so that we might finally be rid of this war. My people, the Itholeans, are under siege at this very moment. They are dying from lack of water or food, from arrows and fires. I came here looking for help. I was not received as warmly as I'd hoped. But I am hopeful that you will aid me now."

Chief Golar stood behind Agonya off to the side. He stepped forward as she gestured to him. "Your Chief has agreed to help me. And I have agreed to marry Ashkii in return. Already we have sent some of you to petition your brothers and sisters in the other villages. Chieftess Mazali has agreed to watch over the village while you are gone, to protect those who remain behind."

Agonya's skin started to shine more brightly as she embraced all the scents around her. "Do not be afraid. I do not think our enemy will attack this village again for a while yet. She realizes that the conditions have changed, and she fears it. I came to you, a cripple. I will leave on my own two feet. Do not be crippled by fear any longer. Stand! Be brave! Let us each do our parts well!" Agonya let her glow fade then motioned for His Honor to take over.

Chief Golar took her place and started assigning duties to different warriors while Agonya and Ashkii headed to see the Korin prisoners.

From the outside, their prison looked like every other home in the village. Ashkii hopped right up to the roof without pause. Agonya bent her knees too, but when she straightened up and pushed off the ground, she only went up a half a meter before falling back to the ground.

"Here I thought the queen who glows can surely jump onto a roof,"

Ashkii teased before jumping back down.

"Oh please! There are plenty of things you can't do. I could point out that I only started walking a few hours ago; and when I'm not actively using my power, my strength is not what it used to be."

"Of course, forgive me. Would you like me to find you a ladder or carry you up?"

"I'd rather not wait for a ladder. You may carry me."

Ashkii picked her up and jumped, landing on the roof gracefully. "Do you want to jump down yourself, or would you like me to carry you again? Though, I suppose you could use this ladder," he said, lifting a rope ladder from the roof.

"You mean there was a ladder here the whole time?"

Ashkii grinned. Then just to show off, he jumped in, rolling into a ball and doing a flip in midair, and still managing to land on his feet.

He was trying to charm her again. Well, it wouldn't work. Retaining her dignity, Agonya descended the ladder and stepped onto the dirt floor. Turning around, she saw the Korin captain chained to the wall next to his companion. He stared at her in disbelief. The rawness of their wrists showed that they had been trying to break free of their bonds.

Agonya straightened her brown woolen dress and inhaled the scents in the room. The orange glow surrounding her flared brighter as the earthy fragrances filled her up. This was the man who had captured her and chased her and almost captured her again. He was a Korin officer and the reason she needed the Montanes to help her.

"Do you know who I am?"

"Y-You're the princess," the captain sputtered. "How are you doing that?"

Agonya smiled at his remark. "I *was* the princess; I am the queen now, and you will address me as such."

"Forgive me, your Highness," the captain corrected.

Agonya clasped her hands in front of herself and started to pace the room. "What are your goals? Other than finding me and taking me to your commander." She paused directly in front of the Kor who glanced sideways at Ashkii.

Ashkii cleared his throat nervously. "Your Highness, we should kill them and get going."

"Kill them?" Agonya turned to look at him. How could he be so callous? Had he just waltzed in here planning to kill these men the whole time he flirted with her? It was unbelievable. "I didn't come here to kill them," she said coldly.

"You didn't? We can't take them with us. They'd slow us down! And we can't leave them here to escape and do who knows what to the village. I thought–"

"You thought wrong," she interrupted, even though everything he said about them screamed at her to just kill them and be done with them. "You're right we can't leave them behind. It isn't safe. But we can't just kill them because it's convenient."

"What about sending them with my father?"

"No, he doesn't need another responsibility. He has enough to do, and I do not trust him to keep his word once I'm gone." Oh, he would gather the other Montanes and arm them for war but she knew he wouldn't fight the Kors unless he had no other choice. She would just have to deal with that later. One problem at a time.

Agonya turned back and studied the Kor. Why had she come? There was hatred in his eyes, but she could also smell fear. She could use that. The other Korin was just the same. She knew in that moment that she had to bring them with her whether she wanted to or not. Then, she pressed her thoughts on both of their minds. "Don't even think about crossing me. You heard the Montane. He's ready to kill you and be done with you. I will let him kill you if you try anything." Speaking aloud to Ashkii, Agonya added, "They come with us."

* * *

A few minutes later they were on the roof, the cool morning breeze on their faces. Brynn and Maya were right on schedule. They each sat on top of an elephantus. Brynn pulled a third creature behind him. The elephantus' back was level with the roof. No need for that show-off to help her down.

Agonya cut the Kor's feet free and pushed the captain onto her elephantus, making him sit in front. She saw Ashkii out of the corner of her eye. He did not look happy about this arrangement. She wasn't happy with him either.

"Well? What are you waiting for, Ash? Put that Kor with Brynn and you can ride with Maya."

Ashkii shook his head. "I think you should ride with Maya and let Brynn and I do the guarding."

Like always, he had to speak his arrogant mind. "No. Every minute we sit here is a minute lost."

"Then, I will guard this one. Brynn, would you mind riding with Maya?"

Brynn nodded and moved to sit behind Maya on her elephantus.

Ashkii urged his elephantus forward. Agonya kicked the back legs of the elephantus she was sitting on. He lurched forward. A few of the warriors standing nearby snickered at her as she passed. She was probably doing it all wrong. How was she supposed to know how to ride one of these things? She'd only learned they existed the day before!

Once they were out of the village, Agonya decided Ashkii had had enough time to comply with her wish. She would rather send him back now before they were too far from the village. Closing her eyes, and sniffing the air she smelled his sweet musky scent and thought, "Ashkii?"

He gave no acknowledgement that he heard. Agonya didn't want to yell at him. He was in the front, and she was in the back. She tried again to make her elephantus go faster. Whatever she did worked. She passed Brynn and Maya, then slowed her elephantus to keep pace with Ashkii and Kyler.

"Do I need to tear it down for you?"

Agonya could hear his teeth grind together as he tightened his hold on the reins, accidentally signaling to his animal to stop.

"Sticks! Watch what you're doing, will you?" Kyler rubbed the back of his head.

"Remember who you're talking to, and I might," Ashkii replied, rubbing his forehead at the same time.

"I had one condition. You have yet to fulfill it." Agonya passed Ashkii. She was perfectly content leaving him behind.

"I hate it." He grumbled as he caught back up to her.

"Are you a child? Throwing a tantrum because you can't have your way? You will turn around right this instant if you don't get your act together." Agonya started to glow faintly again. She was going to have to figure out how to get emotional without glowing. It was quite embarrassing. The only good thing about it was that it had a disconcerting effect on others.

Ashkii shut his mouth and galloped ahead. It wasn't so much galloping as it was lumbering, but at least they were going fast. They were out of Tafka and taking a path that zigzagged further up the mountain.

Agonya focused again on Ashkii's mind. She couldn't trust him to do it without a little encouragement. He still had a wall there, but this time she noticed a little hole near the bottom. "Ashkii?" she thought.

"What is it?" he snarled back in his thoughts.

“I know it’s hard to be so vulnerable, so thank you. It isn’t exactly what I asked for, but it will do. I am glad you are coming despite my other feelings about you at the moment.”

No answer. Fine! He could be silent if he wanted to. Agonya didn’t like the idea of being in his mind any more than she had to. Not just because it was the polite thing to do either. He had betrayed her!

Agonya tightened her fingers on the leather reins and stared at the back of the Kor’s head. He was taller than her. That made it difficult to see around him. It didn’t matter. She knew what was in front of them. Ashkii and Kyler on an elephantus, that’s what. Ashkii was making her mad. She needed to think about something else.

Agonya landed her thoughts on Blackthorn, he was the reason she was doing this. If she couldn’t save him in time, then what was the point of doing anything at all? She used to wake up every morning excited about life and what the day held in store for her. Her days had been filled with oils and perfumes and sneaking out of the palace, defying her father, rendezvousing with Hodel and drinking tea with important people. But now life was about surviving. Her father died, making her queen; she was not prepared for that. He also started a war she had to finish. He sent her out of the city to protect Blackthorn. So far, it looked like she was doing a magnificently horrible job at all of it.

“Sooo, your Highness? Are you going to tell me where we’re going? These plants and animals are interesting and all that but I’m tired of not knowing my destination if you know what I mean.”

“Dahel, is it?”

“You can call me Jaylen if you like.”

“Okay, Jaylen, I’m not going to tell you. You don’t need to know. All you need to know is that you’ve failed and won’t be returning a hero after all.”

“Is that what you think? How do you know I’m not exactly where I want to be?”

“Because you are the one in the ropes. You are the one I will kill if you even attempt to escape or do something rash.”

“Me? Do something rash?” Jaylen raised his tied hands so she could take a good look at them. “Yeah, right. I’m more worried about you doing something rash and uncalled for.”

“You should be. I’m not in a very friendly mood. I have been cooped up for far too long and disrespected and underestimated and--”

“Whoa! I get the point! You’ve had a rough life, is that it? Full of anything you could possibly want at the tip of your fingers, people to boss around and wait on your every need.”

He was right. Why was she even talking to this guy about her problems? She was only paralyzed for a few weeks after being a prisoner after her father died. Then Blackthorn was taken from her. He was right. She was queen now. She commanded people to do her will. Being able to walk and run and go wherever she wanted gave her the confidence she could make things right.

“You’re awfully quiet all of a sudden.”

“I don’t need to talk to you. You’re just trying to find out more information, any information you can use to your advantage. I will put a gag in your mouth if you keep pestering me.”

“Look, I get it. You don’t like me. Fine. We are sharing an elephantus together for who knows how long. Might as well make the most of it. Did you know that man up there, Ashkii? He has the package somewhere in the village?”

“What package?” Agonya feigned any knowledge of it, but she already knew Ashkii had taken it from her.

“Oh, you know what I’m talking about. Is that where we’re going, to retrieve the package?”

So, he wanted the package, did he? Did he know what was in the package? She smiled. Through his arrogance, assuming he had information for her that might change her mind, he had shared the flavor of his perfume.

Chapter 28

The wild horvelina just kept getting madder and madder. Krillin squeezed his eyes shut. He couldn't imagine that it could go any faster than it already was, but he'd thought that on several occasions, and it had proved him wrong. At first, he thought he wouldn't feed the beast so long as it kept running. The whole point was to get there as fast as he possibly could. Now that a whole day had passed, riding on its back without a break, he wanted to feed the damn thing just so he could have a rest. Anything to stop holding on for dear life! He didn't even know if he was going in the right direction anymore. This was a bad idea. A very bad idea.

A low rumbling noise could be heard in the distance. Krillin assumed it was still the river off to his left. He had this sinking feeling though that he had passed the turn off to the village. Concentrating as hard as he could, Krillin peeled off one finger at a time until he could move his hand to his bag. The creature chose that moment to jump over a fallen tree tossing Krillin into the air. He didn't get a chance to fly very far before he crashed into a massive pine tree and fell to the ground.

The beast realized she'd finally gotten rid of that annoying person on its back and turned toward the fallen man. Pawing the ground, it charged.

Krillin clutched his pounding head. He barely had time to register that this massive beast was barreling toward him. He tried to roll out of the way, but his longbow tripped him up. The beast closed the distance with ease.

"Aahhhhhhhhhh!" Krillin opened his eyes a moment later to realize he wasn't dead. The horvelina hadn't been charging him after all. She wanted Krillin's food from his bag. His bag, torn off his back by branches during his short flight, was being ripped to shreds by the beast.

Krillin stood up and almost fell right back down from a sudden dizzy spell. He leaned against the murderous pine tree until he was able to clear his head. Then he approached the animal, another bad idea. He was sure of it. He bent down and helped separate the contents of the bag, so the beast had easier access to the food. While it ate, Krillin gathered up what was salvageable and tied it all together. Then he went and collected his arrows that were scattered across the area of flight. Was this what it felt like to be an arrow? To be pulled back and let loose unexpectedly, to fly through the air not knowing how far it would be to the target. There was always a target for the arrow to strike even if its master was aiming for something entirely different; the arrow always hit something. It never just kept flying and flying.

His map was poking out from the middle of a small bush. He picked it up, studying it to see where he was. A path was visible in the direction he'd come from, not too far away. So, he went to it and looked both ways. The landmarks on the map were nowhere to be seen. He'd have to find the river to see how close to it he was.

The more he walked the less weird it felt to be walking on solid ground again. His legs didn't know what to do. He really had no idea what he was doing, trying to read the stupid map. It barely made sense to him. Maybe he should just head northeast off the path and hope for the best.

The horvelina looked up. All the meat was on its way to one of the stomachs inside the massive beast. Krillin took a step. The horvelina did too. Krillin took another step and another. No way was he going to fight that thing again! But the beast continued to follow him. Krillin glanced around. Would an arrow even pierce through that thick skin? He was too close for that. He needed to get up higher in case it decided to skewer him with those ivory tusks.

Krillin got a running start and leaped into the air, grabbing a low hanging branch. The oak branch cracked. Krillin fell back toward the ground, but the ground wasn't under him anymore. The horvelina was. Krillin landed on top with his legs on either side of the beast's rounded body. "Oww!"

"Sticks!" This creature wouldn't leave him alone! So long as it didn't run like it had before . . . He had no way of guiding it. The baited stick he used last time was lost in the chaos of flying. Without a word or action from Krillin it got back on the path and started trotting the way they were going before their breakdown.

So much for heading northeast. Krillin looked down at his hands. He still had the map in them. It was crinkled up and probably ruined but maybe not. Krillin tried to spread it out while they trotted. He was still nervous not having both hands hugging the beast's neck while he was moving, but he didn't seem to be in any danger of falling off at the moment, so the next task was to find out where he was and where he was going.

* * *

The elephantus whacked vines and bushes out of its way. Its tusks swung from side to side enlarging the path as it went. The vegetation didn't slow down the beasts at all. The only time they slowed was when they came to a tight curve, but once around it, the elephantus could move like nothing else. At this rate, they were sure to be able to catch up to Aiden. The advantage they had was that no one quite knew where to find Dana, not even Aiden. Their hope was that Dana wouldn't find him before they found him.

There was no stopping for meals. Agonya ate and then fed her captive the leftover morsels while they lumbered up the mountain as fast as they could. What they would do if Dana found him first, Agonya hadn't a clue. She could do a little magic, but Dana was better, faster, stronger, and had way more experience than her.

To be logical about it, which was not Agonya's strength, if Dana got what she wanted, what would she do? She might send Aiden back home with a gift of her gratitude. Or she might just kill him and take Blackthorn back to her secret home or wherever she was hiding all the other Kindroots. That is if they weren't already dead. If she found Aiden, would she know they were on the path looking for him, too? Maybe if they were close to her home . . .

"Did you hear that?" Jaylen asked.

"Hear what?"

"Shhh . . ."

There was a rumbling sound approaching from behind. It sounded like running water, but it couldn't be. They were going uphill. "What do you think it is?" Agonya whispered back.

"I don't know, but whatever it is, it's getting closer and louder. My instinct is to get off the path."

"Ashkii? Brynn? Do you hear that?" Agonya called out so they would hear her from the back of the group.

Maya turned her head at Agonya's call. Her eyes widened in alarm. She started saying something, but she was too far away for Agonya to hear. Ashkii heard though because he tucked the reins to the side and stood on the back of the elephantus, locking a spear into place.

Swoosh! The spear flew over their heads and was gone. Agonya strained her neck to see what was so urgent. A horvelina was galloping toward them. There was no sign of the spear Ashkii had thrown.

Swoosh! An arrow flew over her head, this time coming from the horvelina! Agonya turned her head to see where it went. The arrow was embedded in Ashkii's hand. He dropped back down to a sitting position but facing the rear. Unfortunately, he also dropped his atl when the arrow hit.

Agonya couldn't afford any more weapons flying passed her. She remembered controlling the horvelina before, why not now? She linked minds with it. This was the same horvelina that had attacked them before! Agonya got over her shock and forced it to a stop and then motioned for the others to stop too. She pulled back on the reins and slid off the back of the elephantus before it had halted completely. She inhaled and let the energy flow all around her. She sensed the captain's movements and entered his mind before he could take off with her smelly steed. "Stay put!"

He shifted so he could turn around and watch her. She ignored him. Whoever shot that arrow didn't aim to kill. It was a warning shot. One that would prevent another from accidentally hitting him or her. She couldn't see him very well. Easy enough to change. She strode towards the beast who stood motionless under her command. That was something new. She still had control of the horvelina and was able to get inside Dahel's head at the same time. Hmmm. She could use that.

"Who are you and what do you want?" Agonya demanded as she reached the side of the horvelina.

A tall man sat up and slid down to meet her. "Krillin Boged at your service, your Highness." He bowed low and smelifed her hand.

Wow! When was the last time she was treated with such respect? He was wearing the garb of her soldiers. He must have been sent from the city. "You have come a long way to find me. What was so urgent that you had to come so far in the middle of battle?"

"A message from Lord Commander Huren himself, your Highness." Krillin reached inside his cloak and pulled out a scroll with the wax seal of Huren and handed it to her.

Agonya broke the seal and unfurled the paper.

> Your Majesty,
> I write this to you in deep distress.
> I fear you are in danger.
> A Mons attempted to kill Sir Besnek
> I'm most certain they were the ones
> behind the King's death.
> I hope this finds you in time.
> Do not trust the Montanes!
> Your Humble Servant,
> Lord Commander Huren

Shock and dismay filled Agonya. She closed her eyes and dropped the note. Her chest tightened like someone was squeezing a lemon. She had known of their treachery when they took Blackthorn from her, but this? Her father! Agonya wanted to crumple up into a ball on the ground and weep. To weep for her father. To weep for the friendship she wanted to have with Ashkii but couldn't have. To weep for the choices she'd made.

Turning around, Agonya saw Brynn slipping off his elephantus to come to her side. Maya was wrapping Ashkii's hand. Dahel and the other Kor were still astride their elephantus. She had to be strong. She couldn't let Ashkii see this note. Agonya bent down and picked it back up to burn at the first chance.

"You did well, soldier, bringing this to me. I'm amazed that you found me. My journey has drifted like a perfume on the wind. Will you stay by my side and help me in my quest?"

Krillin bowed again. "It would be my pleasure, your Highness."

"Then let us ride. Time is of the essence." Agonya walked back to her elephantus and climbed up using the small rope ladder that hung across its back.

"Meet our newest companion, Krillin Boged and his horvelina." She pointed back to Krillin who was ready to ride. She would have to ask him how he had tamed that wild creature.

While that intrigued her it couldn't keep her attention. Not after what Huren told her. She missed her father. He was not always a nice man, but he had looked out for her and at the end had shown he loved her still somewhere underneath his act. Had Ashkii done the killing? No, she had to believe it wasn't him. His betrayal, stealing Blackthorn, was already too much to bear. Huren's note meant there was another Mons in the city. But even so, Agonya couldn't help thinking about that night.

Agonya gasped. Ashkii had been the one to 'fight' the assassin off their backs when they were escaping. No one actually saw what he did or how he did it. What if he had convinced the assassin he would take care of the problem himself. Was he planning on killing her once he got what he wanted?

"Your Highness? Are you all right?" Dahel interrupted her meandering thoughts.

"What?"

"It's just that, well, you seem sad. I know I'm not the one you want to talk to, but if there's anything I can do–"

"You know, you sound like a decent fellow, but then, I remember how you kidnapped me and tied me up and tortured my friend and would have done the rest of us if we hadn't bested you and escaped. Then, I remember how you hunted us, twice. The second time you dragged me out of the shelter and would have killed my friends if I hadn't bested you again." Agonya paused. She wasn't being very decent herself. Maybe she should give him a break, but he was someone she could talk to about his treachery because it was known to everyone. She wasn't able to confront the one she really wanted to yell at because she needed him to think she was willing to trust him again if he did the right things.

The right things. What was the right thing to do? "I must apologize. You didn't deserve that."

"Apology accepted. I think I did deserve it. I did all those things, even now I'm constantly thinking about how to turn this in my favor."

"I know. That is why I'm constantly keeping my eyes on you."

"I thought it was because of my sensual smell and charming, good looks!"

Agonya smacked the back of his head.

"Ouch! That hurt!"

"Don't expect an apology. You deserved it."

"Want me to watch the prisoner, your Highness?" Krillin called from behind her.

"I don't think two can ride on that thing and I certainly don't want to. Thanks for asking, though." She liked this Krillin guy. He offered what he didn't have to her because he was a proper gentleman, unlike Ashkii and the captain.

Agonya watched the trees go by one after the other. The higher they went the fewer and farther between they became. There were different trees, too, beautiful trees that smelled minty. Agonya had never seen them and had no idea what they were called. The trees reached their skinny arms high, dangling their circular golden leaves for the wind to blow through. Every once in a while, she would hear a creaking and groaning sound coming from their trunks. They weren't trustworthy. Agonya feared one of them would tumble over on top of them unexpectedly.

Huren had warned her. These trees were trying to warn her of a possible betrayal. What were they warning her of? Was it Golar? She already knew Golar wouldn't help fight the Kors. She had to hope this untrustworthy man wouldn't join the Kors in fighting her people. But unless she forsook Blackthorn and rode back to the city herself, she wouldn't be able to stop him if he did. And if she did that, she would become the very thing she despised. She had to trust in someone. Huren was there. He would lead them to victory. She had no choice but to trust him with the very lives of her people. He trusted her to protect Blackthorn. Protect Blackthorn she would, even if it killed her to do so.

Chapter 29

Lord Commander Huren studied the barren fields from the ramparts. Several of his soldiers were still recovering from the battle that happened four days before. Twenty-nine would never recover, never smell life again. A bold move from the Kors, to attack in the dark. He still hadn't figured out what they were trying to distract him from. It all looked the same out there as before, except now there were broken arrows, spears, and shields littering the ground.

He hoped his messenger would find the queen in time. The chances of it were not good. Perhaps the Montanes hadn't shown their hand yet, there was a small chance they were still pretending to be friends.

Friends were lacking these days. The councilors couldn't seem to agree on anything. Lady Velia was going on and on about Huren's lack of security in the city, and how it was his fault the water was poisoned, and the wheat had turned moldy.

The people were starting to sell their most valued possessions for a little extra food. Which meant some of his soldiers were turning a blind eye to what the people were doing, or they themselves were profiting from the whole thing. The few times Huren tried to do a surprise inspection nothing had come to light. How was he supposed to enforce what 'wasn't' happening? He couldn't be everywhere at once.

Huren sighed and started his descent back into the chaos of the city. He might have to go out onto the battlefield to put up a good fight or they would die protected by these stupid walls. What had Azurarus been thinking?

A loud voice interrupted Huren's thoughts as he reached the streets. "The end of the world is here! Are you prepared?"

Huren saw a dirty old man. His clothes were ripped, and he continued to cry about the defeat that was surely to come to anyone who would listen. Striding over to him, Huren asked, "Man, why have you given up? We'll pull through. Winter is almost here. Surely, they'll be the ones to give up and go home."

"The prophecy says we will be laid to waste like the carrion of the birds. There is no hope for us. Pack your bags and flee! The caves in the Acrid Mountains would be better." The man's wild eyes couldn't get any wider.

"What prophecy? I haven't heard of any prophecies." This man was crazy! Lord Tanish had never mentioned any prophecy and if anyone was going to, it would be him, a priest by trade.

"The patron of Rotten Fragrances has prophesied, my Lord! We are doomed!"

Huren thought about throwing the man in prison to keep him quiet, but he wasn't committing a crime. Huren shook his head and walked away. One good thing that man accomplished was to talk Huren out of his own nonsense. He decided to visit the distribution centers one more time. He was going to put a stop to this pilfering one way or another.

* * *

Krillin felt bad for shooting the Montane's hand, but he didn't really have a choice if he wanted them to stop firing at him. Ever since the queen welcomed him with open arms, all they'd been doing was riding in pursuit of who knew what. Although she'd invited him to join her quest, she hadn't offered any explanation as to what they were doing. In fact, she wasn't talking with any of them, except the tied-up Kor sitting in front of her, and even then, just a little. She mostly seemed annoyed with him and kept to herself.

It was good to see the Kors were with the queen. That made his job easier. Krillin could help them escape once he knew where the package was that he'd been told to find and return.

He found her Highness . . . unusual. She emanated fragrances, and he was unsure whether he had only imagined it or if her skin glowed at times. Then there was the matter of Jerky. She tended to keep running because she loved it so much, so her unexpected halt made him wonder if something, or someone, had made her stop. It was like her Highness knew he would stop because she started sliding off her elephantus before it had even happened. Other than that, she seemed like any other person of nobility, entitled to everything. Her politeness was an act, Krillin was sure of that. There was no such thing as good nobility.

Krillin turned the bend in the path to find the others at a standstill. Stretched before them was a huge meadow and a small lake of acid laying to the north of the path that went straight across the meadow.

"What's going on?" Krillin asked. They hadn't stopped for dinner. So, why now?

She turned around to face him. "You should know that we are pursuing someone who is trying to give an evil sorceress exactly what she wants. I do not fancy being so exposed, not to mention we've been awake for two whole days without a rest."

"She finally speaks!" the Kor who'd been riding with her smiled.

"Yes, I suppose you ought to know that too. Don't think you're going to get any more out of me." Then, she turned to the old balding burly man. "Brynn, what do you think we ought to do? Should we camp here in the cover of the trees, or do we chance it and hope to get to the other side before we're noticed?"

The man with the injured hand spoke over Brynn's reply. "It looks like Aiden is here, your Highness. See? Right there in the middle."

"Ashkii's right, your Highness. There's someone out there. Maybe he's hoping to be noticed," Brynn agreed.

"Very well, I guess there'll be no resting until we talk to him," she hesitated, then asked, "Ashkii, this is why you came, is it not? Come with me while the rest of you stay here on the alert. Don't follow us unless we are in danger, but even then, make sure you aren't seen unless absolutely necessary. Krillin. Brynn. I'm counting on you to keep an eye on these prisoners. Maya, don't worry. I'll be back before you know it." Then she and Ashkii got on the same elephantus and rode into the clearing.

The sun was setting, making it harder and harder to distinguish between one shape and another. All Krillin could do was wait. He hated waiting. When he was pursuing the queen, he was moving and doing something; but just sitting and waiting, like when he was in the city and waiting for the battle to start? It was torture.

Krillin turned toward Brynn. "How did you get picked for this mission?"

Brynn shrugged. "I've known Ashkii for many years now and really, it's by chance that I got to join this little group. Don't regret it in the least."

Krillin smelled his aroma, just a little bit like earthy oak firewood, not bad.

Brynn waved his arm toward Maya. "This splendid lady is Maya. She is the queen's lady. She keeps us together, I think." Brynn winked at Maya who turned a deep red.

"I do what I can."

Krillin nodded toward the two men still sitting on the elephantus all tied up. "And who might our prisoners be?"

"Oh, them. Well, that there is a captain of the Kors, or so I've been told. The other one is one of his soldiers. I don't rightly recall their names though, but it doesn't matter."

"Our names don't matter? I'm Captain Jaylen Dahel if you please. And this is the Lord Commander's personal guard, Kyler."

"If he's the Commander's guard, why's he with you?"

"Uh guys?" Maya interjected, "What's going on out there? Are they fighting? Do you think we need to help?"

Brynn and Krillin both turned to look. Ashkii and the man they were trying to stop, were threatening the queen. That didn't make any sense. Wasn't Ashkii on her side?

Brynn didn't hesitate but climbed up next to Kyler and trotted out to help. Krillin looked around. Now was the perfect time to free the captain. Krillin moved into action and approached Maya. "What do you think, should I stay here with you or go see what nonsense is happening out there?"

"Brynn will take care of it." Maya seemed relieved he was offering to stay. She didn't realize what he was planning though.

"Sounds good to me." Krillin walked back to the horvelina and shuffled through his belongings, sneaking a rope into his cloak and a few other things. He straightened up and walked back to Maya who was biting her lip watching the scene unfold in the field.

Krillin wasn't interested in that. As he stood behind Maya, he quickly threw his rope around her. She gasped and started to call for help. Krillin pulled her back and tied her to a tree. He stuffed his extra shirt in her mouth to quiet her. Then he checked her pockets and folds to make sure she didn't have a knife or anything to free herself.

"It's nothing against you, my lady. I just have things I have to do, and I can't worry about you trying to stop me." Krillin double checked his knots and then climbed up to the captain.

"I'm already tied up," the captain held his hands in the air to show he couldn't be tied up a second time.

"Shut up and let me untie you." Krillin fumbled with the knots for a minute before giving up. He pulled a blade out of the bag resting on the back of the creature and sliced through the captain's bonds. "There! Now we just have to find the package."

"The package?"

"That's what Bannon said. He said she had a package and that I was supposed to help you capture the princess and the package but if we couldn't save the princess just the package would do. Is this her bag?" Krillin was already pulling everything out. Nothing looked like it had value beyond what it was.

"I think the package in question is out there." Captain Dahel pointed at the fighting in the meadow.

"You take this elephantus and I'll get Jerky."

"Jerky? What kind of a name is that?"

"She likes jerky." Krillin shrugged and slid down. He ran to the horvelina. Then they raced to join the fight.

Chapter 30

Agonya was nonplussed. She knew the Montanes couldn't be trusted, but this? Almost as soon as she and Ashkii reached Aiden things turned sour. Aiden was sitting on the grass, staring at nothing. Ashkii started to explain the situation and that Aiden should give Blackthorn to Agonya, when he suddenly stopped talking and moved into a protective stance guarding not Agonya but Aiden!

She reached into his mind. The little hole he'd made was blocked up again. "Ashkii, let me in. Why are you doing this? I thought you decided to help me instead of hinder me."

Aiden stood up and prepared to fight Agonya as well. She couldn't get in his mind either. Agonya eyed the bag strapped across Aiden's back. She hoped Blackthorn was in there.

"Blackthorn? Are you here?"

There was no reply. Why wasn't he answering?

Ashkii clenched his jaws together so hard that Agonya snapped her eyes back to him.

"Go, your . . . H-Highness." Every word was forced out like it was the hardest thing for Ashkii to say.

"Not until you give me the Kindroot." Agonya held out her hand. Immediately, both men unsheathed their daggers.

Agonya reached for her own, but her bag was back with her elephantus. How could she have come out here so unprepared? She knew it was dangerous. Sticks! There weren't even sticks on the ground to defend herself because the trees were over fifty meters away in every direction!

Ashkii and Aiden took a step forward. Ashkii waved his daggers through the air. He didn't even notice his left hand bleeding again. How many times was he going to betray her?

Then she smelled it. Oakmoss. Rotten eggs.

Ashkii wasn't betraying her. Dana was controlling them. Agonya checked the wall around her mind even though she knew it was solid. Daggers swung towards her from every direction. Agonya ducked.

She had to get Blackthorn without hurting them. Guilt gnawed at her insides. She was the one that made Ashkii vulnerable. Twisting away from the attacking men, Agonya ran toward the elephantus. She moved to climb up, but Ashkii jumped in front of her.

She inhaled sharply, a deep breath in and smelled a clump of lemongrass at her feet. Instinctively, she pulled the citric scent inside. Then, she pushed her magic around her like a cloak. She began to glow again which stood out even more so than before in the darkening sky.

Aiden charged at her again and would have stabbed her in the gut if her shield of magic hadn't protected her. Instead, his daggers dropped to the ground. Ashkii jabbed at her from the other side. His daggers couldn't penetrate her shield either. But the force of them made Agonya fall backwards. She scrambled up and faced the two men who were now standing side by side, blocking her escape route.

Out of the corner of her eye Agonya saw Brynn lumbering towards them across the meadow. Turning from the Montanes, Agonya ran as fast as she could towards Brynn. If she couldn't get past Aiden and Ashkii, she'd try a different tactic. As she ran, Agonya quickly got inside Brynn's mind.

"Brynn! I'm going to try to build a wall around your mind before Dana gets in! She's controlling both of them." She didn't wait for a response but started creating a solid wall around his mind. She was halfway done when he was right next to her reaching a hand down to help her up. She jumped and grasped his hand at the same moment. Brynn pulled her up behind him and she continued to work on protecting his mind. Before she could finish, Dana's fog crept in. Agonya inhaled the smells around her, searching for more power to push Dana away. She felt Dana push back.

"Get away from him!" Agonya cried with all her strength and pushed Dana's magic fog out of his mind and sealed the wall. Like before when she used too much magic too soon, she found her strength leaving her. She slumped against Brynn.

"We must get Blackthorn! Aiden's bag . . ." She had to stay awake! No way was she going to give up so easily.

The next thing she knew Kyler was pushing and shoving Brynn trying to get to her. She totally forgot about Kyler. She'd been so focused on saving Brynn's mind she didn't even realize Kyler was sitting in front of him. Good thing Brynn was so strong, and Kyler was still tied up. Brynn easily knocked Kyler off the elephantus. He was almost trampled by Ashkii's elephantus running up next to them. He saw him in time though and veered away. Ashkii jumped down and cut Kyler's bonds. Kyler quickly climbed up and Ashkii followed, while avoiding the use of his injured hand.

In the meantime, Brynn and Agonya were approaching Aiden and his steed. Brynn gave Agonya the reins and jumped. He flew through the air, catching hold of a rope ladder. Climbing up, Brynn grabbed the bag hanging on Aiden's back. He tried to rip it off, but Aiden flattened himself, pinning Brynn beneath him. Brynn wrapped his free arm around Aiden's neck. Aiden choked and tried to pull Brynn's arm away.

Agonya reached into Aiden's mind and pried at the wall. Before she could breach it, Aiden lost consciousness. Brynn yanked the bag off Aiden's back and tossed it to Agonya right as her elephantus started picking up speed across the rest of the meadow. Ashkii and Kyler were right behind her; they passed Brynn and Aiden wrestling again and started to gain on her.

"Fight *her*, Ashkii. Not me!" Agonya shouted to him. She couldn't do it for him, but if he was able to build that wall in the first place maybe he could push her out. Agonya searched the bag Brynn tossed to her. Her hand felt something smooth and square, like glass. Digging further, her hand found the hilt of a knife. She grasped the leather and pulled it out just as Kyler jumped onto her elephantus. Agonya swiped at his feet. He stumbled and was falling but he was able to grab the rope ladder and climb back up. Agonya cut the rope. Kyler fell underneath the huge feet and was crushed, his insides spilling out of his chest.

The cheese and bread Agonya ate earlier involuntarily came up and out of her mouth. She tried to wipe it away from her mouth but couldn't. She had to keep going. And she was. Her elephantus was going somewhere. He sped up, faster and faster. He was out of her control. Agonya's heart sank. She had risked everyone's life by coming here for no reason. Blackthorn wasn't inside the bag. Dana must already have him.

They were almost to the trees. Ashkii followed close on her tail. She had no idea how Brynn was faring against Aiden, nor what the others were doing, whether they had decided to join the fray or not. She could only hope Maya was safe.

* * *

Maya was safe, safely tied to a tree. But she was none of Jaylen's concern. He was focused on steering his elephantus after Krillin and his horvelina. Praise the Patron of Fortune that Krillin was on his side! He rode into the treeless meadow not knowing what to expect. Only that with Krillin, they were evenly matched.

Jaylen approached two men fighting on the ground and slowed to get a better look. It was the balding Itholean and was that Kyler? No, the man looked too pale to be Kyler and didn't have any piercings. But then, where was he? An elephantus stood a few meters away, eating the grass unaware of the fighting going on around it. Jaylen peered toward the trees on the other side of the meadow. The queen was almost to the trees. "Krillin, over there!"

Together, they bolted after the queen. The horvelina pulled in front, faster than the elephantus, and yet Krillin was able to prepare his bow without losing his balance. Jaylen had seen good cavalry men, but Krillin was incredible. Would he make the shot?

The arrow soared through the air with as much speed and strength as the horvelina! Jaylen paled when he saw its target. It wasn't heading toward the Montane in pursuit of the queen, but the queen herself!

"Krillin! No! We want her alive." His words fell flat on the wind. Krillin was twenty meters away, closing the gap, and reloading his bow.

It hit him all at once like one of those storms they'd had recently. He felt it clawing its way into his mind. 'No!' He wasn't going to let her in again. How was she doing this? She was so far away and didn't even know he was pursuing her. But something felt different, more sinister and angry. Jaylen squeezed his eyes shut as if that would protect his mind and emotions. The smell of rotten eggs nearly made him gag. He hated eggs in all their forms.

There was no fighting it. He was trapped inside his own body. His eyes opened without his consent, and he urged the elephantus forward as fast as it would go. Images of slicing her beautiful head off her shoulders invaded his thoughts. 'Noooo! I don't want to!' He tried to pull the reins to stop the beast. He couldn't. He tried to roll off its back, but his muscles wouldn't work properly.

He had to outsmart whoever was behind this. But how? Just wanting to do the opposite of what he was doing wasn't working. He was getting closer to her every second. He knew that when he reached her, he would indeed slice her head off if he didn't figure out how to beat this mind control. He hadn't figured it out when she had been the one to put him to sleep either. What made him think he could do it now? Was that why the Mons had turned on her?

There was no time to ponder. Jaylen was approaching a body lying on the ground. He tried to not look at it; he knew it was Kyler. Jaylen swallowed the lump forming in his throat. Whoever was trying to control him couldn't stop his body from reacting to the death of his companion.

Jaylen rode into the darkened trees. What light remained from the sun was blocked by the thick pines towering over him. He thought he saw Krillin and the Montane who wouldn't work with him up ahead. They hadn't killed her yet either. Did that mean, they were fighting against this mind invasion, too?

Jaylen tried to focus on how angry he was about Kyler's death, but it was hard. Pictures of joining the other two to surround her, to cut off her escape flooded his mind. Then he was circling around. Her elephantus must have run off without her after she fell. Twigs and leaves stuck out of her hair, and she was covered with scrapes and bruises. He didn't know how much more of this she could take. He tried to stay on the elephantus, but his muscles were forced to jump down. His hand moved to the hilt of his sword.

Ashkii stood to his right pointing two daggers at her, his left hand was dripping blood all down his arm, but he didn't seem to notice or care. Krillin stood off to his left muttering. Jaylen strode forward without conflict! He wanted to go forward and apparently so did whatever was controlling his mind. Surely, for different reasons though. He wanted to hear what Krillin was saying.

"Pine . . ." Krillin's arm shook, "lavender . . ." the arrow slipped, "mint . . ." it was back in place, "pine . . ." he drew back the arrow, "lavender . . ." he let go, "mint." It flew too high. "Pine." Krillin forced out each word as though it were a sword stabbing an opponent. Jaylen's eyes widened in surprise. Krillin was fighting it and winning!

Jaylen's sword was suddenly in his hand. He didn't even remember the thought process for charging, but he was doing it. He lifted the sword and swiped it through the air. He swiped it too early and missed. The queen ducked and tried to roll out of the circle. Ashkii was waiting for her. She cried out in pain as a dagger sliced her arm. He'd thought it had sliced her arm but when she stood back up it wasn't bleeding.

She heard Krillin and turned to look at him. Jaylen's body moved forward on its own. Jaylen tripped on a root, breathing in a handful of dust. He coughed and sputtered. It was so hard to breathe. The queen jumped over him and ran. By the time Jaylen got back up she had disappeared into the trees. Krillin was still muttering and shooting arrows in all directions except hers. Ashkii, too, disappeared into the trees.

Jaylen sealed his mouth shut and pinched his nose the moment he started to smell the air again. His mind was clear! Just like that. It was the rotten egg odor that triumphed over him. He bent down and scooped up a handful of dirt and threw it in Krillin's face. He choked and breathed it in. He shook his head and quickly pulled his cloak across his face, hooking it on a button so it would stay in place. Such a useful design!

Brynn chose that moment to ride up next to them. "Why's he untied? I thought you were guarding him."

Krillin took a moment to answer and when he did, he made no sense. "I don't . . . justice for . . ." Krillin trailed off.

"I got loose and good thing, too" Jaylen interrupted. Krillin was going to ruin his cover if he wasn't careful. "Your little queen is in trouble."

"One wrong step and you're back in ropes, mister." Brynn frowned, pointing his finger at Jaylen's chest.

Jaylen saluted Brynn and ran after her. There was no time to think about what Brynn might or might not do because Jaylen was starting to gag again. He bent down for a third time and scooped up dust. His throat was so dry, and the dust made it worse, but thinking about water constantly was a lot better than thinking about killing the queen.

"Cover your face with your cloak," Krillin jogged up next to him.

"Got any water?"

"I left it behind. Why? Will it help defeat this sorceress?" Krillin didn't wait for an answer but saw something that made him detour to retrieve it. He came back with leaves.

"What are those for?"

"Mint," Krillin plucked a pinecone from a tree as they ran by, "pine. Just need lavender."

Jaylen laughed. "These will help us?"

"Yes. These have fragrances that will help."

"They are better than rotten eggs, I guess." Krillin was a little bit weird but hey if he had an idea Jaylen wasn't going to stop him.

Brynn rode past them, his spear ready to throw at the first sign of danger. Why wasn't he affected? Brynn didn't have a cloak or anything protecting his breathing. Jaylen didn't have much time to ponder this oddity because a drank jumped out at him, screeching at the top of its lungs. Jaylen unsheathed his sword and rolled to the side, slicing through the air as he went. The blade found its mark, cutting the creature's head clean off. Jaylen rolled to his feet and kept running.

Two more dranks came up behind him. Krillin spun around, still running, and shot both at the same time. Jaylen faced off still more approaching from the side. These must have been what attacked the village. They had that same screeching sound he'd heard from inside the aromatic house.

"What are these?" Krillin asked as he killed yet another.

"I heard someone call them dranks." Jaylen thrust his sword into another, cutting off its high-pitched scream. "These creatures attacked us in Tafka. Although I didn't see them, I heard them. I think they can spray acid or something."

"I don't know how to defend against acid." Krillin notched a few more arrows. "I don't see any more. Do you?"

"No. But I think I see an elephantus and people over there."

"What's the plan? Just going for the bag or helping protect her?"

Jaylen hadn't given it much thought. "Wait and see what happens. If they've already subdued Ashkii, they may want to tie me up again. Our rides are back in the meadow so maybe we should pretend until we have a better way of escape."

"I'll follow your lead, Captain."

Jaylen nodded and slowed down as he approached the company, sword at the ready.

Chapter 31

Huren stood just outside of the storage house and listened.

"You promised me." That was Lord Bykan's voice.

A guard answered him. "I know I promised the pomelo cedar perfume to you, but another lord came and bought it. What about this one? Look, it's even in a glass bottle."

Lord Bykan yanked the offered bottle out of the guard's hands and held it up to the light. "Very well. But next time, I won't let you off so easily."

Huren didn't need to hear any more. "What is the meaning of this?" he bellowed from the doorway. He stepped forward into the food distribution room. Here was the proof he'd been looking for. They were monopolizing the food distribution. This was completely unacceptable!

"Lord Bykan, explain yourself." Huren rested his hand on the pommel of his sword in case anyone decided to try to worm their way out of this.

"Lord Commander Huren! I did not expect to see you here. But I'm glad that you came. I've been meaning to have a word with you about all these ridiculous rules."

"You agreed to those ridiculous rules to begin with. Why didn't you speak your mind before we set the rules?"

"I didn't oppose them at the time. To be frank, I still think it's good to have rations. I just think it would be better to refine the way it's handled. The little nuances, if you catch my drift."

"Then you need to schedule a council meeting. You know the rules. There are consequences for breaking them. I can't start making exceptions. That goes for you too." Huren pointed at the two guards trying to fade into the corner of the room.

"Oh, but, really, you can't seriously be considering punishing me? Why, I'm a lord after all."

"Yes, and a lord who should know better. And these two have disobeyed their commander's orders. I can't have insubordination." Huren turned to his personal guards who had followed him into the room and were standing at the ready. "Take these two to the dungeon and I'll take care of Lord Bykan. Paytah, I want you to stand guard until I can arrange other matters."

"Yes, sir." Two of his guards surrounded one of the pilfering soldiers and his other two did the same to the second.

"Wait." Huren held out his hand to stop them. "I want your names."

The first looked at his feet when he spoke. "I'm Victor Nalel, sir."

But the second actually had the gall to look him in the eyes. "I'm Eli, sir, Eli Haven."

"You reported Krillin. Hypocrite." Huren spat on the ground and watched Joshua lead them out of the room to await their fate in the palace dungeons.

Huren tried to rub the wrinkles off his brow to no avail. "Come along, Bykan, let's get this over with. Do I need to tie you up or are you going to come willingly?"

"I'll come so long as you listen to reason."

"It's not me you have to worry about. The other councilors might not be as understanding as I am and to use your term and be quite frank, I'm not seeing a good reason." Huren gave him a slight push to get him moving and they walked out the door. He paused to lock up the room then they started walking to the courtyard.

He should have known it was Lord Bykan behind the stealing. Bykan never could live without the least bit of comfort without complaining about it to the whole world. He always had to have the latest item on the market.

"You know, it's because of them that I do it." Bykan nodded at the little children curled up on the ground, moaning from hunger.

"It's because you do this, that they don't get what they need," Huren countered.

"No, they don't get what they need because their parents don't give it to them. They keep all their shares for themselves."

"Or they sell it to someone like you." Huren sped up so he didn't have to keep looking at the babes lining the streets. The problem was Lord Bykan was partially right. They needed a better system so that their children were better taken care of. Everyone was feeling trapped in the city. Emotions were running high. Fights cropped up around just about every corner these days.

"Turn here." Huren headed towards the temple.

"Lord Tanish? Of all the council members we have to go to Tanish?"

"Lady Pelipa was the one you wanted to visit? I'm sure she would be the most understanding." Huren watched Bykan's face to see if his inclinations were right. Those two seemed to get along a little too well. The rumors were that they were a couple. Perhaps she was the reason for Lord Bykan's law-breaking.

Bykan didn't give anything away though. His face remained the same. "She at least wouldn't have some crazy religious ideas. She might actually give some credible solutions."

"You think I don't have better things to do with my time than deal with your foolishness? That is for all the councilors to discuss. No. I'm looking for answers to something else."

Lord Bykan raised both his eyebrows in curiosity.

Huren ignored Bykan and knocked on a very plain oak door.

* * *

Lord Tanish opened the door and ushered the men inside. After leaving Lord Bykan in the other room under guard, Huren followed Tanish into a smaller room at the back of the building. A small round table stood at the far wall.

Closing the door behind them, Tanish turned to Huren. "Tell me, friend, what brings you to my table? I am rather curious, since you don't like my advice very much."

Huren smiled. "I always see the other side to the argument, that's all. You think for yourself instead of going along with the group for peace's sake."

"I'm not the popular one, am I?"

"Ha! That's an understatement. But really, we should get to the point. First of all, Lord Bykan is here or in the other room because I caught him bribing my soldiers for extra food and perfumes."

"Oh. I suppose you want me to send messages for a council meeting."

"Yes, that would be greatly appreciated, seeing as how I'm containing the smoke."

"And second?"

"I was wondering if there have been any prophecies I ought to know about."

Tanish spit his tea out. "What brings this up? I thought you weren't a religious man."

"I may not be religious, but I believe in the god of Jedrek.

I saw a man earlier today who was going on and on about the end of the world. My first thought was that he was crazy, but I thought I'd double check with the expert, just in case."

"Did he say which patron this prophecy came from?"

"The patron of Rotten Fragrances."

Lord Tanish leaned back in his chair. "With the foreboding storms emitting that rotten egg scent, that doesn't surprise me. I'm not convinced they have anything to do with a god though."

"What do you think is causing them? And what do they mean?" The first storm that emitted rotten eggs was when they were on the battlefield. It was after that battle that King Azurarus decided to retreat.

"I think there is some sort of sorcery happening."

"Sorcery? You can't be serious. Magic is a thing of children's tales."

"Huren, why do you think Azurarus always burned incense? What do you think caused the queen's death? And have you not noticed how adept our new queen is at getting out of trouble?"

"Wait. Let me get this straight. Are you saying the royal family can all do magic?"

"Remember that package? Do you know what it was?"

Huren frowned. "He wouldn't tell anyone that! I begged him to tell me, but he refused even when he wanted to hand it off to me for protection."

"Exactly, that package screams magic to me. It's what our enemies are after, and I think they can do magic of their own. This last storm, mind you, had me feeling angry the entire time it lasted. And I never feel angry." Lord Tanish exhaled in an attempt to control his emotions.

"You certainly know how to argue for one who never feels angry." Huren had to laugh.

"Arguing and being angry are two very different things. I like to look at every side of the problem and this is a problem. Didn't you feel angry during the last storm? I mean more than usual and all the time." Tanish sipped his hot lemon water.

"I am angry most of the time these days so it's hard to say whether I was angrier or not. Lord Bykan for one is making me angry, the children fainting in the streets makes me angry, the king's death makes me angry." Huren sighed and pushed his chair back. "If you don't know of a specific prophecy then we must get going."

"I only know the histories." Lord Tanish set his cup on the table and walked Huren to the front door. "Oh, and Huren, magic is real. Of this I am certain."

Chapter 32

The men surrounding Agonya were all dangerous to her. They weren't currently trying to attack her, but that didn't mean Dana wouldn't seize control of their minds again or that they wouldn't try something of their own accord.

Ashkii slid his daggers into his cloak and stepped forward, holding his hands away from his body. "You're safe now. We won't hurt you."

"Give me a moment." Agonya stepped back, clutching the useless bag that Brynn had ripped from Aiken's back. Where was Blackthorn? She'd come all this way and he wasn't here. Ashkii had misled her again. How stupid could she be? Agonya turned away from the men and moved further away. She needed to think.

Opening the bag in her hands, Agonya tried not to think about how quickly Ashkii had turned against her in the meadow. Agonya inhaled the forest smells and peered inside Aiken's empty bag.

But it wasn't empty. A large amber square reflected her image up at her as if she were looking in a copper mirror, but it wasn't copper. Agonya reached inside and let her fingers glide over the cold odorless glass. Why was it square? All the glass she'd seen were vials, holding perfumes, but this had straight edges.

Agonya traced the sides. It was a solid box. She pulled her hand away ready to face the men and find Maya, but her finger caught on one of the edges and the top of the box lifted a fraction and fell back into place. For the briefest of moments, she thought she smelled something that wasn't there before. Something was in the glass box. Agonya pried the glass lid open. A sweet fruity scent escaped. "Blackthorn?"

A small leafy branch stretched up and out of the box. "Agonya?"

She touched the soft leaves and felt a huge weight of worry and fear flow out of her. She had found Blackthorn. The fight wasn't in vain. "I thought you weren't here because you didn't answer me. How–"

"I'm sorry. The glass blocks me from using magic. Will you help me out of here?"

Agonya reached her sweating hands into the box and slid her fingers around Blackthorn's pot. Not wanting the men to know she'd found "the package", Agonya was careful not to pull him out of the bag, only out of the glass. "I'm so sorry, Blackthorn. If I hadn't drawn strength from you when the Kors attacked us, you would have been able to defend yourself."

"It's not your fault. I'm glad you didn't hold back when our lives were in danger. If you had, we wouldn't be having this conversation."

This time Brynn stepped toward Agonya. "We can't stay here, your Highness. It's not safe."

Agonya reluctantly set Blackthorn down and withdrew her hand from the bag. Knowing that she had found Blackthorn and that he was alive helped her to think about what needed to happen next.

Glancing at the Korin captain standing beside Krillin, unbound, Agonya turned to face him. "I'm tired," she said. "Tired of being a prisoner and of imprisoning others. And since you did resist killing me, I'm not going to tie you up."

"Can you tell me what just happened? I thought you were controlling my mind until I was being forced to attack you. Don't worry, I think we're all done fighting for now."

"Yes, well, the short of it is that the Sorceress Dana turned you all against me. And one hint of it happening again, either from her control or your own choice, I will bind you."

Jaylen grimaced. "You know that I have orders. Perhaps we can come to an arrangement without fighting."

"One step out of line and we will subdue you. Now. I don't know why Dana stopped attacking us, maybe she ran out of strength. While we have this chance to rest, we should gather the elephantus and make sure Maya is well." Agonya began to walk back towards the meadow.

"One more thing, if I may," Jaylen said, falling into step beside her. "I'd like to bury my friend."

"Granted. Brynn? What happened to Aiden?"

"Dead, your Highness. It was self-defense. He would have killed me if I hadn't choked him first."

"Very well. We ought to give him a proper burial as well. Let's get going."

Brynn climbed onto the elephantus and beckoned for Agonya to join him. Once Agonya was seated, Ashkii jumped up and sat behind her. But there was nothing for Krillin and Jaylen to ride.

"You'll have to walk back. I'll send Brynn with another elephantus as soon as possible. Krillin, don't let him out of your sight."

The elephantus jerked forward and Ashkii instinctively grabbed onto Agonya's waist. Filled with irritation, Agonya was about to forcibly remove his hands when she saw blood dripping onto her dress.

"Ashkii, your hand!"

He let go and tried to pull his hand away from her. "It's nothing."

Agonya grasped his hand in hers and let the magic flow. She could feel her strength leaving her, not that she had much to begin with. That fight had taken most of her energy, she didn't even know she had this much to give to Ashkii. Slowly the wound in his hand closed and the redness of the infection started to fade.

“My hand–”

“You can thank me later. I need to rest.” She was done talking with the traitor Montane. What she really needed was to finish her conversation with Blackthorn.

“It is my fault,” she sent to Blackthorn. “What did they do to you?”

“I passed out helping you fight that Kor. When I woke up, I was in that accursed cage. I tried connecting with you, but I couldn’t smell you. They didn’t harm me. All I need is water.”

Agonya searched for a water skin. “Aha. Here you go.” Agonya lowered the opened water skin into the bag and watched Blackthorn’s roots climb out of his pot and dip into the water. He looked so dull. The instant he touched the water he started to glow. His drooping orange leaves perked up and his colorful berries began to round out their shrunken forms.

“Agonya, find Maya.”

“Is she okay?”

“She is, but she needs you.”

Agonya searched for Maya’s scent wishing she’d done it earlier but knowing she hadn’t had the time. Agonya called her name over and over on the winds of the fragrances.

“Agonya!”

Praise the god of Jedrek. Maya was safe.

“Krillin is the one who stole my candle! He is the traitor!”

“Your candle? What candle?”

“You know, before we left Ithol, before your father died.”

Maya didn’t need to say anymore. Agonya knew exactly what she was talking about. “Are you sure?”

“Positive.”

“But he just saved my life,” Agonya protested more to herself than to Maya.

“He tricked me and tied me up. Then he set Jaylen free. He’s definitely working for the Kors. He even said something about his orders from Commander Bannon and needing to find a package.”

Agonya groaned. That was the last thing Agonya wanted to hear. She didn’t need more traitors surrounding her. What was she going to do?

“What’s the matter?” Ashkii asked.

Agonya ignored him and sent her thoughts to Maya. “Does he know what the package is?”

“No, I don’t think so. Neither does Jaylen but they rode off before I could hear the whole conversation.”

“Are you hurt?” Agonya would lose it if he had hurt Maya in the process.

“No, just uncomfortable. I don’t think he enjoyed tying me up. He just needed to, so he could free Jaylen and get the package.”

“I’m coming to you now as soon as I can.”

There was so much she needed to think about.

“Agonya?”

“I’m fine, Ashkii. But he isn’t.” Agonya pointed to Kyler's body, lying mangled on the open field.

“I'll start burying him.” Ashkii made to get off the elephantus, but Agonya stopped him.

“No, I need you to get Krillin and the Kor. It’ll take too long if we have to wait for them to walk all the way back.”

Brynn directed their elephantus towards the others grazing in the meadow. Ashkii jumped the distance between the animals, landing softly on its back. The elephantus didn’t seem to notice Ashkii at all.

Brynn steered their elephantus toward the other not too far away. When they were close enough, Agonya balanced on her feet and jumped onto its furry back. Her feet slipped and she started to fall backward. Agonya clawed at the ropes in front of her and pulled herself up. Why couldn’t she be as smooth as Ashkii who was already galloping beneath the trees?

Alone with the only one she trusted, she turned to Brynn. “I need you to bury Aiden while I go untie Maya.”

“What? Maya's tied up? But, that traitor! I'm going to kill the Kor.” Brynn’s hand flew to the shaft of his spear.

“Krillin tied her up. He also freed the Kor. Don't do anything rash, Brynn. He will pay for his crimes but for now he thinks I don't know of his treachery which means he will work with us until he gets what he wants. I intend to get as much from him as possible. I suppose as soon as he discovers I’ve found Maya he might try something. That's why I need you to keep an eye on him, on both of them.”

Then mostly to herself, she added, "While I'm sorry about the loss of that soldier, I am grateful he is one less man I have to worry about betraying me."

Brynn nodded. "You can count on me, your Highness."

"Thank you." Agonya rode off toward the spot where she'd left Maya. She made it sound so simple and easy just now, but Agonya really had no idea how everything was going to work out. She wanted to be friends with everyone, to end all this fighting and manipulating.

"Blackthorn, I think you ought to go into hiding. It's you they want."

"I don't ever want to leave your side again, but I understand why you would say that. Dana is coming for me. She knows I'm here. We need to move quickly."

"How soon do you think she'll get here?"

"She could be here within the hour."

"That soon?"

"I can smell her if I concentrate hard enough."

"We should be quick then." Agonya slid the bag with Blackthorn in it over her shoulders before sliding off the elephantus. It was darker under the trees, and it took her a minute to find Maya. As soon as she saw her, Agonya rushed over and cut her bonds.

"Are you all right?"

"I've been thinking, seeing how I haven't been able to do anything else for a while."

"Yes?"

"I think we ought to make it look like a wild animal got me. If I'm dead, then perhaps Krillin will think he got away with it. Then I can spy on him without him noticing me."

"How are you going to keep up with us? We've all got elephantus and a horvelina to ride."

"I've got an idea about that too."

What Maya said, seemed to make sense. The longer Krillin believed she didn't know about him, the longer he would pretend to work for her. Agonya couldn't afford another fight. Not right after the last one.

"Very well. How are we going to do this?"

* * *

Krillin walked fast but not without looking for lavender, the last ingredient he needed in case the sorceress tried to invade his mind again. He had been sure magic didn't exist. That was until someone else started controlling his actions. He recognized that blend of odors: the oakmoss, rotten eggs, and an odor he couldn't name but was still familiar with. It wasn't the first time he'd smelled the combination. That storm had reeked of it.

"I think you're safe, Krillin."

"Huh?"

"She doesn't know you're working with me. That means it'll be easier to find that package we're looking for."

"She will know as soon as she sees Maya though. I imagine the next time we see her she'll want our heads." Krillin pictured her Highness finding Maya all tied up and becoming outraged. It would not be a good thing to be around when that happened.

What was happening with her body glowing? He assumed it meant she could do magic, just like whoever had been trying to control his mind. "What do you know about what the queen can do?" Krillin asked.

"One time she made me fall asleep."

"Really?"

"She got in my mind like the sorceress did but it was different."

"How do you mean? It sounds the same to me." Krillin smelled lavender, so he dashed away to pick it.

"Krillin?" Jaylen called after him.

"I found it," Krillin said as he bounded back to Jaylen's side.

"Found what?"

"Lavender. Here, take some."

Jaylen hesitated but took what Krillin offered him.

"These should help protect us, I think. From the sorceress, and the queen."

Jaylen's eyes widened. "How do you know?"

"I know fragrances." Wasn't it obvious? "How was it different?"

"You know fragrances?" Jaylen chuckled. "If I put any fragrance in front of you, you would know what it is?"

"Yes."

"What if I mixed lots of fragrances? Would you be able to tell me all the ones I used?"

"Yes."

"I'm impressed. I've never met anyone who could do that."

"How is the queen entering your mind different from the sorceress?" Krillin was getting so tired of asking the same question over and over again. Why was Jaylen so interested in his ability to know smells? What he really needed to know was how the two experiences were different, and if he needed other ingredients.

"I think the odors were different and oh, I don't know! It just was."

A lot of help he was. As they continued to step over tree roots and duck under branches Krillin started mashing all three, the mint, the pinecone scales, and lavender in the palms of his hands.

"Here, grind these up and mix them together." Krillin handed some to Jaylen. He might as well help. There were two of them that needed it.

"What do I do with it when I'm done?"

"Hmmm. I think I have some vials in my bag back on Jerky."

Just then the big man with the balding head rode up on an elephantus.

"Get on."

Jaylen climbed up first then Krillin, being careful not to drop the leaf mixture he was working on. It was a short ride to the meadow.

"There he is." Brynn turned towards Kyler's empty shell.

"Wait. Can we go to Jerky first?"

"What's jerky?"

"She's the animal I was riding. I need some vials from my bags."

"What do you need vials for? We are in a bit of a hurry."

Jaylen extended his open hand for Brynn to see. "Krillin thinks this mixture will help us if the sorceress comes for us again."

Brynn studied it for a moment, nodded and changed directions. Jerky wasn't too far away and the elephantus made quick work getting to her. Krillin jumped down and landed on Jerky's back. He patted her to reassure the beast. Then he searched pockets until he came up with a couple empty bottles.

"I'll follow on Jerky." Krillin didn't want to be far from an escape if he could help it.

They retrieved Kyler and met Ashkii who was already digging a hole for Aiden. The dirt smelled dry and grassy. A comforting smell, Krillin worked contentedly. Jerky even helped, loosening the dirt with her tusks and Krillin would move it out of the way.

When he looked up, everyone was staring at him. "What? Did I do something wrong?"

Ashkii laughed. "No! I've just never seen a horvelina help a human before! You're a good team." The others joined in the laughter. "Oh, and I think that's enough."

Krillin stood up and brushed his hands on his pants, hopping out of the grave meant for two. Two men he didn't know. He had met Kyler briefly before he rode into battle. He seemed like a nice enough guy.

"I'd like to say a few words." Jaylen raised his voice.

"Where's her majesty? Shouldn't she be here for this?" Krillin looked to Ashkii and Brynn.

Brynn was the one who spoke first. "She went to make sure Maya was okay. They should be here soon."

Krillin's heart skipped a beat. He knew this was coming, but he wasn't ready for it. Jaylen must have sensed his anxiety because his scent grew stronger even though he stood calmly.

Krillin squinted into the growing darkness and sniffed the air. The queen rode her elephantus towards them. She was alone. Where was Maya? Maya couldn't have gone anywhere. She was tied to a tree when he left her. Krillin closed his eyes. Maybe he just couldn't see her riding behind the queen.

He could smell Maya's scent but only the queen slid off the elephantus and joined the men standing around the large grave. Her face was streaked with tears and mud.

"Where's Maya?" Brynn whispered. He must be afraid of the answer. Krillin certainly was, but not for the same reason Brynn was. Krillin was afraid he'd been the cause of harm to her and that he was found out and would soon have to be the cause of death to most everyone standing around him. He only had a few arrows left. Most had been used trying to avoid killing her majesty. He didn't know why he had worked so hard not to kill her. She wasn't needed alive. In fact, her being alive just made his life harder. On the return journey back to the meadow Krillin had spotted a few arrows and was able to retrieve those but he was nearly out. Not enough for the three he would kill, if they tried blocking him. If he was really fast, he might succeed, but . . .

"She," Agonya sucked in a deep breath, "Maya's dead." Agonya covered her trembling mouth.

"Dead? Impossible! How? Where?"

"A drank." Agonya's voice cracked as she said it.

Brynn was nearly on his elephantus when the queen stretched out her arm, blocking him. She looked up at her own elephantus to where Maya was wrapped in a blanket. Krillin immediately went to Brynn's side. This was his chance to make sure he wasn't suspected.

"Help me move her," Krillin tugged on the Itholean's hand to get him to snap out of his shock. It didn't matter that Brynn was from Ithol. Krillin remembered feeling like that twice in his life. The key was to keep moving. If you stopped, you might never start moving again.

They carefully lifted her down into the grave, her black hair tumbling out of the blanket. She was so light and smelled of acid, like that creature that attacked them earlier.

Brynn fell on top of her, weeping as though she had been his wife or sister. He started to unwrap the blanket. The queen was at his side in an instant.

"Let her rest in peace. Remember her the way she was the last time you saw her. Finding her like this . . . I won't ever be able to get that image–" the queen choked on her words.

Brynn stood and wrapped his arms around her Highness. "I won't look. You do not need to see her again like that. It's just that, I loved her. I loved that she couldn't wash our burns because she didn't want to cause us more pain. I never told her . . ." Brynn trailed off, letting the tears fall silently now.

The queen walked back to the elephantus and came back with something in her hands. It reeked! Krillin gagged. She held it up for them to see and then tossed it in the grave. "May these scents help us to remember the pain of losing our friends."

"We remember," they said in unison.

The queen wiped her hands clean on some grass before pulling out a bottle of perfume from her pocket. She uncorked it and waved the minty aroma around for everyone to breathe in, dumping just a few drops into the grave. "May these scents help us to heal though our friends cannot be healed."

"We will heal."

One by one they waved their hands across the grave and inhaled the blended scents. Then they finished covering the dead beneath the dirt.

Krillin kept glancing at the queen while he worked. Even if a drank had killed Maya, wouldn't she have seen the ropes he'd used to tie her up? Maybe acid burned them away. She must know that Krillin was the one who left Maya defenseless against any animals that might venture her way or she wouldn't let him remain free. It was his fault her friend was dead. For that he was truly sorry, but he was safe for now and could try to find that package without killing anyone else.

Chapter 33

Agonya could only dredge up her worst memories for so long. She'd had to do it so the others would believe the lie. Brynn almost discovered the truth, but he still didn't know what they had buried next to Aiden and Kyler. When Maya made her chop off those lovely locks of hair, Agonya had felt a twinge of sadness at the loss. But it worked.

Agonya turned her back on the grave. "It's time. We need to get back to Ithol."

Brynn wiped his tears and followed her to the elephantus. Krillin was already on his horvelina.

"Where's Aiden's elephantus?" Agonya could only see three from her vantage point, the ones they'd ridden to find Blackthorn on. Of course, she knew where the stray one was.

"Must have run back home," Ashkii said with a shrug. "Here, we can share one." He gave her a boost onto the elephantus he'd chosen to ride and climbed up behind her.

Jaylen and Brynn each got their own and they were soon all headed back down the mountain path the way they'd come before.

"Is there not a quicker way to Ithol from here or must we go back through the village to get there?"

“I have a map, your Highness, perhaps it’ll show us another way.” Krillin pulled out a very battered parchment and studied it for a moment. “We can take this trail for a bit. Once we reach this spot,” he pointed to somewhere on the map, “we can veer off to the southeast. We’ll have to cut through the forest without a path for a little while, but we’ll eventually meet back up with one that will take us straight there.”

“Good. We’ll follow you since you know where to turn.”

Ashkii held their elephantus back for Krillin to pass, then they continued lumbering forward. Agonya wasn’t quite sure what to expect. Would Golar hold his end of the bargain? She doubted it. That meant she probably didn’t have to keep her word to marry the man sitting behind her. Even with his betrayals his blue poppy musk put her at ease. Agonya inhaled deeply and tried to identify the other scents around her besides Ashkii’s. Could she count on him to do the right thing? He seemed to have changed but she had to find a way to help her people with or without him. They needed her now more than ever.

“How are you holding up?” Ashkii’s arms were extended on either side of her, holding the reins from behind.

“How do you think?”

“I think you are not showing your grief because you don’t want to think about it.”

“I cannot think about it,” Agonya agreed. “I have to think about what happens next. I have to think about the people suffering in Ithol. I am their queen, am I not?”

“Yes, but even queens can mourn for the loss of their friends and family.”

Agonya didn’t quite know how he wanted her to respond. Was he saying she needed to cry more? There would be time for that later. Hopefully, she wouldn’t have to cry for Maya for a long time to come. Her father, on the other hand . . . and her mother. She couldn’t remember ever having a good cry for her. Whenever she did start crying for her mother, she tried to think of something else, to shove that memory down every time it tried to pop into her mind. Not even when she forced herself to cry for Maya did she think about her mother. She had cried for her father instead.

“You’re forgetting that I am a queen whose country is at war. Maybe if I was the same person you met before we left the city I would listen to your advice, but I’m not. I still cannot trust you.”

“But I didn’t kill you!”

“Ha! Neither did Captain Jaylen Dahel.”

“What didn’t I do?” The Kor called from behind them.

Sticks! Agonya had to be more careful. “You didn’t kill me, right?” She couldn’t afford to let him hear anything of importance.

The Kor leaned forward so as not to yell. “Nope, didn’t kill you. Isn’t that why you didn’t tie me up again?”

Ashkii ignored him as if he’d never entered the conversation. “What I meant was even though Dana was in my mind and trying to make me kill you, I resisted.”

“I appreciate you not killing me, but it doesn’t mean I trust you. Just like Jaylen back there, he was fighting the sorceress too. He avoided killing me, but that doesn’t excuse his past behavior towards me, and it doesn’t excuse your past behaviors either.”

“I let down my guard to show you I was trustworthy and now you’re saying that’s not enough. To make myself vulnerable to her in the first place and what for?”

“You did do that. I am sorry I put you in that position in the first place. It couldn’t be helped. I haven’t said a word about your wall since then. If your stealing,” Agonya lowered her voice, “him, was the only thing you’d done to let me down then I might have called it even.”

“What else have I done?”

Agonya could tell his whole body was tensed up now even though she was avoiding touching him at all costs which was proving to be difficult.

“How did this become all about you, Ashkii? I thought you were concerned for me about what I was going through.”

“I was, I am. I didn’t mean to,” Ashkii couldn’t find the right words.

Agonya took the reins from Ashkii so that his arms would stop brushing against her and ignored his pleas.

“Why so silent, your Highness? I feel like I was just getting to know you,” Jaylen called up to them.

"Be content with what you heard and be quiet." He couldn't have heard her whispering, could he?

"He heard you, but he doesn't know what it means," Blackthorn offered. "He is curious though if what you were talking about is the package."

"Here I go again," Agonya thought to Blackthorn. "Will I ever learn to keep my mouth shut?"

"Sometimes I think all this secrecy is a bad thing. What if more people knew the truth?"

Agonya had to think about that. Maya knew and that had made all the difference. But she couldn't trust anyone else. "Have you been keeping track of Maya? I fear she's taken on too much."

"She's not far behind. I smelled her as we passed. You did well in disguising her scent. I don't think any of the others noticed."

That was a relief. Agonya worried about that. "What can you tell me about Krillin? It makes me sad that I can't trust him either."

"I like him. He is one of the reasons I think secrecy might not be the best approach all the time."

"What's so different about him? Why him and not the others?"

"He says what he means," Blackthorn replied. "He does what he says, but more importantly there's a reason he started working for the Kors and it is not a bad one. I often think the Itholeans have not proved themselves as a people worthy to defend."

Agonya regretted sighing as soon as she started, but it was too late to stop. Ashkii was sure to question her about it. But he just wrapped his arm around her instead. Agonya stiffened. Didn't he realize he was already standing close to the edge? Agonya clenched her teeth and took a deep breath intending to try and be civil about her reprimand to him. When Blackthorn spoke in her mind. "Ashkii isn't worthy of defending."

"You're right. He has betrayed us. But how can you be so sure that he'll do it again? I had to build a wall around my mind just like Ashkii. I think that's why he had a wall in the first place, because of her. It doesn't excuse his actions of taking you from me. I was devastated when I discovered you were gone, but he helped me find you again."

"You think he might be like Krillin then? Unaware of what he was doing?"

"Oh, he knew what he was doing to an extent, but he was also following orders. He didn't know you either. Not knowing a thing can blind someone to the right thing to do."

"Is that why you are so slow to act?"

Agonya sat up straighter. "Ashkii, you want my trust, do you not?"

"I do."

"There are things that'll need answering before that can happen. I'm not sure that now is the time and place to ask those questions." Agonya motioned to the presence of the others in front and behind them.

"There is a way around that," Ashkii began.

"Wait? You would do that?" Agonya twisted around in her seat to look him in the eyes, to make sure he was serious.

Ashkii turned away to look at the trees passing by. "Yes," he whispered.

"What did I tell you, Blackthorn?" Agonya thought excitedly.

"Be careful. Don't get too excited. He could still be trying to trick you. Remember how he befriended your father and yourself?"

"You were just saying secrecy wasn't always the best idea, right? I should find out what happened."

Blackthorn didn't reply. He tended to do that: just stop talking to her before Agonya was ready to be done, or he would interrupt whatever conversation she was having with others and expect her to switch between the two. He had no concept of conversation etiquette. But she loved him for it.

"I'm waiting."

Agonya let his voice pull her back out of her own thoughts. "Is it a one-way street? Can't you come to me too?"

"While I have mastered the wall, I have yet to acquire the ability to reach out the other way."

"Here it goes, then," Agonya closed her eyes and breathed in his scent.

Ashkii shifted behind her. She sensed he was uncomfortable. Too bad. He could deal with it. He had made her uncomfortable earlier too. As she approached his mind, she could tell that his whole wall was down, not just that tiny little section that would be easily filled if need arose.

"Ashkii? Can you hear me?" Agonya thought.

"What do you think?" he snapped.

"Sticks! I can't even ask a simple question without a mean response."

"Sorry. So why is it you can't trust me apart from the fact that I took the Kindroot from you."

"You were planning on doing that from the moment we met, right?"

"Yes."

"Why didn't you take him in the beginning? You could have stolen him and left us as captives in the Korin camp. You would have been rid of me and done what you set out to do at the same time."

"Ahh. That's not exactly what would have happened. I'm not saying I know what would have been or anything but say I had wanted to steal him from you; the first chance at doing so would have been at Brynn's while you were sleeping. I could have taken him and gone home before the captain even arrived. In that case I wouldn't have known you were going to be captured and therefore I couldn't be sure you wouldn't follow me, then my cover would have been ruined."

"But even before that you could have left me to be killed by that assassin in the city."

"These are all reasons why you should trust me, not why you shouldn't."

"But you knew that assassin, didn't you?"

"What? How could I have known him? Are you saying I didn't kill him to protect you? Unbelievable!" Ashkii threw his hands in the air.

"He was a Montane."

"I don't believe you."

"That's why I can't trust you. You won't even admit you knew the assassin. You didn't kill him. You convinced him or planned with him for you to pretend to kill him to make it look like I could trust you in the first place. Which means you wanted me alive for some reason that I haven't quite figured out."

Ashkii tried to keep his mind blank, but Agonya could feel his agitation building. He knew she could feel it too. There was no hiding this time. If he really wanted her to trust him, he'd have to come clean.

"How do you know this?"

"I can't tell you that. Many lives are at stake."

"Yes. I knew him. No. I did not kill him. Yes. We planned to make it look like I saved you. You think we were just going to hand the Kindroot over to Dana without doing a little research of our own?"

Now it was Agonya's turn to pull away. "I'm an experiment, am I?"

"Yes. No. It started out that way. But you are too kind and noble and beautiful. The hardest thing I ever did was taking the Kindroot from you and delivering it to my father. You've got to believe me. I didn't want to."

"Is your father doing what I asked of him?"

"I do not think so."

"What do you think he will do now?"

"I can't be certain but if I were to guess. I think he will be preparing to stop your return to Ithol. He probably didn't expect you to succeed in retrieving the Kindroot and knew it was too late to stop Dana the Sorceress from taking it. The next best thing is to take you hostage again."

"You don't think he learned from the first time? He can't keep me hostage!"

"You don't know my father like I do. You can be sure he is coming up with a way to do it."

"You'll have to help me then. Help me find a way around whatever Golar is planning."

"The easiest answer is for you to marry me."

"Unless Golar helps my people, you know I cannot. I will not do that if he breaks our covenant."

"They are beyond our reach. You must know that by now. Even if we convince the other tribes to join us, we are still too few to battle the Korins and win."

Agonya wouldn't hear anymore. She sat up straight and noticed their elephantus was now at the back of the procession.

"Agonya, wait!" Ashkii had to use his voice to get her attention.

Agonya didn't care anymore. Ashkii was still only concerned about himself. "I don't want to hear it," she replied out loud.

"You've got to understand."

"No. What you need to understand is that I am their queen. If I cannot defend them, what does that make me? Why would a marriage between us help if I do not have a people to call my own?"

"I know someone you could marry that would save your people," Jaylen said.

"No one asked you."

"No, but seriously, Prince Lucas is mostly agreeable. Somewhat arrogant but agreeable."

"I cannot marry my own cousin."

"Why not? Afraid he'll kill you like your father killed our princess?"

Agonya stiffened. "Is that what you think? That my father killed my mother?" The very thought was outrageous! She couldn't contain the raging river inside her. It bubbled out of her, making her glow brightly in the darkness of the night.

"Whoa! Calm down. I was just saying what was true. Everyone knows how it happened."

"Is that so? Were they there to witness it?"

"King Reid was."

"Did you ever stop to think that maybe King Reid is a liar?" Agonya punched her words at him. Ashkii put his hand on her shoulder as if that would help her calm down. She shook it off.

"No, you didn't, did you? Well, I was there. Did you know that? Did you know I watched my mother die right before my very eyes? To the contrary, my father wasn't anywhere near us when it happened. Uncle Reid is the reason she died. He killed her with his greed."

"You say it was his greed that killed her? How's that even possible? He went to visit his sister because he loved her and wanted to make sure she was well."

"Ha! He has blocked the scent from your nose if you believe that dung. He came because he wanted something that my mother had. He tried to force her to give it to him. It wasn't hers to give. She resisted and died because of it."

"If he really is the reason she died and you saw the whole thing, why didn't he kill you too?"

Agonya sat back down. When had she stood up? "Because I was hiding behind the vines. I'd been playing hide and seek with . . . with Maya. He didn't know I was there."

Jaylen rubbed his chin. "If that's true, then that might explain why King Azurarus attacked us first. That part of the story always did feel a little off. I still think you should marry Prince Lucas. Even if what you say is true, no one will listen to you unless you meet the King's demands first."

"I cannot marry his son. I will not, unless there is no other way. I would rather die to protect what my mother died protecting than surrender."

Chapter 34

The descent down the mountain was uneventful. No more dranks, and no scent storm. Except, there was one night Brynn woke up pale as a ghost, vomiting the previous night's dinner of roasted squirrels. By the morning, he was feeling better and no one else seemed to be showing any signs of sickness.

For the most part, the men didn't bother Agonya with any more questions. She did not offer anything either. Instead, she worried that she'd said too much. If they'd changed their minds about her, they didn't let on.

Ashkii, if anything, was kinder to her since their talk, offering to do the little things for her, like helping her up and down the elephantus or giving her the best part of the meals. The others didn't object. In fact, this worked in her favor. Agonya was able to sneak extra food to leave out for Maya, who was keeping an eye on Krillin and Jaylen. If they left the camp together, Maya would follow them to hear what they said. She had to constantly disguise her scent so Krillin wouldn't smell her. So far, it was working. He hadn't noticed her.

Their conversations mostly obsessed with finding the package. Their talk about it was changing though. Maya told

Agonya she thought they were less inclined to take whatever it was from her than before. They didn't agree with each other most of the time and that was the only reason they were still behaving for the most part. Until they agreed on the right course of action, they were stuck escorting the queen. It was the surest way to get back to the battle where they wanted to be anyway. There was time enough for binding the queen and stealing the package once they were within riding distance of the camp.

After a few days of traveling like this, Agonya heard water flowing swiftly in the distance.

"Do you hear the river? It can't be far now." Agonya mused.

"Two days' ride from here," Ashkii replied.

"What's the point of having a map?" Krillin muttered, stuffing the map he'd been pulling out back into his bag. "Do you have one in your head?"

"You think you're the only one with a talent? I know this land extremely well."

"Speaking of my talent, I smelled something these last few days. At first, I attributed it to our elephantus, but I can definitely smell someone following us."

"Are you sure?" Agonya tried to keep the panic off her face. Was this it? The time for Maya to be discovered?

"Positive. Maybe I should go check it out."

Agonya's heart sped up. "I'm sure it's nothing," she said, trying to dissuade them from investigating. Then she reached out to Maya's mind to warn her.

Krillin sniffed the air. "There's definitely another elephantus behind us. And it's not alone," Krillin said again.

"Come. You can show me where this scent is coming from," Ashkii jumped onto Jerky and sat behind Krillin.

"Maya!" Agonya screamed in her thoughts. "Disguise your smell and get away from the elephantus!"

Agonya hated for Maya to be discovered, because then she would lose her advantage over these men. But she couldn't do anything except wait and watch Ashkii and Krillin disappear on the path directly toward Maya.

"No need to be frightened," Jaylen said, as he walked over to her.

"What makes you think I'm scared?"

"Maybe, it's the way you're biting your lip," Brynn said.

Agonya stopped biting her lip. "I just don't like splitting up."

"We could follow them if that'll make you feel better."

"That's okay. I'm sure it's nothing. They'll be back before we know it."

"In that case," Brynn said. "I suppose we ought to discuss what the plan is once we reach the city."

"Yes, what is your plan?"

Agonya stood between the two men who were both staring at her expecting her to have some brilliant idea. She still didn't know what they were going to do once they got there.

"I suppose that depends on what we find once we arrive. Whether we sneak in or not. If Golar keeps to our covenant, we'll be able to join in the fighting. Unfortunately, I have a feeling he will break it. One night of being more powerful than Golar isn't enough for a man like him to suddenly take orders from a woman like me. We should scout out what's up ahead before going too much further." Agonya's thoughts were all a jumble. There were too many possibilities.

"Got it!" Krillin called.

Ashkii rode the elephantus into camp behind Krillin. "Looks like Aiden's."

"I'm still on edge," Krillin admitted. "I think there was a rider too but we couldn't find him."

"I told him the rider he smelled was Aiden's lingering scent."

"Well, I suppose I don't have to share an elephantus now. We each can have our own."

"Ashkii, Her Highness suggested we scout out what lies ahead before going any further," Brynn said. "You're probably the best one to do that. Since you know this land."

Ashkii turned to Agonya. "Are you okay with me going? Do you trust me?"

"I don't trust you. But I think I have no choice but to rely on you. Go. Be quick. Don't be seen by anyone."

Ashkii turned the new elephantus off the path towards Ithol and disappeared into the forest again.

"What do you think, Blackthorn? Can I trust him?"

"I do not know. For me, it is still hard to trust any human. However, what you said the other day about dying for me and that scent that you chose to follow to come rescue me when you could have gone with the Montanes to reinforce Ithol has earned my trust in you. Now, whether or not you can trust him, I think you can learn something of what lies ahead. Perhaps, Maya can follow him."

Agonya would have thought her failure to keep him safe would have revoked his trust in her. "I really meant what I said, Blackthorn. I will die protecting you if I must."

"Hopefully, it won't come to that."

Inhaling, Agonya sorted through all the scents around her until she found Maya's disguise. "Are you okay? I'm sorry I screamed at you. I'm afraid I must ask you to go ahead on foot."

"No worries, my lady. I'm happy to do it. All this riding is tiresome. It'll be nice to stretch my legs."

"The closer we are to the city the more danger there will be. I'm sure of it. Do you think you can go ahead of us and see what we are up against?"

"I haven't been caught yet."

"Oh, and you should know that Ashkii is scouting out the situation and should report back."

"I'll be careful. Don't worry."

Chapter 35

Huren was stewing about the council's decision to pardon Lord Bykan. It was ridiculous. For once in his life, he agreed with Tanish against all of the other councilors. They didn't understand their situation clearly. They thought the winter weather would come and force the Kors to retreat before they ran out of food. But Ithol was no longer the Paradise it used to be. And even though it was cold enough for snow, there was no moisture in the sky. The Kors weren't going to back down anytime soon.

Huren stepped inside one of the food storage rooms, the one Bykan had been stealing from. The ground under his feet shook and rumbled. He braced himself against the doorframe. The rumbling grew louder and louder. It didn't take more than a moment to regain his balance and rush back outside to see what was happening. Dust rose into the air about a hundred meters away. Right where the city wall had been standing a moment before. It was crumbling even as he gaped at it.

He snapped out of his shock. "Go! Blow the horn! Defend the city!"

Huren ran as fast as he could toward the wall. The whole city was in chaos now. Women and children were crying and screaming, some of them getting trampled by others trying to get away.

He saw a soldier nearby. "You there!"

"Yes, sir?"

"Help the women and children get to safety."

"Yes, sir!" the man turned back.

"The palace. Take them to the palace grounds," Huren commanded.

The soldier nodded and started to gather those who couldn't or shouldn't fight. Huren continued running.

He saw stones crushing a man here, a woman there and even children. There were people all along the path of destruction crushed by chunks of the wall. There were dead Itholean soldiers lying on top, fallen from the great heights of the wall to their deaths below.

Moments later, Kors started pouring into the city as fast as climbing over rubble and dead bodies would allow. Huren drew his sword and moved into the familiar stance. His heart pounded and he could smell the scents of war. He was ready for it, ready to fight, ready to not be so useless anymore. As soon as he got close enough to the enemy, he would strike them down.

Huren shouted out orders to his soldiers as he saw them, forming groups to block streets and alleyways. Then the advancing enemies were on him. Sweat ran down his body. He swung his blade.

A group of about ten men surrounded him. They fought well. He was proud of them for responding so quickly. It felt good to finally hold a sword in his hands. To feel the raw strength and power flow through him. No more sitting behind desks and trying to please the council.

"This is it," he thought. There was no escape now. Either they were strong enough to push the Kors back or they weren't. For now, though, they were strong. A bit disorganized, but the few he had been able to shout orders to, obeyed quickly and it looked like others further down the line were following suit.

A horn blew in the distance. Late. But it blew, nonetheless. It rang long and clear and deep. No doubt everyone in the city heard it. If they didn't know already, they knew now.

Huren glanced up from his most recent kill, looking for the next enemy. There were hundreds of Kors charging the city. He watched one of them chase down one of the fleeing women. Why wasn't she beyond the breach yet? Huren ran towards the man, sword in his hands. He aimed and thrust it into the Kor's chest and out the other side. Huren pulled it out, kicking the body away from him. The next Kor was swinging a sword at him before he could re-position himself in a proper stance. Huren's blade deflected the attack. The force of the blow knocked him off his feet.

One of Huren's guards engaged the attacking soldier, giving him time to scramble back to his feet.

"Thanks," Huren grunted between breaths. The guard merely wielded his sword at the Kor and tried to push him back. Huren joined him, moving with ease over the broken rocks. He felt his uniform snag on the Kor's blade. He ducked and rolled into the man. The man lost his balance and his guard stepped forward, stabbing his sword into the Kor at last.

As far as Huren could see, the Kors were being held back at the edge of the city. His men were fighting, holding their ground. Then, a terrible shattering sound clashed in the heavens.

Every man paused and looked up at the sky. "Was that thunder?" Huren asked to no one in particular. A moment before, the sun had almost been at its highest, but now it was completely gone! Clouds cloaked the sky, and something started to fall to the earth. Not rain. Sort of like a mist but not that either. This was something new. It was terrifying.

Huren thought about retreating, hiding from whatever was coming his way but that wasn't him. He was a fighter. It was his duty to protect the city. He braced himself. Everyone had forgotten about fighting in those few seconds, even the Kors. The mist was more like smoke, its smell was repugnant. Mist didn't have a smell. Whatever this was was suffocating. People started dropping to their knees. Coughing filled the air. Huren tried to hold his breath so as not to breathe in anymore, just long enough for him to think clearly again.

A few others had their heads on straight. Huren with those few brought their cloaks or scarves up to cover their faces. It blocked most of that stuff but not all of it. Huren wanted to throw up the mush he'd eaten earlier, before his daily rounds. The odor was strong. Too strong. Bile rose up inside of him. He dropped his cloak, and the bile forced its way out of his body, projectiling out of his mouth a good meter onto a nearby Korin soldier.

After momentarily cursing at his luck, the soldier charged at him. Huren grasped the man's arms before his sword could penetrate his armor and pulled. Using the man's own momentum Huren rolled backward and kicked him hard as he left the ground. Huren continued his roll so that he was upright again in time for the next idiot. But no one else came for him. What in blazes was going on? Why wasn't anyone fighting?

He smelled it before he saw it. Huren took a step forward to try and see what it was. It ranked of putrid meat, worse than whatever was falling from the sky. Were those dogs? They were too large to be dogs. The darkness made it hard to see their true shape. They didn't charge like the soldiers. Whatever these creatures were, they just walked right past the Kors, straight into the city. Hundreds of them climbed over the rubble.

Then as they neared the Itholean guards, they leaped and attacked as if they could tell the difference between Kor and Itholean. Their teeth latched onto the men and shook them all about. One man's sword flew from his hands as he called out in terror. Huren ran towards him. Where were his blasted feet? Why wouldn't they move quick enough? Several meters lay between him and this creature. Was that a thorny devil? None of this made any sense. Thorny devils lived in caves and tunnels far up the mountains. They hated being out in the open. Why didn't they attack the Korins? How did they know who to attack?

The thorny devil took a bite out of the man's chest and tossed him aside. It turned toward Huren. The eyes were dark, almost as if they didn't exist. Huren knew they were there though because he felt them boring a hole in his head.

Screams filled the streets. In that short moment, the other thorny devils stepped over the dead soldiers and started attacking any Itholean in its path. Huren started, not believing what he was seeing. He had to do something.

"Don't just stand there, you idiot!" He told himself.

"For the Queen!" Huren raised his sword and charged the nearest creature. Seeing their commander move to action his soldiers did the same.

Sweat poured down his back as Huren fought creature after creature. They weren't just thorny devils as he'd originally thought but there were dranks too. Their screeching only added to the terror now flooding the streets.

❋ ❋ ❋

The queen had been easier to capture than Krillin expected. His scented mixture was working, and she couldn't control their minds. And with the Montane out of the way the older Itholean was easy to subdue and leave behind. They hadn't been able to take the package from her yet because she still had magic that could burn their hands. Jaylen learned that the hard way. So, she was tied up and slung in front of Krillin over Jerky's back.

Jerky stumbled underneath him, and the queen started to glow. "Did you feel that?" Krillin asked, ignoring Agonya's attempt to speak through her gag.

"Yeah. Was that thunder, too? But I don't see any clouds."

"What are you doing?" Krillin gasped. The cloth in her mouth was starting to smoke. The next second, it caught on fire!

Krillin cried out in alarm and started slapping her face. He pulled at the rag which now came loose with only the slightest yank. He threw it on the ground in front of Jerky who then trampled the fire out.

"Please, let me sit up," Agonya gasped and coughed.

Krillin helped her upright. "What were you thinking?"

"I was thinking we could talk about this whole tying me up while I slept and treating me like a prisoner after the way I welcomed you." Agonya raised her bound hands and tried to push the long black strands of hair out of her face.

She had a point, but Krillin had already made his choice before meeting her. She had been kind to him, so he pulled her hair back and tied it in a knot. "I know you must think of me as cold-hearted, but I'm only doing what I must."

"But why must you? What do you get out of kidnapping me?"

Krillin's body stiffened. He didn't like thinking about his past when he didn't have to. "Your father killed my father."

"You're kidnapping me because you can't return the favor?"

"No. Itholean guards killed my brother."

"So, both your father and brother were killed? What happened? There must have been a reason."

"If you stop asking questions, I can tell you that it was only for the crime of being different," he spat.

"What do you mean? Different in what way?" She seemed genuinely interested.

"He's one of them, the ones we don't talk about. His forehead was broad, and his eyes were far apart. He had a wide mouth and a small nose. He also walked different, and his words came out slurred sometimes."

The queen nodded in understanding. "I'm very sorry for your loss. Please, tell me how it happened."

Krillin wasn't quite sure what made him do it but he told her his story. Although this wasn't the first time Krillin had told someone his story, it felt like it. She seemed to understand in a way that Aekan and Lord Commander Huren hadn't.

"Your wish, then, is to make sure those soldiers get justice?"

"Yes. Your father let them kill Sani. He let them kill my father. I don't blame you. But I agreed to work for Aekan, because he promised he'd help me. I have no other choice but to bring this package to him." Krillin surprised himself that he wasn't worrying about her reaction to all of this. Usually he always felt anxious, especially around those in authority.

"You must smell that I am not like my father in many ways. I could forgive you for your crimes and see that these men were punished, if you were to help me now."

She seemed to think that was good enough. But Krillin had only known her for a short time. He wanted to believe her. He kind of liked her. As far as he could tell, she had the power to do what she said and she worked hard not to abuse that power, which was the only reason he felt so comfortable telling her his story.

“Wait a minute,” Jaylen cleared his throat, “that’s all very fine, but you forget that I am a captain of the nineteenth battalion of the first division in the army of King Reid.”

“Sure, but can you seriously tell me that bringing me in, a captive, and stealing from me will get you what you want?”

“It isn’t a matter of what I want. I have orders and I can’t ignore them.”

“Krillin has orders, too. As do I. So, which are the better orders?” She seemed to think she could convince them to trust her to do as she said she would.

“Even if,” Jaylen replied, “Krillin and I help you, what makes you think you can fulfill your promises to him? Your city will surely fall, and your kingdom will be no more.”

A loud horn sounded through the air, emphasizing his point.

“The fighting has begun.” Krillin’s voice urged them forward.

“I admit,” the queen said, “everything smells rotten.”

“You can’t stop us from taking the city.”

“I can try. If the city falls before we get there, I must do what I can to ensure as many lives as possible are not lost. I will do what I must. I have not been idle in my thoughts as you might think. Why should I tell you what I’m going to do?”

“The captain makes a good point, your Highness,” Krillin countered.

“I can’t help you make your choice but think about it. King Reid killed his own sister and then lied about it. He started this war to get what he wanted. He will not rest until he has it. Is he the type of leader you want justice from? What about justice for my mother? You are not the only one to suffer losses.” She shifted on the horvelina’s back.

He knew that what Jaylen said was most likely true and that he should stick with the winning side, but he couldn’t just switch sides at the last moment, if it looked like the other side would win. Would she really forgive him his crimes? She didn’t even know the extent of what he’d done.

Before Krillin could think any further on it, the aromas of many people blew in his face. He jerked his head up and looked every which way. He couldn’t see them. Krillin retrieved the bow off his back anyway.

“What is it?” Jaylen hissed.

“People.”

“Where?”

“Everywhere. Mostly in front but I smell them moving to surround us.”

“Untie me now and we might be able to get out of this mess,” the queen demanded, sticking her hands under the tip of Krillin’s arrow.

“No, don’t listen to her,” Jaylen said. “Let’s turn around, go back the way we came. We can find another way to the camp.” Jaylen steered his elephantus off the path so he could turn around.

Either they were Montanes or Kors. Krillin didn’t think they were Kors. In fact, both Captain Dahel and the queen assumed they were Montanes. He didn’t know much about them. Best to follow the captain’s instinct on this.

Krillin turned Jerky around and they rode as fast as they could back the way they’d come. The queen continued to plead with him to cut her bonds, saying that they were making a mistake.

Krillin pulled on the reins. Several elephantus blocked their path. He glanced to the side; the river ran swiftly past. They couldn’t go that way.

“Hand over the queen and you can continue on your way,” the Montane in the middle said. He was shorter than the others. His pale skin was covered with tattoos and his blonde hair was cropped short.

Captain Dahel trotted forward. “Who are you to command queens?”

“I am Hinto, second in command to His Honor, Chief Golar. It looks to me that you’re holding her against her own will. Let her come with us and you may go.” Hinto leveled his spear at Jaylen. His men mimicked him so that there were many spears now pointing at them.

“You did not seem to want to let us go when you held us captive a few days ago. How can I know you won’t just imprison us again once you’ve got her?” Jaylen replied.

“You are not as dumb as you look. Back then, you were intent on stealing her yourself and we could not let you do that.

But if you give her up willingly, we will let you return to your people over that ridge there."

"And have you done what I have asked of you?" the queen chimed in, sitting up taller.

"Your Highness, we have not yet been able to do so."

"Why not?"

Hinto shifted uneasily. "We were about to when Ashkii over there told us of your predicament."

Krillin followed the Montane's finger and saw Ashkii sitting on an elephantus, almost completely hidden by the trees. The queen saw him too. Krillin saw the disappointment on her face, but it was more than that. She looked hurt by the Montane's actions.

She really shouldn't have been shocked by it. In Krillin's opinion, she was too trusting of everyone.

"Agonya, come ride with us," Ashkii called to her. "We will ride into the city together."

She shook her head. "Why should I believe you?"

Hinto stepped closer. "I do not think you are in a position to negotiate. You will come with us if you have any hope of saving your people."

The queen's glowing aura let off a faint hint of berries, "I'm afraid you are mistaken, if you think *you* are my only hope."

"What was her hope?" Krillin wondered. Her father was dead. She was on the verge of losing her kingdom. The Kors wanted her dead or alive. The Montanes wanted her. Ashkii betrayed her. Krillin wasn't sure if they cared about her health one way or another. Did they want that package, too?

Krillin broke the awkward silence. "Why do you want her anyway?"

"The queen is one of a kind, as you can clearly see. And we promised her we would help. We will not let you take her to the Kors."

"She has something you want, doesn't she?"

Hinto's mouth tightened for a second before he smiled, "Hand her over or face the consequences. I am growing tired of all this talking."

The Montane didn't answer the question, but Krillin knew what Hinto wanted. And it wasn't the queen's safety.

Everyone she knew turned their backs on her and yet she still tried to convince them to do the right thing. Krillin was her hope. It was up to him to make the right choice.

Krillin didn't understand what it was she was trying to protect, but he knew it was important and if there was anyone that should have it, he trusted her the most. He didn't trust Captain Dahel or the other Kors, even though he'd turned to them for help. He didn't trust this man, Hinto, in front of them. He smelled of betrayal.

Krillin could see the other Montanes closing in on them but ignored them. "Your Highness, give me your hands."

He sliced through her bonds in one sweep then he rolled off Jerky, cutting the rope around her ankles as he did so.

"What are you doing, soldier?" Jaylen cried. "Watch out!"

The queen jumped down off the horvelina, surrounding herself in a bubble of magic. Several spears bounced off her shield and one or two others pierced Jerky's skin. The horvelina reacted in anger, charging at the elephantus. Her movement surprised the Montanes who were only focused on the queen and her companions. They quickly lost control of their animals who were getting tangled up with each other in their haste to avoid the deadly tusks.

"Quick! Up here! We can get away." Jaylen kicked the elephantus into motion, riding up next to Krillin. No thought was needed. They both ran and jumped up grasping the rope ladder, pulling themselves up.

"Your Highness!" Brynn broke through the Montane's ranks riding his elephantus.

"Brynn!"

The Montanes recovered from their surprise. While they formed a line, Krillin notched an arrow.

They charged. All of them but a few who were doing something Krillin couldn't see. Then he heard it and loosed his arrow over the charging Montanes. It struck one of the Montanes attacking Jerky, but he was too late.

There was nothing Krillin could do. "Jerky!" Krillin called as they got further and further away. Jerky couldn't follow. Spear after spear stuck out of her in so many places. She collapsed on the hard earth, squealing in pain and anger. Krillin couldn't hear her anymore. No! Not again! Jerky was his friend. He hadn't saved her. He let his friend die just like he let Sani die and his father! Krillin was overcome with grief. He nearly fell off the galloping elephantus.

The queen put out a hand to catch him. "Krillin. Are you hurt?"

He heard her words but couldn't understand. Thump. Thump. Thump. The beats of the animals' feet hitting the ground was so loud.

"Here, take this."

He felt something in his hand. Long and slender. At one end was a sharpened stone and feathers on the other. He tightened his grip on his bow. Automatically, he put the arrow in his hand into the bow. With his eyes closed tight, he aimed for the pounding feet following them and fired. Arrow after arrow until there were no more feet behind them. Each arrow shot was for Jerky. That was the best he could do.

"They're not following us anymore."

"We're not in the clear yet," the captain said. "Look."

Krillin opened his eyes. Several tribes of the Montanes blocked the only way to the city and camp. They were in wide open fields now. No trees for protection. The city was within sight behind the Montanes. Plumes of smoke rose from Ithol. The battle had begun.

"We're never going to be able to fight them all. I'm out of arrows."

"No need." The queen pointed off to the side. "That way."

The captain steered the elephantus in the direction she pointed. "Krillin, I'm going to have to report you for hindering our mission."

"How else were we going to get away from the Montanes?"

"We could have done it," the captain insisted. "As soon as we reach the city, we're going to turn her Majesty over to Commander Bannon."

She laughed. "You can try, but I'm going to help my people with or without you."

They galloped across the field until she motioned for them to stop. She slipped off. "Come on!"

Krillin looked up once his feet hit the ground, but she was gone! Where on earth did she go? He could smell her. He followed her scent, motioning for Jaylen, who was just as perplexed, to follow. Soon, they were descending into the ground. Brynn brought up the rear.

"Go, your Highness. I'll guard the entrance. Hurry!" Brynn held his sword, ready to pierce anyone who dared to follow them.

Chapter 36

A small round object landed in the tunnel entrance. Smoke began to rise from it a moment later followed by shouts from above.

"Run!" Agonya cried. "Come on, Brynn! You won't do us any good if you can't defend yourself."

Jaylen grabbed Brynn's arm and shoved him in front of the group. Brynn hastily stuffed his recently acquired Montane daggers back into their sheaths and ran. They ran as fast as they could.

Behind them, the Montanes dropped into the tunnel one after the other, not bothering to wait for the odor bomb to clear. They had their cloaks covering their noses, protecting them.

Agonya tried not to breathe in the scents from the odor bomb, knowing they would put her to sleep. Instead, she reached into her bag and grabbed the first bunch of leaves her hand touched. She lifted the bunch to her nose and inhaled deeply. There was a faint scent of rose currants on the lemongrass. She felt the tiredness in her legs leave her as the strength of the fragrances filled her up. She ran faster.

She, also, began to glow. She wasn't sure if that was a bad thing or not. On the one hand, the light rising off her skin helped them see where they were going. On the other, it helped the Montanes see where they were going too.

Another odor bomb bounced on the ground just behind them. The Montanes were gaining on them. They had to keep going. Brynn started to slow down.

"Stop! Wait!" a Montane called to them. "We just want to talk!"

What could they say that Agonya hadn't already heard? They didn't want to talk. They wanted to make her a prisoner again. They didn't want to help, when clearly the city was in danger.

Agonya, not wanting to yell while she ran, spoke to the man in his head. "Come with us, help us fight and then I'll be ready to listen."

She cut him off when he started to say it was too dangerous. She didn't want to hear such nonsense. She ran faster. Touching Brynn's arm briefly, Agonya tried to give Brynn the strength he needed to keep going.

The feet following them fell back. And Agonya listened to the steady beat of their own to help her keep going. She didn't know how long they'd been running when her muscles seized up. She gasped for air. She couldn't smell anything but dust. Exhaustion hit her like a bag of clay. Agonya had to stop and take a breath. She glanced back over her shoulder.

"Did they stop following us?" she asked.

Jaylen answered with a nod.

"Let's walk for a bit. Then, we'll run again. We can alternate between the two so we aren't completely useless when we arrive."

Agonya started walking deeper into the tunnels. It wasn't strictly a straight shot. She remembered getting lost on the journey out of the city. She glanced back at the men to warn them about the thorny devils. "Krillin?"

He was still back where they'd stopped running. Jaylen jogged back to him. "Are you hurt, soldier?"

Krillin was crouched down, rocking back and forth on the dirt. He shook his head and kept mumbling incoherent words.

Jaylen put his arm around him. “It’s all right, Krillin, the tunnels don’t go on forever. We’ll get out. You just need to put one foot in front of the other.”

Jaylen pulled Krillin up to standing. “He’s got tunnel sickness. The quicker we get out of here the better.”

Brynn walked over to his other side. “Can you stand?”

Krillin didn’t respond.

Agonya crouched next to him and looked him in the eyes. “We need to keep moving. The Montanes may still be following us.”

Then the faintest whisper left Krillin’s lips. “Run. Run. Run.”

Agonya helped him to his feet, and Krillin started to run with each repetition of the word. They all joined in and were chanting “run” together. It seemed to be working even for Agonya. If he focused on the one task, he could forget his fear of the tunnel. So, she pushed forward despite her exhaustion.

They ran until Agonya could smell the rotten egg. They must be very near the city exit. “Quick, cover your noses. She’s here.”

The men didn’t hesitate, they had no desire to be controlled by the sorceress again. Then, they climbed up into the empty room.

Agonya could see fires burning, in the darkness, in the streets. A few people, women and children included, ran by crying and screaming.

The sun no longer shone like it had when they entered the tunnels. The storm was back. This time more potent and mixed with something sweet.

Agonya checked the wall around her mind. Safe.

The four men were moving toward the door to the street. Agonya held out a hand to stop them. “Once we go out there, you’ll have to make some hard decisions. Some of us might not make it. While we’ve had our differences, I want to thank you for helping me get here.” Agonya smelifed each one of them, breathing in their fragrances. Then, she motioned for them to follow her into the storm.

As she drew near to the first intersecting street, she heard a woman scream. Agonya dashed around the corner to find a

Korin soldier grabbing the woman's wrists, his face covered in shadows. Agonya rushed forward.

"Get away from her!" Agonya glared at the soldier and stepped up right beside him.

He laughed. "Get in line, pretty lady. I'd be happy to satisfy you too."

The soldier on the edge of the Korin camp flashed before her eyes. Agonya clenched her teeth and banished the memory.

"Whoa!" The soldier let go of the woman and backed away. Before Agonya could channel her powers towards him he fled.

"Quick, Krillin, shoot him before he gets away!" Captain Dahel shouted. "Krillin?" he spun around but Krillin was nowhere to be seen. The captain cursed and ran after the man.

Agonya turned towards the woman whose eyes were wide and her body was stiff.

"It's okay now. You can get inside where it's safer," Agonya said, but before she finished the woman turned tail and ran. Echoes of "unnatural" and "stench" bounced off the walls behind her.

Agonya turned towards Brynn. "What just happened?"

"I think you frightened her, your Highness."

"What?"

"You're glowing again."

"Oh." Agonya looked at her hands. The look on the woman's face, the one of terror had been for her not the Kor. Agonya began to walk. She didn't have time to worry about how others thought of her.

Brynn kept pace with her, passing the surprisingly empty street.

Where was everyone? Indoors? No. Agonya heard children crying. She rushed towards the sound. They were huddled behind rain barrels. What could she do?

Brynn blocked her path. "You can't save everyone, your Highness."

He was right. Children would slow her down. She needed to get to the battle and then there wouldn't be time. "Brynn, there's something I need to tell you." Agonya quickly glanced around to make sure they were alone. "Maya's alive. We faked her death because I didn't know who I could trust. She's safe."

Brynn stared at Agonya, unable to speak. Then, he swept her up into a big hug. "Thank you."

As quickly as he scooped her up, he set her down. "I can't tell you how much that means to me. What do we need to do so that I can see her again?"

"I need to find the Lord Commander Huren and the other council members. If you want, you can leave me. Maya is still outside of the city. She was keeping an eye on Ashkii."

"I will not leave you until I know that you are safe. If Maya is not in the city and hasn't been discovered by the Montanes, then that is good. Come. Let's find the battle, then we might actually be able to fight someone and win."

Agonya let Brynn guide her further down the street. She saw people peeking out from behind closed curtains as they passed. Their faces were gaunt in the candlelight. She'd been away too long. "I have to save them," she whispered.

"Don't worry. I'll get you to the Lord Commander."

Agonya wanted to believe him. So, she let him lead the way. She didn't have to do this on her own, just like Blackthorn had said.

* * *

"Come back here, soldier." Jaylen called after the fleeing man. Sticks! Where was Krillin? Jaylen slowed down. His sides ached. It was amazing he could still stand up. He had to keep going. If that soldier recognized him, he would be in deep trouble.

"Soldier, I gave you an order!" Jaylen shouted.

The man hesitated a few house lengths ahead of Jaylen. That was enough for him. Jaylen closed the gap quickly. The soldier realized his mistake and tried to pick up his pace. Jaylen caught the man's arm.

"Get off me!"

"Not until you give me a report of the city? I've just returned from my mission and need to know where the Lord Commander is so I can report directly to him my findings."

Jaylen wasn't sure this would work but an idea had been forming in his mind while running.

When Krillin had cut her bonds, he knew he couldn't bring her in on his own. He also knew that he couldn't fight against his people. He was a captain. He had responsibilities. Jaylen didn't know what to think about the queen's claims, but he had to try to work with her to convince her to surrender.

"We undermined the wall, sir," the soldier said, finally seeing the captain's symbol on his cloak and saluting him. "The wall collapsed just like we planned. Their army is in disarray. It has been quite easy to get in and to do whatever the hell we want."

"The Commander?" Jaylen didn't dare let go until he got what he wanted.

"He'll be back at the command post set up outside the city walls."

"Anything else I ought to know?" This man wasn't telling him something important.

He shook his head in reply. "No, sir. The battle is won."

Jaylen let go of the soldier.

"Who was that woman? Why didn't you attack her or come to my defense if you really are a captain?"

"She is my mission, lad. The Commander will be pleased to know I have brought her back." Jaylen smiled and strode back the way he'd come, leaving the confused man to do as he wished. The seed was planted. No one could question his loyalty now.

* * *

The queen and Brynn weren't where Jaylen left them. But he knew where they would be going. He just had to find his way to the palace in the dark in a city he'd never been in before. He headed towards the lights in the distance. Before too long, Jaylen saw them turning a corner. He ran after them but when he reached the street they turned onto, he saw them about to disappear again. "Wait! Your Highness! Brynn!"

The queen turned back. The force of her beauty hit Jaylen. She was radiant. He caught her scent of sweet cinnamon and myrrh and noticed there was hardly a tear on her dress.

"Your Highness," Jaylen began again. "The wall to the city was undermined and has collapsed. That must have been the first thunderous sound we heard. It looks pretty bleak for the city."

The queen's glow started to fade, and she looked more normal again. "To the wall we go."

"If I might make a suggestion. . ."

"Go on."

"It might be wise to surrender."

The queen stepped out of his reach. "Surrender! There's no way I'm coming with you. Surely, you know that. If you are still intent on fighting for that liar, go."

"I don't know that he is the liar you say he is. And Ithol has already fallen."

She ignored him and continued the way she'd been going. He followed. What choice did he have? The closer to the wall they got the more bodies he had to step over. She would see he was right. He just needed to give her time to accept the truth. Jaylen glanced at the body he was stepping over and gasped.

"Your Highness! Look!" There was little light to see by, but he could see chunks missing from the bodies and burn marks like what he'd seen before from those creatures that breathed acid.

Agonya stumbled to her knees. "Dranks."

"Yes, and something else by the looks of it," Brynn added, pointing to a little girl lying face down on the ground. A whole leg missing, completely ripped off.

The queen's hands flew to her mouth when she saw the girl. "How can you even consider surrender when this. . ." she trailed off. She wasn't looking at the girl anymore.

Jaylen followed her gaze. He unsheathed his sword and moved into a fighting stance, but before he could do anything else Brynn flew past him towards the thorny devil.

It growled and swung its long spiky tail in front. Jaylen watched the tail hit Brynn and fling him into one of the shop walls. Jaylen took advantage of the creature's distraction and slid underneath its scaly body. His sword dug in, making a large slit the length of his belly. The creature tried to retreat but the sword held fast. This thing had spirit. Jaylen yanked the sword out and scrambled back to his feet. He tried to wipe its guts off his face, but it just spread making it worse. That's what he got for going underneath the odorous thing.

"Captain, over here, please."

Jaylen saw her Highness bending over Brynn. "Is he?"

"He's alive if that's what you mean, but he won't be going anywhere anytime soon. Help me move him inside, off the street."

"Come with me," Jaylen said again, sliding his arms under Brynn's shoulders.

Agonya lifted the legs.

"Your Highness, there is something bigger going on than my army against yours. Please, listen to reason. You must see that surrendering will cause the least death and damage." Jaylen kicked the door behind him open.

"Another one! Quick!" Agonya cried, trying to push him to move inside faster. His boot caught on something, and he couldn't get it free. Jaylen fell. Brynn cried out in pain as his body jerked towards the ground.

Too late. A thorny devil ran into Brynn, chewing clear through his torso. Jaylen couldn't move. He felt his heart speed up but he couldn't get out from under Brynn's shoulders.

The devil chomped down on Brynn's innards and tossed them aside. Then it turned to Jaylen, still on the ground. Its green eyes held Jaylen in place. He yanked the hilt of his sword but couldn't get it free. This was it, the end of his life. All his plans ended here because he was weak. Jaylen closed his eyes and prepared to be torn apart.

He heard a ghastly scream and opened his eyes. The queen was glowing orange and pushing two daggers between the thorny devil's spikes into its chest. She jumped, using her weight to drive the daggers in further.

Jaylen felt his body return to normal and pushed himself off the ground. That had been close. Too close. She saved his life even though she had no reason to.

Before Jaylen could thank her, the queen slumped to the ground, placing her head between her hands.

Jaylen knelt beside her unsure of what to do. "You saved my life," he said, unable to say the words he wanted to say.

She didn't look up.

"I'm sorry, your Highness. Brynn was a good man." Then, after a moment of silence, he added, "All the more reason to surrender now before other good men die."

She lifted her head and glared at him. "You are wrong. This is the reason I will keep fighting. Leave me alone, if you're not going to help!" She stood up so fast, Jaylen didn't have time to process what was happening. The queen pulled Brynn's daggers out of the thorny devil. Then she ran, illuminating the fallen men, women, and children she passed.

"Wait!" Jaylen couldn't lose her. He needed her to surrender.

***

"Blackthorn," Agonya cried out as she ran. "What do I do now?" Everything was wrong. Sure, they got away from the Montanes but ever since they stepped out of that tunnel, she'd been losing people one after the other. What made her think that she, Agonya Kanti Nakai, could do anything to help?

"Be careful, your Highness. You don't know when another thorny devil will come around a corner or a Korin soldier for that matter." Blackthorn's steady voice gave her strength.

Agonya continued to run even if what he said was true and she very well might run into more trouble. That's what she was hoping, wasn't it? She wanted to find the trouble in the city so she could put a stop to it. She had to get to the real battle. The battle that had left this section of the city with nothing but dead and dying people. The battle that Brynn promised to get her to safely.

It was only a short distance now to the eastern gate. Agonya slowed down and peered around the next corner. If she still had any people to save, they weren't here. Korin soldiers stood guard all along the collapsed wall.

"Come with me," the captain's low voice startled her. She forgot he was following her.

"And surrender? No way!" Agonya struggled to free her arm from his grasp. "Let go of me."

"If you won't come willingly, I'll have to force you to come. It's for your own good."

Really! The gall of this man. He tried to bring her hands together, but she was already grabbing the rope from his bag with her free arm.

Jaylen caught her arm and pulled her closer to him. "I'm immune to your mind control trick."

"Is this how you repay me? I just saved your life and you're trying to tie me up?" She channeled her magic to his hands, burning them again. He let go but didn't cry out. Agonya yanked the rope free and ran back the way she'd come. She had to get to the palace which would be the most defensible position inside the city and most likely where the battle was happening now.

Agonya heard the captain curse. He called out but it wasn't to her. He must be calling for backup. Agonya ran faster. She ducked between two barrels on the corner and peeked through them. Jaylen stood with three more soldiers.

"I tell you, it's the princess," he said.

"You mean for us to believe the princess is roaming these streets?"

"May the patron of fortune find favor with her," another said.

"A thorny devil will most likely rip her head off," the first said.

"I don't see anyone, um, Captain?" the third soldier strained to see anything among the shadows. The idiot was holding his torch in front of him, blinding him, more than illuminating anything around him.

"Captain Dahel, and yes, she turned there."

Agonya tried not to breathe as the four made their way to the intersection. Would they notice her? They stopped right next to her. "Please. Move on," Agonya pleaded in her mind, checking to make sure she wasn't glowing.

"Look, Captain, if the princess is really here–"

"She's here."

"If she is, then she can't go too far without being noticed and we've got all the exits guarded so she can't escape, right? Let her go. We'll get her eventually."

"I can't do that. I will go after her even if you don't. You're free to go back to your post."

Agonya heard three sets of boots return the way they'd come. Jaylen still stood there. She only assumed he was watching them leave. Every second he stood there felt like an eternity to Agonya. In reality, he was only there for a few seconds before picking a path.

When he was far enough away that Agonya was sure he wouldn't hear her, she crept out of her hiding place and went a different way. She knew these streets well. And she had lots of practice hiding from her personal guards. Before she could stop it, images of Brynn's mangled body crowded out any pleasant memories she had been having. Her smile faded.

She might be good at hiding, but everything else, she did wrong. She failed every one she tried to help. Even Krillin, who she hadn't hurt directly, had gone a separate path from her because he knew she couldn't keep her promises. And Brynn! He would never see Maya again.

"Not your fault, your Highness." Blackthorn broke the image in half when he spoke in her mind.

Agonya let the tears fall as she walked.

"No, perhaps not. I've got to keep trying, trying to protect the others."

"Of course you've got to. I'm just saying you don't have to carry that particular burden around with you while you do what you have to." Blackthorn started to glow and would have lit the path in front of her if he hadn't been in her pocket. "One step at a time, little one. One step at a time."

Chapter 37

“Run. Run. Run. Run.” Krillin didn’t run even though he wanted to. They were out. He was out of the stinking never ending tunnel. He hadn’t felt trapped like that since . . . since he’d watched his father executed.

Jerky. Jerky was executed. Just like his father, Jerky died for him. Fought for him.

He watched the queen dash off down the street. He started to follow but a whimper from behind made him pause. Krillin turned. Had he imagined it? He took a few tentative steps and heard it again. What would his mother do? Krillin started to tell the others where he was going but when he glanced back at them, they had their weapons drawn and were shouting at someone. Never mind. They didn’t need him.

Krillin gave in to the incessant voice in his head and ran.

A little girl not much older than Anya was hiding in a tiny alleyway, weeping. Krillin wasn’t sure what to do. Should he talk to her? What would he say?

“Are you hurt, little girl?”

She looked up at him with red eyes and rubbed at them as if that would wipe the redness away. “Who are you? Are you going to hurt me?”

"No, I don't want to hurt you. I heard you crying. Do you need help?" Krillin stumbled over his words. She smelled of dirt and blood.

She was silent, just staring at the wall. "They killed them right in front of me," she whispered.

The disconnected way she spoke, as if it was someone else speaking, shook Krillin to the core. "Killed who? Who killed them?"

"The Kors. They killed my family. You're not one of them, are you?" she asked, backing away from him.

"A Kor? No. I'm not a Kor."

Her shoulders relaxed but the haunted look on her face remained. Krillin didn't know why, but he felt drawn to this girl. "I worked for them once."

Oops. She was backing away again except she didn't have anywhere to go. "I mean, I'm not working for them anymore. I was told to find the princess."

The little girl hugged her knees close to her chest.

"I found her," Krillin kept speaking. "She's beautiful and kind and smart and well she's the reason I decided not to help the Kors anymore." He hadn't really thought about it till just then, but yes, what he told this little girl was true. There was no need to go back to help the captain. If he didn't go back, he wouldn't have to choose between the two. Nothing against Captain Dahel but . . .

"Why did you work for the enemy in the first place?" she asked in that strange, disconnected way.

"Huh?" Krillin rubbed the back of his neck. "They killed them."

She didn't ask any more questions but the way she looked at him, like a cat watching shadows.

"We killed them," he said, remembering all those dreams where he just stood by and watched the beatings over and over again. It was beginning to dawn on him just what he had done, what he had failed to do. "I let my brother die. Then my father. I didn't do anything to stop them. I killed them." The weight of guilt and understanding pushed Krillin to his knees, and he buried his head in his hands. All this time he'd been blaming the Itholeans. Yes, those guards dealt the killing blows, but he, Krillin, did not speak up. He had failed to protect Sani. It was

Krillin's fault. Every choice he had made since then had been wrong. The queen was right, he didn't want the Kors to win the war, but he didn't want to help her either.

A small arm draped across his back. Her scent was more than dirt and blood. He could smell it now. It was the smell of home, the smell of his mother. Krillin let her scent fill his mind.

"Thank you, um . . ."

"Amber. I'm Amber."

"Thanks, Amber. I'm Krillin. Do you want to help me find my mother and sister? It might be dangerous."

"I would like that very much. I like you, Krillin. Your smell is pleasing." Amber rose from her crouched position and waited for Krillin.

They were going to make things right. At the very least, Krillin was glad to have a friend again. Someone who understood him. Someone he could protect. This time he would do it. He wouldn't stand by and watch. Not anymore.

* * *

"Post men at all the entrances and some in the gardens too."

"The gardens? Aren't they sealed off, sir? I think it would be a better use of the men at the main weak spots."

"You heard me, Captain. The wall around this place is not nearly as tall as the city wall." Huren shook his head. The enemy was sure to climb over the wall if it wasn't defended.

"Sir?"

Huren turned to find a servant man holding a tray with refreshments on it.

"Thanks." He needed something to eat and drink after hours of fighting. Everyone was exhausted. That this servant thought to bring him something was amazing. He didn't even know he needed it himself until it was there. "Do you know if my men are being taken care of, too?"

"Yes, sir. All the royal servants are tending to the needs of everyone who made it inside. Mikkah has set up a healing center for the injured. A few of the people have come forward with healing knowledge. We've also led the women with children to the west wing, to be furthest from the action."

"Very good. And the Councilors? Where are they meeting?"

"The courtyard, sir, like always." The servant bowed and backed away.

Huren sighed and went to join them. His captains and lieutenants knew what to do. Now he had to calm the councilors and their pettiness. The moment the city wall had fallen, Huren knew they'd lost. It was only a matter of time before they had to surrender, and Huren needed to make sure those idiots went about it the right way.

* * *

The closer to the palace the more homes and buildings lit up under relentless flames. The firelight revealed exactly what Agonya feared. The Korins were gathering for an assault on the palace, her home, the place Agonya knew so well. She knew every secret it held. The memories too. Her whole life was tied to this place. The good and the bad days alike.

Agonya pushed back her stray hair to rest behind her ear and motioned for the others to remain hidden. They were still many blocks away from the palace but there was no way through. Not only were there thousands of soldiers blocking their way but thorny devils and dranks too. They could hear the frustrated screeching and smell the acrid muck drifting down their little blind alley.

"Are you sure you don't want to try to leave the city another way?" Agonya asked the crowd of Itholeans gathered around her. She'd found them as she picked her way across the city and couldn't leave them behind. There had been a mix of emotions when they first discovered who she was, some revered her, some were angry but now that she was there, in the city, none of them wanted to be left behind.

The man standing in the back spoke first. "Your Highness, there is no other way out is there? This is our last hope."

"There is a way," she said. "Listen, there is a tunnel that leads out of the city. You could try to use it but there is another army on the other end. You could try to hide inside the tunnel until the battle is over or see what the Montanes will do with you. They may or may not be kind to you."

All the children gasped along with several of the women and even men at the mention of the Montanes.

"If there is such a tunnel as you say, then why are we trying to get into the palace?"

"Because I didn't leave Ithol to save myself. I had a mission to bring help back to you. I failed to bring the help I wanted to, but I am here and there are things I can do to help. If I can't save you, I will do what I can to protect as many of you as I can. I cannot leave now, but you can. In fact, I encourage you all to save yourselves."

"I will stay by your side, your Highness. Wherever you go I will go." A young man who was probably just underage stepped forward. "Tyler, at your service."

A few more men and women stepped up to join him, each offering their service to her.

"And the rest of you wish to escape whatever will come of this day?"

An old man, leaning on his walking stick, straightened his tall shoulders. "I will guide anyone who wants to find the tunnel, just tell me where it is."

Agonya smiled. His courage was brighter than the fires wreaking destruction all around them. And it gave her hope. "It is good. If you would go with this man, I encourage you to do so. You will find the tunnel in a home not far from here. Old rugs lay across the top of a trap door. But be careful down there. I do not think it is free of all dangers."

Agonya proceeded to tell them the exact street and house. Then she watched them head back into the heart of the city. "May the god of Jedrek be with you," she whispered after them.

There were five who remained by her side. She nodded to them. They followed. They would have to go the long way around.

"Do any of you have weapons?" she asked.

"I have a knife," the older woman said, patting her large pocket on her stained dress.

The others shook their heads.

"Then we'll have to keep our eyes open for any we might find along the way. Look for fallen soldiers. We must arm ourselves if we are to get past our enemies."

Agonya led the way, winding through the streets so that they would end up near the gardens. That was the only way in now. She hoped the enemy wasn't completely surrounding the palace walls yet. They would not know of the hidden door that she had used to flee the city in safety.

They passed a few dead people here and there. None of them had weapons. All of them reminded her of Brynn. Dear sweet Brynn. She couldn't think about it. She had to get inside the palace. She had to fight for what was left of her people. What was left? Not much by the looks of it. What made her think she was able to make things right or to bring an end to the war? She didn't have any spices to help her. Her bag was empty now. She'd used up the last of it to get away from Jaylen.

Jaylen. That man thought he knew what was best. Sure, he hadn't known the truth when he went to war and chose the wrong side. Agonya hoped she'd convinced him, like she had Krillin. But his helping her was only for his own benefit. Not even the knowledge of the truth was enough to change his mind. Without that, what could Agonya do for these Itholeans who for some reason or another had decided to fight alongside her even if they lost, even though they would probably lose.

"Turn here." Agonya motioned for them to follow, then froze.

Snarling escaped the drank's teeth. Then another one noticed and left its prey, the fallen soldier in the street.

Almost immediately Agonya was surrounded. Everyone took up defensive stances to protect her. The dranks crouched, ready to spring and started to scream. The woman with the knife advanced fast. She ran right up to the two screaming creatures and slit one of their throats. She wasn't fast enough. The second one squirted acid all over her. Tyler grabbed it from behind and flung it against the wall.

Agonya rushed forward to help the woman. She took the knife from the lady's limp hands and tossed it to Tyler. Then, she started to remove the clothing that was burning the woman's flesh. Someone handed her a cloak and Agonya wrapped the woman inside, covering her nakedness.

"Come," Tyler said. "We can't linger here. With the noise those things made there will surely be more any second."

"Can you walk?" Agonya asked.

"Yes."

Agonya helped her stand, and they walked as fast as they could.

"Over there," Agonya said. "We're almost there!"

"Almost where?" an oily voice spoke from the darkness off to her right. A man dressed all in black stepped from his hiding place. He didn't have a visible weapon, but he still looked creepy. She noticed he had the distinct smell of metal and was that cardamom perfume?

"Who wants to know?" Agonya stopped running, a meter away from the man.

"Pardon me, for the intrusion, miss. You can call me Aekan."

She had heard that name before. Was this the man Krillin had worked for? "Aekan, it's really none of your business. You look as if you are exactly where you want to be and therefore have no business looking to be somewhere else."

"Ah, yes. The princess most certainly has better things to do than stand around all day talking to strangers. Please don't let me keep you," he gestured for her to keep moving.

How did he know who she was? Something was wrong. She couldn't let him follow her and see where they were going. She couldn't take him with her either. Agonya nodded to Tyler and Ryker, who stepped up next to Aekan, intending to search him for weapons.

Aekan had other ideas. He moved so fast, bending this way and that. He slipped through their outstretched hands and had their hands tied behind their backs in no time at all. Four more men were there, having tied up the rest of the Itholeans with Agonya. She was left standing alone in the middle of them all.

"You really shouldn't have done that," Agonya said in the calmest voice she could muster.

"I'm dying to find out what you've been up to all this time and where you're headed now. It's just my luck to have crossed paths with you here." Aekan stepped up right next to her. A little too close for comfort. His perfume masked his sweaty body odor, not well enough.

"I could show you some of the things I've done."

Agonya was in his mind. She saw a woman and child huddled in a corner. She saw his cruel intentions. She saw his next move. Then, she changed it.

* * *

Krillin stepped over the little boy he'd brought to his mother for care. He was dead now. How long had he been lying in the room, forgotten? His tiny body was liquefying. The stench filled the whole room. Krillin gagged. But his stomach was empty. He had to look. He had to find out what happened to his mother and to Anya.

Krillin stumbled into the adjoining room. Empty. What now? Did he just give up looking for them? They had to be somewhere.

The smell overwhelmed him, and even though his stomach was empty he found something to vomit. Krillin tried to flee the sickening stench, but he stumbled. When he looked up, he saw dead flowers. They were different from the ones he'd received that one day. Krillin walked over to the flowers. Sure enough, a note was tucked inside, addressed to Krillin Boged. He took it and fled the room.

"Run. Run. Run. I just need to get away," Krillin told himself. He was so intent on getting away that he ran smack into Amber.

"Ow! What'd you do that for?"

"Uh . . . Sorry," Krillin stepped back, "I didn't see you there."

"I'm not hiding, you know."

Krillin nodded and unfolded the note addressed to him.

"Where's your mom and sister?" she asked, trying to put on a brave face.

"They're not here. But I have a note from Aekan. Remember the man I told you about? The one who works for the Kors?"

A shadow crossed her eyes and Krillin could smell the fear returning.

Krillin kept talking, hoping to distract her from the memories that plagued her. "He wants me to keep working for him. He took my family to make sure that I do. There's no mistake this note was meant for me." Krillin crumpled the note and tossed it aside.

"He's going to kill your family if you don't do what he says?" Amber's voice had a hint of anger in it.

"Yes. But you should stay here, where it's safe. He might kill you, too, if you come with me."

Amber shook her head. "You need me. I will go."

"It's too dangerous."

Amber folded her arms and looked into his eyes, her own were still red from crying. "Nowhere is safe. You told me you killed your brother by not doing anything to stop his murderers. I did the same when my family died. But I'm not going to kill your mother and sister too."

"Fine. You can come. But you must obey me." Krillin knew he shouldn't let her come, but it would have been like leaving his little sister behind unprotected.

Amber swallowed whatever else she was going to say to convince him and ran down the alley after him. "How far is it?" she asked.

"Not far, you know the apothecary with the funny-looking woman who smells like too many things. I can't make up my mind if she smells bad or good. Know the one?"

"Yes. I like that neighborhood. Lots of hiding places."

"I'm going to need more arrows, too, before I try to defy Aekan. And don't drink anything he might try to give you. It'll probably be poison." He was the one responsible for that little boy's death and countless others. Krillin tried to slow down so that her short legs could keep up with him. She was only a kid after all. Even as they ran, Krillin questioned his decision to let her come. He liked having someone to work with even if she couldn't do much. But then again, who was he to say she couldn't help. Her family was dead, and their prospects of survival looked bleak.

It was more of the same on every street. Dead people here and there and occasionally a cat or a dog. Krillin thought he saw something that looked like a drank but it couldn't be, could it? Those lived on the mountains.

"Um, have you seen any strange animals? I mean the kind that don't normally live here?"

"Yeah. Didn't you see them? They came like a pack of dogs, howling at each other whenever they saw new prey. Then there were those spiky ones." A shiver ran down her back.

"I thought I saw a drank turn that corner over there." Krillin slowed his pace to a crawl. "They burn."

"Yeah. You're right. We should avoid them." Amber crept ahead of Krillin and crouched down to peer around the corner, "It's gone." Amber stood up, knocking a barrel as she did so, which in turn bumped a pile of trash that made a horrible metallic sound like pots and pans banging against each other. She started to scream.

Krillin grabbed Amber and lifted her off her feet. He slung her onto his back and ran. They had to get away as fast as they could from that spot. "Shhh. They'll find us. Shhh."

He could smell them coming. Not just one but four or five of them were closing in.

Krillin turned and pushed open a random door. Once through it, he pushed it shut again. He had to peel Amber's arms from his chest to set her gently on the floor. She was okay, just frightened. Then, he looked around. Whoever owned this house was well off.

Krillin spotted a chair on the other side of the room. He pulled it up next to the door. It wouldn't hold the door shut but it would at least tip over giving them warning that someone or something was coming in. Krillin wasn't sure if the dranks could smell specific people or not. If they could, there would be no outsmarting them.

"Krillin." A soft voice came directly behind him. Amber wasn't curled up on the floor anymore. When had she moved?

Krillin turned to face her and saw what she was holding: a bow and arrows.

Chapter 38

Only one councilor was missing, Huren's oldest friend. Sir Marko's absence troubled Huren but didn't surprise him. They had fought side by side in the Neroli Wars, and if anyone was going to be missing in battle from this group, it would be Sir Marko. He was not one to hide. Unlike the other councilors.

Huren ignored his twisting gut and strode to the center of the courtyard. "Ladies and Lords, you all know why we are here and what we must do. The only question to answer is how. How are we going to–"

The main door slammed open. Huren's eyes widened in disbelief. She couldn't be here. Had he been wrong about the Montanes? Or maybe she got away from them in time. There was something different about her. Queen Agonya Kanti Nakai glided into their midst. Even with the dirty torn dress and hair escaping from her braids she was beautiful and regal. Every head turned toward her.

"Your Majesty," Lord Tanish said, bowing before her.

"Your smell is pleasing, Lord Tanish." The queen took his hand and smelled it. "I apologize for being late. I came as quickly as I could. I'm glad to see," the queen paused as she took in the men and women standing before her, "most of you are still alive and working together."

Huren started to move forward, but she gave him the slightest shake of her head. "Tell me how the war is going. I know that the palace is our last defense and that we have lost many lives today. What else should I know?"

"How did you get past the Korin soldiers?" Lady Kanuna asked the question burning in Huren's own mind.

The queen turned toward the beautiful councilor, but she didn't seem upset by her question. "Sometimes," she said, "people are too concerned by what is in front of them that they don't see what is behind them."

An idea began to grow in Huren's mind. But they were about to surrender. He couldn't afford to hope. They were done fighting. But the queen's words were true. If they were able to attack from behind, they might have a chance. No. He shook his head. They weren't behind them any longer. "Your Highness, we have lost more than half our soldiers and way too many citizens. The Kors offered us a chance to surrender only an hour ago."

"What were their terms, Lord Commander?"

"The same as before." Huren swallowed his hesitation. He had to tell her the whole of it. "They want you and a package they said you would know what it was. And if we didn't have you and this package, they would settle for pillaging our wealth and taking us as slaves."

The queen clasped her hands behind her back and began pacing back and forth. There really wasn't anything for her to think about was there? Huren could only see one option. There wasn't much hope for anything else.

"Now that I am here," the queen stood still and faced the worried councilors before her, "and yes, I do know what package they seek, we can fulfill their terms. Though, I think they will make us slaves and plunder our wealth either way. Will you fight one last time, with me?"

Gasps and many shaking heads erupted across the courtyard. What was she thinking? They had clearly lost. What more could they do?

"Your Highness," Huren said, "What are you proposing, exactly?"

The queen's skin began to glow softly. Was that frankincense he smelled? A feeling of calm washed over him. Then the calm became determination. Huren looked around at the other lords and ladies. They too looked determined to help their queen.

"I'm going to need all the perfumes, incense, and candles we can find. And we're going to send as many men as you think we can back the way I came. We're going to attack from front and behind."

He was confused. Why did he feel like this would solve all their problems when he knew it was folly? All the other councilors looked just as confused.

Then, someone said, "Ah, perfume, why didn't I think of that?", causing the others to chuckle in agreement.

The queen walked over to Lord Bykan and held out her hand expectantly. He glanced around nervously before handing her the perfume bottle in his pocket. She knew more than most people gave her credit for. Huren smiled to himself because she had seen what he had not about Lord Bykan.

Opening the bottle, the queen breathed in the rising scents. "This is a very fruity perfume, Lord Bykan. I wouldn't have expected both citrus and non-citrus scents to be together, but the neroli and apple fragrances will work perfectly." Then, she began to glow a faint orange. A shield surrounded her, growing larger and larger the more she breathed in the perfume. "Attack me," she said.

No one moved. Then someone who had entered the room with her rushed forward with a food knife. As soon as the knife touched the orange shield it bounced off and the woman stumbled to the ground. Before they could retain the lunatic, the queen stepped forward, letting her shield disappear and knelt next to the woman.

That's when he noticed the woman was badly burned, probably from dranks. "Hold out your hand," the queen commanded. Everyone gasped when they saw what Huren had seen. Then, miracle of miracles the queen held the woman's hand in her own and the burns began to turn pink and heal over with new skin!

One by one, the councilors came forward and offered whatever they had on their persons.

“We’re going to knock some scents into the Kors,” Lord Bykan whooped.

Lord Tanish handed her his own stack of incense. “I’ll go find Mikkah, your Highness, so we can start collecting whatever else is here in the palace.”

Lady Velia stepped forward with a stiff bow. “Your Highness, I do not think this is the wisest course of action.”

“Sweet Velia, since when have you been concerned with wisdom? For as long as I’ve known you, you have forsaken her at every turn. Why now, do you seek her favor?”

Velia flushed either with embarrassment or anger, Huren couldn’t tell which. Then she found her voice. “I beg your pardon, your Highness, but you have returned to us at the end of a war you haven’t been a part of and now you tell us to fight! Whatever these tricks are that you have learned will not be enough. What do you know of our struggles? What makes you think you have the right to play chance with our lives?”

A few other councilors nodded at that sentiment. Whatever determination they had felt earlier seemed to vanish. Several months ago, they would not have even listened to one word she spoke. It was fair for them to know why they ought to do it now.

“You’re right, Velia. I have failed you all. It wasn’t a choice that I made willingly to leave you here to suffer. Do not think for one moment though that I have not suffered as well.” Her face shone regally as she spoke. “I have not suffered unnecessarily. I am not the silly little girl that you knew. I am your queen. You should address me as such whether you want to or not. I do not take it lightly that some of us might die by trying to fight one last time. Know this, for I think it might be of some comfort to you, with me here, if we must surrender in the end, I will do what I must to save your lives. I am a bargaining tool you did not have before. But until we can fight no longer, I will not surrender so willingly.” The queen turned away from Velia and searched the room until her eyes met Huren’s.

“Yes, your Majesty.” Huren bowed.

“Faithful Huren. Thank you for your message. It came to me at just the right time. For that I am in your debt. I have brought you a portion of that debt. He awaits you in the prison cells. Perhaps he will have answers for you in our defense."

"Your Majesty?" What was she talking about? She brought a prisoner for him to question?

"Time is of the essence. Go."

"Yes, your Highness." Everything changed the moment she walked into the courtyard. For the first time since her father's death, Huren had hope.

* * *

Agonya paced the sunroom. All the plans were in place. The soldiers were waiting on her. The perfumes were procured. And she felt none of the confidence she showed her councilors.

According to the plans, Agonya had to try and help all her people who were out fighting the real battle without being next to them. She knew it could be done; that's why she said she could do it. Dana the Sorceress was proof that it could be done. There were whispers that she was being a coward, hiding in the sunroom.

"You're not a coward even if I think what you're doing is too dangerous." Blackthorn was sitting on a table near the fire pit in the center of the room. Agonya thought letting him out of her pocket was too risky, but he had insisted his disguise would be fine considering all the other plants in the room.

Agonya smiled. It was nice having Blackthorn back and she hadn't changed the colors of his berries when she hurt him trying to heal Brynn. Every single one of his berries were a different color and a different fragrance! That must just be the way his berries ripen. But what did his fragrant berries have to do with defeating Dana? Agonya sat down to face him.

How could she possibly think she was strong enough to fight Dana the Sorceress? Yes, she had defeated a man who called himself Aekan in the streets, outside the palace, against all odds, but that also meant she had used quite a bit of her energy. How was she supposed to use her magic in places she wasn't present? The only time she'd been able to do that was to connect her mind with another, and even that didn't always work for her.

"What choice do I have? Even if I'm not strong enough to defeat the sorceress?" Agonya directed her thoughts directly to Blackthorn.

"You're not strong enough." Blackthorn agreed. "But you are not alone. I know I said it was too dangerous, but I will do what I can. Perhaps together we will be strong enough. But we can't forget what can and will happen if we mess up."

"A sacrifice I am willing to risk, at least for myself. I will break our bond if it becomes too much. You are the one thing I cannot risk." Agonya poked the coals in the fire. She didn't have time to think about whether or not it was a good idea. She had to prepare for battle.

"Now, what do you think?" Agonya swept her hand toward the incense and perfume laden tables. "You know these better than I do. Which ones will be of most use to us?"

"Frankincense and lavender will help our soldiers be brave. The lavender will also be good to intercept Dana's rotten eggs." Blackthorn scanned the table, at least that was what Agonya thought he was doing when he turned his trunk from side to side. "Sandalwood, too."

"What does that do?" Agonya asked, walking over to pick up a stack of incense.

"Sandalwood should increase your range; how many will be affected by the magic."

"Excellent." Agonya turned to the servant standing in the corner. "Go tell the commander I'm ready, please."

The short elderly woman curtsied and left them alone.

"I have confidence in you, Agonya. Together, we will be able to do a lot of good. Here, take some of my berries." Agonya remembered the first time she saw his berries. They were all small and green, but they had gotten bigger and changed colors during their journey. There were red berries, purple, orange, blue, all sorts of colors. As Agonya looked at them, three began to glow brighter than the rest.

Agonya crossed the room and gently picked them.

"I will let you know when to use them."

"Is there anything else we ought to discuss before we are no longer alone?"

"There is the one . . ."

"Yes, I've been thinking about that. I think it is best if you do not come with me when we surrender."

"Will you abandon me?" Blackthorn jumped in alarm. "I thought we could find a way to hide me again. I do not wish to leave your side."

"Nor I you. We both know that I will be thoroughly searched. They will take you from me whether we want them to or not. If that happens then she will have won in the end. She mustn't be victorious. I believe there is a way that will not leave you abandoned even if I can't be with you, perhaps someone else can."

***

"The incense is burning at all the gates and around the whole perimeter of the palace walls, your Highness. Just like you told us." A young soldier stood at the door of the sunroom.

"Good. You may go back to your post. Let the commander know, I have begun." Agonya walked over to the fire pit, directly beneath the open roof window, and sat on golden pillows as close as she could get without catching fire.

Agonya heard the door close as he left. "Blackthorn?"

"Remember what we discussed. The clouds first, then the animals. Let the soldiers deal with the soldiers."

"Right." Agonya closed her eyes and smelled her surroundings. She reached out past the stone benches and pillars in the courtyard, past the walls and up past the roof. She followed the smell of frankincense all the way to the halls where it burned. She focused on each one, moving all the way around until each one had a little bit of her magic intertwined with the incense.

"This better work," she told Blackthorn in her mind.

"It'll work. Trust me." Blackthorn rested on a table behind her, giving off a faint glow of enthusiasm. "Until now, we haven't had the proper tools. But now, I think we have a slight chance of making a difference."

"Nice to see you're not all pessimistic anymore."

"Oh, I'm still pessimistic. I don't think we will win the war."

"But we can try to make it even."

"*Try* is the key word."

"Okay, I'm trying now." Agonya poured the first perfume into a brazier over the fire. A tiny stream of smoke started to rise. Agonya drew it towards herself with her hands, breathing in the subtle blend of lavender and sandalwood.

Blackthorn reached out to her, bonding his magic with hers. The power inside of her was incredible. Agonya didn't know what to liken it to. She needed to get it out of her soon. Already her muscles were getting weaker.

Together they pushed upward with all the force Agonya dared to use. The magic rose in a straight bright path all the way to the oppressive clouds above. She could feel when it hit the clouds. A few shouts could be heard off in the distance, beyond the palace walls. She wondered if they would attack now.

The clouds didn't separate or disperse like they did two months prior. Agonya felt a great weight press down on her. Rotten eggs and oakmoss mixed with her own lavender and sandalwood. She could smell each one individually and as a blend.

"Go away!" she thought. "Leave us be!"

A smoke-like vapor started to descend directly over the sunroom. A voice came from the perfume that swirled around Agonya and Blackthorn. "Give me what I desire, and I shall leave you to die in your own time."

Dana. She wasn't in Agonya's mind per se and yet somehow Agonya knew only she could hear her.

"I can't do that. He is not mine to give to you."

"Don't be foolish, child! You are his guardian, are you not? The best way to protect him is to bring him to me. I will end this war if you do this for me. Think of all the people you will save from slavery or death."

"Ha! Do you think me so naive that I would believe all your lies?"

While Agonya spoke to the air, she felt it push down on her. Agonya grabbed a bench to keep herself upright.

A sweet tangy orange scent filled Agonya's mind, pushing out all the other demanding scents.

"Blackthorn? Is that you?"

“You can do this, your Highness. Don’t grace her with your words. Fight back. Use the next perfume.”

Oh. Agonya had completely forgotten about her stash of perfumes. They had picked these specially for this occasion. Agonya grabbed the next one in line and dumped it in the brazier. This time the aroma was hearty like a good possum stew. Her strength was renewed. Agonya reached out with her magic, feeling her way through the vast cloud above and pushed back the vapor still swirling around them.

Several minutes passed. Agonya searched for the edges of the cloud. It seemed like it spanned the whole city and beyond. Agonya dumped the third perfume on the fire and added its earthy musk odor to the mix. There. The edges. Agonya focused all her strength and attention on the cloud as a whole and infiltrated it to its core. She felt Blackthorn lend his strength, giving her just enough to penetrate the thickness and make the clouds break apart right down the middle.

“What are you doing?” Dana screamed. “NO! You can’t do this. You shouldn’t be able to do this!”

Agonya ignored her just like Blackthorn said to do and redoubled her efforts until the sun peeked through. It wasn’t much, but the sun was still in the sky even though it felt like the middle of the night.

Despite all her efforts and even though the vapor creeping around her was gone, Agonya only made a small part in the cloud to form two clouds.

“Your Highness!” someone called from the doorway. “The thorny devils are breaking down the wall with their tails. What do you want us to do?”

“Give me time. I’ll do what I can.” Agonya dumped the fourth perfume on the fire and brushed the stray hairs out of her face.

The fresh scents revived her body. The first three perfumes were a faint hint upon the air. Yet Dana’s scent was present still. Agonya searched for the thorny devils. She tried to remember their reptilian smell to help find them.

Their heads were full of rage as they swung their tails at the wall and rammed their heads into the gates. Agonya drew their rage away from their minds and replaced it with sleepy thoughts. Then the anger swirled around inside her! How was she supposed to calm all that anger! She wanted to kill everyone!

"NO! I won't do it."

"No?" Dana replied with a laugh. "Of course you want to do it. Go on. Let go of all that wrath."

Blackthorn burst into her thoughts, picture after picture of Maya, Brynn, Ashkii, her mother, her father, filled her mind. One. Two. Three. Four. Agonya breathed deeply between each count. And with one huge push forced all the anger up and out towards the clouds. They broke apart.

Agonya sighed. She couldn't rest. She'd only put a handful of thorny devils to sleep. There were still so many. Not to mention the dranks!

"Focus. You did well. You gave your soldiers breathing room." Blackthorn's words made sense, but still. So few?

"Okay. I'll try again." Agonya dumped the next perfume on the fire. She fought. She put thorny devils and dranks to sleep until she ran out of perfume. In between each attack she sent the creature's anger, Dana's anger back onto her own creation. The clouds were nearly gone. A good thing too. Her perfumes were empty.

Agonya's heart raced beneath her rib cage. "I can't do this, Blackthorn! I can't." A well of tears burst out of her. Agonya collapsed on the floor.

"Your Highness!" a servant raced to her side. Agonya saw his concerned face for only a second before everything became black.

Chapter 39

The commander was set up at the back of the troops, doling out order after order and receiving reports.

"Sir, something is wrong with the thorny devils," a runner was saying.

Lord Commander Bannon ignored the runner and stood up when he saw Jaylen standing in the back.

"Captain! Glad you could join us for our victory!" Bannon grinned.

His grin didn't last long though. Jaylen watched his brow wrinkle.

"Where is she? And what have you done with my guards?" he asked.

"My apologies, sir. Kyler and Ryker both died in battle." Jaylen covered his nose in respect.

"And the princess?" The anger in the commander's voice was evident to all within hearing. Several people backed up trying to pretend they weren't in the vicinity.

"I brought her back to the city."

Bannon towered over Jaylen and waited for him to explain.

"She escaped. But she won't be leaving the city, sir."

"I see." Bannon controlled the anger pulsing through his veins. "You will join your men at the front gate."

"Sir, she has powers."

"Nonsense. You are just making up excuses." Bannon turned back to the messenger still waiting to finish his message. "What was it you were saying about the thorny devils?"

The messenger straightened up, glancing briefly at Jaylen. "Um, they are falling asleep, sir."

"Falling asleep? Are you sure?"

"Yes, sir. We can't wake them up."

"How many?"

"Twenty-three, sir." The messenger shifted to his other foot. "It's like magic, sir."

Bannon stopped pacing and looked the messenger in the eye, "You are certain of this?"

He nodded.

Bannon forced himself to look at Jaylen. Finally! He was ready to listen.

"Tell me what you know about her powers."

* * *

Krillin felt the smooth handle and smiled. Amber had found the bow. He didn't need it, but it was a beautiful bow nonetheless, and it didn't hurt to have two. If the string broke on one, he'd have a backup. They also found plenty of arrows to restock his quiver which was getting low after his encounter with the Montanes. Krillin was able to retrieve his arrows from the two dranks and thorny devil that he'd killed on their way to the apothecary.

Amber walked next to him carrying five knives in one of the satchels they'd found. She looked so grown up, even though she was Anya's age.

Fear bubbled up inside him at the thought of Anya. She was probably waiting for him at the shop. That or she was dead. He didn't want to think about the latter.

"Turn here. The shop is the second to last on this street."

Amber gagged. "I can smell it!"

The street was empty except for dead dranks.

"Ewww! Gross!" Amber pinched her nose as they walked past the carcasses.

"I'm afraid they both reek of awful memories."

"Memories? What do you mean? I didn't know memories had smells."

"It's just something we say when it smells bad."

"Oh."

Krillin saw the disappointment on her face. She really was hoping memories had a smell. That was a new thought indeed. Maybe they did. After all, the queen could control minds and Dana could control even more than that. How did they do it? Could anyone do it?

"Krillin?"

"Huh?"

"Ready?"

Krillin inhaled the many rotten and bloody scents around him and entered the shop. It was just like he remembered. Bottles lined the shelved walls and bins of dry powder of all different colors sat underneath. There was also a table with a scale and random plants strewn across it. Sitting at the table was an old woman, the funny looking one he told Amber about.

Krillin cleared his throat. The woman jumped in her seat and looked up, knocking one of the bottles off the table. She reached for it but it hit the ground, spilling its contents everywhere.

"Sticks! That was one of the most difficult scents I've acquired." The woman threw up her hands.

"Sorry. I didn't mean to startle you. Have you noticed the birds are flying?" Krillin hoped she would be the one he had to deal with. She was a little strange but not intimidating.

"That nonsense!" She waved his hand to shrug it off. "Paradise is coming. Blah, blah, blah."

Krillin relaxed a little. He wasn't quite sure what to expect. The note had said if he ever returned to the city, his mission complete, that he should come here. But it hadn't mentioned his mother or sister. And if Aekan wanted him to continue fighting . . .

"I'm here because of this." Krillin held out the crumpled note.

The old woman didn't even look at it, instead she rose from the table and left the room.

Krillin glanced at Amber. She had the same worried look on her face that Krillin felt. They only had a moment before two big burly men entered the room.

"Krillin?"

"Yes, sir."

"Aekan left instructions for you, if you were to return in his absence. He should be back by morning. He said you were to go report directly to Lord Commander Bannon for duty."

If he could just get the information he needed and get out of there without conflict, they would never know he didn't intend to report to the commander. "Where might I find him?"

"In front of the palace if he hasn't captured it yet. I'm sure he'll be hard to miss."

Krillin steered Amber toward the exit.

"Oh, one more thing. Aekan said to reassure you that Sari and Anya are safe."

The other guard did it so fast, Krillin thought he'd imagined it. But the guard had glanced at the back room, smirking as he did so. Were mother and Anya there? They were his only reason for answering the stupid note. Amber nodded in silent agreement.

"Thank you for taking care of them for me? Now that I'm back, I'm sure I can relieve you of that burden."

"Not until you've given your report to the Lord Commander," the largest man replied. The two widened their stance and loosened their sword sheaths.

Krillin made his calculations. But before he could enact them, another man led his mother and sister out of the adjoining room. They looked unharmed apart from being watched over like prisoners.

"Krillin! You're back!" Anya exclaimed. She tried to run over and give him a hug, but the man who led her out grabbed her shoulder, stopping her mid-step.

"Let her go," Krillin growled. How dare he prevent Anya from welcoming Krillin who had done everything Aekan had asked of him.

"It's okay, Krillin. We're safe here."

It was so good to hear his mother's voice. Krillin knew her words were true but only until he didn't do what the Kors wanted him to do. And he didn't want to play their game anymore. "It's not okay. I've done my part and it's time to move on. The battle is won. Let us be on our way."

One of the guards grabbed Anya's hood. "They stay here."

Krillin pretended to give up. He waved at his mother to stay. Then, he and Amber started for the exit. Just as he reached the door, he whipped his bow and arrow off his back and shot the guard holding Anya square in the chest, knocking him backwards.

Krillin notched a second arrow that would have hit its target straight on, but the guard was able to block it with his sword. What the man didn't anticipate was the little girl running forward and stabbing him again and again with a butcher knife. He tried to knock it out of her hands. That's when Krillin's third arrow struck.

Krillin walked up to the fallen men and retrieved one of their swords. He stuck each of them through, making sure they were dead. It wasn't much of a fight. He thought it would be harder.

The old woman looked at Krillin with wide eyes, grabbed as many supplies as she could and dashed out of the shop.

"Do you have everything?" Krillin asked the girls.

His mother dashed into the other room and was back in a moment with two sacks. Krillin took them from her and the four of them walked out of the apothecary together.

The moment Krillin's foot touched the street, something assaulted his senses. He clasped his head between his hands and fell to the ground. He couldn't think.

A memory came to him, a horrible memory. Was he imagining it? No. He had to get up. He had to help his family. He felt hands on either side of him, pulling him up. He heard voices speaking, but he didn't know what they were saying.

"Krillin," his mother's kind voice whispered in his ear. "It's not real. Only a memory. Come on. Stand up."

That memory. He hadn't thought about it ever since . . . It was just a memory she said. How did she know? She wasn't part of that memory. Oh. Krillin allowed them to help him stand.

The old woman stood not too far away and was about to spray something else into the air, but Krillin, even in his grogginess, launched an arrow at her. She was quick and ducked behind a rain barrel.

A small hand tugged on his. They began to run. They ran as fast as they could away from the apothecary. Once out of the reach of the woman's perfumes, Krillin's mind cleared. He knew he couldn't hide from the past anymore. The fact that he was as guilty as those guards for his brother's death was true. He'd have to do the best he could to make sure he didn't contribute to Anya's death or his mother's or Amber's for that matter. She was family now.

"Come. I know a way out. We will not be taken captive or forced to do their will." Krillin didn't slow down, and the girls kept up with him. They were going back to that tunnel. The tunnel that made him feel trapped. He wouldn't feel trapped now. He was sure of it.

* * *

Huren led his men out of the garden gate. Thirty men at a time. He had to make sure each group made it out safely. The first troop he sent around to the right and the next to the left. They would attack from all directions if they could. Huren smiled. It was good to have a feasible plan of attack after so many months of just reacting to the Kors. He kept alternating troops to the right and to the left until all three thousand men made it out.

Huren stationed the last couple of troops to guard the garden gate. Then he took off around the perimeter of the palace and hoped the queen was able to deal with the thorny devils and dranks like she promised. She certainly showed potential when she created that shield out of thin air and healed that woman's hand but neither one of those things meant she could stop the creatures from attacking them. He made sure to avoid detection as best as he could. Each troop knew exactly where they were supposed to go once they left the palace.

Huren turned to his personal guards. "Everyone's in place. Blow the horns!"

He heard the shouts as they charged toward the large command tent, but he ignored them and barreled down the street, silencing Korin soldiers as he went with a quick thrust of his sword or a slash across their throats. In a matter of minutes, he was within reach of the command center. He raised his arms, clasping his sword with both hands and slashed down through the canvas in front of him.

Aekan, it seemed, had told him the truth. He only needed to have two fingers removed. The Lord Commander of the Korin army stood talking with a lesser officer. He turned as Huren pushed his way into the tent. Huren met his eyes and leaped over the chairs that stood between him and his enemy.

Unfortunately, the commander was fast. Their swords met the moment Huren's feet touched the ground, and the dance began. Soon every man in the tent was engaged in battle.

The commander was good, but not as good as him. Huren jumped on a chair and knocked another one into the man with the flat of his sword, giving him just enough time to make his footing surer. The commander tried to knock the chair out from under him, but Huren merely used it as a springboard and aimed his sword at the commander's neck. He pushed off the chair which flew backwards as he left it. He sailed toward his enemy, but the commander dodged out of the way.

Huren landed and ducked beneath the Kor's blade. Twisting his sword backwards, Huren jabbed at the air behind him. He felt resistance at the tip of his sword.

The Korin commander cursed and backed away. Huren moved into a better fighting stance and was about to lunge forward again when he noticed one of his closest guards, lying face down on the ground only a few feet away. Huren's sword missed the mark but left a large gash in the commander's side, nonetheless. He couldn't think about his friend, he had to get the job done.

Huren knocked the man on to his knees and was about to run him through when he felt the cool sharp tip of a sword resting on the back of his neck. He looked up. Did he dare kill the commander? Huren glanced around the tent. Korin and Itholean alike lay sprawled across the ground. The battle was over and there were more Kors than Itholeans standing.

"Looks like your little attempt to overcome us has failed." The Lord Commander stood up and pushed Huren's blade away.

Huren let it drop to the ground and raised his hands. Then he knelt and bent his head forward, exposing the back of his neck further. There, on the ground, he closed his eyes and breathed in the pungent smells of blood and sweat. The blood and sweat of his men, his friends. And the image of King Azurarus beheaded in his chambers filled his mind. The last time they spoke, the king had known he was about to die. And now, Huren knew it was his turn. "I'm coming to join you, old friend," he thought.

And he was okay with that. Despite the months of frustration about not being able to fight back, to make the Kors hurt, or even to defeat the lord commander of the Kors, Huren knew their attack dealt more damage than they had all summer. Between knowing that and the knowledge that his queen would pick up where he left off, Huren was ready to die.

* * *

"Lord Commander! Sir! General Gad requests backup."

Jaylen watched the messenger fold over, out of breath after delivering his news. But before he could wonder what it meant another messenger arrived.

"Lord Commander, General Tumu requests. . ."

Messenger after messenger came, all with requests for reinforcements before the last had finished speaking. Jaylen stared, open-mouthed at the sheer number of messengers now filling the front of the tent. A total of twelve generals needed help.

Jaylen turned his gaze from the messengers to the man on his knees, waiting for death. Then, before realizing he was overstepping his place, Jaylen got in the Itholean's face. "Did you come here because of her? Is this her doing?"

He knew the answer but had to ask. It was one thing for her to use her powers against Jaylen but on this scale . . . Organizing this attack was incredible. He was in awe. He'd assumed she was an ignorant queen who happened to have mysterious powers over the mind but didn't really know what was happening between their two kingdoms. He had dismissed her pleas to listen to her, simply because she hadn't shown him she knew how to lead a kingdom, let alone an army. But now he saw that she hadn't had the opportunity to show him.

Jaylen wiped his sword clean and wondered if she really was right about this war and if so, what did that mean for him?

Lord Commander Bannon ignored Jaylen and sent as many troops as was possible for reinforcements. Then, he looked at the Itholean commander still poised for execution and sheathed his sword.

"Bind him."

Jaylen was the first to move. He started to pull out two pieces of rope from his bag, but one was missing. He sighed. She had taken the other. He tied the Itholean's hands behind his back.

Bannon sent the messengers back to their generals that help was on its way and for each of them to give a report of their losses.

When Jaylen looked up, he found he was alone with the lord commander.

"Captain Dahel," he said, "you told me she used magic the first time we spoke. I didn't believe you. You told me again. I still brushed it off as an excuse for your failure. While you were gone, I received a message from King Reid explaining why the thorny devils and dranks weren't to be feared. They were going to fight for us. And when the creatures started to appear and they didn't attack us, that's when I knew that magic was real, but that still didn't necessitate that she had power. Then that messenger said the thorny devils were falling asleep and I knew. I owe you an apology."

Jaylen straightened up and wiped his hands on his pants. "Don't worry about it. I hardly believed it myself, sir."

Bannon shook his head. "What do you suggest we do, Captain?"

Jaylen bit his lip. "I know every Itholean life is important to her. She will do anything to save their lives."

"But that would seem like we're the ones surrendering."

“Not if we use him,” Jaylen gestured toward the man in the chair, “as a bargaining chip.”

“Yes. If I’m not mistaken, he is the lord commander himself. Very good, Jaylen. Send the guards back in on your way to deliver our demands.”

Jaylen pressed his dagger in the man’s side, forcing him to walk in front of him.

Bannon stopped him at the tent flap. “Spread the word to keep as many of the Itholeans alive as possible.”

Jaylen sniffed the air as a sign of acceptance and strode from the tent. This was it, he was going to be known as the one who made the Itholeans surrender.

* * *

“A Kor at the front gate brought him all tied up and said they were willing to let him live if we surrender.”

“Perfect.” Lady Velia’s voice seethed with anger. “Our queen did this. And look at her!”

Agonya heard voices talking and tried to wake herself up. Where was she? Agonya felt cushions beneath her and smelled a fire burning. The last thing she remembered was fighting in the sunroom. Uh! She must have failed. They were right. She wasn’t strong enough. She couldn’t even sit up properly. No. No. No. Not again!

“Your Highness, I’ve arranged everything,” Blackthorn said as if nothing was at all wrong. “You’ll be back on your feet in no time.”

“What are you talking about? Arranged what?” Agonya couldn’t see him from her bed on the floor. Was he still on the table? She was out of scents and her magic had eaten up all her strength. “How long have I been out, Blackthorn?”

“Not long.”

“I’ll go give them our terms of surrender,” Lady Velia was saying.

“Wait!” Agonya shouted, not realizing her voice still worked properly.

“Your Highness. You’re awake.” Lady Velia threw her hands in the air while at least five others rushed to her side.

“I’m awake. What’s this I hear about surrendering?”

Velia flushed. “Your plan failed. That’s what. The Kors want us to surrender in exchange for Commander Huren’s life and the lives of the other soldiers they captured alive after that nice little attack you ordered.”

“How do we know they’re telling the truth? Do we have proof he’s still alive?”

A messenger stepped forward. “I’ve seen him, your Highness.”

Agonya tried to push herself up. “Are the Kors waiting at the gate for an answer?”

“Yes, your Highness.”

“Bring me that plant over there, please, and make sure the fire is stoked.” Agonya waited for the servants to bring Blackthorn to her side.

Agonya sent her thoughts to Blackthorn. “I can’t negotiate peace like this. Do we have any orinberries?”

“No, but you haven’t used all of my berries yet.”

Agonya reached into her pocket and pulled out the last glowing berry. She held it in her hands and lifted it up to her nose. When she breathed in its scent, she caught a whiff of the fire. The smoke encircled the berry, knowing exactly where to go as if the berry was calling it to itself. The smoke turned bright orange as it whirled in her hands. She breathed it all in.

The fruity smoke blended into her well of magic, scraping whatever was left off the walls. From there she could see it spreading to the tips of her toes and the tips of her fingers. Every last muscle got a taste of it.

“Blackthorn! How are you doing this?” Agonya felt betrayed. “All this time and you could have healed me without the orinberries!”

“What would you have done if you knew the power of my berries when you were first paralyzed?”

“I would have picked them all to ensure they worked so I could have my feet back.”

“Exactly, but they weren’t ripe and wouldn’t have worked properly. And you would have harmed me further. You could have killed me in your pursuit of good health.”

He was right. There was a time when she had resented her father for making her protect this Kindroot. A time when she just wanted his power and knowledge to get her strength back.

"My fruit can do more than heal you, but not until you proved yourself to me, did I even consider telling you this. I would have told you, then, on the trail when you told the Kor you'd rather die for me, but you did not need them then. And only recently have they ripened enough to work properly."

"Thank you for teaching me about my powers despite my untrustworthiness. If I have learned anything, it is that Dana must not get her hands on you, or she will steal from you and continue to torture all of you for as long as you live."

Agonya stood up from her cushions, tucking Blackthorn into her travel cloak.

"Your Highness." A young servant rushed to her side as if Agonya was going to fall over at any second.

"I'm fine." It was time to go find out if Huren lived. On the way, she could hide Blackthorn.

Seeing every eye in the room focused on her, Agonya added, "I'm terribly sorry I couldn't stop this war that my father started. Just as I promised, I am going to do everything in my power to save those that can be saved. And even though we surrender today, we will find our freedom again. I promise you that."

No one spoke. For the first time ever Agonya felt like their queen, and they respected her for it.

Chapter 40

Ashkii waited in silence on the ridge overlooking the Fertile Basin. It seemed like the longest wait of his life. He hated it. He waited, not because he wanted to, but because he had to. He was a prisoner of his father's, and he could not do as he wished. So, he watched and waited. Depending on what happened, they would either ride into the city where he would see her again or they would go back home to wait some more.

He was so stupid letting himself be discovered! He could have been by her side by now if he hadn't become restless waiting for information to report back to her. He was a failure as a Tafka warrior and a failure as a traitor.

She didn't understand what he had done for her. She didn't know that while she looked at him, sitting on the elephantus, the tip of a knife pricked his back to make sure he didn't do anything rash. The look on her face when he pleaded with her to see reason pained him. Part of him was glad she got away from his father. Then again, thinking about that meant she was back in the city in even more danger than she was before.

Ashkii wanted to scream! Standing on the edge of the battle, and not being able to do anything about it was mere torture. The clouds were one, covering the entire breadth of the city and the surrounding plains. Not a star or moon could be seen. The minutes floated by like perfume on a breeze. All he could do was watch in silence.

"Look!" several hands pointed to the heart of the city. The palace lit up and not by the light of the fires burning throughout the city but there was a source within the palace walls that shot light into the sky all the way to the clouds which reflected the light back onto the palace beneath it.

Ashkii caught his breath. He knew she was fighting back, just like she had fought back when she was a captive of his father. They all understood this power was hers. They also knew that the clouds were not natural, but the Patron of Life had put them there to aid the Korins in battle.

Her light cut the clouds in two and faded. "She wasn't strong enough," they whispered. Ashkii wanted to tell them they were wrong, but he couldn't break his silence. So, he stood and watched.

The light reappeared. This time it spread into the clouds and through the clouds, breaking them into mist that floated away into the night. Then the horns sounded. Itholean horns. If it hadn't been for the victory over the sorceress' clouds, Ashkii would have despaired at those beautiful horns blowing in the night. But now, he hoped. He knew she wouldn't win this battle, but she might win the next one. It was only a matter of time.

Ashkii waited until the night was finally over.

The sun began to rise above the horizon. Thorny devils and dranks filed out of the city as if they were soldiers in an army. They didn't go far though. Just outside of the gates the creatures lined both sides of the road and watched the people stream out of the city.

The sorceress must have gotten more powerful than Ashkii thought possible. No one seemed bothered by the fact that they were surrounded by these creatures who would attack them faster than they could blink if they got the chance. They just walked.

Which was exactly what the Montanes expected to happen. They were just surprised it had taken so long for the Itholeans to surrender. Ashkii couldn't turn away from the prisoners of war. She would be among them. He needed to see she was safe.

The lord commander left the city first with his Korin guards. Agonya came next just as the sun became a full circle of brightness. Her silky-smooth hair piled beautifully on her head, and her white dress sparkled in the sunlight. She was a queen. And yet a captive. And all Ashkii had done was mess things up. He messed up so badly there was nothing he could do about this outcome. But as soon as he figured out how, he was going to escape his father and find Agonya. He was going to make this right.

"Load up," Chief Golar said, as he rode through the warriors ranks. "We're going home."

Fear rose up inside Ashkii at those words. He wanted to run down to her, to fight for her. His father's command meant one thing. Their assassin had been spotted, blending in among the people. Ashkii had to fight his fear. She wasn't weak. The assassin would have a hard time killing her. He might actually die in the attempt, and that too caused fear in Ashkii.

"Don't do it," Ashkii whispered, breaking his silence. A few minutes was all he needed. He could mount his elephantus and ride down to her and if he couldn't take her away from there, he could at least warn her of the danger. Then again, he'd have to get past all those horrible creatures to do it. Ashkii felt someone standing behind him.

He turned to see who it was. Hinto grabbed his wrist while Skah grabbed his other wrist. They were going to bind him, to make sure he didn't try anything stupid. Yeah well, he wasn't stupid. He knew he couldn't save her. So, he let them tie him up. They raised him up and Hinto jumped up behind him and picked up the reins.

She was so far away now, no more than a speck in the distance. Ashkii had to focus. If he was cooperative, his father might loosen his bonds before reaching the village. He just had to wait for the right moment. And while he waited, every step of the way, he would remember. He would remember every smell, every smile, every laugh, every argument. He would remember everything about the woman he loved.

❋ ❋ ❋

Maya watched her mistress from her hiding spot. Agonya left the city, surrounded by enemies. How had it come to this? They used to enjoy so many wonderful parties every week, perfumes and oils and food and cloth in abundance. Now there was hardly anything left. What was left would surely be taken by the Kors as they plundered the city on their way out.

Maya could also see the Montanes. Ashkii had betrayed her yet again. But she thought he hadn't done it willingly this time. She knew Ashkii loved Agonya even if he kept messing it up. In some ways, Maya understood how difficult family could be. The fact that Ashkii's family was his weakness was not a new thing.

Her own family stopped talking to her a long time ago. Agonya was her family now. Maya had done exactly what Agonya asked of her, not because she had to, as her servant, but because she loved Agonya like a sister. She took comfort in the thought that Agonya didn't go into the city alone. She had Brynn with her. Poor sweet Brynn! He had truly mourned her death. Not just as a friend but as if they had been lovers. Lovers! She did not think of him as a lover. He had been a good friend, yes, but a lover? He was almost as old as her father. Yet she could see herself coming to love him anyway.

Maya sighed as she watched the last of the prisoners of war leave the city, now slaves and homeless, exiled. The Montanes, too, were almost gone from sight, retreating up the river into the forest.

The sun beat down on Maya, directly overhead and still people poured from the city. A few more hours passed. It looked like they were gone now. Would there be any survivors left in the city? Maya didn't know.

She stood up and moved to pull her hair back into a braid. Oh. Yeah. She let her hands drop to her side. She kept forgetting how she had chopped it all off. There wasn't enough of it to weave a braid or even to pull back in a ponytail.

She sighed and walked toward what was left of the city. There was no point in hiding now. The remaining Kors wouldn't care if one more Itholean was there. Who was she anyway?

Sure enough, a handful of guards stood at the gate to the city. The one that hadn't broken when the adjoining wall fell. They didn't stop her or even question her. Maya passed the gate and worked her way through the devastated streets. Young and old alike lined the streets with expressionless faces. None were living. Maya listened for movement, any indication that someone lived here still. She felt like she was falling into silence.

No one stirred. The houses were silent. The squares were silent. The dead were silent. But as she made her way past them, their voices started to scream at her. Each one told their own story of how they died and what atrocities happened to them before their death.

Maya stopped up her ears with her fingers as if that would silence the voices. But every face whole or not yelled at her to turn around, to flee the city.

Maya kept on. She tried not to look, only to keep going. She would find the palace and rest there. At the palace, she would be able to take a bath and if there was any food left it would be there. Not to mention a nice warm bed. That was all she wanted at the moment. Rest. She was so tired. When was the last time she had slept?

She stumbled and made the mistake of looking at the ground. No! It couldn't be! Not Brynn! This wasn't happening. Maya squeezed her eyes shut and shook her head. But when she opened her eyes again, she saw Brynn's eyes looking back at her, but he couldn't see her. The sobs welled up inside of her. Maya tried to swallow them.

She heard his laughter and saw his crooked grin. She heard his weeping when he thought she was dead. Maya rubbed her eyes, but even her tears couldn't silence his voice. He told her how much he loved her and if he had lived, would she marry him? He wanted to grow old with her and raise children together.

Maya tried to say that she would, but her words failed her and all she did was fall to her knees and weep.

"Maya," a faint but familiar voice called to her.

She looked up expecting to see her, but she wasn't there. Maya knew she wasn't there. She had left with the Kors, a captive. Even after all their conversations inside their heads it always surprised her to hear Agonya's voice.

"Your Highness! I thought we'd never be able to talk again. I'm so sorry for not protecting you. Please forgive me." Maya couldn't hold back another sob.

"Maya, sweet Maya. You did what I asked of you even though it was the hardest thing to do. I knew that you would have more chance of survival if you were not at my side. I knew I would be forced into exile if I went back. This was my choice. Thank you for loving me so!"

Maya hiccupped and straightened a little at her words. Brynn. He was still in her arms. She could feel Agonya watching her in her agony.

"Don't despair! He died a good death. Oh, Brynn! He was ever so courageous. He fought a thorny devil. That's how he got hurt. I tried to save him. As we . . ." It was Agonya's turn to choke up. "As we tried to move him to safety another one came out of nowhere and ripped him from our hands! I'm so sorry! I never wanted him to die. He stuck with us through everything! He loved you so much, you know."

"Yes, it took all my self-control not to tell him I was alive. Thank you for telling me how he died."

"I told him."

"What?"

"I told him you were still alive, at the end. He knew you lived. He smiled one last time before the end. He had hope one last time."

Maya was speechless. Of all the gifts her queen could have given her: this, this was beyond anything she could have hoped for.

"You are my hope, Maya."

"Me? What can I do?"

"The Kors have only taken the soldiers and councilors as captive. As for the people, they are free to continue living here under Korin occupation. I know it won't be easy but I need you to be their leader now, look after them. Check the tunnels and set up a base in the palace. It has the least damage and plenty of beds for everyone. More importantly, Blackthorn is waiting for you. You'll know where to find him. Please take care of him for me."

Agonya's voice was getting harder and harder to hear. She must be getting further away.

"I will." Maya was glad to have more instructions. For the brief time that she didn't have any commands to follow she wasn't sure what to do and felt lost. Agonya had given her a purpose again.

"I will come back. I expect to see you all alive and well upon my return. I love you, Maya. You are like a sister to me. Until I return."

Her mind was silent again. This time though it wasn't only the emptiness of loss but also hope. Not a lot of hope but it was there. It was something she could cling to. She might not ever be able to share a laugh with Brynn again but perhaps she might with Agonya.

A voice broke the silence. "Miss? Are you hurt?"

Maya looked up to see an elderly man extending a hand to help her up. He was accompanied by a small group of people: some women, some men, and even some children.

"Yes." Maya wiped her eyes. "But not physically. My mind and heart are broken, but there is also hope."

Maya grabbed the man's hands. He was stronger than she expected. He pulled her up with ease.

"I'm so glad to see you all here alive. Come. Let's go. There is much work to do. I'm Maya, by the way. What's your name?"

"Misu," he said.

Maya grasped the old man's shoulders and sniffed, first the right, then the left cheek. He smelled of dirt. And peppermint. "Your smell is refreshing."

"As is yours," he replied with a grin. "Shall we begin?"

Acknowledgments

Thank you for reading my story! Without you, this book would just grow dusty and smell of rotten eggs.

Thank you, to my family, Ryan, Oliver, Phillip, and Jeremy, who have put up with my writing habits and have been the most supportive family I could have asked for. You put up with me through five years of learning to write and helped me find the resources I needed to grow as a writer. And I know you will continue to stick with me through all the ups and downs.

Thank you, to all my beta readers: Janell Benson and Paige Smith (my very first readers and the ones who told me my book was worth pursuing), Ryan Guyer (my wonderfully fragrant husband), Jamie Paul, Autumn Montoya, Sarah Weatherby, Ron Bartlow, Molly, Brandon Hoffman, David M. Donachie, Emmy, Marilyn Lorance, and Gail Harris. I can't thank you enough for all the feedback and encouragement you gave to me. Your feedback helped shape this story into its current scent.

A huge thank you, to Dr. Karen Renner and Dr. Lisa J. Hardy who were also beta readers but who were more than just beta readers. You were my first writing group and your friendships are irreplaceable. You both have taught me so much about writing and communicating, and loving, not to mention the enormous help you gave me in editing this particular book and getting it ready to print.

Thank you also to GhostMadeofToast, Emmy, Lamorach, Shepsus, Hituro, and PplRPpl2 who are a part of my writing Discord group and helped me figure out how to make the cover of this book.

A big thank you to Caylene Finnicum who was my brainstormer and sprinting buddy and cheerleader through much of the writing process! And to my mom who made it possible for us to meet by sending me to the writing retreat.

And of course, thank you to Sara Lorance who is a part of the family and has been one of my biggest supporters!

About the Author

J. L. Guyer currently lives with her family of boys in Flagstaff, Arizona where she received her Bachelor of Arts in English from Northern Arizona University. She loves writing, reading, being outdoors, and napping.

You can learn more at her website, www.jlguyer.com, or find her on social media: Facebook @J. L. Guyer and on Twitter @JLGuyer1.

CPSIA information can be obtained
at www.ICGtesting.com
Printed in the USA
JSHW051651101222
34604JS00002B/3

9 798218 094621